C0-AON-065

Watch the skies, watch the government, watch your neighbors, and you may soon discover the truth about alien visitations to our world. And while you are watching and waiting, why not take the time to explore the possibilities that await you in such imagination-provoking stories as:

"Secret Service"—It should have been the start of an incredible career, but instead she was stuck baby-sitting the former President, a job with no future. At least that was what she thought until she discovered that even a man who has lost his mind might still have some secrets worth knowing. . . .

"Chasing the Mist"—Going to the therapist had changed his life, but he never suspected just how much it had been changed until his recurring dream became a surprising reality. . . .

"Renewing the Option"—When he'd boarded the train, he'd been looking forward to getting home, but now he wasn't sure he'd ever reach his destination . . . he wasn't even certain what his destination was!

THE UFO FILES

WITHDRAWN

THE UFO FILES

Edited by Ed Gorman
and Martin H. Greenberg

BP BOOKS, INC.
new york

www.ibooks.net

A Publication of BP Books, Inc.

Copyright © 1998 by Ed Gorman and Tekno Books

Reprinted by permission of DAW Books, Inc.

Distributed by Simon & Schuster, Inc.
1230 Avenue of the Americas, New York, NY 10020

ibooks, inc.
24 West 25th Street
New York, NY 10010

The BP Books World Wide Web Site Address is:
http://www.ibooks.net

ISBN 0-7434-8742-7
First ibooks, inc. printing July 2004
10 9 8 7 6 5 4 3 2 1

Cover art copyright © 2004 by Scott Grimando

Printed in the U.S.A.

ACKNOWLEDGMENTS

Introduction © 1998 by Ed Gorman.

Ordinary Aliens © 1998 by Gregory Benford.

The Observer © 1998 by Robert Charles Wilson.

Diplomatic Exchange © 1998 by Will Murray.

Secret Service © 1998 by Edward Lee.

Survivals © 1998 by Nina Kiriki Hoffman.

Emma Baxter's Boy © 1998 by Ed Gorman.

Chasing the Mist © 1998 by Tracy Knight.

Amid the Walking Wounded © 1998
   by Dallas Mayn.

Outside Looking In © 1998 by John Helfers.

The End of Winter © 1998 by R. Davis.

Heirloom © 1998 by Jim Combs.

Bug-Eyed Methodists © 1998 by Bob Morrish.

Some Burial Place, Vast and Dry © 1998
   by Peter Crowther.

Daddy Dearest © 1998 by Jack Cady.

Renewing the Option © 1998
   by Elizabeth Engstrom.

The One That Got Away © 1998
   by Kristine Kathryn Rusch.

The Man with X-Ray Eyes © 1998
   by Richard T. Chizmar.

Closed: Due to Curiosity © 1998 by Robert Randisi
   and Marthayn Pelegrimas.

Here's Looking at UFO, Kid © 1998
   by Lawrence Schimel and Mark A. Garland.

CONTENTS

INTRODUCTION

The debate over whether or not extraterrestrial beings exist and if they have or have not visited Earth yet is never going to be decided one way or the other until a spacecraft lands on the White House lawn, ignores the Secret Service, and plants their flag while waiting for the President to show up.

Until that happens, however, the believers and nonbelievers will still argue over abductions vs. hypnotism, spacecraft vs. weather balloons, Little Green Men vs. government conspiracy. For every report of an abduction, there is one where the photos are revealed to be faked, for every Air Force sighting, there is an expert who claims that it was nothing but the planet Venus or an unusual "cloud formation."

All of this is great for writers, however, for until the aliens do land and prove their existence to us, people can imagine whatever they want. And that's what we've assembled here. Twenty-three stories of mysterious sightings, enigmatic aliens, and the everyday Earthlings who may or may not have seen them.

From a young girl who suffers nocturnal visits from silent extraterrestrials to aliens who just want to go out on the town to aliens who encounter a place as strange as any far-off planet—the city of Hollywood—the range of man's thoughts about unidentified flying objects, from fear to fascination to indifference, can be found in the following stories. So sit back, relax, and take a trip into the world of UFOs.

And keep watching the skies. . . .

ORDINARY ALIENS
by Gregory Benford

Gregory Benford is a professor of physics at the University of California, Irvine, where he conducts research in plasma turbulence theory and astrophysics. He has served as an adviser to the Department of Energy, NASA, and the White House Council on Space Policy. Benford is also the author of more than a dozen novels, including *Jupiter Project, Against Infinity, Great Sky River, and Timescape.* A two-time winner of the Nebula Award, Benford has also won the John W. Campbell Award, the Australian Ditmar Award, and the United Nations Medal in Literature.

Roswell, that should have been the tipoff, Dad thought.

The wreck hadn't been impressive at all. The aliens, unimpressive short guys. When the government finally released their findings, there were no surprises.

By then it was all old news anyway. The UFOs were in the skies in full, plenty of them, the main expedition finally arrived. Nobody cared about the one scout craft that they had lost decades before, not even the aliens. The one minor scientific detail—that they had bred short, pale aliens to fit the small ships, so the expedition aliens were bigger and different—got space on page three of the newspaper for one day, tops.

Their craft was good, sure, but the Air Force had figured it out pretty quickly. Somebody said they used most of what they learned in the F-16 fighter planes.

Roswell should have suggested that the aliens weren't super-creatures. In fact, Dad thought, it should have indicated that they were just like most people, with all that implied.

It was the third time something had knocked on the

door that evening. Slow, ponderous thuds. Dad answered it, even though he knew what would be standing there.

The Gack was seven feet tall and burly, as were all Gacks. "Good evening," it said. "I bring you glorious word from the stars!"

It spoke slowly, the broad mouth seeming to shape each word as though the lips were mouthing an invisible marble. Then it blinked twice and said, "The true knowledge of the universe! Salutations of eternal life!"

Dad nodded sourly. "We heard."

"Are you certain? I am an emissary from a far star, sent to bring—"

"Yeah, there've been two others here tonight already."

"And you turned them away?" the Gack asked, startled.

Junior broke in, leaving his homework at the dining room table. "Hey, there've been *hundreds* of you guys comin' by here. For *months*."

The Gack blinked and abruptly made the sound that had given the aliens their name—a tight, barking sneeze. Something in Earth's air irritated their large, red noses. "Apologies, dear ignorant natives, from a humble proselyte of the One Patriarch."

Dad said edgily, "Look, we already heard about your God and how he made the galaxy so you Gacks could spread his holy word and all, so—"

"Oh, let the poor thing finish its *spiel*, Howard," Mom said, wiping her hands on a towel as she came in from the kitchen.

"Hell, the Dodgers game'll be on soon—"

"C'mon, Dad," Junior said. "You know that's the only way to get 'em to go away."

The Gack sniffed appreciatively at Junior and started its rehearsed lecture. "Wondrous news, O Benighted Natives! I have voyaged countless of your years to bring . . ."

The family tuned out the recital. As Dad stood in the doorway, he could see dozens of Gack ships orbiting in the night sky. They were like small brown moons, asteroid-sized starships that had arrived in a flurry of fiery orange explosions. Each had a big flat plate at one end. They were slow, awkwardly shaped, clunky—like the Gacks themselves.

They had come from a distant yellow star and all they wanted was free rein to "speak to the unknowing," as their emissary had put it. In return they had offered their technology.

Dad had been enthusiastic about that, and so had every government on Earth. Dad's half-interest in the Electronic Wonderland store downtown had been paying very little these last few years. An infusion of alien technology, whole new racy product lines, could be a bonanza.

But the Gacks had nothing worth using. Their ships had spanned the stars using the simplest possible method. They dumped small nuclear bombs out the back and set them off. The ship then rode the blast wave, with the flat plate on one end smoothing out the push, like a giant shock absorber.

And inside the Gack asteroid-ships were electronics that used vacuum tubes, hand-cranked computers, old-fashioned AM radio . . . nothing that humans hadn't invented already.

So there would be no wonder machines from the stars. The sad fact was that the aliens were dumb. They had labored centuries to make their starships, and then ridden them for millennia to reach other stars.

The Gack ended ponderously with, "Gather now into the outstretched loving grasp of the One True Vision!"

The Gack's polite, expectant gaze fell in turn on each of the family.

Mom said, "Well, that was *very* nice. You're certainly one of the best I've heard, wouldn't you agree, Howard?"

Dad hated it, how she always made *him* get rid of the Gacks. He began, "Look, we've been patient—"

"*They*'re the patient ones, Dad," Junior said. "Sittin' in those rocks all those years, just so they could knock on doors and hand out literature." Junior laughed.

The Gack was still looking expectantly at them, waiting for them to convert to his One Galactic Faith. One of its four oddly shaped hands held forth crudely printed pamphlets.

"Now, now," Mom said. "We shouldn't make fun of another creature's beliefs. This poor thing is just doing what our Mormons and Jehovah's Witnesses do. You wouldn't laugh at them, would you?"

Dad could hold it in no longer. The night air was cold and he was getting chilly, standing there. "No thanks!" he said loudly, and slammed the door.

"Howard!" Mom cried.

"Hey, right on, Dad!" Junior clapped his hands.

"Just shut the door in its faith," Dad said, with a little smile.

"I still say we should always be polite," Mom persisted. "Who would've believed that when the aliens came, their only outstanding quality would be patience? The patience to travel to other stars. We could learn a thing or two from them," she added sternly.

Dad was already looking in *TV Guide*. "We should've guessed that even before the Gacks came. After all, who comes visiting in this neighborhood? Not that snooty astronomer two blocks over, right? No, we get hot-eyed guys in black suits, looking for converts. So it's no surprise that those are the only kinds of aliens who're damn fool enough to spend all their time flying to the stars, too. Not explorers. Not scientists. Fundamentalists!"

As if to punctuate his words, a hollow thump made the house creak. They all looked to the front door, but the sound wasn't a knock.

Another booming came down from the sky and rattled the windows.

When they went outside, the night sky was alive with darting ships and lurid orange explosions.

Junior cried, "The Gack ships! See, they're all blown up."

"My, I hope they aren't hurt or anything," Mom said. "They're such *nice* creatures, truly."

Among the tumbling brown remnants of the Gack fleet darted sleek, shiny vessels. They dove like quicksilver barracuda, sending missiles that ripped open the fat bellies of the last few asteroid ships.

Dad felt a pang. "They were kinda pleasant," he said grudgingly. "Not my type of person, maybe, and their technology was a laugh, but still—"

"Look!" Junior cried.

A sleek ship skimmed across the sky. A bone-rattling boom crashed down from it.

"Now, *that's* what an alien starship oughta look like," Junior said. "Lookit those wings! The blue exhaust—"

Behind the swift craft huge letters of gauzy blue unfurled across the upper atmosphere. The phosphorescent words loomed with hard, clear purpose.

GREET THE CLEANSING BLADE OF THE ONE ETERNAL TRUTH!

"Huh?" Junior frowned.

Dad's face went white.

"We thought the Mormons were bad," he said grimly. "Whoever thought there might be Moslems?"

THE OBSERVER
Robert Charles Wilson

Robert Charles Wilson is known and acclaimed for his emotionally touching, finely tuned science fiction. His novels include *Gypsies, The Divide, The Harvest* and *Mysterium*. He lives in Toronto, Canada.

I've never told anyone this story. I wouldn't be telling it now, I suppose, except that—they're back.

They're back, after almost fifty years, and although I don't know what that means, I suspect it means I ought to find a voice. Find an audience.

They won't confirm or deny, of course. They are, as ever, enigmatic. They do not speak. They only watch.

I was fourteen years old when my father decided to send me to spend the summer of 1953 with my uncle, Carter Lansing, an astronomer at the then-new and marvelous Mt. Palomar Observatory in California.

The visit was billed as therapy, which I suppose is why Carter agreed to suffer the company of a nervous teenage girl for two consecutive months. The prospect, for me, was both exhilarating and intimidating.

Exhilarating because—well, it must be hard to imagine what plush iconography was contained in that word, "California," at the dawn of the 1950s. I was a Toronto girl in the age of Toronto the Good; I had passed a childhood in chilly cinderblock schools where the Queen's portrait gazed stonily from every wall, in the age of Orange parades and war privation and the solemn politics of nation-building. I knew the names of Wilfred Laurier and Louis Riel. My idea of a beach was the gray pebbled lakeshore at Sunnyside. Oatmeal breakfasts and snowsuits: *that* Toronto.

California, by contrast, was somewhere between New York City and Xanadu. I had seen its picture, in LIFE or at the movies. Blue Kodak seas, palmettos, Spanish missions with terracotta roofs; William Randolph Hearst bathing with movie stars in Venetian tile pools.

It was initimidating for much the same reason. I had trouble imagining my awkward and pasty-white body tucked into its one-piece bathing suit and salmon-pink rubber cap for a frolic on the sands of Malibu. Surely everyone would laugh?

And intimidating because of my uncle Carter, the family celebrity. The *smart* brother, my father called him. Carter had attended MIT on a scholarship. Carter had been tutored by the famous, had excelled, had been groomed for his ascension into the elite of the astronomical community. His picture had been in *Time* magazine, smiling, handsome, the opposite of the neurasthenic cartoon "scientist," a young and vital genius. He knew Igor Stravinsky; he knew the Huxleys.

Whereas my father managed a branch-plant greeting card business entombed in a Leaside industrial park.

So there was the daunting possibility that Carter had agreed to take me as an act of *noblesse oblige*: some restorative Altadina air for a crazy Canadian niece. For the girl who sees monsters. The girl who floats through walls.

He met me at the airport, unmistakable in his leather flying jacket and sunglasses. We said hello, and that was about all we said during the long ride that followed, apart from a brief session of how-are-you, how's-the-family. I was dazed by the overnight flight but fascinated by the passing landscape. California was much browner than I expected, much drier and dustier, much more provisional, like something under construction. The earthmovers and oil wells outnumbered the palms.

At least until we climbed into the hills where Carter lived. Here the houses were painted in pastel colors, the lawns immaculate and gleaming. Automatic sprinklers gushed rainbows into the vertical sunshine. Dwarf palms blessed arched doorways. We parked at last, and Carter carried my luggage into his house, which was clean-smelling and shady and cool as some ancient arboretum.

"This is your room," he said, dropping my suitcases on the plush carpet. It was a small room, spare, the bed merely functional, but a palace as far as I was concerned. The window looked out on the garden; the heads of bird-of-paradise poked over the sill, Picasso birds, with a dab of sap for an eye. The air smelled warm and somehow safe, somehow forgiving.

I asked, "Does the window lock?"

Carter's smile faded abruptly. "It locks," he said, "but you might want to leave it open a crack these summer nights. There's jasmine in the garden. Smells good."

"But it locks—the window *does* lock."

He sighed. "Yes, Sandra, it locks."

I thought at first they couldn't find me, that I had evaded them.

"Them." *They* or *them*—I had no other words. We didn't talk about "the grays" in those days, as we do now, when every encounter is shoehorned into the typology of the abduction scenario. I had no name for them, for the same reason children in those times referred to their genitals as "thing" or "down there." Code words for the unspeakable.

Because events happened to me that were impossible, and because I described these events in great detail, I had been taken to doctors, who called me "nervous and imaginative" and wrote referrals. So I'd learned the painful equation. Talk + diagnosis = punishment. I was tired of my mother taking the blame. (My mother died when I was ten years old, and I was supposed to resent her for dying, but I didn't; I only missed her.) I was tired of my father's obstinate, stony disbelief, his dutiful mustering of a sympathy he clearly didn't feel.

And I was tired of the nights, the fear. Let California wash all that away, I thought. Smother it with eucalyptus musk and bury it in cypress shade. Take me a few degrees closer to the warm equator. Show me some southern stars. Let me see the sky at night and not be afraid.

Days passed. I was alone more often than not, but

never lonely. The sunshine was blissfully exhausting. And sleep was sweet, at least for a while.

"I'm having some friends over," my uncle announced.

Late July. We had fallen into a fixed routine that suited us both, Carter and I. We ate dinner each night at eight, an impeccable meal prepared by Evangeline, Carter's housekeeper. Tonight was no exception. In the last weeks I had seen more of Evangeline than of my uncle. Evangeline was a large black woman with a dignity and reserve as imposing as her waistline. I thought she liked me more than she liked Carter, but Evangeline's true feelings were hard to divine.

She put a bowl of peas on the table, gave me an inscrutable look, turned back to the kitchen. Carter wore his making-conversation-with-Sandra expression, as if he wanted credit for his patience.

"That sounds nice," I ventured.

"The thing is, Sandra, it's more or less an adults-only affair."

I wasn't especially disappointed. I had figured out how it was with Carter Lansing. He didn't dislike me, but he had no common ground with a teenage girl. Nor did he care to develop any. When I was forced to beg a ride to the drugstore to buy sanitary pads, he had turned chalk-white and treated me like an invalid.

(Years later I would learn that my uncle was gay and that my visit had doubtless put a crimp in his social life, and that everyone knew this fact about him save myself. Had I known, I might have understood. Or perhaps not: I was in some ways exactly as conventional as he expected me to be.)

A gathering of Carter's adult friends: How tedious, I thought. "I'll lock myself in my room. Listen to the radio."

"No need to lock yourself in anywhere, Sandra. I'm just afraid you'll be bored. It's a pretty stuffy group, actually."

"I'm sure you're right."

He was completely wrong.

* * *

In the morning I wrote in my pocket diary:
*Another night. No sign of THEM. Am I FREE AT
LAST?*

Don't be misled. I admired my uncle. I envied his
work.

I had read about the observatory on Mt. Palomar; I
knew more about it than I admitted to Carter. (Sensing
that this aloof god would not appreciate my worship.)

The Hale Observatory was new, the freshest and fin-
est outpost on the frontier of human knowledge. It was
the first 200-inch telescope, the Big Eye, a monument to
contemporary technology. Designed and built at Cal-
Tech, it had been wheeled up the mountain—insured for
$600,000 by Lloyds of London—in 1947, just six years
ago, and it was formally dedicated to George Ellery Hale
in 1948. At the dedication ceremony, a CalTech trustee
had read "*Benedicite, Omnia Opera Domini*" from the
Book of Common Prayer, and it must have seemed appropriate: The telescope would look deeper into the
heavens than anything before it, some 500 million light-
years deeper.

And at the helm of that telescope (encased, most
nights, high up the barrel of the device, like a dove in a
dovecote, in heated clothing) was Edwin Hubble, the
aging astronomer who had scaled the expansion of the
universe, who had peered into the most ancient history
of the sky.

I met Edwin Hubble at my uncle's party.

Palomar drew celebrities, and there were celebrities at
the house that night, though I didn't recognize them. I
spent most of the evening in the kitchen with Evangeline, helping her spread sturgeon roe over crackers for
the guests. We held our noses and shared our amazement that intelligent adults would eat such trash. And
while Evangeline served the guests, I peered at the action through the crack of the kitchen door.

She caught me looking.

"That's a funny bunch," she said when the door was
safely closed and we were alone again. "That half-blind

Englishman with the big glasses and pretty little mouth, that's Aldous Huxley. A book writer."

I said I knew the name. Secretly, I was thrilled—authors!—but I let Evangeline think I was unimpressed. (Perhaps she wasn't altogether fooled.)

"The mannish-looking woman is his wife. That old man with the foreign accent? Name's Stravinsky, writes music. The little bitty lady in the easy chair? Anita Loos. And the gray-haired gentleman, that's Mr. Edwin Hubble himself. Just back from England."

I knew about Hubble, too.

I had done the kind of reading my teachers called "precocious." This was the Hubble who was charting the universe, calculating the volume of infinity; the Hubble of the red shift, the expanding-universe Hubble.

He didn't look at all like a scientist. He looked like an aging athlete—which he also was. (He played basketball and football in school and won letters. He still liked to fish and hike, though he had suffered a debilitating heart attack in 1949.) He smoked a plain black pipe, which rode in his solid jaw like a prosthetic device, and he looked as stern and unforgiving as a high-school vice-principal.

I opened the kitchen door wider.

Evangeline's eyes widened with it. "Best not go in there, honey."

"It'll be okay, Evangeline."

I appeared in the midst of this mixed-drink-driven crowd like, I suppose, the unwelcome ghost of vulgar America in my Capri pants, my gull-wing glasses, my hideous braces. Conversation stopped.

Carter rushed to introduce me, but I saw the indignation in his eyes. "This is Sandra, my niece. She's staying with me for the summer. If you're looking for food, Sandra, there's plenty in the kitchen."

"Nonsense," announced a strong, high-pitched voice. Anita Loos, author of *Gentleman Prefer Blondes*, posed in an easy chair like a cynical munchkin. "Sandra—it *is* Sandra, isn't it?—don't let Carter chase you away so soon. My God, a *niece*. Of all things."

I thanked Miss Loos but walked directly to Hubble,

who was at the window gazing down into the Hollywood lights, pipe in hand. "Dr. Hubble," I said.

He turned and looked at me, glanced uncomfortably at Carter, then offered his huge hand.

I took it eagerly. "You discovered the expanding universe," I said.

"Well, not quite."

"But you know more about it than anyone else."

"Did your uncle tell you that?"

"No."

"No? Are you interested in astronomy?"

"Kind of."

Wrong answer. He nodded dismissively and turned away. The window opened on a constellation of city lights: Los Angeles, a city Huxley had once called "the great Metrollopis of the West."

"The universe is expanding," I said, "but there's no center. Wherever you are, *that's* the center. Here or a million light-years away, wherever there's an observer, he's at the center of the universe."

Hubble turned back. I had his attention again. He frowned at me. "Yes?"

"Is that right?"

"More or less."

"Well, I don't understand. Everything I've read talks about an observer. The observer is at the center of the universe. But what's an observer, exactly? Why is an *observer* at the center of the universe?"

He exhaled a great blue cloud of smoke into the jasmine-scented air.

"Bring a chair," he said. "Let's talk."

We talked—solemnly, intently—until Hubble's wife Grace came to drag him back to the party. Carter looked daggers at me from across the room.

But then Hubble turned back and said the words that left me breathless:

"You must visit Palomar," he said. "You must see the telescope."

That night they came again.

The party was over; the house was silent and quite

dark. I woke and was motionless, not only paralyzed but suspended—it seemed to me—between the tickings of the clock. The sense of helplessness, of vulnerability, was absolute. Moonlight shone through the window, and I remember dust motes hovering in that pearly light like weightless diamonds.

They were all around me—perhaps a dozen, gathered around the bed.

Huge, their eyes. Black, and unblinking, and sad.

A great part of the terror resides in those eyes. Powerful, these creatures, to come through walls, to move so silently, to immobilize their victims, float them perhaps into shining spaces, probe their bodies with the casual indifference of a woman rummaging in her purse for a lost key. . . .

But their eyes are so sad!

To all the obvious questions—what are they, what do they want, *why me?*—there was no answer but that ferocious and hungry nostalgia, the sadness of their eyes.

By daylight I might wonder: Are they sad for themselves? Or are they, somehow, sorry for me? But at night the questions are wordless, moot. That night in California they took me nowhere, only gazed at me, their huge heads bobbing, their eyes, all pupil, sad and frank as a child's eyes.

I could only lie motionless in bed and draw weak, stertorous breaths. I was afraid they would take me away with them, to the places that cloud memory, to the palace of unbearable light.

But they only peered at me until suddenly they were gone, and I could draw my breath at last and scream, scream until Carter burst into the room, scream until he put his hand against my cheek and said in wide-eyed wonder. "Sandra! My God! Sandra!"

In modern quantum physics, as well as in astronomy, there is an entity called "the observer." Seldom defined, "the observer" hovers over physics textbooks like a restless ghost. An electron is a particle or a wave, depending on "the observer." "The observer" collapses the wave function. "The observer" turns future into past, makes history of possibility.

But what's an observer? It was the question I had posed to Hubble, the question that still nags, even now, so many years later. What *is* an observer? Where do *observers* come from?

A week later Carter drove me to Palomar, up the breathless heights of the mountain.

Hubble had made the arrangements; Carter's own feelings about the visit were mixed. He didn't have enough seniority at the Hale Observatory to bring in a tourist—an adolescent girl, of all things—and he was still afraid I would embarrass him or, worse, annoy Edwin Hubble himself. At the same time, I had already attracted positive attention: not a bad thing.

He had been treating me with a little more respect since the party, though my occasional night terrors continued to frighten him.

(Join the club, I thought.)

We drove up the steepening slope along black asphalt switchbacks, even stopped for lunch at the Palomar Gardens, a restaurant halfway to the Hale Observatory. It was owned, I later learned, by George Adamski, an amateur astronomer and publicity-seeker who would later author a flock of books about "flying saucers." Watch the skies.

"He doesn't like children, you know," Carter said, talking about Hubble over cheeseburgers at the Gardens. "Keeps to himself. Likes to fly-fish, for Christ's sake. You know he was hit by lightning?"

"Really?"

"He was out in the woods somewhere, probably with his boots in the water and a fishing rod over his head. They say his heart nearly stopped. Some say he hasn't been the same since."

I think this was meant to intimidate me, but it only succeeded in making Hubble seem more vulnerable— more like myself. Maybe I'd been struck by lighting, too; maybe that's what was wrong with me.

We drove on to the observatory. The staff treated me like visiting royalty, gave me the tour. Palomar was about as romantic as an industrial plant, with the exception of the telescope itself, a heroic act of engineering, a 500-ton machine floating on pressurized oil. The horse-shoe mount was so immense it had been shipped to California from Westinghouse by way of the Panama Canal. The mirror, hidden in a steel iris like the bud of a night-blooming flower, had been the subject of bomb threats—it had been trucked up the mountain under police guard, to protect it from lunatics who believed the sky would open and rain fiery vengeance if stripped of all its secrets.

I looked a long time at the elevator that lifted an astronomer up to the observation perch, imagined Hubble disappearing into the throat of this grand and terrifying creation.

Of Hubble himself there was no sign, until I was escorted to a long trestle table in a concrete chamber where the staff took meals. He was there, alone, all furrowed brows, sketching on a paper napkin. I learned later that his presence was something of a novelty: The altitude was supposed to be bad for his heart; he hadn't been up the mountain for months, and his first telescope run in nearly a year was scheduled for September.

I sat down and drank Coke from a chilled bottle and he showed me what he'd drawn: a single dense much-penciled *O* at the center of the paper.

"O for Observer," he said.

"And the napkin is the universe?"

"The observable universe. Here at the edge, farthest from the observer, the red shift becomes infinite." He peppered the napkin with dots. "These are stars. But here is the observer's dilemma, Miss Lansing. He occupies the center of the observable universe, which is bounded by its own primordial past." He tapped the napkin. "From the observer's point of view, what part of the universe is the oldest?"

The speed of light is finite. Most of the stars the observer sees are younger than his own sun, younger still the more distant they are. A star ten thousand light-years distant is ten thousand years closer to the beginning of the universe, ten thousand years *less old* than the observer's own space. So I tapped the dot in the middle.

"Precisely! Here at the edge is the youngest universe, perhaps the universe moments after its birth. *The past.*

While here at the very center is . . . the *present*. So where on this map, Miss Lansing, do we find the *future*?"

I shrugged.

"Not shown," he said. "Very good. And yet, time passes. The universe expands. It *emanates*. The future, not yet existent, emerges from this point, this absolute spaceless point. . . ."

"From the observer?"

"From the observer as a spaceless point in his own subjective universe."

"From me?"

"From any observer."

I thought about it. "From my eyes? From my brain?"

He smiled quizzically and shrugged.

I was dazed by the idea of time radiating from my skull like lightning bolts from the RKO radio tower at the beginning of certain movies. The future was deep inside me. But I could only see the past: My eyes looked out, not in.

I thought about it while Hubble ate his lunch, taking delicate spoonfuls of soup.

"Does the universe expand," I asked, "or does the observer shrink?"

He smiled again. "The statements are commutable. It amounts to the same thing."

We shrink into the future, *collapse* into it. Nowadays people talk about black holes, singularities. The observer collapses into his own singularity, shrinking away from the universe at large.

I said, "If there was such a thing as a time machine—"

"If there was such a thing as a time machine, you would be able to pop out of your own skull and look at yourself."

I didn't want to imagine it. Too frightening.

"You're a very bright girl," the famous astronomer told me.

"Thank you."

"A very astute observer."

He lit his pipe. I blushed.

The night terrors abated but didn't stop. What did ebb, and quite quickly, was my uncle's patience.

I don't blame him. He had surrendered enough to me that summer: his privacy, his social life. But I stopped calling him at night, smothered my screams, clammed up at the breakfast table, because I couldn't bear the weight of his impatience. His impatience was obvious and caustic; it erased the glow of Hubble's approval, cast me back on my own troubled past.

He left me alone more often. Usually Evangeline was in the house, and on rare occasions we were allowed to borrow the car, see Hollywood, Sunset Boulevard, the ocean. Mostly, though, I wandered through the house while Evangeline worked in the kitchen. I watched KTLA from Mt. Wilson on my uncle's TV set, played Sinatra on his hi-fi rig, raided his library. (I read Huxley's *The Perennial Philosophy* and *Beyond the Mexique Bay* and understood neither.) At lunch, I assembled mile-high sandwiches and took them into the backyard, sequestered myself under an acacia tree with a magazine or just let the California sunshine make me drowsy.

My father phoned once a week. I told him I was having a great time. Had "the problem" come back? No, I said, and I don't think Carter contradicted me.

And by my own impoverished standards I *was* having a good time. "The problem" was at least in remission. Perhaps I was lulled into susceptibility.

I think Carter was lulled, too. I think that's why he left me alone in the house that August night.

Carter was an astronomer on a day schedule. Most of his work involved the tedious comparison of photographic plates, and I think he chafed at his junior status at Palomar. He must have needed a night life, God knows; if not with the stars, then with the constellations of human bodies at certain clubs along the Sunset Strip.

But he left me alone, and even after fifty years I find it difficult to forgive him.

He called an hour after Evangeline had served dinner and driven herself home, and though there was still plenty of daylight, the sun was westering; the shadows were longer, and I had begun to feel nervous. On the phone he sounded strange, perhaps a little drunk. He wouldn't be back until tomorrow, he said, and would I be all right?

And what could I say to that? I wanted to beg him not to leave me alone, but that would have been abject, cowardly. So I said I would be okay, probably, and hoped the quaver in my voice would communicate some of the terror I was feeling. But he didn't hear it, or didn't want to hear it. He thanked me lugubriously and hung up the phone. And that was that.

What do you do in an empty house, when you're alone and don't want to be?

The obvious things. I turned on all the lights, plus the TV set. Messed up the kitchen making popcorn. Watched *All-Star Revue* and *Your Show of Shows* and *Hit Parade*, by which time it was eleven o'clock and the street outside was quiet and I could hear crickets in the garden and the nervous whisper of my own breath. I stayed up later, smoked one of Carter's cigarettes and tried to enjoy a Charlie Chan movie but dozed in spite of myself. I remember deciding that I really truly ought to go to bed, but that was as far as I got. I slept on the sofa with my head on a velveteen cushion. And woke again, and the house was still ablaze with light, but my watch said it was two A.M., and the television was all snow and static—radio noise, cosmic rays, random electrons. I turned it off.

I remember thinking I should have closed the window blinds, that the house would be more secure that way. I stood up, yawned, went to the big picture window. Outside, the date palms danced in a fierce dry midnight wind, perhaps a Santa Ana. No human life was visible.

I tried to think of something nice, something comforting. I called up the memory of Hubble, of Hubble telling me I was "a bright girl." But that only reminded me of our conversation, which had been, to tell the truth, a little creepy. The universe was expanding, or I was shrinking, "the statements are commutable," and the future was inside me, and what if I could look in that direction?

What would I see, if I could turn my eyes inside out? I would see the future into which I was dwindling.

Perhaps a blackness as illimitable as death, a dark consuming nothingness.

Or would it be full of stars?

Or would it be a looking glass world, like Alice's: deceptively familiar, except for. . . .

For what?

And then I heard a noise from the kitchen.

The wind had blown open the back door. I closed it and locked it. If Carter had forgotten his keys, he could pound on the door. Maybe I'd let him in. Maybe not.

I turned at a suggestion of a shift in the light, and saw—

(The words are impotent. Powerless.)

Saw one of *them*.

It came through the wall. This was the kitchen wall where Carter had hung a Monet print and where Evangeline kept, lower down, a rack of hanging copper pans. It came through all these things without disturbing them, though one of the pans bumped gently against its neighbor, as if a breeze had touched it. The creature was indifferent, gray, only a little taller than myself. For a moment, I stared transfixed. It moved through the wall as if against a trivial resistance, like a man walking through surf. Then it was wholly in the room, and its head rotated in an oiled motion, and its vast black deep sad eyes locked on mine.

I drew a breath but didn't scream: Who would hear?

Instead I ran from the kitchen.

Not that there was anywhere to go, any safe place. Maybe I could have fled the house altogether, but if I opened the big front door, *what might be outside?* The night was too large; it would swallow me.

The visitor didn't instantly follow me into the living room, and that gave me a space to think, although the house was suddenly full of minor, deeply ominous sounds. I wanted tools, weapons, barricades. There was only my uncle's black telephone and, next to it, his Rolodex of personal numbers.

To my credit, I did the sanest thing first: I called Evangeline's number. There was no answer. Evangeline had found somewhere to go this Saturday night, or else she was a very deep sleeper.

I thought about dialing the operator and asking for the police—I could say I'd seen a prowler—but I knew the police would come and listen with dreary patience and tell me to lock the doors, and then I'd be alone again.

From the direction of the bedroom I heard a rustling sound, the sound of leaves in autumn, restless mice, cat's claws on glass.

I had reached the state of calm that borders on panic, when thoughts are crisp and weightless and nerves light up like neon tubes. I flipped through the Rolodex again, found Edwin Hubble's home number and dialed with a trembling finger.

Grace answered after seven rings. She was in no mood to comfort a frightened teenage girl. Nor would she put her husband on: "This is completely inappropriate, Sandra, and I'm sure your uncle would agree," and I was about to give up and run, just run when Hubble's deep voice displaced hers: "Sandra? What's wrong?"

Suddenly it seemed possible the whole thing had been a humiliating mistake. I had dreamed the monster in the kitchen. And even if not, what could I tell the stern and unforgiving Edwin Hubble, how could I enlist his sympathy for what he would almost certainly consider an adolescent fantasy?

But I needed someone in the house. Above all else, that.

I mumbled something about my uncle being away and "There's something wrong here, and I'm sorry, but I don't know what to do, and there's no one else I can call!"

"What sort of problem?"

Big silence. I listened for monsters. "It's hard to explain."

I think he heard in my voice what Carter hadn't: the sweaty tremolo of fear.

Miraculously, he said he'd be right over. (I heard Grace protesting in the background.)

"Thank you," I said.

And put down the phone reluctantly. No voice now

but my own. The house all echoes and stubborn shadows.

I was in a frenzy of embarrassment when, some twenty minutes later, Hubble's big Ford pulled into the driveway. There had been no more visitations. The kitchen was empty; I asked Hubble to look, and then I looked myself.

We didn't talk about what I thought I had seen, or if we did it was only in the most indirect, delicate way. He seemed to know without being told. I wondered if Carter had already briefed him on "my problem."

He cased the house, and then we sat at opposite ends of my uncle's long living room sofa. I asked him whether he was ever scared, perched in his supernaturally powerful telescope at the top of a mountain, staring into the bottomless deeps of space.

He smiled. "You know, Edith Sitwell once asked me the same thing. I was showing her some photographic plates. Galaxies millions of light-years distant. It terrified her. The immensity of it. To be such a mote, less than dust among the stars—to see oneself from that perspective."

I had no idea who Edith Sitwell was. (An English writer; she had been in Hollywood to consult on a script about Anne Boleyn.) "What did you tell her?"

"That it's only terrifying at first. After a time you learn to take comfort from it. If we're nothing, then there's nothing to be frightened of. The stars are indifferent."

The words were not especially soothing, but his presence was. Even at the end of his life, Hubble was still the former athlete, six foot two, almost two hundred pounds. A guardian, powerful and benign. I wondered why he had come so willingly. He was supposed to despise children and he had little sympathy for weakness.

I wonder now if he was suddenly conscious of his own mortality. He must have known he was nearing the end of his life; this visit might have been the random kindness of a dying man. Or maybe he just missed late nights, mysteries, the hours before sunrise. Maybe he'd been away from the telescope for too long.

Certainly he remembered what it was like to be alone and afraid. He told me about a summer job he'd held when he was seventeen ("Only three years older than you!"), working with a survey crew in northern Wisconsin, trekking into what was then a virgin forest. He talked about the campfires and canvas tents and sextants and the way the sky opened like a book in the silence of the great woods. "Sometimes," he admitted, "I saw things. . . ."

"What kind of things?"

But he wouldn't say. He changed the subject. "Time for bed," he told me. "Past time."

"But you'll be here?"

"I'll be here. It won't be the first dawn I've seen, you know, Sandra."

I slept while Edwin Hubble kept watch for me.

I slept in the dark, and woke to a harsh and terrible light.

The palace of light.

Should I call it a flying saucer? An unidentified object? I don't know if it's either of those things; I've never seen it objectively, as a sky-ship, a vehicle, though there have been accounts (and I do recognize the details) in which people describe it that way. Still, the words trivialize the experience. Was I taken up into a "flying saucer?" Surely not; surely it wasn't one of those silver-domed art-deco totems from the cover of *Fate* magazine.

No, it was . . . the palace of light.

The palace of light.

I was taken up through the beams and tiles of the house, lifted above the roof in a slow delirium of terror, and then I was in the palace of light. I had been here before, but every visit is as fresh and terrifying as the first. The light was soulless, sullen, and everywhere at once. It hurt my eyes. *They* gathered around me, a dozen or more; they turned their sad and quizzical eyes on me, queried my body with probes and syringes of solid light.

The ordeal was endless, worse because there seemed to be no malevolence in it, only a bland curiosity. And, of course, the sadness. I wondered: Why don't they weep?

This time, though, the experience was different. My body was paralyzed, my eyes were not, and when I looked to my left I was astonished to see Edwin Hubble floating above a pedestal of light, equally helpless, equally bound and paralyzed. But his eyes were wide open.

I remember that. His eyes were wide open, and he seemed . . . *not afraid.*

He seemed almost at home with these creatures—with their sadness and their curiosity.

But I was not. I closed my eyes and prayed for dawn, begged for unconsciousness, begged for a door back into my daylight life.

When I woke, Edwin Hubble had gone.

What woke me, in fact, was the sound of the front door. It was Carter, home from the night's revels. The window was full of morning light and fresh with the smell of jasmine and acacia and a few warm ions from the distant sea.

I spent the day in a frenzy of apprehension: Hubble would say something to Carter, lodge a complaint; I would be disgraced, humiliated, sent home to another round of psychiatric torture.

But I don't think Carter ever found out Hubble had visited that night; or if he did, he was too ashamed to make an issue of it. He was the one who had been AWOL, after all. I was only a child.

But I don't think he knew. When he came home from Palomar the next day he was an uncommunicative as ever.

And I was, as ever, frightened of the dark. . . .

But here is the strange fact: *They didn't come back.*

Not that night, or the night after; or any other night in California or in the decades since.

(Except lately . . .)

They didn't come back. I had lost them, somehow. I had learned to evade them.

I had learned not to let my eyes turn inside out.

* * *

I didn't see Edwin Hubble again that summer—not until the last day (the last hour, in fact) of my visit.

It was a Saturday, end of August. Uncle Carter drove me to the airport. I sat silently in the passenger seat of the car, whispering good-bye to the dwarf palms and the tindery hills and the bobbing duck-billed oil rigs. We arrived half an hour early.

I was astonished—though less astonished, I think, than Carter—when Edwin Hubble met us at the luggage check-in, gave us a wide grin, and steered us to the lunch counter while we waited for my flight to be called.

Hubble said he hoped I had enjoyed my stay and my visit to the Hale Observatory. Pleasantries all around, but there wasn't really much to say or time to say it. At last, my bewildered uncle excused himself and lined up for a second cup of coffee.

And I sat at the table with the famous astronomer.

He touched his finger to his lips: I was not to speak.

"If you look into the uncreated world," he said quietly, "it looks back at you. Maybe you think, *why me? How did they find me?* But it's a mirror world, Sandra. Maybe they *didn't* find you. Maybe you found them."

"But—!"

"Shh. It isn't wise to speak about this. You have a knack for turning your eyes inside out, so you see them. And they see you. And you're afraid, because they're from the uncreated future, from a place, I think, where the human race has reached its last incarnation, from the end of the material world. Perhaps the end of all worlds. And they're sad—melancholy is the better word—because you're like an angel to them, the angel of the past, the angel of infinite possibility. Possibility lost. The road not taken."

My uncle was heading back to the table, too soon, with tepid black coffee in a waxed-paper cup.

Suddenly I wanted to cry. "I don't understand!"

Hubble touched his lips again. He was solemn. "One doesn't have to understand in order to look. One has to look, in order to understand."

Carter stood beside the table, glancing between the

old astronomer and myself. "They're calling your flight," he said. "Did I miss something?"

Edwin Hubble died that autumn, still making plans for the Hale Observatory, still probing the limits and implications of the red shift. He suffered a fatal heart attack at the end of September—the 27th, if I recall correctly. He had been on the mountain for the first time in months, making long photographic exposures of NGC 520, and he was looking forward to another run. I cried when I heard the news.

My uncle continued his career in astronomy, eventually left Palomar for a tenured position at CalTech. He died, too, halfway through Reagan's second term.

George Adamski, who owned the diner halfway up the mountain, went on to publish several accounts of gaudy flying-saucer jaunts around the solar system. Crank books, clearly, though I sometimes wonder what prompted his change of career.

Aldous Huxley, whom I had met briefly at my uncle's party, experimented with mescaline and wrote *The Doors of Perception,* his own inquiry into what he called "the antipodes of the mind." His book dwells at length on light, the quality of light, the intensity of light. He died of throat cancer on November 22nd, 1963, the day Kennedy was shot.

And I went back to Toronto, finished school, left home, married a petroleum chemist, raised two children, and nursed my beloved husband through his own long struggle with cancer.

I live alone now, in a world 1953 might not recognize as its linear descendant. The multicultural, information-intensive, post-industrial present. The Great Metrollopis of the World. The world is full of frightening things.

But I am not afraid to look at what I see.

Lately they have come back.

They have come back, or, Hubble might say, I have gone back to them.

There is no explanation. They are the perennially anticlimactic, the ever-unknown. The world expands, or I am shrinking, and sometimes my less than 20/20 vision turns inside out, and in the long empty nights I see them moving through the walls; I have even visited the palace of light, and the palace of light is as terrible and enigmatic as ever.

And they are as sad as ever, their eyes more poignant than I remembered, but—is it possible?—they seem, in their alien fashion, somehow *pleased* with me.

Pleased, I think, because I'm not afraid of them anymore.

I look, in order to understand. The understanding is elusive, but I suppose it will come, perhaps at the moment I reach the final dwindling point, the event horizon of my own life, when the universe expands to infinity . . . and will they be there?

Waiting?

I don't know—I understand so very little—but I am not afraid to look: I am a good observer at last. My eyes are open, and I am not afraid.

DIPLOMATIC EXCHANGE

by Will Murray

Will Murray is the author of nearly 50 pseudonymous novels in the long-running *Destroyer, Doc Savage,* and *Executioner* series. He is a regular contributor to *Crypt of Cthulhu* and *Lovecraft Studies*. Other short fiction by him is found in *Miskatonic University* and *100 Wicked Little Witch Stories*.

It was to have been a night launch.

The pines of South Dakota's Black Hills stood out in spectral relief as under converging floodlights, the flight crew pumped propane-heated air into the stirring bag of aluminized Mylar. It swelled, lifted, and slowly drew erect, a fifteen-story teardrop emblazoned with corporate logos surrounding the scarlet legend, *ARGOSY III*. The balloon shroud shed frost flakes, which the January wind carried to Ray Starkweather's rugged expectant face.

Standing by the open hatch of the canary-yellow gondola, he was oblivious to their cold bite. His black eyes ranged the silvery envelope, searching for telltale rips or tears that would doom his latest attempt to solo around the globe by high-altitude balloon. He saw none.

His flight crew drew back from the growing envelope, binoculars trained on the shimmering giant inflating.

It was cold in the Stratobowl, the pine-girt natural crater where for sixty years balloonists had ventured into the stratosphere from its wind-sheltered protection. The chill touched him, but Starkweather barely felt it through his blue fleece-lined flight suit. Where he was going, high in the thin, dry reaches of the atmosphere, mere cold was a minor inconvenience.

From his walkie-talkie, voices crackled.

"North visual check, green."

"This is south. Bag appears pristine."

Starkweather rogered them all in turn as the bag reached its full inflation. Elasped time: four hours, twenty-two minutes.

"Time to go, Ray," chief meteorologist Paul Sampson said, clapping him on the back. "Good luck."

Starkweather ducked into the hatch, dogged it, and took his command chair. If the winds and Fate were right, he was twenty-plus days from landfall in aviation history.

The gondola lifted with a gentle lurching sway that was arrested by the ground crew. Then it went straight up, silently into the cobalt sky, where not even eagles dared.

It was Ray Starkweather's third attempt. And his last. Corporate funding had run out. If he failed this time, the money boys with their De Roziere balloons and pressure cabins would conquer the last unaccomplished achievement in aeronautical history.

Altitude sickness had scotched his last attempt. First time out, the bag had split, dropping him into the shallow waters off Cape Cod. But that had been a lucky break. An hour later, and he would have gone to the bottom of the Atlantic, trapped in the fragile plastic pod.

This time—

This time the hanging gondola grazed the tops of the pines with a skeletal scraping that made the skin on the soles of his feet bunch and creep.

"What the hell?" Starkweather got on his radio. *"Argosy III* to Stratobowl Base. *Argosy* to Stratobowl. Why am I dragging along the treetops? Come back."

"Ray, you're not getting proper lift."

"I see that, dammit! Why not?"

"Bag appears to be wavering. West face. Possible leak."

"Impossible!" Starkweather bit back.

"I see rippling. Envelope is definitely rippling!"

Then the unnerving scraping became a clawing and crackling as the gigantic balloon settled into complaining pines. Inside, eyes pinched in pain, Starkweather pounded the tacky pod walls as defeat overcame him.

The gondola landed on its side, shrouded in hundreds of pounds of collapsed Mylar. They had to rescue him from the sadsack tangle. The worst part of it was the uncontrollable nosebleed he earned when his face banged a bulkhead on impact.

Dawn found them still at the site, going over the envelope for punctures—all localized on the west face of the shroud.

"This is ridiculous," Starkweather was muttering darkly. "We doubled up on the Mylar ply this time out."

Paul said: "Ray, let's face it, *Argosy*'s a glorified picnic basket supported by an overblown sack of hot air. Something was bound to go wrong—just like last time."

Starkweather said nothing. He was fuming.

Someone gave out a yell. Starkweather was the first to the scene. A crewman had spread out a section of envelope and barked, "Found a puncture!"

Starkweather eyed it. "Looks like a B-B hole to me."

"Well, we can take it up with the manufacturer, but what's the point?" Paul said disgustedly. "We're history."

"The wrong kind of history," Starkweather said ruefully.

The corporate sponsors had fled by the time they dragged the flaccid envelope back into the shed. Nursing a Styrofoam cup of black coffee, Starkweather regarded it like a beachcomber contemplating a beached whale.

Later, he would be certain he hadn't heard the footsteps coming up from behind. Yet he turned as if expecting someone. Almost as if a scene from a film were being reenacted, and he was a minor player.

The man wore black. Suit, tie, wing tips. His face was a pale, expressionless mask under anthracite-lensed sunglasses.

"Ray Starkweather." His voice matched his taste in clothes. A mortician's voice.

"Yeah?"

"Del Vincent. National Reconnaissance Office. On behalf of the Department of Defense, I have a proposition for you."

"Do I know you?"

"We've never met."

"You look familiar."

"I have that kind of face," Vincent said. He was all business and got to the point:

"The National Reconnaissance Office is prepared to underwrite your next attempt at a global circumnavigation. I'm authorized to supply you with a state-of-the-art De Roziere hybrid balloon and solar-powered pressure cabin. All you have to do is carry an NRO instrument package on board."

"If you have that kind of equipment, why do you need me?"

"Balloonists with stratospheric experience can be counted on half a hand. And for security reasons, we require an American."

Defeat had laid its cold touch on Ray Starkweather too heavily for him to jump at the opportunity. He was still trying to place the man's face.

"NRO. That's an intelligence organization, isn't it?"

"Correct. I'm with the Cryptic Events Evaluation Section. For this mission, U-2s and Zircon satellites are useless. We're interested in atmospheric lightning. You know what that is, of course."

"Yeah. Red sprites and blue flashes. They shoot up from the backs of storm clouds. All the way into the ionosphere. No one knows much about them, except they have something to do with the global electrical circuit. What's NRO's interest in that stuff?"

"Classified. All we want from you is to make your attempt. No interference from us. Just maintain mission secrecy. Film the phenomena using low-light videography. And activate an instrument package at the agree-upon time and locality."

"I see." Starkweather downed the last dregs of bitter coffee. He crushed the cup and threw it aside. "De Roziere balloon, you say? With one of those, I can compete with Branson and the big money boys."

"You'll be able to climb above weather into the jet stream. Take advantage of the Coriolis effect to sweep you along. And you won't be risking oxygen starvation, like your last time up. I understand the hallucinations make LSD pale."

Starkweather winced. He still had nightmares of what

he thought climbed into *Argosy II* with him. "Okay, I'm game. How soon can we start flight preparations?"

"The equipment is in inventory. We launch whenever you say."

"You make it sound like my answer was in the bag."

Vincent gestured to the deflated Mylar. "Three strikes, and you've been handed a fresh bat. How could you say no?"

Starkweather grunted. "What movie did you steal that line from?"

"I make up my own dialogue. We'll be in touch."

After Vincent left, Paul strolled up and asked, "Where have I seen that creepy guy before?"

"In your dreams. He's the angel that put us back in business." Turning to his crew, Starkweather shouted, "Gather up that useless sack. We have preparations to make."

The De Roziere was impressive. It consisted of a 200,000-cubic-foot helium balloon constructed of the same polymer that keeps potato chips crisp in their bags, nestled inside an aluminized Mylar sheath filled with hot air. A smaller helium balloon supported the shroud.

The capsule, painted International Orange, resembled an aluminum oil drum bulging with integral propane tanks. Its skin was festooned with dark photovoltaic panels and TV cameras. The forward end was Control. The hatch end was filled with a cramped bunk and mini-toilet. The plexiglass bubble over the control position was a bonus feature.

"Not bad," Starkweather said, slapping the gleaming skin with his hand. It rang dolefully. "And I like the no-logo look."

"It will get you there. And back," Vincent said humorlessly. "Let's get you acquainted with the equipment."

"Where's the package?"

"When you're ready to launch, it will be there."

Starkweather shook his head. "That won't be for at least a month. We have to check everything out. Prefly the rig."

"No need. This bird has been aloft. NRO certifies it as airworthy."

And it was. Three weeks to the day from *Argosy III*'s ill-fated flight, Ray Starkweather was overseeing a dawn launch from the shelter of the Stratobowl.

Under halogen floodlamps, the envelope inflated like a dream. Starkweather watched it with a calm confidence he couldn't put his finger on.

"I feel like I've done this before," he muttered.

"You have," Vincent said. When Starkweather eyed him speculatively, Vincent added, "*Argosy I, II,* and *III.* Remember?"

"Not what I meant. I have this nagging *déjà vu* feeling."

Vincent said a tight-lipped nothing.

The envelope was by now clearing the pine tops. Starkweather felt his chest inflating with the helium of excitement. The balloon reared up like a squid standing on stringy tentacles.

Vincent snapped open a cellphone and barked, "Bring the package."

A team of stone-featured, white-coated tech types hustled from a waiting RV. The package was long and square, like a child's toybox of burnished copper. They carried it to the waiting hatch and carefully slid it under the bunk, locking it down.

"That's it?" Starkweather blurted out.

"That's it."

"But it's sealed. How do I activate it?"

"It's self-activating."

Starkweather looked doubtful. Vincent laid a cold hand on his shoulder and said, "It's time."

"Something's not right about this."

"Everything is going according to plan. Good luck."

The hatch clanged shut. Starkweather took his seat, went through a last-minute electrical check, and in short order the capsule was aloft. Not a jar. Smooth as silk.

It cleared the tree line and sought the dawn in an ethereal silence that banished all concern.

From Control, Starkweather looked upward often, checking the huge supporting envelope. It was as stable as if fixed in amber. The capsule felt like a warm womb. There was no sensation of rising, no bouncing. It was perfect launch weather. Calm below sea level, with a prevailing easterly wind to carry him away.

The day-long passage over the Atlantic states was uneventful. Blue water came into view through the side and floor ports as twilight fell and the helium balloon began losing lift in the cooling air. The autopilot kicked in, blowing propane-ethane flame into the Mylar shroud. It puffed, filling with hot air. Until the sun returned, the autopilot would blast hot air into the bag whenever the altimeter dropped. Then helium would take over.

Time for another radio check.

"*Argosy IV* to Base. Over."

"*We read you,* Argosy IV." It was Vincent's cold voice.

"What are you doing on my radio, Vincent?"

"*We have an interest in your mission.*"

"Dammit, let my people do their jobs."

"*After the package is activated.*"

There was no winning this argument, so Starkweather let it ride.

The *Argosy* soared through the troposphere. Weather was with him. It was no more bumpy than a typical roller-coaster ride. High cumulus clouds came level with the capsule, then fell away as the bag strained toward the stratosphere. Hours passed. The sun sank fully beneath the sharp curvature of Earth. The heavens took on the mood and hue of indigo.

Starkweather monitored his systems. Thirty-six hours in, and no malfunctions. Weather reports came in with clocklike regularity. Global Positioning Satellite feeds told him exactly where he was. Strategically placed video cameras allowed him to monitor the Mylar shroud for problems. He detected none.

Finally, it was time to punch into the jet stream.

He disengaged the autopilot and turned on the overhead burner full blast. The altimeter climbed in jumps.

The transition was rough. The jet stream was active. The dome of the sheath bumped fast-moving air, bounced back. Starkweather fed the bag additional lift. Bump. Bounce. Like a beachball scraping along the roof of an underground river. Helpless, the capsule twirled like a yoyo on a string.

On the third attempt, *Argosy* achieved penetration. The capsule swung wildly. G-forces buffeted Starkweather about the cramped cabin as the Coriolis effect snatched *Argosy* along. Twenty minutes of rough weather, then bag and capsule settled onto course. A willing prisoner of the jet stream, she was carried inevitably eastward at a brisk 250-plus miles per hour.

Above lay what scientists ruefully called the ignorosphere—the lower ionosphere. Sunlight, when it returned, would be intense. Starkweather began wishing the topside bubble were tinted. Still, he'd trade a sunburned neck for an electrically warmed capsule anytime. He still had nightmares about cat-eyed gremlins that had climbed aboard when oxygen starvation got him during *Argosy II*.

Vincent broke into the long peaceful lull of a violet-orange dawn.

"Stratobowl Base to Argosy. *Copy."*

"Argosy receiving. That you, Vincent?"

"The same. According to the latest satellite feed, you're over the British Isles."

"That's what my instruments confirm."

"Approximately 40 kilometers due west of your position, there is electrical storm activity," Vincent advised.

"Roger."

"Look for red sprites. They've been known to shoot 100 kilometers into the E-ledge of the ionosphere. You may hear a popping and clattering on your radio. If we lose contact, remain in your control chair. No matter what happens. Do you understand?"

"Where else am I going to go—to bed?" Starkweather shot back acidly.

"Remember your instructions."

Over Scotland, the clouds began gathering. Starkweather watched them from his high, serene vantage point. They looked like a herd of dark angry elephants on the march. From time to time, they broke into fitful eruptions of light as they discharged electricity earthward.

He broke out the low-light videocam and got down

on the floor, where the sealed porthole looked straight down. If he was lucky, he'd capture one of the three-millisecond-long red sprites as it jumped off the back of a thundercloud and sought the high electron density of the E-ledge. If he was *really* lucky, he'd snag one of the rarer blue jets.

The camera whirred, disturbing the eerie silence of near-space.

The sky turned red in all directions.

"Gotcha!" Starkweather said.

The red suffused the inside of the capsule like atomized blood, lying like a gory shine under the flat floor port. Strangely, it remained steady. And deepened.

Something—a tingle of buried memory—made Starkweather look upward. He got a face full of hot red light. It was deepening, as if coming closer. From on high.

"What the—"

Dropping the camera, Starkweather regained his chair. He snapped on the radio. "*Argosy* to Base. Come back."

"*Vincent here.*"

"Vincent, have you ever heard of a red sprite of long duration?"

"You have a red contact?"

"Yeah," Starkweather poked his head into the clear dome, craning in all directions. "Seems to be originating from the ionosphere. It's filling the atmosphere in all directions like a red sprite, but it's constant."

"*Good. Right on time.*"

"What's right on time?"

"*You are. Listen up, Starkweather. No matter what happens, do not panic. Everything is normal, whatever you see, whatever happens, is supposed to happen. Understand?*"

"What are you—"

"*We've been through this before. Nothing will hurt you.*"

"We've been through *what* before? Put Paul on."

"*Paul's on ice now that we're into the classified phase of the mission.*"

The intense red burned Starkweather's furious face. "What *is* this crap? This is my endeavor, Vincent!"

"*Relax. We're approaching the exchange point. Remain*

in Control. Whatever happens, do not enter the bunk compartment."

"What do you mean, *we?"* Starkweather muttered under his breath.

Soon the radio was popping and hissing like a cat spitting hot grease.

Starkweather lifted his voice. "I *sput* to know what's going on."

Vincent came back, his voice breaking up.

"Starzzziiiii pop! sput."

"What?"

Crackle. *"Remain in Control.* pop! *package* pop! *will take* pop! *of itself."*

A sound came through the capsule's insulated skin. It made Starkweather's heart leap into his throat and brought him back into his seat, sweating.

It sounded like someone was undogging the hatch. It was impossible. Not up here. The metallic sound continued. He checked his oxygen gauge. It was good. This wasn't oxygen deprivation playing with his mind.

"Oh, my God!"

Starkweather jumped for the door. If the hatch came open here at twelve thousand feet, it was all over. Asphixiation. Death by freezing. He squirmed in, lunged for the inner hatch wheel, grabbed it in both bone-white hands.

The wheel was turning. Definitely turning. This was no hallucination. He set his feet and wrenched it around in the opposite direction. The wheel responded. Then, stubbornly, it reversed direction again.

Sweating, Starkweather pitted his strength against the impossible external force attempting to undog the hatch. It proved too much for him. It was like fighting an inexorable machine.

At his back, the control room radio was sputtering and popping. Vincent was trying to raise him.

"Remain calm. This crackle *all planned. You are in* sput *danger. Do you understand? You are* pop! *no danger."*

Then the hatch mechanism gave a cold clank, followed by a long hiss that told Starkweather the pressure seal had been compromised.

Cursing, he recoiled, fell back into the waiting bunk.

Slowly, the hatch opened. His eyes were fixed on it. Red radiance seeped in, blinding him. He expected to be sucked out. But there was no turbulence. No violent rush of air.

The hatch fell all the way open and the cabin pressure remained undisturbed.

"I'm dreaming," Starkweather muttered sickly.

Then the dream took on a surreal quality.

A pair of cat's eyes loomed in the red light. They floated into the cabin, resolving into a mincing mannikin that paused as its feet slapped pertly on the cabin floor.

There were three of them. Four feet high, dressed in coverall outfits resembling aluminized Mylar. They had two pipestem arms and two spindly legs and one head possessing an impressionistic humanness, but were as alien to humankind as the smooth face of a painted Easter egg.

Their feline eyes fell on Starkweather, then shifted to the package racked beneath the bunk. One gestured. The other two came forward, ignoring Starkweather.

Together, they pulled the copper package out from under the bunk, touching the top with a crystal wand that flared at the tip. The lid split at midsection. One end hoisted up.

Inside, resting in funeral-parlor white satin, lay a corpse, thin-fingered hands resting on its tiny chest.

It resembled one of the three creatures, except the eyes looked like scars in old wood and the smooth gray features had fallen in and dried like old autumn leaves.

Mutely, they reclosed the box. The crystal wand flared blue, and the box simply levitated up to and out the hatch.

The sentry at the hatch stood aside as it passed. His ovoid head dipped in a brief gesture of respect, eyes thinning.

And out in the thin air of the high stratosphere, a pulsing scarlet globe hovered like a Christmas tree bulb. It irised open, receiving the coffin in silence. Thin-eyed humanoids took possession.

The radio continued to sputter.

"Starkweather, I need to hear pop! *voice. Starkweather,* crackle *are you?"*

The leader fixed Starkweather with his unwinking eyes. And a chill went through him—a chill of remembrance.

"Where have I seen you before?" he croaked. It was no vague *déjà vu.* He had looked into those eyes before. Somewhere, some time. . . .

It hit him like a hammer in the center of his forehead.

"Christ! Your eyes. You're one of my damn altitude-sickness gremlins!"

In response, the being gestured thinly toward the control cabin.

Stumbling back, Starkweather retreated into the cabin. He fell wooden-legged into his chair and picked up the mike.

"Starkweather here," he croaked.

"Report."

"Package . . . is gone. . . ."

"Good."

"Vincent, Vincent, I'm not alone up here," he breathed.

"Check your oxygen. Sounds like a touch of altitude sickness."

"I've got my ass hanging out in space, breathing unbreathable air with a goddamned UFO holding *Argosy* up like a puppet."

"Damn."

"I saw what was in the coffin."

Vincent's voice tightened. *"I'm disappointed in you, Starkweather. We did better last time."*

Starkweather kept his back to the frightening openness at his back. "What last time?" he demanded.

"You think you kept ditching because of equipment failure. That was us. We set you up. The last time I punched a handful of B-B shot into your damn envelope to bring you down."

Starkweather's fingers whitened on the mike. "Why? Why?"

"Back in '47, one of their saucers crashed in New Mexico. We ended up with three bodies. One year ago, they opened diplomatic contact with Washington. We agreed

to an exchange, one body at a time. They didn't trust us, or us them. So we worked out a way to do the exchange on neutral ground. The stratosphere. We needed someone who could make the exchange and be cut loose with no knowledge of his role. They're not ready to reveal their presence yet. And we need to keep the lid on for domestic political reasons."

Awe threaded Starkweather's voice. "This changes everything. We're not alone."

"That's old news. But never mind that. I want you to calm down. The transfer is done. It's out of your hands. Just sit tight."

"For what?"

"Wait for it."

Starkweather felt something cold touch his sweating temple. His right eye caught a clear flash of crystal that flared violet.

And in his fading consciousness, Vincent's voice was saying dispassionately, *"That was gray corpse number two. I'll be in touch about number three. . . ."*

The bedside telephone rang and rang and rang.

Half-asleep, Ray Starkweather fumbled it off its cradle. He shivered. He had shivered for six days ever since the British rescue helicopter had plucked him out of the cold waters off the Shetland Islands.

"Ray Starkweather?" a voice asked. He sounded like a funeral director asking after the dearly departed.

"Yeah . . . who's this?"

"My name is Vincent. Calling from the Pentagon. National Reconnaissance Office. Congratulations on being the first solo high-altitude balloonist to almost circumnavigate the globe."

"I almost drowned trying . . ." Starkweather shivered again.

"Nevertheless, we admire your guts. And we believe you have the stuff to succeed. The NRO is prepared to offer you equipment, crew, and funding to stage another attempt. In return, you will carry a classified instrument package on your voyage."

"You make it sound easy. I'm broke, suffering from hypothermia and my crew has left me in disgust."

"The equipment is in inventory. A De Roziere hybrid balloon. We can launch whenever you're up to it."

"You sound like my answer is a foregone conclusion."

"Four strikes, and you've been handed a fresh bat. How could you say no?"

Starkweather grunted. "What movie did you steal that line from?"

"I make up my own dialogue. We'll be in touch."

As he hung up the telephone and sank back into the hospital bed, Ray Starkweather stared at the ceiling. "I know that line from somewhere. . . ."

Sleep refused to come. But his shivering went on all night long. In his mind's eye, he kept seeing disembodied cats' eyes floating in a mist like luminous blood.

Weird how oxygen deprivation played tricks on the mind. Why, Starkweather wondered, did his imagination conjure up damned gremlins every time. . . .

SECRET SERVICE
by Edward Lee

Former cop, tank gunner, and pump jockey, Edward Lee
has had nine horror novels published, *Ghouls, Incubi* and
Creekers among them. In addition, he has had dozens of
short stories, reviews and commentaries published in genre
magazines and major anthologies. His *Hot Blood 4* story,
"Mr. Torso," was nominated for the Horror Writers' Associa-
tion's Bram Stoker Award. He lives in Crofton, Maryland.

"Victor four, six, forty-six delta, romeo nine, nine,
forty-nine tango, echo eight, seven, forty-seven
sierra," the old man muttered.

He looked up, however briefly, and caught Karen's
eye, one of his own eyes long since obscured by cata-
racts. He smiled shakily, deepening the furrows of age.

Garand took Karen's arm, then loudly said to the old
man, "Ms. Lavender will be back shortly, Mr. President.
She still has some processing to finish."

"It was, uh, nice meeting you, Mr. President," Karen
said.

The old man held his smile on Karen. "Yes, yes, nice
meeting you, too, young miss. We'll watch TV?"

"Sure, Mr. President, all the TV you want," and then
Garand pulled her aside and took her back into the
house.

Some President, Karen thought through a smirk.

To be more correct: a *former* President. It was difficult
to believe that this broken, half-blind old man sitting in
a lawn chair, one Rowland Wilcox Raymond, had served
two terms as the Chief Executive of the United States
of America. *What a rip-off,* Karen thought.

"You see what we mean?" Garand said.

"Alzheimer's and a half," Karen said. Former President

Raymond had been diagnosed several years ago—she remembered hearing it on the news. He was ninety-two now, and in otherwise perfect health.

"He just seems so . . . I don't know. Like someone's grandfather."

Garand chuckled dryly. "Well, in that case, Granddad has a big mouth."

"A big mouth?" Karen inquired. "What do you mean?"

Garand shrugged. "He used to be the President, for God's sake, privy to the most sensitive information in the world—and now he's got Alzheimer's. Talk about a classified nightmare. Anything he might say, right off the top of his head, could jeopardize our national security."

"Oh, come on," Karen scoffed. "He can't remember anything important, can he? He's ancient."

"Ancient?" Garand shook his head. "Those numbers he was reeling off? They were permissive-action suffixes. You know. ICBM launch codes."

Fuck, she thought. However profane, it was a pale thought, and a hopeless one. Almost ten years on Uniform Branch—night duty at the goddamn Oman Embassy on Massachusetts Avenue. The closest she'd ever gotten to the White House was seeing it on a post card. All right, so her performance ratings weren't that high, and the 2.5 at Maryland probably didn't help, but— *It's because I never slept with the Field Supervisors,* she felt sure. *That's why I never got promo'd to White House duty. Sexist pigs. Their brains are in their Jockeys.* The only reason she'd joined the Secret Service in the first place was to guard the President—the *real* President—a critical service, a job with prestige and honor. *And because I don't do the nasty with every pantload in the upper office, I get ten years of night shifts for a bunch of Arabs . . . and now . . . this . . .*

Well, at least she got out of Uniform Branch, and the 2000-acre ranch in Sacramento was nice. But when she'd asked for the Presidential Security Detail . . . this wasn't quite what she'd had in mind.

"I can fly anything God can make," the President said.

"I should've put USAEUR on Defcon One. Fuck 'em. The ice cream—*that's* the answer."

"Senile *and* crazy," she whispered to herself.

"What's that, missy?"

"Nothing, Mr. President. I was just saying that it was very *hazy* today."

"Ah, yes, you're right. It was the Texas Mafia. LBJ knew all about it."

Karen wiped spittle off his chin, refilled his anti-spill cup with Kool-Aid. After a week, she'd stopped being appalled. What was the point? "All you gotta do is stay with him until eight A.M," Garand, the Case Agent In Charge, had instructed. "Feed him, change channels for him, like that. Since his diagnosis, his sleep schedule's changed, a typical symptom of Alzheimer's. He's awake all night long, likes to watch TV."

Great, Karen thought. *My illustrious career forges on . . . with reruns of* Three's Company *and* Golden Girls.

"But *don't* let him out of your sight. He's crafty. There were a couple of times when he got out of the house at night. We don't want the President getting off the property and winding up on Route 40. Can you imagine if someone picked him? He'd be spouting off our MIRV targets, or telling someone that Brezhnev was actually murdered with Prussic acid contact poison administered by a U.S. Army field operative."

Karen's spirit felt like a stone dropped in a well. *Plunk.*

"Cheer up," Garand said. "At least he can go to the bathroom by himself. Well . . . usually. Oh, and you don't mind cooking, do you?"

Garand had the audacity to give her a card file of the President's favorite dishes. "Did you enjoy your dinner, Mr. President?" Karen asked, taking up the empty plate.

"Oh, yes, I'd like dinner very much. I would like corned beef and cabbage, and potato rolls, please. And the Green Giant brand lima beans."

Which was what he'd just devoured in a considerable portion only moments ago. Karen sighed.

"TV, TV! Magnum!"

Not a professional notion but an honest one: She saw herself wringing his neck. At least then her life would be interesting, not this busy-work executive nanny stuff. Porridge was more interesting. A ten-pound bag of fertilizer was more interesting than this inept tragedy that was her life. Returning from the kitchen, she found the President finnicking with the lock on the french doors.

Pain in the ass. "Just where do you think you're going, Mr. President?"

"I'm meeting North and that ghoul Casey at the Old Executive Office Building. I've got to tell them to shred everything." He blew spit bubbles as she guided him back to his chair. "Casey wants one of his ops to hit Woodward. George thinks we should, and frankly, you'd need a crowbar to get into Hayworth's pants. God knows I tried."

Back in her seat, her mind blanked. These slips of senility weren't even funny anymore; by now she'd heard it all: senseless prattle laced with startling utterances. "No, no, it was *Bobby* who did it—she was pregnant. Peter Lawford watched the door." "The *Thresher* was sunk by a nuclear torpedo, but it really was an accident." "It was Teddy and Dodd—Remember? The waitress at La Brasserie?—we told them we'd pay the girl off if they abstained on the Companion Bill to H.R. 214." All this and disturbingly more. Undisclosed missile sites, top secret radio frequencies, a White House nuclear self-destruct device, Mach 7 aircraft, secret listening posts, electromagnetic pulse beams aimed at a row of townhouses in Reston, Virginia, C.I.A. heroin routes into Burma, and Vince Foster was really executed in Crystal City. On and on.

She didn't even care anymore. The system seemed to work for everyone else, leaving her with the shaft. What, a pissant COLA raise every year and a 401K? That's what life was all about? *I'm a Secret Service Agent in good standing, and they make me be a baby-sitter! I have to wear a fucking apron. I do dishes!*

Sometimes she could just lump it all. Forget about duty and service. Do something for herself for a change. At thirty-five she wasn't getting any younger.

The clock ticked on like her life: without event. When

she looked, the President was picking his nose with one hand and scratching his crotch with the other.

Yeah, to hell with this. Start over again. Do something for me!

"Alexander Haig was Deep Throat," he babbled. "Rogers assured me we could hide all our ADMs and W-79s from SALT II and the Russians would never know."

"What's that, Mr. President?"

More spit bubbles. "I was just saying, I had sex with Faye Ray once. They invented AIDS at Fort Dietrick in 1976, said it would wipe out the ghettos in five years."

Jesus.

Occasionally she nodded off and caught snatches of plush dreams. Lying on a beach in Cancun. Traveling Europe. Making love and having babies.

"You know the protocol. I need the SAC commander to authenticate confirmation of hostile intent. I don't *care* if our airspace hasn't been violated yet. What, I'm supposed to wait? Give me the discriminators! I'm the President!"

Her eyes fluttered open. She moaned. Now he was fervently pressing buttons on the remote as Tom Selleck switched to Jay Leno, then Jerry Springer, then Beavis. "I need those discriminator passwords! Goddamn Andropov! I'll bury him! Watch me!"

Yes. A real life instead of this farce. A nice house, a two-car garage. A white picket fence and a dog in the yard. Hubby mowing the grass on lazy Saturdays while she baked cookies . . . She was nodding again, words rupturing the sweet dreams.

"—million dollar offer posted last year, but so far, no takers."

A million dollars would be nice, too, to make the dream just perfect.

"—verifiable evidence. How do you *prove* something like that?"

A handsome husband who never cheated on her . . . Attractive well-mannered children who got good grades and didn't get into trouble . . .

Yes, it would be so nice . . .

The dream morphed into the face of a stuffy show

host and a gaudy background made to look like a TV news room. The dream was gone. She was awake again.

"From Ubatuba, Brazil, to Roswell, New Mexico, the mystery may never end, even with countless thousands of eyewitness reports. What's really happening out there? And just *what* is the government trying to hide from the public?"

Great. Now it was this UFO claptrap. One hokey flop after the next. At least Magnum was good-looking, killer butt, gorgeous pecs. And those eyes!

But when she turned her head to check on her charge . . .

"Oh, my God, no!!"

The President was gone.

I can't believe it! I fell asleep! How could I be so stupid!

She dashed to the kitchen, then the den, then the south hall. Nothing, and they were all locked accesses. If he'd wandered down to the foyer, the recept team would've seen him right away. Just as she was ready to hit the elopement alarm—

snick-snick-snick

An odd sound to her left. Toward the bedroom. *Maybe the President's finally decided to take a shit on his own.* From the TV, more words droned on: "Fantasy-Prone Syndrome, systematized hallucinosis, shared delusional ideas of reference, and, of course, the primal human instinct to *believe* that we are not alone in the universe. The same can be said of every religion to ever exist. It's a functional mythology . . ."

Karen winced as a heel snapped off her shoe when she turned toward the bedroom, then a sudden pinching cramp reminded her that her period was starting and it felt like a gusher. This was not her day. But then she heard the sound again, another *snick-snick-snick,* followed by an even stranger wet, crackly peeling noise.

She limped into the bedroom, stopped, and frowned. "What are you *doing!*"

"The TV. Didn't you hear?" He was on his knees, his tongue licking the corner of his mouth as he dug at the floor with a pocketknife. He was peeling a tile off the floor!

"Mr. President, would you please give me a fucking break?"

He didn't hear her, removing the rest of the split tile. "Now I remember! LeMay gave it to me when he was Chief of Air Force Operations. I thought I'd better hide it."

Karen peered over. There was a deep hole in the floor, beneath the tile, and from the hole the President had removed a white one-foot-square metal box.

"Give me that," she said, exasperated. She wrenched it from his crabbed hands. "Oh, yes," came more blabber, "we knew the Walker spies were selling our sub frequencies. Army INSCOM people found the mail drop. It was in Odenton, Maryland."

You dick. "Come on." She guided him back to the TV room and sat his ass down. "It was a phone pole they'd mark with white tape," he continued with his tale. "Our men would take the Walker material and switch it with disinformation and fake codes."

"Shut up," she said. She sat with the box in her lap. Red letters warned: RESTRICTED, DO NOT REMOVE UNDER PENALTIES IN ACCORDANCE WITH THE INTERNAL SECURITY ACT OF 1950, USC 790. Her eyes narrowed in curiosity when she opened the box and withdrew an old, yellowed document:

T-O-P S-E-C-R-E-T

HEADQUARTERS, ARMY AIR FORCES
WASHINGTON

06 JULY 47

SUBJECT: ISSUANCE OF CLASSIFIED ORDERS

TO: Commanding General
        Air Material Command
        Wright Field, Ohio

1. Notification of confidential orders to be received by the following USAAC and cleared civilian personnel:

Lt. General Martin T. Chizmar, 0-12366, AC
Major General Richard E. Gorman, 0-14963, AC
F.B.I. Director J. Edgar Hoover
F.B.I. SAC Edward L. Greenberg

2.   All above personnel will report to Air Material Command, Foreign Technology Division, in compliance with Emergency Orders via AR-200-1.

3.   These orders will be assumed by all personnel as expeditiously as possible.

RE: Confidential material to be transported to AMC, FTD, via USAAC 1st Air Transport Unit, from 509th Bomb Group, Roswell Field, New Mexico.

BY COMMAND OF THE PRESIDENT OF THE UNITED STATES
FM:

DALLAS MAYR
Lt. Colonel, Air Corps
Executive Military Dispatch
Office of AC/FS-1
THE WHITE HOUSE

Hmm, she thought. The TV rambled on: ". . . the incontestable fact remains, with all the countless thousands of abduction and eyewitness reports, not one shred of evidence exists to verify the existence of extraterrestrial visitations to our planet. If these things were really happening, someone, somewhere would've produced genuine proof by now."
She picked up another document.

TOP SECRET
SPECIAL ACCESS REQUIRED/EYES ONLY
TEKNA/BYMAN/UMBRA/SI

 DEPARTMENT OF THE AIR FORCE
WASHINGTON DC 20330-100

OFFICE OF THE SECRETARY

25 May 1974

SAF/AAIQ
1610 Air Force Pentagon

TO: THE COMMANDER IN CHIEF

SUBJECT: CLASSIFIED REQUEST PER MEMORANDUM (GAO Code 701034); AFR 12-50 (CLASSIFIED) Volume II, Disposition of Air Force Records and Material

(a) Identify pertinent directive concerning crashes of air vehicles not of terrestrial origin, investigations, wreckage/debris/dead bodies—retention, recovery, and evaluation.

Dear Mr. President:
Per your request relative to the above memorandum, i.e., the incident concerning the Low Frequency Radar Array (LFRA) detection on 18 April 1974 and disposition thereof. The most notable debris and, of particular sensitivity, all anatomical and post-autopsied remains, have been properly redeposited amongst selected sites within protected districts of the Army, Air Force, Navy, and Federal Reservations, via recent amendments to AFR-200-1, and so ordered by the MJ-12 Directorate.

T 46294

Attachment (To):-MILNET
          -U.S. Air Force Joint Recovery Command
          -NSA (Interagency Liaison Office)

Signed,

Timothy M. McGinnis, Major General 0-7
Commander, Air Force Aerial Intelligence Group
Fort Belvior, Virginia, MJ-12/Detachment 4

Karen's eyes felt pried open by hooks. *This can't possibly be for . . . for . . . for . . .*
Real.

"And so ends another edition of *Extraterrestrial Border Line.* Until next time . . . keep watching the sky."

Next was not a document but a strange wedge of heather-gray material. Thin as newsprint yet sturdy as sheet metal. It wouldn't even bend when she pressed against its corner, nor could she scratch it with the President's scout knife. When she held the flame of her cigarette lighter to it, it didn't warp, melt, or even blacken, and it didn't conduct any heat. A yellowed sticker, barely readable, stated: PROPERTY OF U.S. ARMY AIR CORP, AIR MATERIAL COMMAND, C/O WATSON LABORATORIES, RED BANK, NEW JERSEY. Another sticker read: EVIDENCE: CORONA, NEW, MEXICO, 198NE, 224S, 5 JULY 47.

Holy . . . shit . . .

A song, now, in the background: "What'choo gonna fix? Hot Pockets!" She snatched the remote. "Turn that shit off, you asshole!" she said to the President.

"Mr. Gorbachev?" he replied. "*Bring down this wall!*" He blew some spittle bubbles as if in contemplation. "Oh, my. I—I think I've got poop in my pants."

Karen may have been able to make a similar claim when she looked back in the box.

"Point Six, this is Team Leader!" Garand shouted into his walkie-talkie. "Report!"

"Team Leader, this is Point Six. We're clear."

"Team Leader, this is Point Four. Clear."

"Team Leader, this is Point Five. Clear. He ain't in the friggin' house."

Garand's mind raged as he fumbled to jack back the slide of his P-226 9mm pistol. The elopement alarm blared like an air raid siren. "Point One, you better get me a fly line to Edwards on the priority band. We're gonna need a tac team out here, and a couple of choppers."

"Roger, Team Leader."

There it all went, like smoke right before his eyes. *My whole life! Twenty years in executive protection and I'm gonna go down in history as the guy who lost President Raymond. With my luck, the old fucker probably got picked up hitchhiking out on Route 40 and he's halfway to L.A. by now. He'll be walking into the Hard Rock Cafe telling everyone about the Aurora spy plane, and how we broke Syria's star-net cipher codes and never bothered to tell the Israelis!*

Another thought just then, a strangely reassuring one.

Maybe I oughta just put this roscoe to my head right now and drop the hammer. . . .

But before any such consideration could become more transitive, his radio barked. "Team Leader, this is Rover Point. We've got him. He looks okay."

Thank you, God. Thank you thank you thank you. . . .

"Oh, man! You're not gonna believe this! He shit his pants! You should see this, Cap! President Raymond's standing here shaking shit out of his pant leg!"

"Maintain proper radio acumen, goddamn it," Garand said. "What's your loke?"

"Past the west lawn. Talk about close. He was hitchhiking along Route 40."

Thank you, God, thank you . . . "Bring him in. Is Lavender with you?"

"No, sir," the radio replied. "No sign of her anywhere."

"My name is Karen Lavender of the United States Secret Service," the woman said. Billings glared up. *Another kook, but . . . not a bad looker.* Nice figure under the businessy dress, nice hair, nice legs. "Look, lady, I'm in makeup right now, we're taping in five minutes and

I'm on a tight shooting schedule. You wanna be on the show, fine. Go talk to the line producer."

The woman looked flushed, dizzy, out of breath from some weird kind of excitement she was trying hard to suppress. Her eyes shone hard, steely. Very serious. "I don't want to talk to the line producer, I'm talking to you."

Huffy bitch, ain't she? "Yeah?" Billings challenged.

"Yeah. I'm here to collect the million dollars you're offering for incontrovertible proof of the existence of extraterrestrial life."

Then, onto Billings' makeup table, she set down a big white metal box about the size of a portable television. *Looks like one of those military courier cases, and very official looking markings.* Then he checked out the documents, and the best piece of "debris" he'd yet seen. *Yeah, this is damn good work.* But still, in this day and age? Forgery had been honed to a state of the art. "Look, lady, there's hackers out there who can make documents with their PageMaker that look better than this. And this piece of crash debris? *You* may think it's part of a UFO, but I can tell you, it ain't nothing but treated titanium. Believe me, I've seen it all before, a million times. Where'd you get this stuff anyway?"

"I stole it from the private residence of former President Rowland Raymond."

Billings chuckled. *She's good.* "Uh-huh, and I just rode the Merry Go Round with Hillary and Bill."

"There's one more thing in the box," she said. "Take it out. Look at it."

Yeah, she's a huffy bitch, all right. Sort of reminded him of his wife.

Billings peered in the box. She was correct. An acrid redolence, like formaldehyde maybe, seemed to eddy from the open box.

When he reached in, it was a heavy-duty clear plastic bag that he removed. A sizable parcel, with some heft to it.

Billings' guts sank.

The bag contained a severed alien head.

SURVIVALS

by Nina Kiriki Hoffman

Nina Kiriki Hoffman has been nominated for several awards for her fiction, the most recent being a Nebula for her novel, *The Silent Strength of Stones.* She also has stories in *Tarot Fantastic, Enchanted Forests,* and *Wizard Fantastic.*

Sensitive is not the first word most people think of when they see me.

Favorite color of leather: black. Favorite color of lipstick and nail polish: black. Piercings: three holes in right ear and two in left. Tattoo: in progress. Black barbed wire bracelet around my upper left bicep. My friend Lurica works on it when she has time and access to her dad's tattoo parlor without anybody finding out.

It really hurts. But I love it.

My mom named me Deborah, and she and my stepdad Reg call me Debbie. Totally suckoid name! Like, what *doesn't* Debbie do? I am *so* not Debbie.

Anyone who's a friend of mine calls me Shrinka.

Sensitive is what my flying saucer guy, Speedy, calls me.

He also calls me Shrinka.

I was pretty messed up the night I met Speedy. Lurica and I and some guys I didn't really know went out to Pata Lake to watch meteors. It was August and we had the guys with us because they were either old enough or sneaky enough to get a car; but their drugs were awful.

We parked at the end of the dirt road that runs through the picnic grounds by the lake. The air was hot and still and full of weedy lake smell. I did not like this location. I was afraid skinny-dipping was in store. I hate dark water; you never know what's under the surface. I'm not fond of nudity either. Unlike "Debbie Does," I have little to be proud of . . . yet. I'm fifteen. Maybe something will still happen. Sometimes I doubt it, though.

Then again, my vision had started to blur. Things whipped close and then away, and I saw little sparkling lights all around. The base of my neck tingled. It was entirely possible that soon I wouldn't even know if I was naked and/or in water.

Guy One—I forget his name; he looked like a lot of guys I know, pale, with long, stringy hair, zits, sweaty hands, and very sad taste in clothes—Guy One had a bottle of tequila and thought this was a good reason for me to let him touch me. I have my standards. I don't mix drugs and alcohol, and I'd already chewed the blotter paper Guy One gave me outside the 7-Eleven. I pretended to drink with Guy One and let him grope me outside my clothes until he drank enough all by himself to pass out.

Guy Two looked just like Guy One, only he was a little skinnier. Lurica seemed to like Guy Two much more than he deserved. They squirmed around together on the ratty blanket we had found in the trunk of the car.

By the time Guy One passed out, the sky had changed from dark blue-gray to a disgusting shade of pea-soup green, and the stars were intensely bright and pulsing in time to the metal music in my brain. The stars that were shooting sounded like *piyow piyow* ricochets. I liked the sparkling, smeary trails they left. I mean, for a drug effect, not too bad. What I didn't like was how pukey I felt.

One of my other standards is don't puke on anything you own. I also believe you shouldn't puke on anyone until you're sure you don't like them. So I staggered to my feet and wandered into the woods.

It was an even bet at any step of that journey whether I would stop to spew or keep walking. There was a path, and lots of bushes and brambles and trees, some of them with branches that slapped. The landscape alternated between black shadow trees against a neon sky, and blazing silver and gold trees with diamond leaves. The zipper tabs on my black leather jacket jingled as I walked, and I could almost make music from that. If my head and stomach hadn't hurt so much, I probably would have enjoyed it.

I got out of sight of the car and Guys One and Two and Lurica. I stumbled away from the path and couldn't figure out how to get back to it. Brambles tore bigger holes in my fishnet stockings and scratched my legs up. I could feel it, but it didn't hurt me until later.

I turned around in hopeless circles, holding my stomach and staggering back and forth. Then my knees cracked into something smooth that tilted away from me at a forty-five degree angle. At which time my stomach had something definite to say.

The first thing I did when I met Speedy was throw up on him.

The throw-up didn't stay on him, though. It slithered off and dripped to the ground.

I collapsed facedown onto this smooth, cool, tilted surface, my mouth burning from stomach acid, my head pounding, my stomach sore. I felt totally dizzy. I laid my cheek against the surface and took some deep breaths, wondering how long it would be before I felt like living.

I heard a voice.

Stirfry! (Although that didn't seem like something a person would say—but I wasn't sure I was hearing right.) *Local life-form! Unplanned encounter!*

I mean, I was hearing something that *meant* things like that, all snarled up with a bunch of other impressions: hunger, sleep, startled, huddledness, sniffing the air, worry, and a taste kind of like lime Jell-O right out of the package. Hunger was strongest.

"Sorry," I said, patting the metal beneath me. "Didn't mean to puke on you. You startled me."

Why is it talking to me/us? Concerned/scared, and other impressions that didn't seem to belong to me, even though I wasn't always sure who was feeling what when I was this messed up.

I took some more deep breaths, then rolled over onto my back. The nausea was wearing off. A rush of feelings/thoughts flowed into me from the metal at my back, too fast for me to understand them. It was like taking a big gulp from a mug of something before you know what it is, or even if it's cold or hot. First just a strange texture on my mind, and then a sense of cool, bubbly stuff settling in among my own thoughts, only I didn't know what I was thinking.

I opened my eyes and looked up.

Tree branches above me twisted and snapped like witches' fingers. Leaves wavered even though there was no breeze, flashing day-bright spots of green, red, blue. The pea-green sky sparkled with the trails of falling stars. Air whispered over my face, chilling the sweat jewels on my forehead.

I ran my hands over the smooth hard surface I was lying against. Cold, metallic, yet there was this prickly layer over it, like dropping my hands skin-deep into a pool of sleep. "Hey," I said. "Hey, little guy. Who are you?"

Must act. Must master and standardize encounter. A wave of exhaustion came to me with that thought.

The metal I was lying on began humming and thrumming soft and steady, like a refrigerator. All the while I could tell it was worried and upset. I still felt floaty and sluglike, though.

Lights flashed somewhere nearby. I looked down. Along the edge of the thing, lights blinked, fast, slow, white, red, soft orange, pale green. They made light splashes and shadows on the trees and bushes and the sides of my legs.

I pushed away from the thing, took a couple of steps back, then turned to look at it.

Oh.

I got it.

Finally.

It was a flying saucer. I'd been lying on a flying saucer.

"Awwwwrrright! A flying saucer! Awesome!

Just about the best drug effect ever!

It was a lot like the ones in fifties movies, about twenty feet across, two plates face-to-face with just their edges touching, with a smoked glass upside-down bowl on top. Along the rim where the plates met, lights chased each other, alternating colors and pace. Too cool.

It rose.

"Wait!" I yelled, like a total dweeb. "Don't go!"

Turned out it was just stretching its legs. It had hunkered down like a chicken on eggs, almost flat to the ground; and now it rose until its rim was higher than my head. I looked at its underside. Smooth, metal-looking all the way across, but right in the middle a little round vent. Four sturdy little telescoping legs with square feet on the ends, dug into the dirt.

The humming rose in pitch, and a ramp dropped down, spilling reddish light on the flattened, burned bushes under the saucer. Narrow stairs led up the ramp and inside.

A short, bald, gray alien guy with creepy big black eyes and a silver suit stood at the top of the ramp. "Greetings, Earthling. I come in peace! Come inside," he said.

Only it wasn't him talking.

It was the saucer.

I didn't know how I knew this. I just knew it.

I remembered some slides we had looked at about fish in school. Some kinds of fish on the bottom of the ocean have their own bait. They dangle something that looks like a worm in front of their mouths, and when little fish come to eat the worm, the big fish snap up the little fish.

The gray guy waved his arms and smiled. "Come inside. I won't hurt you."

"Excuse me," I said. My mouth still burned from the puke. I coughed and swallowed. "Ex*cuse* me, but you are so, so wrong. It so, so *will* hurt me to go in there. I'm not some dumb piece of Kentucky Fried Chicken. I realize that if I go in your mouth, I come out the other end as crap."

"My mouth?" mouthed the smiling little alien in the doorway.

I punched the saucer. "Quit playing with your puppet," I said. Then I shook my hand. Punching something so hard only hurt me.

The little gray guy stiffened, then stood still, his arms dangling. No expression on his face. A puppet.

I won't hurt you.

I could feel how hungry it was, and how scared.

"What are you scared of me for? I got nothing!" The only people I ever successfully scare are shopkeepers. I think it's the leather jacket, maybe the black lipstick and nail polish. I figure they figure I'm the type who shoplifts.

Well, maybe I scare some other grown-ups. Like, say, my parents. Especially my stepdad.

The saucer's thoughts shifted around again, a kaleidoscope of impressions—hunger, fear, *no; standard situation; can be dealt with,* licorice, the cold of snow against bare feet, and then kind of a firming up.

Come inside, it thought.

"No." I backed up. I couldn't tell if this was actually happening or was just a wild scenario the drugs were feeding me. I'd had pretty out-there dreams before, but this one fed so many senses, I couldn't tell it from things that happened when I was straight.

A raw ray of white light stabbed out of the door behind the little puppet guy. It shone on me, and then I couldn't move.

No, no, no, I thought, as the light pulled me toward the ramp. *No. Don't. Leave me alone. I get to choose!* Then, *Why the heck not? It's not like I'm going anywhere anyway. It's not like I have big life plans. It's not like anybody cares.*

When I woke, I was walking on a path through nighttime woods. None of the drugsight was awake in me; the sky was dark and the trees were darker, and I felt tired and sick. My mouth tasted metallic and sour.

I couldn't remember much of anything, not where I was nor how I had gotten there. Not until I tripped on the edge of the blanket and fell across Guy One, who was so far gone he didn't even stir when I oofed down onto his stomach. Lurica and Guy Two were all tangled and passed out.

I remembered we had come up here to watch falling stars, but I didn't know why I had been in the woods. I curled up next to Guy One because he was warm and the night was cold. I fell asleep.

*   *   *

"Are you all right? Shrinka, wake up! You're scaring me!"

I opened my eyes. Lurica's face hung above me, a pale oval framed by chopped-short cherry Kool-Aid colored hair, with a dim ceiling somewhere above her.

I was ready to go right back to sleep.

She shook me. "Stop it! You've been asleep for almost two days! Wake up now!"

I rolled my head and looked around. The room was dim, the curtains closed. The air hung heavy with heat. A lamp nearby spilled yellow light. I lay on my own bed, on top of a tangle of dirty sheets and blankets, and I was still in my leather jacket. I was broiling. I wiggled my toes and realized I was still wearing my black cowboy boots, too. I felt sticky, sweaty, greasy, and totally unclean. "Two days?" I mumbled.

"Yeah! It's a good thing your mom is gone for the weekend! What's the matter with you? I know that stuff was bad, but it didn't knock *me* out," she said.

"What's the matter with me?" I said, and then I remembered. That dumb saucer, messing me up even worse. Who did it think it was?

Then I felt scared. I knew it was hungry. I knew it ate people. I knew it had made me go inside of it. Had it eaten me?

I lifted a hand and held it above my face. I flexed the fingers. My hand looked and acted like a hand. Not that that proved much.

I remembered more. Floating through the air, right into the saucer. It felt like something I had done a thousand times before, and I guessed I probably had, in dreams. Landing on a padded table, not being able to move a muscle. Lights. Finally some lights flashing fast and slow into my eyes, and some more thoughts. Vanilla pudding. Sand sliding across sand. Hunger. Regret. *You are one of us.*

Oh. Right. I was *so* sure.

Go home unchanged. Forget we ever met.

As if!

"I have to go back to the lake," I said. I sat up. Many parts of me groaned.

"You have to eat something, ditsel," said Lurica.

As soon as she said that, I realized I was famished. We went downstairs and made bologna, mustard, and Wonder Bread sandwiches. I ate three of them, and drank a lot of milk. Then I took a long, hot shower.

"What's the matter with you?" Lurica asked me while I dressed. "What happened?"

"Do you have a car?"

"You know I don't!"

"Who do we know who has one?" I thought through our friends. Actually, we didn't have any other good ones besides each other. But there were a couple of boys we could probably get to take us to the lake again. Or we could pick someone up at the basketball courts or the 7-Eleven or the Coffee Nudge.

I put on lipstick. Just wait till I hit sixteen. I would *force* Mom to teach me to drive, or blackmail Reg into it, and then I would hit the road. Maybe Lurica and I, together. We'd be so gone only dust would be left.

But right now I needed help. I had to get back to that flying saucer. I had things to say to it. It better still be there.

You are one of us.

Oh, yeah?

Something clicked in my head. I remembered more.

Nope. I didn't need to get back to it. I would make it come to me.

"What?" Lurica asked me. "What, what, *what?*"

We stood on the back porch. It was a hot, sticky Sunday night. Stars twinkled through haze. Out in front of the house, engines growled along the Gut, the street where kids cruised up and down in unmuffled cars and checked each other out. Before us spread the overgrown back lawn. The house actually has a huge back yard, with a high wooden fence. Reg wanted to raise Dobermans. This was one in a series of dreams he had that never came true.

I wished I had some more acid. All the colors and weird time effects, the sounds that I could see, the way doubts washed out of my brain and I accepted whatever I experienced. Somehow that would make this easier— less hard to believe.

Light came on in my head and I saw images—strings of symbols that I could read, even though they weren't in English. I read along one of them and then sent my thoughts twelve miles north, to Pata Lake.

Hey. You. Come here, I thought.

I could feel the saucer waking, puzzled, frightened. And still so hungry.

What's the matter with you, anyway? Why can't you find anything to eat? I thought. Well, it had found me; but it had spit me out again.

Resisting life system/style/map.

I felt cold prickles all through me. Attached to what it was saying, a horde of other impressions: abandoned, searching without hope for the crossover point into another place, hunger deep and wide and gnawing; disgust with its own kind; a yearning to be some simpler other thing that did not need what it needed, did not do what it did; the bite of vinegar, the smell of woodsmoke; and a weariness so deep it was smothering.

"What the hell are you doing?" Lurica asked, shaking my shoulder and pulling me back to the porch. I lost contact with the saucer.

"Shut up!" I said.

"Hey! I didn't come here to watch you go into a trance!"

"So go, already."

She gripped my shoulders and stared into my eyes. "Shrinka. I did not get that stupid boy to load you into a car, I did not force him to drive you home, carry you upstairs, and get us food, just so you could be mean to me. I did not sit by your side for two days, worrying about you and washing off your face while you sweated so you could be mean to me. Stop zoning out! You're scaring me again!"

"I'm sorry," I said. She was the best friend I had ever had. She had done her best to save my life.

"So *what* is going on in your head?"

How to explain this? Lie? Just say what I was actually thinking? It was pretty weird! But it was the truth. "Um. I'm talking to the flying saucer I met up at the lake."

"No way!"

I just looked at her.

She swallowed, and said, "Is it talking back?" Not like she believed me, more like—let's find the limits of the delusion.

"Uh-huh." I went over and sat down on one of Mom's green plastic Adirondack chairs. "I want it to come here."

"Why?"

"It has some splainin' to do."

"If you can talk to it in your head, why can't it splain in your head?" she said, flopping down into the chair beside mine.

Sometimes Lurica is so sensible I want to strangle her.

Well, the saucer *had* explained. It was trying to die because it didn't want to do what flying saucers did anymore. Which was eat people.

Though why did I think that? I'd heard of saucers stealing people for a while and putting them back. That wasn't like eating people.

I was sure eating people was what saucers did, though. Something I had figured out when I bumped into this one. Something I still believed.

Weird.

And what about *you are one of us*, huh? No way was I a flying saucer.

I felt my arms, touched my face, just to be sure. No metal here!

Well, maybe Lurica was right. I could do all my talking long-distance. I sent out a thought. *What did you mean when you said I was one of you?*

I was asking one particular saucer a question. I knew that saucer's mind, in a way; had spent some time feeling it out. This time I touched someone or something else.

Whowherewhat? It was interested, this stranger.

I got out of there fast!

"What did it say?" Lurica asked me.

I shivered, even though I was hot. "It was some other one," I said. "I think I'll just forget it."

We sat and watched the few stars that could shine through the haze. "Thanks for saving my life," I said eventually.

"Hey, anytime. You'd do the same for me."

I heard Mom's, and Reg's VW van pulling up in front

of the house. Had we cleaned up the kitchen after we made the sandwiches? I wasn't sure. Mom got so irritated about dumb things like that. Lately everything I did irritated her, though. Not that it had ever been much different.

"Who left this mess in here?" she yelled as soon as she hit the kitchen. "Debbie! Where are you?"

"Out here," I muttered. I guess she heard me through the screen door.

"You march right in here, young lady, and clean this up! A fine welcome home!"

I sighed and put my hands on the chair arms, ready to rise.

Lurica's hand clamped on my wrist. She stared up.

I looked up, too.

A flying saucer hovered. It made no noise. Underwaterish colored lights flashed around its rim, faint and eerie. It lowered slowly down our lawn, its four legs with their little square feet extending below it. Finally it rested on its landers.

It looked different from the one I had seen before. bigger and scarier and somehow meaner.

"Debbie!" Mom shrieked, coming closer. She banged open the screen door. "You get in here this instant— Oh, no! Not again!"

I glanced over my shoulder. Mom stood in the doorway. Her face had gone white. Reg was right behind her, and he was staring, his mouth open wide enough to shove an egg into it.

"Not again, not again," Mom moaned, and slowly collapsed.

Light beams shot from the saucer, four quick bursts, enough to paralyze each of us.

Who are you? I thought. This wasn't the same sick, hungry, frightened saucer I had seen at the lake.

A ramp dropped. This time there was no figure at the top of it. A light came out and surrounded me, carried me inside.

Well. Guess Mom wasn't lying when she said she never knew my father. All this time I thought she was just a slut.

While I lay on that table in that dim, warm room without being able to move, and something studied me, I studied it back.

You are one of us.

Strings of symbols lined up in my mind, and I read down them.

I wasn't a flying saucer. But I wasn't strictly human either.

Yuck. Talk about alienation.

Anyway, I didn't have any of the stuff they needed to extract from humans to survive, or if I did, they knew I needed it for myself. So they put me back in that chair on the porch.

Then they grabbed Lurica.

No! I screamed, at least in my mind. I still couldn't move any of my voluntary muscles. *Stop that! Put her down!*

For a moment she hovered, stalled, halfway between the ship and the porch, caught in the soft yellow light like a mandarin orange in lemon Jell-O.

Then the saucer pulled her toward it again.

Stop it! Leave her alone! She's my best friend! Hurt her and I'll—I'll—

What the heck could I do to something made of metal that could fly away? Conk it with a baseball bat? Squirt it with a hose? Throw pepper at it?

Sure. Just as soon as I could move again.

Let her go!

A soft hum sounded. I could move my eyes enough to look up.

The little saucer from the lake—smaller than the one sitting on the ground, and still hesitant, hungry, and frightened—hummed and hovered above the yard.

I heard some of the car engines in the Gut stutter and die. Car doors slammed. People yelled to each other, and footsteps sounded on concrete.

The Pata Lake saucer flashed lights and hummed. Then a beam of light shot down and cut through the light holding Lurica. She fell and sprawled facedown on the grass.

The bigger saucer started its engine, retracted its land-

ing gear, and shot straight up. The little saucer barely
sideslipped in time.

They chased each other away while people tried to
get in through the gate. Reg had padlocked it shut. Some
people peered over the top of the fence. Probably standing on the trash cans, I thought, and heard one go over.

Some kid scrambled over the fence and came and
shook me. "Are you okay? What happened? Was that
a flying saucer? What's wrong with you?" He ran and
turned Lurica over, asking her the same questions. No
satisfaction there either. He checked out Reg and Mom,
and then he went in and phoned 911.

He didn't stick around long enough to answer questions, and he took Mom's purse when he left. But at
least he phoned.

Ace Holmes was the guy I liked least from our old
class at Whitman Junior High. He was big and athletic
and good-looking and mean. He beat up anybody
smaller than he was, which was pretty much everybody;
he pinched girls in the halls and made rude remarks;
and he was smart enough to know how to zero in on
other people's weaknesses. Lurica and I had tried and
tried to ignore him, but he was totally excellent at figur-
ing out how to bother us.

He'd spent two years in ninth grade, which meant he
was the only kid in our class who had a driver's license.

It wasn't easy to get him to take me up to Pata Lake
a couple nights later. I had to pretty much promise him
I'd put out. I was glad it was a struggle to get him to
go, though. I didn't want to like this guy.

He didn't want anything romantic, like a blanket on
the grass; he wanted backseat service. But when I ran,
he chased me, all right—straight into the woods, where
I knew my little saucer was.

Open up, I thought. *And get ready to paralyze. I've
brought you something.*

The saucer rose on its legs. *What? Who? What? Why?*
Lights flickered along its rim.

"Wha—?" said Ace, stopping to stare.

Take him, I said.

By this time the saucer was so hungry it was almost dead.

"What the heck *is* this?" Ace demanded.

"What does it look like?"

"Uh—uh—"

Take him. Eat him. He's all yours, I thought.

I think Speedy hated me for a while after that. I had used his weakness against him: He was so close to the edge that his survival instincts kicked in, and he couldn't stop himself from taking Ace inside and getting whatever it was he needed.

I think it's the part of a person that dreams certain kinds of dreams.

I waited in Ace's car. In fact, after a while I fell asleep. I woke up when the engine started. I looked over and saw that Ace was sitting in the driver's seat. He stared out through the windshield and never looked at me. He flicked on the lights, turned the car around, and headed back to the highway. No talking. No sideways glances. Nothing. It was like sitting next to a robot.

Robot Ace obeyed all the speed laws and traffic rules. He stopped the car in front of my house and let me out, then drove off as soon as I shut the door.

I went inside, sat down on my bed, and had a huge fit of shakes.

We started high school the next week, right at the bottom of the ladder again.

Nobody noticed anything different about Ace. Maybe he looked a little bleary-eyed some mornings, but we all did. We were coming down off summer nights and parties. We had to learn to get up early again.

I wondered if Ace had nightmares, but I didn't ask.

I didn't want to know.

I was looking for the next person I could take to Pata Lake.

EMMA BAXTER'S BOY
by Ed Gorman

Ed Gorman has garnered acclaim no matter what genre he
writes in. Britain's *Million* magazine called him "one of the
world's great storytellers." Reviewing his western work, the
Rocky Mountain News said, "Quite simply, Ed Gorman is
one of the best western writers of our time." A review in
The Magazine of Fantasy & Science Fiction said, "Gorman
is a skillful writer (who turns) the reader's expectations upside down, which is refreshing and disquieting." He has
won several awards, most notably the Shamus and the
Spur, and has been nominated for the Edgar, the Stoker,
and the Golden Dagger. His work has appeared in such
diverse magazines as *Redbook, Ellery Queen's Mystery
Magazine,* and *Poetry Today*.

The night rain didn't slow them down any. Sheriff Dan
Gray had his lantern, and his breed deputy had his
own lantern, too.

They had gone through the house, and now they were
searching the outbuildings: barn, silo, chicken house. In
the barn, you could hear the restless horses above the
hiss of cold November rain.

Joel Baxter and his wife Emma stood on the porch
of the farmhouse, just beneath the dripping overhang,
watching the lawmen set about their work.

Joel was a scrawny man in his late twenties. He shaved
only once a week, which left him with a heavy growth
of dark, gristly stubble. He had guilty, frightened blue
eyes and more of a tic than a smile. He wore bibs and
a flannel shirt and a corn cob pipe was stuck in the
corner of his mouth.

Emma was twenty-five. She'd been pretty but went
early to fat. Her prettiness was hidden now in her fleshy

cheeks. She wore a gingham dress, a soiled apron, and a red woolen shawl. The temperature could be no more than thirty. When they talked, their breath was silver.

The Baxter farm was on the outskirts of Dade Township, which was a small community of merchants that served the surrounding agricultural areas. The sheriff and the breed worked out of there.

Joel watched as the sheriff and the breed came together in front of the silo. They were talking, their words lost in the sibilance of the rain. There being no moonlight, their expressions were hard to read. They both wore ponchos heavily oiled for just such a downpour, ponchos and wide-brimmed Texas hats.

Emma said, "Maybe they'll want to search the house again."

"It'll be all right."

"But what if they do?"

"They won't, Emma. Don't get all excited now." Emma had a tendency to do that, to get all excited whenever the root cellar was threatened. Nobody knew about the root cellar but her and her husband. She meant to keep it that way. She had lost two babies to miscarriage. She didn't plan to lose this one to anything.

The sheriff and the breed came over and stood below them on the ground.

"You wouldn't have any coffee, would you, Emma?" the sheriff said.

Joel looked at her. He knew what she was thinking. Let them in for coffee, they just might start searching the house again. This time, they might just find the trapdoor to the root cellar.

"Sure we do," Joel said. It would look funny, turning the sheriff down.

A few minutes later, the three men sat at the kitchen table, the large kerosene lamp casting off smoky illumination. On the counter beneath the three-shelved cupboard a large piece of pork soaked in brine. Also on the counter was a bottle of New England rum, which Joel had bought for Emma in town earlier that day. She used it to wash her hair with, which kept it clean and free of prairie mites. The pride she'd once had in her face and body, she now had in her auburn tresses.

She brought them steaming hot coffee.

The breed said, "Thank you very much, ma'am." The breed was always polite. The priests had educated him. He was clean, too, and never looked insolent the way most breeds did.

She went into the bedroom to sew. Women were not welcome when men were talking. She kept the door open, though, so she could hear them.

"There's a child out here, somewhere," the sheriff said. "I don't see no reason to keep bullshittin' us about it, Joel. You've got a kid of some kind on these premises." The sheriff was a fleshy, white-haired man whose white beard was stained a chestnut color around the mouth from chewing tobacco. He had a bad pair of store boughts that clicked and clattered when he talked too fast, so he made a point of speaking slowly and distinctly which strangers mistook for him being wise and deliberate in his words.

"Mrs. Calherne drove by up on the hill in her buggy the other day," the sheriff went on, "and she seen Emma and a kid playin' in the yard here. She was too far away to see what the kid looked like. But it was a kid, all right."

"She must have bad eyesight, Sheriff, that's all I can figure."

"Bad eyesight?" the lawman said. The breed never talked except to say thank you. "Then we must have a lot of people around Dade Township with bad eyesight because this is about the tenth, eleventh party to see a kid in your yard."

Emma had to be more careful about where she took the kid out. He'd have to remind her of that again.

"One of the other ones who saw the kid, saw him a couple of times, matter of fact," the sheriff said, "was my deputy, Frank Sullivan. He was real curious about why somebody would want to keep their kid hidden the way you folks do."

The sheriff looked over at the breed. "Then one day Sullivan, he told me he was going to come out here and look around when he knew you folks was in town. Well, he did that, Joel, two weeks ago it was, and nobody's seen him since. He come out here and then he disappeared. Now what the hell's that all about, and why are you keepin' this kid of yours a secret, anyway?"

Joel said, "I don't know what happened to your deputy, Sheriff."

The sheriff looked at the breed again. then back at Joel. "Where's the kid, Joel?"

"What Kid?"

"You know what kid. The kid a whole lot of people have seen from a distance, but you won't admit to."

"There isn't any kid," Emma said, as she entered the kitchen.

She stood next to the stove, watching the men. "I don't know what those folks think they're seeing but it isn't a kid. I guess I'd know if I had a kid or not, wouldn't I?"

The sheriff sighed. "He's here somewhere. I'm sure of it."

"You looked everywhere," Joel said.

"Maybe not everywhere," the sheriff said. "Maybe you've got a secret place, something like that."

"No secret place," Joel said. "Where would there be a secret place?"

Thunder rattled the farmhouse windows. In the lightning that followed, Sheriff Gray's face looked lined, old, dead.

"Guess we have searched it pretty good," he said. He sounded too tired to move. He sighed. "Maybe we'll push on back to town," he said to the breed. The breed nodded. "I appreciate the coffee, Emma."

"Yes, thank you," the breed said. The priests on the reservation had done a good job of educating him. He sounded a lot whiter than most white men.

They stood up and shrugged into their ponchos and shoved their hats down heavy on their heads and said a few more good nights, and then pushed on into the cold, slashing rain.

When they were sixty seconds gone, Emma said softly, "My heart was in my throat. The breed, he kept looking over there by the stove."

"I think you're imagining things, Emma. I didn't see him looking over there once."

Her reaction was immediate, angry. "You don't give

a damn about your own son, do you? *You* want them to find him, don't you? You know what they'd do to him, don't you? They'd kill him? They'd take one look at him and then they'd kill him, and you wouldn't give a damn, would you, Joel? Your own son and you wouldn't give a damn at tall."

"They're not gonna quit lookin' for their deputy," he said quietly. "They're gonna come back here, and they're gonna keep comin' back."

"That all you got to say?"

"That's all I got to say."

"I don't suppose you're gonna go down there with me and say good night to him and say his good night prayers with me. That'd be askin' too much, wouldn't it?"

"Yes," he said. "Yes, it would."

She took the lamp and walked over by the stove and lifted up the small hooked rug and bent down and lifted the metal ring on the trapdoor.

The root cellar stank of dirt and cold. They'd kept vegetables fresh down there, but the coldness muted all the other odors. His grave would smell like that, Joel knew, dirt and cold. This was the smell of eternity. Darkness, rot, nothingness.

She went down the steps quickly, pulling the trapdoor closed behind her.

Joel stood there, listening to the noises the child in the cellar always made. He had never heard anything like these noises, a very low keening followed by a kind of sucking sound.

Without the lamp, the house was dark now, a lonely, empty dark.

Joel went into the bedroom and stripped to his long johns and lay down and listened to the rain thrum on the roof. He wished he could pray. He wished he still believed. He didn't know what they were going to do about the root cellar.

He rolled over and went to sleep. There was no sense waiting up for her. Sometimes, she stayed down there till dawn.

Sound woke him.
What kind of sound?

He sat up, listened, reaching for the Navy Colt on the floor next to the bed.

Kitchen. Table. Somebody bumping against it.

Hiss of rain.

It could be Emma, but instinct told him otherwise.

He eased himself out of bed, tiptoed to the bedroom doorway that looked out upon the one large room that was both living space and kitchen. He glanced out the window. A lone horse was ground-tied by the silo.

The trapdoor. Somebody crouching there. Opening the door six inches to peer into the dank darkness below, the keening sound louder suddenly, agitated. Lamplight flickering up from the cellar.

"Joel?" Emma said from the root cellar. "Is that you up there?"

The crouching man heard him then. Started to turn, started to stand.

"Better come up here, Emma," Joel said.

"What's wrong?" Emma called.

"The breed came back."

"The breed? I tole you, Joel. I tole you."

The keening sound became mournful then, the way it always did when Emma left the root cellar and came back upstairs, mournful and frightened and impossibly lonely.

She came up, bringing light in the form of the lamp.

The breed stood next to the stove.

"You saw it, didn't you, when you were looking down there, in the lamplight I mean," Joel said.

"I didn't see anything," the breed said in his perfect English. His poncho and his hat stank of rain.

"Maybe he didn't see, Joel," Emma said hopefully.

"Oh, he saw, all right," Joel said. "He saw all right." Then, "Where's the sheriff?"

"He's outside waiting for me. I don't come out pretty soon, he'll come in here."

"Oh, my Lord," Emma said. "What're we gonna do, Joel?" In Emma's voice, he could hear her fears: Now her third child would be taken from her, too. Emma Baxter, it seemed, was never to be blessed with a child she could keep.

"You're lying," Joel said. "The sheriff ain't out there."

"Oh? And how would you know that?"

"Because there's only one horse out there."

"That doesn't prove anything."

"It proves it to me," Joel said. Then, "Come over here."

"What?"

"Step away from the wall."

"Why would I want to do that?"

"Because I told you to."

"I only take orders from the sheriff."

Joel decided to get it over with. He crossed the floor in three steps and brought the barrel of his gun down hard on the breed's right temple.

The breed looked startled for a moment. Then he sank to the floor, unconscious.

"Oh, my God, Joel, what're we gonna do?" Emma said. "What're we gonna do?"

But Joel didn't say anything. He just got the rope and tied the breed up wrists and ankles, then dragged him over to the corner.

"We got to put him down there," Emma said twenty minutes later.

The trapdoor was shut. She had poured them both coffee. The breed was still unconscious.

"Emma," Joel said, "you know what we got to do." He sounded sad as Emma looked.

"Oh, no, Joel, oh, no. You don't do that to our son. He's your own flesh and blood."

"Part of him is my flesh and blood," Joel said. "Part of him is somethin' else."

He still recalled the night it happened, a steamy August night, him waking to find the bed empty, Emma gone off somewhere. Him scared. Where had she gone? And then her coming back, telling him she'd heard this strange sound in the sky, and then seen this explosion over the hills in the woods, something falling from the sky. And then her going out there to see what it was. And finding the fire and next to the fire the odd bubbling muck—like quicksand, she kept saying, like quicksand—

and then her stumbling and falling into it, and grasping and gasping to be free of it, the thing boiling and bubbling and sucking her down, sucking her down, and her free finally, finally free.

She'd vomited several times that night. And run a fever so hot Joel was sure she was going to die right there in their wedding bed. But in the morning, she was not only alive, she rolled over when the rooster crowed and shook him gently and whispered, "I'm going to have a baby again, Joel. I'm going to have a baby again."

Her fever was gone, and no more vomiting.

Joel himself went over the hill to the woods that morning. He could see where a fire had burned an area of the forest, a scorched black circle as if a fiery disk had fallen from the sky, but there was no evidence of the bubbling hole she'd described, no evidence at all, though on her dress he could see strange mauve stains, and knew she was telling the truth.

Winter came, and the child was born, and when the midwife delivered it, she screamed and tried to run from the room. But it was too late. Joel buried what was left of her, her flesh so shredded and torn, up in the hills by the deep stand of hardwoods. She was the first person to die because of what had been birthed between Emma's legs. If they killed the breed, he would be the fourth.

"I got to, Emma," he said. "I got to. We just can't go on killing people this way. They'll figure it out and they'll hang us. They'll hang us right down in Tompkins Square the way they did those two breeds last spring."

"He's our son."

"No he ain't, Emma," Joel said gently, "and I think deep down you know that."

"He come from my womb."

"Yeah, but it wasn't me that put him there, and you know it."

She looked at him. He'd expected tears, argument. All she said was, "Then I'll do it, the breed I mean."

He shook his head. "Emma, listen, the breed wakes up, I'm gonna take him into town, and we're gonna talk to the sheriff, and I'm gonna explain everything, how none of this was our fault, and how we want to stop it now before it gets any worse. That's the only thing we can do, Emma. The only thing."

No reaction this time either. She just watched him. She didn't even look angry any more. Just watched him.

The breed moaned. He was coming around.

"I love you, Emma," Joel said. "I want a good life for us. It wasn't our fault what happened. I think Sheriff Gray'll understand that. He seems to be a good man."

"What is that thing, anyway?" the breed said. You could hear pain in his voice. Joel had cracked him pretty darned good on the side of the head.

"You shut up, breed," Emma said. "That's our son is what that thing is. And we're proud he's our son. Very proud."

Now she was crying, crying hard. "You don't call him a 'thing,' either, you understand that?" Emma said.

"C'mon, Emma," Joel said gently, touching her hand. "I'm gonna let the breed go and then we'll ride into town, all right?"

But all she did was weep. Weep.

Joel, more tired suddenly than he'd ever been in his life, stood up and walked over to Emma on the other side of the table and kissed the top of her head, the way he'd do with a child. "It'll be better once we tell the sheriff, Emma. It really will."

Then he went over and crouched down and started undoing the ropes binding the breed.

And that was when the breed shouted, "Watch out, Joel!"

All Joel had time to see was the carving knife coming down in an arc, the huge and terrible blade gleaming in the lamplight, coming down, down, down.

And then the pain in his shoulder, then the pain all over the upper part of his body.

When she was all finished with the knife, Emma dragged Joel over to the trapdoor and pushed him down into the root cellar. His body made a big noise when it collided with the dirt floor.

She did the breed the same way. He was even bloodier than Joel had been. She'd gotten the breed to admit that he'd been lying. He'd come back here after riding back to town with the sheriff.

She gave the breed an extra hard push through the opening.

Then she closed the trapdoor and left her son to his business.

An hour later, Emma hefted the large metal trunk on to the back of the buckboard. Her son would be safe and dry in there, especially after she threw the blanket over it and fastened it down with rope.

Then she climbed aboard and took the reins and set off. The roads were muddy, but at least the rain had let up. She wasn't quite sure where she was going. She just needed to get to another part of the Territory as fast as possible.

She thought about Joel, and that first spring she'd met him, and how he'd courted her with his big, wide, country boy grin. He'd been so nice back then, nice all the time right up to the night when their son was born. And then he hadn't been nice at all. Then he'd changed so much he wasn't like Joel at all.

By sunrise, they had reached the stage road. The rain hadn't been so bad over here. The going was easier, much easier.

CHASING THE MIST
by Tracy Knight

Tracy Knight is a psychologist who uses elements of his work to write stories with keen insight into the human mind. Other fiction of his appears in *Cat Crimes Goes on Vacation, Frankenstein, Werewolves,* and *Murder Most Delicious.* He lives in Carthage, Illinois.

A flock of sparrows surrenders its sanctuary among the branches of an immense elm tree, rising as a sable cloud across the face of the harvest moon.

The crickets and cicadas, chirping alarms of impending winter, fall suddenly silent.

The rustling leaves hush.

Soundlessly, the craft descends through the autumn gloom, turning slowly on its axis like a lazy top. Spindly legs unfold from its body, giving the ship the appearance of a colossal metallic spider.

The craft settles on the ground, a pulsating iridescent cloud encircling its hull.

A door opens on the side of the craft. Out steps a tall man, Nordic in countenance, long blond hair reaching the center of his back, skintight silver suit sparkling with reflected color. He raises one hand, palm out, and smiles.

"Louie. It is you, isn't it?" the Nordic says invitingly. "You've come . . . for the key."

Other creatures scramble out of the craft, nonhuman things: a small entity with glistening onyx skin and marionette limbs, clattering as it walks and hops; an arthropod being, pincers for hands, clicking mandible dripping something thick and dark; a tiptoeing fetus, moist doe eyes dominating its soft face; others, twisted forms that shamble haltingly, unrecognizable as anything alive.

"Louie?"

"For heaven's sake, Louie! You went to that therapist because you were feeling depressed. He said the hypnosis would help you, even make you stop smoking! And just look at yourself!"

Louie Walters lurched out of his reverie and into his kitchen. His wife Charlotte sat across the table from him, her eyes twin smoldering embers, lips pressed tightly together, the first hints of tears belying her angry expression.

Forehead leaning against his open hand, Louie wearily lit up his third Camel in a row, inhaled deeply, and released a thin plume of blue smoke toward the slowly rotating ceiling fan. He absently tugged at one of the straps securing the faded overalls to his portly frame. The border of white hair surrounding his bald spot was uncombed and long, lying over his ears and nearly touching the collar of his T-shirt. He couldn't remember when he'd last had a haircut.

"Tell you what, Charlotte," Louie said, his voice bereft of feeling, "if you want to ride me, throw a saddle on me first." A twinge of regret immediately ignited his gut. He sounded like an ass.

Charlotte didn't bother to dam her tears any longer. They slid freely from her eyes and trickled onto the table, leaving small wet spots on the newspaper spread out before her. "We've been married forty-five years. You've *never* treated me like this. It's like . . . it's like you're a thousand miles away. It's like I don't even know you."

Deep inhalation. Plume release. Dead man smoking.

Without warning Charlotte stood up, seized her coffee cup from the table, and hurled it across the room, where it shattered against the wall.

Louie stubbed out his cigarette, reached up, and pressed his palms against his eyes. "What do you want me to do, Charlotte?" He sounded like a careworn sixty-seven-year-old man, which is exactly what Louie had been before the appointment with the therapist. Now—unfamiliar, unthinkable images erupting inside him—he was also something else. He wished he knew what.

Charlotte leaned down, gently grasped his chin, and brought his eyes level with hers. "What do I want you to do? I want you to talk to me, dammit!" She released him, then stomped out of the room.

"I . . . I don't know what to say," Louie muttered to the empty kitchen.

He closed his eyes and spent a few moments trying to review his life, to rummage for any seeds of personal history that might have given rise to psychosis: his childhood in Bloomington, safe and secure; his forty years as a railroad engineer for Burlington Northern, steady and productive; his marriage to Char, all the joy they'd shared.

It was strange; the memories of his life appeared as unwieldy bundles of imagery with no flow or order, impossible to assemble. Just facts.

Oh, well, Louie thought. *Specters of visiting aliens would purée anyone's mind.*

But the bottom line was this: No. He found no fertile soil of dysfunction in his past from which such hallucinations could grow.

Suddenly, another flashback. Stark images of the craft and its occupants roared through Louie's inner landscape.

He shook his head and rubbed his temples, trying to drive away the terrifying apparitions.

"Louie. It is you, isn't it? You've come . . . for the key."

A minute later, Charlotte returned to the kitchen, nervously patting her tall gray hairdo. "Get up." Her voice was small, scared. "You're coming with me."

"Where?"

"To Doctor Mikelpress' office. I called him. I told him it was an emergency."

Louie nodded sluggishly, rose from his chair.

Embracing her husband, Charlotte pressed her cheek against his chest. "I'm losing you, Louie. I'm losing you and I don't know what to do."

"You're remembering everything now," Mikelpress continued in his soothing voice, sitting on a chair next to the couch where Louie lay silently, deeply in trance, not moving a muscle. "These important, vital memories that inform your life, inform your existence, have too long been hidden from you. They have returned. They are, at last, home." Doctor Mikelpress pushed his gold-rimmed eyeglasses to the bridge of his nose, then ran his fingers through his untrimmed beard. His overgrown brown hair stuck out in a thousand directions, a tendril bouquet.

Louie grimaced ever so slightly, then furrowed his brow. He mumbled under his breath, barely articulating the words. "Yesss . . . the key . . . I'm here."

Mikelpress allowed himself a satisfied smile. "Yes, Louie. The key. And now allow yourself to become completely immersed in those images, allow yourself to review them, each and every detail. These precious memories are no longer lost to you. You own them again. They are your life. They are you."

Louie remained silent for several minutes. A look of peaceful certainty settled across the old man's face.

Mikelpress gently brought Louie out of the trance, reminding him that he would carry the formerly lost memories with him forever, and that he would awaken refreshed, alert, reinvigorated, prepared to face the first moments of this new life.

Louie Walters slowly opened his eyes, let out a deep sigh, then sat up on the couch.

"How are you feeling?" Mikelpress asked.

Louie patted his chest, assessing himself. "Okay. I'm feeling okay."

"It's time you told your wife what we've discovered. She deserves to know."

"It's just . . ."

"What?"

"We've been married forty-five years. Our life, it's been . . . so smooth and steady. Perfect as a storybook. I hate to upset her when I'm not even sure what the hell's going on. But . . . I guess you're right. I *should* tell her."

"Good, that's fine." Doctor Mikelpress slapped his thighs with open palms and stood up. "Should we set another appointment?"

"No," Louie said. "Not right now. I think I'll be okay."

Mikelpress watched Louie walk calmly out of the central office and into the waiting area where Charlotte sat, expectancy filling her eyes. She smiled at Louie, raising her eyebrows as if to ask, "Are you okay?" Without exchanging words, they joined arms and left the office.

Mikelpress said, "They're gone."

The door to an adjoining room opened. Out strode a tall, burly man dressed in a midnight-black suit, equally black hair combed severely around a razor-straight part. On his face he wore sunglasses, a thin mustache, and a taut, chiseled expression. Agent Monte Borgnine asked, "What do you think, Doc? Did it take?"

Mikelpress nodded excitedly, his unkempt hair jitterbugging. "I'm sure it did. He accepted every suggestion, reacted physically. With everything that's been done these past six months, I can assure you the 'memories' are firmly implanted. Just the fact that he thinks he saw me for the first time only a couple of days ago speaks to the procedure's success. It's amazing."

Borgnine shrugged. "It's not difficult remaking people's lives if you use the right combination of chemicals and persuasion techniques. Look at all of the victims of the M-K Ultra program, all the mind control research my agency conducted in the past. In Walters' case it was a simple recipe: ninety days of drug-induced sleep, eight weeks of mind-scrambling with hallucinogens, then turning him over to you last month so you could implant the memories."

"And he added so many details himself. I only suggested the specific physical setting, the craft, the aliens. He came up with the situations, the conversations with the aliens, all on his own."

"Humans," Agent Borgnine said as if discussing a species other than his own, "they take whatever traces of meaning life gives them and weave a story out of them, adding whatever's needed to make it complete. Give them a few plot points, they do the rest."

Mikelpress looked downward, scuffed one shoe against the carpet. He hesitated for a moment, then asked, "So . . . tell me, Agent Borgnine . . . what's the eventual outcome of this? I've implanted the memories you wanted, but now what? Is this some kind of CIA experiment? Are you seeing how long he can maintain his sanity?"

Borgnine handed Mikelpress the roll of bills he was owed for today's session. "Can you keep a secret?"

Mikelpress looked vaguely affronted. "I'm a therapist. I keep secrets for a living."

"I'm with the CIA, that part is true. But this operation isn't authorized. I struck out on my own for this."

"Why?"

"Because the government's taken a long step down a deep shithole. The aliens have been landing for decades now, and last year I discovered that we've made a noninterference pact with them. I don't know what kind of country you want, Mikelpress, but I like the Earth just the way it is. I don't want any melon-headed aliens lumbering around this great nation of ours, doing whatever the hell they feel like doing."

Mikelpress's jaw dropped and his eyes suddenly looked like he'd ingested some of the Agency's hallucinogens. Kaleidoscopic emptiness. "You mean . . . those written accounts you gave me to use as references for the suggestions, and those photos . . . they were for real?"

Borgnine nodded. "Real as life. The Fairfield Bowling Alley, the business district, the clearing with the elm tree, the spiderlike UFO, the aliens. It's all real. I lifted the pictures from an Above Top Secret file, along with the accounts of the people who've seen them land. Fairfield's a hot contact site. So you see, that's the point. Now Louie Walters thinks *he* remembers the aliens landing. He won't be able to resist going there, seeing for himself. I'll follow him at a safe distance. Then when the UFO lands and the aliens disembark, I'll show them what America's made of. They'll fly off this planet so fast they'll fry their antennae."

Mikelpress pulled at his beard, contemplating. "There's a book in this for me."

"Sure, Doc," Borgnine said, dismissively patting Mikelpress on the arm. "Sure there is."

The September day was dwindling to a close, sky darkening early, orange and red leaves luminous against the gray of twilight.

Charlotte kept her hands on the steering wheel and

her eyes on the road even after Louie had told her everything.

"You think I'm crazy, don't you?" he asked.

"Louie, if you haven't driven me buggy during the past forty-five years, you sure as hell aren't going to push me over the edge now."

"I love you, you know that?" Louie said, feeling the first smile he'd felt on his face in weeks. "You're still the woman of my dreams."

She reached over and patted his leg. "So tell me, honey, what can I do to help?"

Louie opened the glove compartment and burrowed through the clutter, finally extracting a road map. He laid it on his lap, scanned it a moment, then punched it with his index finger. "Fairfield! That's where we need to go. When I was remembering today, I saw a sign at a bowling alley, the Fairfield Bowling Alley. Just outside that town is where the craft landed, where I met them. Follow Route 136 until you get to I-55, then head north."

"You want to go there? Now?"

"Charlotte, I need to see this. I need to know it's real. The man, the alien, he said he had the key. That's what I need right now: a key. I want things to make sense again."

Charlotte nodded. "Then that's what we'll do, honey." She turned left and drove into the deepening night.

"I'm not sure you should've come along, Mikelpress," Agent Borgnine said, keeping the Volvo at thirty miles per hour, his eyes locked on the Walters' car ahead. "This could get dangerous, even bloody."

Almost whining, Mikelpress said, "I'm part of this story now, too." He fidgeted in his seat like a kid needing to pee. "Besides, I'll need an ending for my book. Hey, help me think of a title: *Curse of the Spider Craft?* Naaa. *The Fairfield Horror?* Nope. *The Impending Angels?* Hey, I like it!"

Clenching his jaw muscles, Borgnine shook his head. Mikelpress was getting on his nerves. "They're *not* angels, Mikelpress. That's the reason I needed Walters to be my decoy. The reports I stole said that on several occasions the aliens captured and mutilated contactees."

"Mutilated?"

"Skinned and left in a little tattered pile on the ground."

Mikelpress fell silent.

Borgnine chuckled. "Still want to go?"

"Yeah," Mikelpress answered, voice trembling. "Sure I do."

"Tell you what. When we get there, stay behind me at all times. You'll get your story, I'll get the aliens, and you'll be safe. I'm a crack shot. Nothing to worry about."

Mikelpress felt a bead of sweat pop out on his forehead. He did want to go, *had* to go. Already images of mobbed book signings and talk show appearances were dancing in his head.

Still . . . a bloody confrontation? Mutilation? Heaps of tattered body parts?

Mikelpress' thoughts were punctured by Borgnine's voice. "We're a lot like Walters, you and me."

"How so?" asked Mikelpress, wiping his brow.

"Each of us, we're chasing our own little wisps of meaning. I want to be a hero, to repel an alien invasion. You want the prestige and respect you've never had, to write a bestseller. Walters, he wants contact with an alien civilization, to make sense of his life. Meaning is a harsh mistress. She makes us chase her, woo her. Pitiful, isn't it?"

Suddenly the Walters' taillights brightened.

"They're taking the I-55 exit," Borgnine said. "Perfect. We're on our way."

By the time they passed the Fairfield Bowling Alley—crooked black letters on its spotlit marquee spelling out "HAPPY BIRTHDAY, CRAZY!"—Louie was trembling with excitement.

"This is it," he said softly. "I'm remembering it. I'm remembering it all."

Charlotte followed Louie's breathless instructions, turning first down a series of gravel roads, ending up on a thin dirt path that snaked its way between fields of dying corn. Tall weeds and brush whispered against the bottom of the car.

"Okay, okay," Louie said. "At the end of this cornfield, douse the lights."

"We're there?" Charlotte asked.

"Almost."

After flicking off the headlights at the cornfield's edge, she rolled down her window. Except for the sound of the car moving down the trail, the night was silent.

"God, Louie, it's spooky out here. Too quiet."

"Not for long," he assured her. "Not for long, my love."

Charlotte stopped the car at the corner of the clearing and shut off the engine.

"We're here," Louie said. "C'mon, Char."

They exited the car and, arm in arm, walked to the center of the clearing, the sky a gauzy haze of darkness, the cool gentle breeze—suffused with ambrosial scents—fingering their faces. A lone elm tree, tall and proud, stood in the clearing, its two largest limbs splaying skyward as if in celebration of the night and its promise.

"Look!" Louie pointed toward the southwestern sky, where a pinpoint of shimmering light moved slowly. "That's it! It has to be!"

Standing still, he held his wife close to him as they gazed silently at the point of light, which began bobbing and dancing against the black canvas of night. It grew in size with each passing moment, thousands of undulating colors becoming clear.

Soon the craft came into full view. Its rotating hull, larger than a cruise ship, was dark although, oddly, it shone. A sharp humming sound accompanied the extension of at least ten long landing legs.

Charlotte gasped. "My God, Louie. It *does* look like a spider."

"Didn't I tell you, sweetheart? A big, beautiful spider. They're here. They're here for us."

The craft was fifty feet above their heads. Around its hull glimmered an iridescent haze embodying all the colors of the rainbow.

As it approached the ground, Louie and Charlotte

stepped back, the storm of rising wind buffeting their hair.

"Damn, Mikelpress, get your hands off me," Agent Borgnine whispered harshly. They were creeping alongside the final few rows of corn. Seeing the craft descending, Mikelpress had pressed himself against Borgnine's back, as if he were a child accompanying a parent into a haunted house.

He retracted his hands.

"Jeeeee-sus Christ," Mikelpress said. "It *is* real. And it's here. And we're here watching it."

"How many years of education did you get to learn how to discern the obvious, bulbhead?"

Borgnine reached into his suit coat and pulled out a Ruger .44.

"Quite a gun," Mikelpress said, unconsciously brushing the back of Borgnine's coat again.

"Yeah, well, these aren't your basic looters or terrorists we're dealing with. Who knows what it'll take to kill them."

Mikelpress burst into a brief seizure of giddy laughter. "God, this is something. I can't wait to get home and start writing my book."

Borgnine crouched at the corner of the cornfield, peering around it and watching the craft gently land. He reached into a pocket of his suit coat, pulled out a silencer and secured it to the Ruger's barrel.

"Gee, Monte. You're really stocked up for this operation of yours. Even a silencer. Wow."

Borgnine kept his eyes on his gun. "Know something, Mikelpress? I just thought of something. You writing a book: I don't think that's such a good idea. The CIA's liable to figure out which of their agents was the one who saved the world. Can't have that."

Mikelpress lapsed into silence for a moment. Then he said, "Well, I can disguise your identity. No one would ever know it was you."

Borgnine ignored him. "Even more, I don't think it's such a good idea that anyone besides me even knows about this."

Borgnine turned around quickly, pressed the barrel against Mikelpress' throat and fired.

The muffled gunshot sounded like a man spitting air.

Mikelpress pitched backward, thumping against the hard ground. He lay there gurgling for just over a minute, then joined the autumn silence.

Borgnine slowly stood. "But thanks for keeping me company on the drive. Hunting aliens gets lonely sometimes. And it was fun scaring you with that mutilation story I made up, Mikelpress. I enjoy watching bulbheads squirm."

He strode toward the landed craft, toward Louie and Charlotte Walters.

"Now you'll have to excuse me," Borgnine said to the corpse in parting. "I've got work to do."

"Sweetheart?"

"Yes, Louie?"

"In a moment, the side of the craft is going to open. Several creatures will come out, but the main one will be human. Or at least human-*looking*. Don't be scared. Okay?"

"Okay."

"Another thing: Thanks for sticking with me, not only during the past few days when I was acting like a turd, or after I told you I remembered meeting space creatures. Thanks for the whole forty-five years. You've been wonderful to me."

"Aw, Louie." She clasped her hands around his bicep and pulled him close. "I wouldn't have had it any other way."

Whoosh.

A blinding white light flooded from the craft's open hatch.

"Oh, my God," Louie said, eyes squinting, voice quivering with anticipation. "It's him."

Through the ivory glow emerged the Nordic, his long blond hair flowing in the craft's updraft. He stepped confidently forward until he stood directly in front of Louie and Charlotte. His royal blue eyes smiled nearly as much as his mouth.

"Oh, my God," Louie repeated.

"You're here." The Nordic's voice was soothing, rich with bass tones. "We're happy you've come, Louie Walters."

After a sharp intake of breath, Louie said, "So am I. I'd forgotten about meeting you in the past. I just remembered yesterday. I wanted so much to come here and find you. I know it's important."

"Yes it is, Louie."

"This is my wife Charlotte."

The Nordic smiled. "She's been a good partner, hasn't she?"

"The best."

"I know. We've been watching." Spreading his hands, the Nordic said, "Let us sit."

As soon as the three of them had taken their places on the ground, other creatures emerged from the craft. The small onyx being with jerky movements and clicking limbs; the insect man, mandible snapping and dripping, pincers slowly opening and closing to a steady, unheard rhythm; the wan fetus with its sad eyes; the others, some small and nearly shapeless, others tall and angular with only the barest hints of faces or awareness. The creatures huddled behind the Nordic, as if in respect or deference.

"Why have you come, Louie?" asked the Nordic. "Only to see us, to know we're real?"

"That's part of it," Louie said, feeling his chest swell with emotion, "but this is also where I find the secret, the key."

"The key?" the Nordic asked, eyebrows arched.

"Yeah, like I remembered you telling me: the key. I'm looking for the key to my life, to be able to put everything together . . . finally—"

"To fulfill your life's story? Is that it?"

"Yes."

"I understand." The Nordic shifted on the ground, raising a knee and placing his hand upon it. "Louie, perhaps we're *all* looking." He swept his other hand around, toward the other creatures shuffling and skittering behind him. "All of us. I do know one thing, though. This instant, you're revealing the two qualities most necessary for making sense of life."

"What are those?"

"Humility . . . and hope. At least that's what I and my fellow travelers have learned."

Louie let that sink in, feeling such a surge of emotion that he thought he'd cry.

There was a noise behind him.

Hard footfalls in the brittle, dying grass.

"Everyone stay still!" Agent Monte Borgnine bellowed from the shadows. "The first one who moves is dead!"

All heads, human and inhuman, turned toward Borgnine. Everyone complied with his demand, even the most alien of the creatures. No one, nothing, moved.

Borgnine approached, aiming his Ruger directly at the Nordic's chest.

Instinctively, Louie raised his hands above his head. "Who are you? What's this about?"

Borgnine either chuckled or growled, it was hard to tell. "I guess I do owe you some kind of an explanation. If it weren't for you, I wouldn't have been able to trap these monsters."

"What do you mean?"

Still aiming the gun at the Nordic, Borgnine shifted his eyes toward Louie. "Well, I hate to break it to you, old-timer, but you were set up. That's right. Dr. Mikelpress—you'll find him dead out there near the cornfield if you want to pay your last respects—he did a job on you, pardner. You've never seen this craft or these aliens before. He planted the images at my direction. I needed a decoy, a canary in the mine, my friend. Can you say 'tweet'?"

Every muscle in Louie's face went slack. "What?" He looked to the Nordic, hoping the alien would contradict this madman's claim.

The Nordic's expression told Louie nothing.

"Fact is," Borgnine continued, "besides your name, everything you remember about yourself was fabricated by me. *Everything*: your history, your life, all of it. I found you in a State Psychiatric Hospital, Louie, with a head full of liquor and drugs, having just been rescued after making your second leap off the Mississippi River Bridge in as many days. You apparently thought your life was over anyway. I hope you don't mind that I borrowed it."

Charlotte's face clenched with anger. "Don't listen to him, Louie! Mister, I don't know who you are, but you can't fool us with your line of bull! I've been married to this man for forty-five years—"

"Sorry, lady," Agent Borgnine interrupted. Now he was squinting one eye, holding the pistol at arm's length and sighting down the barrel, as if relishing the imminent act of blowing away the Nordic. "I don't even remember your last name. But I do remember you were in worse shape than Louie here. Chronic depression. One step from catatonia. A regular zucchini woman. You'd just come out of a series of ten electroshock treatments at the same State Hospital. I didn't have to pull too many strings or line too many pockets to get either of you out of there and relocate you. Neither of you had any family, anyone to help you, anyone who cared at all. Mikelpress and I did you a favor, if you think about it. You should be thankful. At least you two doomed losers have had a glimpse of a normal life. See what you've been missing all these years?"

"Don't listen to him, Char," Louie said. Ignoring Borgnine's order not to move, he put his arm around her shoulders.

"Answer me this, Charlotte," Borgnine said, sneering. "When is your wedding anniversary?"

Charlotte paused briefly, then clamped her hands over her ears. "Leave us alone! I'm not listening any more!"

"Ha!" Borgnine exclaimed, again turning his full attention to the Nordic and his minions. "She doesn't have a clue. See what a good job we did?"

"Indeed," the Nordic responded flatly.

"Louie and Charlotte, you sit right where you are," Borgnine said casually. "You, Blondie, stand up, right there with your ugly friends. I'll make this quick, I promise you."

With preternatural steadiness and calm, the Nordic stood, clasping his hands behind his back. Resigned, it seemed, to the fate that Borgnine had planned for him.

"I hope your friends in the stars are watching," he said. "I hope they realize that Earth is not the place for you. We have enough trouble managing our own. Take a look at Louie and Charlotte here. Empty vessels with no lives of their own, useless sacks of flesh."

"Damn you!" Louie turned and lunged toward Borgnine. He managed to wrap his arms around the agent's shins.

Borgnine kicked his legs, struggling to escape Louie's grasp.

Suddenly the Nordic brought his arms to the front again. In one hand he clutched a small handgun.

"Mr. Borgnine?" the Nordic said.

Borgnine stopped, looked to the Nordic's face, then to his gun. "What?" he said, as if waiting for an explanation.

Louie released his hold on Borgnine and threw his body over Charlotte's, protectively.

The Nordic shot Borgnine once in the forehead.

After expelling a brief, graceless grunt, Borgnine plunged to the ground. His body spasmed twice before he went still.

"It's okay now," the Nordic said, securing the gun in the waistband of his silver suit. "He's dead."

The couple got to their feet. Louie brushed the dirt off of Charlotte's clothing, then his own.

"That looks like a regular pistol. Where would an alien get one of those?" Louie asked.

The Nordic winked. "It *is* a regular pistol. Let me introduce myself. I'm Agent Ben Cheever. I'm with the NECU, the National Extraterrestrial Contact Unit. We've known about Borgnine's intentions for months, even before he removed the two of you from the State Hospital and started the brainwashing procedure on you both. We've been keeping our eyes on things, keeping watch over you. We knew if he wasn't neutralized, everything we're working to build would be lost."

"You mean . . ." Louie stammered, "you mean this was all a show? You're just a human and the craft is fake and these other aliens, they're—what?—robots or something, special effects?"

"No, these are genuine Extraterrestrial Biological Entities—EBEs," said the Nordic. "We've had contact with them for years. To date we've established ongoing relationships with twenty-three species. But we have a long way to go. They've shared their technology, but our communication with them is still at its most rudimentary level. So we travel together, observe one another, study the Earth as a team. We do what we can. We stay near one another. Someday—perhaps years from now—we'll find a way to push through all the boundaries that separate us. Someday we'll know what our story is to be."

"I see," Louie said. It was all too much, too much to truly absorb and understand. He found himself holding Charlotte more tightly. "What . . . what about us? We aren't . . . we aren't who we think we are, not at all."

"He's my husband," Charlotte said absently, as if she'd forgotten every word of Borgnine's explanation. "I want to live out my life with him, make him happy."

The Nordic—Agent Ben Cheever—said, "Since you already know the truth, you could come with us. I'm sure I can get approval; we've been talking about expanding the EBEs' social circle for years."

As if on cue, the aliens surrounded Louie and Charlotte, gently caressing the couple's hands and faces, brushing against their legs and shoulders, sniffing the air around them, regarding them with innocent, quizzical eyes.

The Nordic laughed. "I think this is a show of approval. You're good humans, Louie and Charlotte. We'd be proud to have you along."

"Thanks anyway," Louie said without hesitation, "but I think we've got a lot of . . . catching up to do." He leaned down and kissed Charlotte's cheek.

"I understand." The Nordic smiled. "Perhaps you can use a lesson from us. Be together. Observe. Stay near. Learn from one another. See what life story you can write. Be coauthors."

Louie kissed Charlotte again. "I'm willing."

"And you know I am," Charlotte said, tears running down her cheeks.

"In some ways, you two are quite lucky," said the Nordic. "You hold a blank piece of paper. You can fashion any story you like. Write the very best one you can, okay?"

"Thank you," Louie whispered. "Thank you for the key."

"I never told you I had the key, you realize. That was a false memory, Louie. That was you."

"Still, as it turns out, I was right."

Hands on his hips, the Nordic walked over to Borgnine's body. "We'll clean up here, then be on our way. You folks go on, okay? But one last thing . . ."

"Yes?" Louie and Charlotte responded in unison.

"You two can keep a secret, can't you? About us, about all of this?"

"No problem," Louie said, "Charlotte and I have enough to keep us busy for quite a while."

Louie and Charlotte Walters turned away from the craft, linked arms as naturally as if they'd had four-and-a-half decades of marital practice, and walked away into the autumn shadows.

Charlotte cleared her throat daintily. "So . . . what's your favorite color?"

"Hmm . . . I forget."

"Make something up."

"Okay. Blue."

"Mine's purple," Charlotte said. "What kind of movies do you like?"

"Westerns. Westerns and the old comedies, back when they were funny."

"I like romances."

"Ack," Louie said, then laughed. "Tell you what: If you watch a Western with me, I'll let you drag me to a romance."

"Deal."

The couple turned and watched as the craft rose into the sky impossibly fast, becoming a burnished pearl in the welcoming darkness, then winking out.

Eyes still focused heavenward, Louie said, "Know something? Even though it's late, I'm wide awake."

"Me, too."

"Suppose we could find a coffee shop in Fairfield?"

"We could try."

They drove into town, happened upon an all-night diner, held hands, and talked until dawn.

AMID THE WALKING WOUNDED

by Jack Ketchum

Jack Ketchum's short fiction appears in *Vampire Detectives, Murder for Mother, Careless Whispers* and many other anthologies. He lives in New York City.

It was four in the morning, the Hour of the Wolf he later thought, the hour when statistically most people died who were going to die on any given night and he awakened in the condo guest room thinking that something had shaken him awake, an earthquake, a tremor—though this was Sarasota not California and besides, he'd been awakened by an earthquake many years ago one night in San Diego and this was somehow not quite the same. The glow outside the bedroom window faded even as he woke so that he couldn't be sure it was not in some way related to his sleep. He was aware of a trickling inside his nose, a thin nasal discharge, unusual because he was a smoker and used to denser emissions. He sniffed it up into his throat and thought it tasted wrong.

The guest room had its own bathroom just around the corner, so he put on his glasses and got up and turned on the light and spit the stuff into the sink and saw that it was blood; as he leaned over the sink, it began leaking out his nose in a thin unsteady stream like a faucet badly in need of new washers. He pinched his nose and stood straight, tilted back his head, and felt it run down the back of his throat, suddenly heavier now so that it almost choked him, the gag response kicking in, and he thought, *now what the hell is this?* so he leaned forward again and took his hand away from his nose and watched it pouring out of him.

He grabbed a hand towel, pressed it under and over his nose, and pinched again. *One seriously major fucking bloody nose,* he thought, unaware as yet of just how serious this might prove for someone who had been taking ibuprofen, eight pills a day for over a month's time, trying to fight off some stupid tennis elbow without resorting to a painful shot of cortizone directly into the swollen tendon—unaware, too, that ibuprofen was not just an anti-inflammatory but a blood thinner, which was why he was not going to be doing any clotting at the moment.

The towel, pink, was turning red. The pressure wasn't working.

If he put his head up, it poured down his throat—he could taste it now, salty, rich, and coppery. If he put his head down, it poured out his nose. Straight up, he was an equal-opportunity bleeder, it came out both places.

He couldn't do this alone. He had to wake her. He crossed the hall.

"Ann? Annie?"

There was a streetlight outside her window. Her pale bare back and shoulders told him that she still slept nude.

"Annie. I'm bleeding."

She had always departed sleep like a drunk with one last shot left inside the bottle.

"Whaaaa?"

"Bleeding. *Help.*" It was hard to talk with the stuff gliding down his throat and the towel pressed over his face. She rolled over, squinting at him, the sheet pulled up to cover her breasts.

"What'd you do to yourself?"

"Nosebleed. Bad." He spoke softly. He didn't want to wake her son David in the next room. There was no point in disturbing the sleep of a fourteen-year-old.

She sat up. "Pinch it."

"I'm pinching it. Won't stop."

He turned and went back to the bathroom so she could get out of bed and put on a robe. He was not allowed to see her naked anymore. He leaned over the sink and took away the towel and watched it slide out of him bright red against the porcelain and swirl down the drain.

"Ice," she said behind him and then saw the extent

of what was happening to him and said, *"Jesus"* while he pinched his nose and tilted back his head and swallowed and then she said, "Ice" again. "I'll get some."

He tried blowing out into his closed nostrils the way you did to pop the pressure in your ears in a descending plane and all he succeeded in doing was to fog up his glasses. Huh? He took them off and looked at them. The lenses were clear. He looked in the mirror. There were beads of red at each of his tear ducts.

He was bleeding from the eyes.

It was the eyes that were fogged, not his goddamn glasses. She came back with ice wrapped in a dish towel.

"I'm bleeding from the eyes," he told her. "If it's the ebola virus, just shoot me."

"Eyes and nose are connected." She hadn't grown up a nurse's daughter for nothing. "Here."

He took the ice pack and arranged it over his nose, tucking the corners of the dish towel beneath. Within moments the towel was red. The ice felt good, but it wasn't helping either.

"Here."

She'd taken some tissues and wrapped them thick around a pair of Q-tips.

"Put these up inside. Then pinch again."

He did as he was told. He liked the way she was rushing to his aid. It was the closest he'd felt to her for quite some time. He managed a goofy smile into her wide, dark eyes and worried face. *Ain't this something?* He pinched his nose till it hurt.

The makeshift packs soaked through. He was dripping all over his T-shirt. She handed him some tissues.

"Jesus, Alan. Should I call 911?"

He nodded. "You better."

The ambulance attendants were both half his age, somewhere in their twenties, and the one with the short curly hair suggested placing a penny in the center of his mouth between his teeth and upper lip and then pressing down hard on the lip, a remedy that apparently had worked for his grandmother but which did not do a thing for him and left him with the taste of filthy copper in his mouth, a darker version of the taste of blood. Annie asked if she should go with him and he said, "No, stay with David, get some sleep. I'll call if I need you." She had to write down their number because at the moment he couldn't for the life of him remember.

Inside the ambulance he began to bleed heavily and the attendant sitting inside across from him couldn't seem to find any tissues nor anything for him to bleed into. Eventually he came up with a long plastic bag that looked like a heavier grade of Zip-loc, which he had to hold open with one hand while dealing with his leaking nose with the other. A small box of tissues was located and placed in his lap. When one wad of tissues filled with blood, he would hurriedly shove it into the bag and pull more from the box, his nose held low into the bag to prevent him from bleeding all over his khaki shorts. The attendant did nothing further to help him after finding him the bag and tissues. This was not the way it happened on *ER* or *Chicago Hope*.

The emergency room was reassuringly clean and, at five in the morning, nearly deserted but for him and a skeleton staff. They did not insist he sign in. Instead a chubby nurse's aide stood in front of him with a clipboard taking down the pertinent information, leaving him to deal with his nose, replacing the half-full Zip-loc bag with a succession of pink plastic kidney-shaped vomit bowls but otherwise treating him as though it were ninety-nine percent certain he had AIDS.

He didn't mind. As long as the pink plastic bowls kept coming and the tissues were handy.

He was beginning to feel light-headed. He supposed it was loss of blood. He couldn't remember Annie's address though he'd written her from his New York apartment countless times in the past four years since she'd moved away and knew her address—quite literally—by heart. He couldn't remember her social security number either. The nurse's aide had to dig into his back pocket to get his wallet. The card was in there along with his insurance card. He couldn't do it for her because his hands, now covered with brown dried blood, were occupied trying to stop fresh red blood from flowing.

The ER doctor was also half his age, Oriental, handsome, and built like a swimmer with wide shoulders and a narrow waist, like the rest of the staff quite friendly and cheerful at this ungodly hour but unlike them seemingly unafraid to touch him even after, having swallowed so much of his own blood, he vomited much of it back into one of the pink plastic bowls. He asked Alan if he was taking any drugs. And that was when he really learned about the blood-thinning properties of ibuprofen. He thought that at least he was probably not going to have a heart attack. He supposed it was something.

The doctor used a kind of suction device to suck blood from each of his nostrils into a tube trying to clear them, but that didn't work, which Alan could have told him; there was far too much to replace it with, so he packed him with what he called pledgets, which looked like a pair of tampons mounted on sticks, shoved them high and deep into the nasal cavities and told him to wait and see if they managed to stop the bleeding.

Miraculously, they did.

Half an hour later they released him. He phoned Annie and she drove him back to the condo and he washed his hands and face and changed his clothes and they each went back to bed.

He woke needing to use the toilet and found that both his shit and piss had turned black. A tiny black droplet clung to his penis. He shook it off. He supposed he'd learned something—a vampire's shit and urine would always be black. He wondered if Anne Rice could find a way to make this glamorous.

The second time he woke he was bleeding again. He squeezed at the pledgets as he'd been told to do should this occur, but the bleeding wouldn't stop. He roused Ann and this time she insisted on driving him to the hospital herself, handing him her own newly opened box of Puffs to place in his lap. Upstairs David continued to sleep his heavy adolescent sleep. It was just as well. The boy was only fond of blood in horror movies.

The chubby nurse's aide was gone when he arrived, but the pink plastic bowls were there and he used them, sat in the same room he'd left only hours before while his doctor, the swimmer, summoned an Ear, Nose, and

Throat man who arrived shortly after he'd sent Annie back home.

By now he felt weak as a newborn colt, rubber-legged and woozy. It seemed he needed to grow a new pair of hands to juggle his kidney-shaped pan, eyeglasses, tissues, and tissue boxes, all the while holding his nose and spitting, vomiting, dripping, and swallowing blood at intervals.

He felt vaguely ridiculous, amused. A bloody nose for chrissake.

What he felt next was pain that lasted quite a while as the ENT man—another healthy Florida specimen, a young Irishman who arrived in pleated shorts and polo shirt—withdrew the pledgets and peered into his nose with a long thin tubular lighted microscope, determined that it was only from the right nostril that he was actually bleeding, and then repacked it with so much stuff that by the time it was finished he felt like a small dog had crawled up and died in there.

A half-inch square accordion-type gauze ribbon coated in petroleum jelly, four feet of it folded back-to-back, compacted tight into itself, and pushed in deep. In front of that another tamponlike pledget, this one removable by means of a string. In front of that something called a Foley catheter which inflated like a balloon. Another four feet of folded ribbon. Another pledget.

He had no idea there was so much room inside his face.

The man was hearty but not gentle.

He was given drugs against the pain and possible infection and put into a wheelchair and wheeled into an elevator and settled into a hospital bed for forty-eight hours' observation. Once again a nurse had to find and read his insurance and social security cards. The drugs had kicked in by then and so had the loss of blood. He didn't even know where his wallet was, though he suspected it was in its usual place, his back pocket.

The bed next to him was empty. The ward, quiet.

He slept.

He awoke sneezing, coughing blood, a bright stunning spray across the sheets—*it could not get out his nose so instead it was sliding down his throat again, his very heartbeat betraying him, pulsing thin curtains, washes of blood over his pharynx, larynx, down into his trachea.* He gagged and reached for the bowl at the table by the bed and vomited violently, blood and bile, something thick in the back of his throat remaining, gagging him, something thick and solid like a heavy ball of mucus making him want to puke again, so he reached into his mouth to clear it, reached in with thumb and forefinger and grasped it, slippery and sodden, and pulled.

And at first he couldn't understand what it was, but it was long, taut, and would not part company with his throat, so he pulled again until it was out of his mouth and he could see the thing, and then he couldn't believe what he'd done, that it was even possible to do this thing, but he had it between his fingers. He was staring at it covered with slime and blood, nearly a foot and a half of the accordion ribbon packed inside his nose. He'd sneezed it out or coughed it out through his pharynx and now he was holding it like a tiny extra-long tongue and it continued to gag him so he reached for the call-button and pushed and fought the urge to vomit, waiting.

"What in the world have you done?"

It was the pretty nurse, a strong young blonde with a wedding ring, the one who'd admitted him and gotten him into bed. She looked as though she didn't know whether to be shocked or angry or amused with him.

"Damned if I know," he said around the ribbon. *Aaand ithh eye-o.*

He vomited again. There was a lot of it this time.

"Uh-oh," she said. "I'm going to call your doctor. He may have to cauterize whatever's bleeding up in there. I'll get some scissors meantime, snip that back for you, okay?"

He nodded and then sat there holding the thing. He shook his head. *A goddamn bloody nose.*

It occurred to him much later that an operation followed by a hospital stay under heavy medication combined with heavy loss of blood was a lot like drifting through a thick fetal sea from which you occasionally surfaced to glimpse fuzzy snatches of sky. In his younger days he'd dropped acid while floating in the warm Aegean and there were similarities. He awoke to orderlies serving food and nurses taking his blood pressure and handing him paper cups of medication. None of it grounded him for long. Mostly he slept and dreamed.

He remembered the dreams vividly, huge segments of them crowded spinning inside his head with unaccustomed clarity of detail and feeling—and then he'd seem to blink and they'd be gone, just like that, his mind occupied solely by the business of healing his ruptured body. Adjusting the new packing to relieve the pressure, swallowing the pill, nibbling the food. Then hurrying back to dream.

There was something ultimately lonely, he thought, about the process of healing. Nobody could really help you. All they could do was be reasonably attentive to your needs. He began to look forward to his momentary visits from the pretty blonde nurse because of all the hospital staff she seemed the wittiest and most cheerful and he liked her Southern accent, but ultimately he was completely alone in this. He'd told Annie not to call for a while after her first phone call woke him; he was fine but he was not up to conversation yet. And that felt lonely, too.

When the black man with the haunted eyes appeared in the bed beside him by the window he was not really surprised. He assumed a lot went on in his room that he wasn't aware of. He'd looked over at the window to see if it was day or night because as usual he had no idea, no concept of time whatsoever, and there he was lying flat on his back and covered to the chin, hooked up to some sort of monitor and an elaborate IV device of tubes and wires much different from his own, his face thin to emaciation, drawn and gray in the moonlight, eyes wide open and focused in his direction but, Alan thought, not seeing him, or seeing through him—and this he proved with a smile and a nod into the man's unblinking gaze.

Possibly some sort of brain damage, he thought, poor guy, knowing somehow that this man's loneliness far exceeded his own, and moments later forgot him and returned to sleep.

*   *   *

Imagine the seats on a slowly moving Ferris wheel, only the seats are perfectly stable, they don't rock back and forth as the seats on a Ferris wheel do, they remain perfectly steady, and then imagine that they are not seats at all but a set of flat, gleaming slabs of thick, heavy, highly polished glass or metal or even wood, dark, so that it is impossible to tell which—and now imagine that there is no wheel—nothing whatever holding them together but the slow steady measured glide itself and that each is the size and shape of a closet door laid flat, and that there are not only one set but countless sets, intricately moving in and out and past each other, almost but never quite touching, so that you can step up or down or to the side on any of them without ever once losing your footing.

It is like dancing. It gets you nowhere. But it's pleasurable.

That was what he dreamed.

He was alone in the dream for quite a while, until Annie appeared, a younger Annie, looking much the same as she did the day he met her over a dozen years ago, sitting across from him on the plane from L.A. with her two-year-old son beside her. Her hair was short as it was then, as was her skirt, and she was stepping toward him in a roundabout way, one step forward and one to the side, drifting over and under him, and he wasn't even sure she was aware of his presence; it was as though he were invisible, because she never looked directly at him until she turned and said, *You left us nowhere, you know that?* which was not an accusation but merely a statement of fact, and he nodded and began to cry because of course it was true; aside from these infrequent visits and the phone calls and letters he had come unstuck from them somehow, let them fend for themselves alone.

He woke and saw the black man standing in the doorway, peering out into the corridor, turning his head slowly as though searching for someone with those wide, empty eyes, and he thought for a moment that the man should not be out of bed, not with all those wires and tubes still attached to him reaching all the way across the room past the foot of his own bed, but then he heard movement on the other side of the darkened room and turned to see the form of a small squat woman who appeared to be adjusting the instruments, doing something to the instruments, a nurse or a nurse's aide he supposed, so he guessed it was all right for the man to be there. He looked back at him in the doorway and closed his eyes, trying but failing to find his way back into the dream, wanting to explain to Annie the inexplicable.

It was almost dawn when the arm woke him.

He had all but forgotten about the arm, the inflamed swollen tendon that had started him on ibuprofen and landed him here in the first place. The drugs had masked that pain, too. Now the arm jerked him suddenly conscious, jerked hard twice down along his side as though some sort of electric shock had animated it, something beyond his will or perhaps inside his dream, needles of pain from the elbow rising above the constant throbbing wound inside his face.

He guessed more drugs were in order.

He was hurting himself here.

He pressed the call button and waited for the voice on the intercom.

"Yes? What can I do for you?"

"I need a shot or a pill or something."

"Pain?"

"Yes."

"I'll tell your nurse."

They were fast, he gave them that. The pretty blonde nurse was beside him almost instantly, or perhaps despite his pain he'd drifted, he didn't know. She offered him a paper cup with two bright blue pills inside.

"You hurt yourself awake, did you?"

"I guess. Yeah, my arm."

"Your arm?"

"Tennis elbow. Didn't even get to play tennis. Did it in a gym over a month ago."

She shook her head, smiling, while he took the pill and a sip of water. "You're not having a real good holiday, are you?"

"Not really, no."

She patted his shoulder. "You'll sleep for a while now."

When she was gone, he lay there waiting for the pain to recede, trying to relax so that he could sleep again. He turned and saw the black man staring at him as before, and saw that the man now nestled in a thicket of tubes and wires, connected to each of his arms, running under the bedcovers to his legs, another perhaps a catheter, two more patched to his collarbones, one running to his nose and the thickest of them into his half-open mouth. Behind him lights on a tall wide panel glowed red and blue in the dark.

By morning it was gone. All of it. Alan was lying on his side so that the empty bed and the empty space behind it and the light spilling in from the window were the first things he noticed.

The next thing was the smell of eggs and bacon. He did his best by the food set in front of him though it was tasteless and none too warm and the toast was hard and dry. He drank his juice and tea. When the nurse came in with his pills—a new nurse, middle-aged, black and heavy-waisted, one he'd never seen—he asked her about the man in the bed beside him.

"Nobody beside you," she said.

"What?"

"You been all alone here. I just came on, but first thing I did was check the charts. Always do. Procedure. You're lucky it's summertime, with all the snowbirds gone, or we'd be up to our ears here. You got the place all to yourself."

"That's impossible. I saw this guy three times, twice in the bed and once standing right there in the doorway. He looked terrible. He was hooked up to all kinds of tubes, instruments."

" 'Fraid you were dreaming. You take a little painkiller, you take a little imagination, mix and stir. Happens all the time."

"I'm an appellate lawyer. I don't *have* an imagination."

She smiled. "You were all alone, sir, all night long. I swear."

Some sort of mix-up with the charts, he thought. The man had been there. He wasn't delusional. He knew the difference between dreams and reality. For now the dreams were the more vivid of the two. It was still one way to tell them apart.

Wait till the shift changes, he thought. Ask the other nurse, the blonde. She'd given him a pill last night. The black man had been there. And he was on her watch.

He dreamed and drifted all day long. Sometime during the afternoon Annie and David came by to visit, and he told David about coughing up the accordion ribbon and what he'd learned about the color of vampire shit. Teenage kids were into things like that, he thought, the grosser the better. That and Annie's cool lips on his forehead were about all he remembered of their visit. He remembered lunch and dinner, though not what he ate. He remembered the doctor coming by and that he no longer wore the shorts and polo shirt as he took his pulse and blood pressure but instead the pro forma white lab coat and trousers. He decided he liked him better the other way.

"Sure," she said. "I remember. You hurt yourself awake."

"You remember the guy in the bed beside me?"

"Who?"

"The black man. I don't know what was wrong with him, but he looked pretty bad."

"You know what your doctor's giving you for pain?"

"No."

"It's called hydrocodone, honey. In the dose you're getting, it's as mean as morphine, only it's not addictive. I wouldn't be surprised if you told me you were seeing Elvis in that bed over there, let alone some black fella."

He *hurt himself awake* again that night.

This time he was batting at his aching face—at his nose. He was batting at the culprit, at the source of his misery. As though he wanted to start himself bleeding again.

What was he doing? Why was he doing this?

His dream had been intense and strange. They were

alone inside a long gray tube, he and Annie, empty of everything but the two of them and stretching off into some dazzling bright infinity and he was pulling at her clothes, her blouse, her jacket, trying to rouse her and get her to her feet while she crouched in front of him, saying nothing, doing nothing, as though his presence beside her meant nothing at all to her one way or the other. He felt frightened, adrift, panicked.

He woke in pain, batting at his face, and reached for the call button to call his nurse for yet another pill, but the black man's big hand stopped him, fingers grasping his wrist. The man was standing by his beside. The fingers were long and smooth and dry, his grip astonishingly firm.

He looked up into the wide brown eyes that did not seem to focus upon him but instead to look beyond him, into vast distances, and saw the wires and tubes trailing off behind him past the other bed where the squat dark form he realized was no nurse nor nurse's aide hovered over the panel of instruments and a voice inside his head said, *No, we're not finished yet; my accident became yours, and I'm very much sorry for that, but it happens sometimes, and for now no interruptions please, we need the facilities, deal with your own pain as I am dealing with mine;* and he thought, I'm dreaming, this is crazy, this is the drug. But the voice inside said, *No, not crazy, only alone in this, alone together here in this room and the nurse cannot see, cannot know, the nurse is not in pain as you and I, you'll only disturb her, you can live with that, can't you?* and he nodded yes because suddenly he thought that of course he could. *Good,* the voice said, *a short time, stop hurting yourself and instead of her, dream of me; you've been doing that already, but she always gets in, doesn't she?* He nodded again and felt the pressure lessen on his wrist. *Stop hurting yourself. She is not the pain nor are you. Rest. Sleep.*

The man sat back on his own bed and rested, adjusted the wires, smoothed them over his chest. The dark female figure resumed her work at the lighted panel. The man's touch was like a drug. Better. The pain was vanishing. He didn't need the call button. Or perhaps he was just living with the pain, he didn't know. One more night, he thought. One more morning, maybe.

Maybe there were things he could do for her and the boy that he hadn't done, things to make it better. But he needed to let go of that now.

He dreamed of a Ferris wheel. Only there was no wheel. He dreamed of a thousand wheels intersecting.

He stepped down and up and forward and side to side.

OUTSIDE LOOKING IN

by John Helfers

John Helfers lives in Green Bay, Wisconsin, writing part-time and doing freelance editing and other literary work to fill the rest of his days. He's contemplating beginning a novel, but must finish the work-in-progress on his hard drive first, which includes writing a Vietnam veteran's memoirs and a possible *Ghosts of Fear Street* children's novel. His short fiction appears in *Sword of Ice and Other Tales of Valdemar, Future Net,* and *Phantoms of the Night.*

The plain blue Plymouth jounced over the rutted desert hardpan. Inside, Ryan shivered as the intermittently-working heater blew lukewarm air over his face and hands. Once night had fallen, the temperature had plunged twenty degrees in an hour, the desert throwing off whatever heat it had clung to during the day to sprawl stark and barren under a cold white moon. But it wasn't the cold that bothered Ryan the most. It was the wind.

Out here the wind just kept going and going. It picked up dust and sand and flung it everywhere, making it sound as though the car were being rubbed by a thousand sheets of sandpaper. The wind caused dunes to pile up in the road, and the gutless wonder of a car the military had loaned him protested every time its tires encountered one. Luckily, Ryan hadn't gotten stuck. Yet.

He grinned ruefully. *The guys back at base are probably laughing asses off right now.* He had already been regarded as somewhat odd for requesting this assignment, but to drive out to the base? Ryan had gotten some strange looks at the motor pool when he had turned in his request. He was used to it. The supply sergeant had told him that the Plymouth was all they

118

had left. Ryan couldn't tell if the man was joking or not, although he had seen a few humvees around the garage. He had just nodded and taken the keys.

Maybe I should have flown in, he thought as the car almost bogged down in the biggest drift he had seen so far. He pressed hard on the gas pedal and the car, as if sensing his urgency, lurched free of the dune. Ryan looked behind him, making sure the green duffel bag was still on the back seat. He looked out at the desert night, the darkness cut only by the arcs of his headlights and the dead white moon. And every few seconds, unaware that he was doing so, Ryan kept looking up at the inky black sky.

It wasn't that Ryan did or did not believe in UFOs. He had never really thought about it one way or the other. Sure, he had heard about the various stories, these people or those people claiming to have been "abducted." He didn't really care what theories were postulated or what the government knew or didn't know. Until the evening he first saw one, none of it had mattered to him.

He had been stationed at McConnell Air Force Base outside Wichita, Kansas. Now that he thought about it, he realized that the Kansas plains and the New Mexico desert had a lot in common. Kansas just had more grass. That night his wing had been scheduled for a routine night flying exercise.

Ryan remembered every detail of that evening. Walking out to the waiting F-16, climbing aboard, settling himself into the cockpit, his copilot right behind him. On the horizon, the pair could see several bright pinpoints of light.

"Whaddya think that is, Ryan?" Jeff drawled.

"Probably more heat lightning," Ryan said.

Takeoff, the part that Ryan loved best. The feeling he got during takeoff was unlike anything else. *Those first few seconds when you're squashed back in your seat and breathing hard because it feels like you're trying to break though a wall that's all around you and the ground keeps trying to pull you down, hold you down, and the roar of the engines drowns out everything, even your thoughts,*

*and old Mother Earth grabs at you one last time and you
haul back on the stick and cut for the heavens and
then . . .*

Freedom. *Man wins again,* Ryan had thought as he
nosed his Falcon up to cruising altitude and settled into
position with his wingman. Neither Ryan nor his navigator spoke as the planes got into position for their
exercise.

Just before the exercise was about to begin, Jeff broke
the silence, addressing Ryan by his call sign. "Lynx, I
got two bogeys at heading two, seven, one, moseying
south. They are cruising."

Looking down, Ryan saw the two dots on his radar
display. He whipped the jet around and hit the afterburners, his wingman close behind. Within seconds the
pair of F-16s had their targets in range.

Ryan clicked on his radio. "Unidentified aircraft, this
is the United States Air Force. You are in restricted
airspace. Change your course to heading two, seven,
zero immediately."

There was no reply from the blips. *In a few seconds,
we'll have them.*

"What the hell . . ." Ryan forgot to finish his sentence
as he flew closer to the unidentified aircraft. On the horizon and growing larger by the second were two bright
green dots of light. They didn't resemble the signal lights
of any aircraft Ryan had ever seen. They didn't flash,
but glowed that steady, eerie green.

"That ain't no heat lightnin' I've ever seen, even back
home," Jeff's voice drawled in his ear.

Ryan snapped his air mask over his face and contacted
his wingman. "Nighthawk, cover the second bogey. I'm
on the leader."

No sooner were the words out of his mouth than the
two lights, by now the size of basketballs, split up, one
going straight up, one heading for the Kansas plains.

Like the precision birds they were, the pair of jets
split up to pursue both targets.

"Lynx, did you see what that thing just did?" Ryan's
navigator asked.

"Yeah, Tex, I did," Ryan said. Their bogey hadn't just
arced into the atmosphere; it had changed its direction

instantly, going from horizontal movement to vertical in the blink of an eye. Ryan was able to pull up on his stick so as to parallel the target's course, but even so, its maneuverability had caught him by surprise.

"Just a few more seconds and we'll be on it," Ryan said, hitting the afterburners again.

"Yeah, assuming we really want to," Jeff said. Ryan ignored him

By now the light was as big as a car door. Ryan was just getting set to pull alongside it when the light disappeared.

"What happened, Tex? Where is it?"

In the back seat, Jeff was looking wildly around in case the light was now following them. Then he checked his radar. "Lynx, you're not going to believe this, but our bogey just stopped dead. It's now a thousand yards behind us, and just sitting there. No, wait, it's moving again, same course as before."

"The son of a bitch is playing with us," Ryan said. *But not even a Harrier can stop that fast. It's not possible. Maybe some kind of experimental aircraft?*

Jeff interrupted his thoughts. "Lynx, I just lost radio contact with base and Nighthawk."

"Well, we're not letting this thing get away without a closer look at it. I'm gonna crawl so far up his ass we'll be able to see what he had for dinner," Ryan said.

"Lynx, I don't think that's such a good idea."

"Noted," Ryan said, keeping a lock on his anger. He was one of the top pilots on the base, but this thing had just made him look like a rookie. What he wanted—no, what he needed—from this thing was a positive visual identification. And there was only one way to get it. "Hang on."

Ryan rolled the F-16 over and started heading back down toward the bogey, which had resumed its course south. He approached more slowly this time, hoping to sneak up on whatever it was down there.

A minute passed, then two. The dead silence in Ryan's headphones was unnerving, but he ignored it and slowly kept pulling closer. By now the light was filling the cockpit of Ryan's plane, bathing the instruments and his face in that bright green glow. Ryan flipped his visor down and nudged the jet lower.

"Holy Mary, Mother of God," he heard Jeff say just before all hell broke loose.

A brilliant ball of light leaped from the craft to the F-16, causing the plane to yaw sharply. Wrestling the stick back to normal, Ryan tried to keep his eyes on the bogey, but was distracted by an explosion of warning buzzers. Looking around, he saw his cockpit gauges go haywire, dials spinning crazily and lights flashing on and off. The control stick froze in his hand.

"Tex, what's going on, talk to me," he said.

"Nothing's working back here." Ryan felt the plane shudder. "Oh, shit, engine one just flamed out."

"Initiating restart procedures," Ryan said, just as Jeff called out to him again.

"Engine two out. This is very bad, Lynx, very bad."

Ryan was running through the engine ignition checklist with one hand while trying to keep the jet level with the other. The F-16 continued to dive, with none of Ryan's efforts having any effect. Ryan felt himself being squeezed back into his seat as the ground rushed closer.

"Tex, I can't even pull the stick back. We'd better eject," he said.

"Affirmative."

With that, Ryan reached behind his head and pulled the eject release handle. The canopy exploded from the plane and the two seats burst out into the night air.

Ryan tumbled through the air for a moment, then jerked upright as his parachute deployed. He could see another parachute canopy below him, so he knew Jeff was all right. Looking down, he saw the F-16 dive straight into the ground, disintegrating in a burst of flame.

Man sure didn't win that one, he thought. The last thing Ryan saw before he hit the earth was the one green light pair up with the second, and both speed off into space.

The Plymouth protested again as it shuddered over the washboard road. Shaking his head, Ryan snapped his attention back to the present as the car's headlights illuminated a large sign near the roadside.

UNITED STATES AIR FORCE
MISSILE TESTING GROUND
WARNING: LIVE ORDNANCE
KEEP OUT

Only a few more miles to go, he thought. The sign reminded him of the aftermath of the Kansas encounter, as he had come to call it.

Of course, the Air Force had investigated. After all, no government agency likes to waste forty million dollars unless they have a reason. Both Ryan and Jeff stuck to their story, that they had encountered some sort of UFO. Their wingman could not confirm their claims, as he hadn't been able to get close enough to his target for a positive identification. When the investigators recovered the jet's black box from the wreck site, all they could ascertain was that the plane experienced a sudden unexplained power loss. They decided the accident was caused by a mechanical malfunction, and that Ryan was not at fault. That was the story released to the press. There was no mention of green lights or flying saucers at all.

After that, life went back to normal. Ryan, however, never sat in a fighter cockpit again. It wasn't that he was afraid to go up. But the encounter had taken the joy of flying out of him. The idea that there was something out there that he couldn't explained distracted him to no end. He thought about the green lights constantly. He had to know what they were doing there.

He requested and received a desk job. He knew the other officers were talking about him behind his back, saying he had lost his nerve, but he didn't care.

Ryan started researching the Air Force files on UFOs. Project Blue Book, Area 51, Roswell, everything he could get his hands on. His research grew into more than a hobby but less than an obsession. However, it did come to the attention of his superiors at the base, who strongly suggested that he transfer someplace where his skills would be put to better use.

Ryan agreed. By now he had learned everything he could, and it was time to move on. Some of the information the military had could only be accessed in one place. Now that he had firsthand experience, Ryan needed to learn more. He requested to be transferred to Washington, and when the transfer went through three months later, he left on the last plane he would ever ride.

"—are about fifteen minutes away from Dulles International Airport. Weather in Washington, D.C., is light fog with a temperature of 45 degrees. We may be encountering some slight turbulence as we come in, and we advise you to remember that the 'fasten seat belt' light is on. Thank you for flying American Airlines."

The announcement jolted Ryan out of his light sleep. He blinked as he heard the stewardess' voice. *That's strange, usually the pilot announces our arrival.* His hands moved to check that his seat belt was still fastened securely around his waist. After all, there was no ejection lever he could pull if something went wrong here.

His window shade was open, and he looked outside. The sky was clear, and he could see to the ground below. Surprisingly, instead of the bright glow of the Washington suburbs, the land was dark, with only the clustered lights of small towns visible. *Maybe the pilot's taking a different route in,* he thought.

Looking around, he wasn't surprised to find most of the scattered passengers in the cabin still asleep. Across the aisle from him a small boy stared back at him, unblinking. The boy's mother had her face by the window and a blanket draped over her body. Ryan smiled and nodded to the boy, who just kept looking at him, unembarrassed.

Probably looking at the uniform, Ryan thought. As he was officially working, he was wearing his dress blues. He brushed an imaginary piece of lint off his lapel.

The plane slapped air as it flew through a pocket of turbulence. The announcement system clicked on, then clicked off again without anything being said. Ryan looked down the aisle toward the front of the plane, and saw a stewardess walking toward him.

"Excuse me, sir, but could you come to the front of the plane, please?" she asked.

"Why? Is something wrong?" Ryan whispered.

"There's a telephone call for you. If you'll follow me," she said.

Who in hell would be calling me here? Ryan had no family, and there was no reason his superiors would be contacting him before he landed.

Ryan unfastened his seat belt and got up to follow the stewardess. He passed the boy on his way, and could feel his gaze as he walked up the aisle. They walked through first class and through a doorway to where the rest of the stewardesses were clustered in a tight knot. One of them, a young blonde Ryan found quite attractive, was dabbing at her red eyes with a tissue. Ryan could see from their faces that this was no ordinary tour of the cockpit.

"What's going on?" he asked.

The stewardess who had summoned him answered. "I think Dulles can answer that better." She pointed at the phone

Ryan picked up the handset. "Hello."

"Who am I speaking to?" crackled a voice on the other end.

"This is Major Ryan Winters, United States Air Force. Who am I speaking to?"

"I'm Brad Gustafson, chief air controller at Dulles International. We gotta situation here, and you're about the only man who can help out."

Ryan didn't reply. Whenever the Air Force used the word *situation*, it was never good. He doubted this would be much better.

"Major?" the voice said.

"I'm here," he said.

"I'm gonna make this short. About ten minutes ago someone in the cockpit of that 747 made an unexplained course change. Attempts to contact the crew have failed. A few minutes later one of the stewardesses called down to us and said that the cockpit door is locked from the inside. Right now the plane is flying as pretty as you please, so it must be on autopilot. We've contacted airports along the way and warned them about your course

change. But if the crew has become incapacitated somehow, someone's gonna have to land that bird."

"Which is where I come in, eh?" Ryan asked.

"Yep," Gustafson said.

"I'm qualified on the F-16 fighter jet. This is a little
bit different," Ryan said.

"Well, just imagine it's an F-16 with a 500-foot rear
end. Don't worry, the autopilot can handle much more
than you think. We'll walk you through programming it
for landing. All you'll have to do is flip a few switches.
Look, Major, you're all we got, and I'll take you over
talking down some know-nothing yokel," Gustafson
said.

Ryan thought of the boy sitting next to his seat. "All
right, just relax, I'm in. After all, I want to get off this
plane alive, too."

"I sure as hell hope so," Gustafson replied.

Ryan covered the mouthpiece and asked the flight
crew, "How much fuel do we have?"

The stewardess who'd summoned him replied, "At
least another hour's worth."

Ryan nodded. He spoke into the handset. "Brad, I'll
see what I can do. But if I can't get through that door,
we're gonna have a big problem on our hands."

"Right now, you are just about the only hope those
people have, so do whatever you have to."

"I plan to," Ryan said. "I'll contact you in ten minutes
or if the situation changes drastically."

"We'll be here," Gustafson replied.

"Ryan out." He hung up the phone, then turned to
the crew. "Any idea what caused this?"

The young blonde spoke up. "When I brought in dinner, I thought I heard Jameson, that's the copilot, mutter
something about lights in the sky."

Ryan looked at her for a moment. "I'm going up
there. Don't come up unless I ask for someone."

He headed up to the cockpit and knocked on the
door. There was no answer. Ryan knocked again.

"Hello? Can anybody hear me?"

"Yeah?" a voice called out from the other side.

"Mr. Jameson? I'm Major Ryan Winters of the United
States Air Force. I'd like to speak to you if I could."

Ryan heard movement on the other side of the door.

"Yeah, what about?" The voice sounded closer now.

"Sir, I understand you've seen some strange lights in the sky. Is that correct?" Ryan asked.

"Maybe. I'm not crazy though, they're out there." The tone of his voice shifted abruptly. "How do I know you're from the Air Force?"

"I've got my identification here, but I can't show it to you with the door closed," Ryan said.

"Well, then I guess you're shit out of luck."

"Mr. Jameson, I want to hear about what you've seen. I want to know about the green lights." Ryan waited. After several seconds, the cockpit door clicked and slid open.

"Step in, slowly."

Ryan did so, his foot coming down on something soft. Looking down, he saw a tray with the remains of one of the dinner choices, now unrecognizable, underfoot. His eyes then moved to the source of the gasping noises on the floor.

The pilot was stretched out in the narrow aisle, taking up just about every inch of remaining floor space. The white of his shirt was rapidly losing ground to the spreading red stain centered in his chest. A sodden handkerchief covered the wound. His eyes were closed, and his breathing was quick and labored.

Ryan looked up, not at the other men in the room, but at the instrument panel directly in front of him. He scanned the dials for airspeed, heading, and fuel remaining, looking for any warning lights. There were none, but the heading indicator showed that the plane was now on a northeastern course, heading toward the New England states. Satisfied that everything else was as it should be, he spoke to the other two men in the cockpit. "Mr. Jameson, would you let the navigator take the pilot out of here, please?"

Jameson didn't say anything, he just looked from the bloody dagger in his hand to the navigator, a man who looked much too young to hold the position. After a moment, he nodded.

Ryan also nodded to the man, who left his chair and worked his way around Ryan to the captain. Bending over, he whispered in the man's ear, then took him by the legs and slowly dragged him out of the cockpit. Ryan shut the door after they were gone, then turned back to the copilot.

"Nice blade. Ceramic?" Ryan asked.

Jameson's face revealed his bewilderment for a moment, then he noticed where Ryan was looking. "No, actually it's a carbon-plastic polymer. Completely undetectable." He looked at the knife as though he had never seen it before.

Ryan nodded. "In case of hijacking?"

Jameson nodded, wiping his free arm across his sweaty brow.

They stood there for a moment. Ryan took a look around the cockpit for the first time. It seemed so claustrophobic to him, all the huge panels of dials and gauges. He would always prefer the F-16 cockpit, where the canopy made you feel as though the sky were close enough to touch, not locked away behind endless numbers and arrows, visible only through a few small windows.

"How much fuel do we have left?" he asked suddenly.

"Enough for another hour and a half of flight," Jameson said automatically. Then his eyes narrowed. "Where's that identification you were talking about?"

Ryan smiled. " Guess the uniform's not enough, eh?" He produced his military card and let Jameson take it. After scrutinizing it carefully, he handed it back. He was backed against his flight seat. His tie was gone, and his headphones were still around his neck.

"Where are we going?" Ryan asked.

Jameson almost looked back at the control panel behind him, the dagger in his hand rising in a defensive position. Ryan held his hands up and tried again. "I only asked because it seemed to be a logical reason why you might hurt the captain."

"I didn't want to, but he wouldn't listen. When they call, you have to go, there's no waiting," Jameson said.

"When who calls?"

"The green lights. They spoke to me again, a little while ago. They told me to go."

"Go where?"

Jameson looked as if he wasn't comprehending the question, but he answered. "Go to them."

"And what will you do then?"

"They will tell me when I get there." Jameson's eyes weren't glazed but seemed to be looking at something far away. His dagger hand, however, remained steady, and there was no doubt that he was aware of Ryan's exact position.

Ryan thought back to his own encounter with the lights. He remembered no communication with the craft, verbal or otherwise. He didn't know whether Jameson was certifiable, or whether he had actually communicated with extraterrestrials. He didn't dare try to neutralize Jameson until he knew more about the situation.

"Are you going with them?" he asked.

"When I see them again, I will know," Jameson said with irritating confidence.

"Why do you listen to them? Aren't you worried that they'll take you away to experiment on you?" Ryan asked.

"Whatever happens to me, it must be better than living here. The same thing day in and day out. Crossing the country without even getting to see it," Jameson said. He looked out the side window, then sighed in relief. "They're coming."

"May I look?" Ryan asked. *Too many questions, not enough answers,* he thought.

Jameson moved to the pilot's chair and motioned Ryan forward into the copilot's seat. Ryan walked forward until he could see out the side window.

A pair of glowing green lights hung off the right side of the plane, growing steadily larger as they approached. They looked exactly like the ones Ryan had encountered over Kansas.

"Just like I told you," Jameson said behind him. "They're coming for me."

Ryan continued watching the balls approach. Jameson was muttering to himself, but Ryan couldn't make out what he was saying. The green lights grew larger, but Ryan still couldn't make out what kind of craft was behind those lights. He needed just a few more seconds.

By now the lights had pulled up alongside the 747,

about one hundred yards away. They paced the airplane perfectly, never wavering or deviating from their course. For one crazy instant, Ryan thought about letting Jameson keep his supposed rendezvous. Or subduing Jameson and meeting the aliens himself. Just as quickly as the thoughts came, he dismissed them. If they wanted to make contact so badly, they would do it in their own way. Maybe this was it.

As the two men watched, the green lights flickered rapidly for a moment, and then both Ryan and Jameson saw the actual alien ships for the first time. Now only a porthole on the nearest spacecraft (for its shape suggested nothing else) radiated that odd green light. And clearly silhouetted in the emerald glow was a humanoid shape.

Neither Ryan nor Jameson said anything. The alien raised its arm and held it for the two men to see for a few seconds; then the green light on both ships intensified until both men had to look away. When their vision cleared, the ships were gone.

Ryan looked at Jameson. The copilot looked dazed, the dagger slipping from his hand to clatter to the floor. He sank slowly into the pilot's chair.

"They didn't say anything. They . . . didn't speak to me."

Ryan also sat down, grabbing the controls of the plane and changing the course of the airliner back toward Washington, D.C. He didn't say anything either.

As Ryan coaxed the Plymouth over a large hill, he saw the base before him. Driving up, the car's misaligned headlights half-illuminated another large sign:

UNITED STATES AIR FORCE
GOVERNMENT PROPERTY
NO TRESPASSING

As if anyone would want to, Ryan thought. The sign was attached to a chain-link fence which surrounded a half-dozen ramshackle buildings with metal roofs. The headlights of Ryan's car revealed not one scrap of color anywhere. Every bit of paint had been scoured clean, leav-

ing naked gray concrete and tin. None of the buildings had
windows and no lights illuminated the perimeter.

There was no guard at the gate either, but there was
one anomaly. A small steel post at the side of the road
with a covered slot in it. Ryan fished his ID card out
and fed it in. After a few seconds, the gate slid open
noiselessly. The post, the oiled gate, and the strands of
razor wire topping the fence were the only indications
that the base was still occupied.

Ryan took back his card and drove to a large building
with a garage door on the side. Getting out, he shielded
his eyes from the lashing sand as he trotted to the door
and struggled to pull it open. Running back to his car,
he drove it in and parked it at the end of a line of old
jeeps, pickups, and two-and-a-half-ton trucks. He turned
off the car, got out, and went back to look at the desert
one last time. It looked no different than it had on the
drive out. He pulled down the garage door, slamming it
shut with a clang.

Ryan walked back to his car, brushing off loose sand
that had lodged in his uniform. He took his hat from
the passenger seat and put it on. Taking his duffel bag,
he slung it over his shoulder and walked toward the far
side of the motor pool building.

A pair of steel metal doors waited for him, framed by
a small shed. A slot similar to the one at the gate was
on the wall. Ryan fed it a different card from the one
he had given the slot at the gate. This card worked just
as well, and the metal doors swung open, revealing a
small room with no other exits. Ryan stepped inside.

The doors closed and the room began to move downward. As it did, Ryan thought about the rest of that
flight to Washington.

He had landed the plane without incident, the autopilot being as easy to program as Gustafson had claimed
it would be. Jameson had been taken off the plane, bab-
bling about green lights and UFOs the whole while. The
pilot was taken to a nearby hospital and lived through
the ordeal. The passengers barely even knew anything
out of the ordinary had happened, save that the pilot
was carried off by paramedics. Ryan overheard some of
them talking about a green flash of light they thought

they saw during the flight. A revised version of the story made the papers: Pilot suffered seizure during flight, plane landed safely, etc. In Washington, it barely made page 12.

In Ryan's debriefing, he made no mention of any green lights. He just told the story as it was: Copilot with a nervous breakdown had stabbed the pilot, Ryan disarmed him and brought the plane down. For his act of heroism, Ryan was awarded the silver Carnegie Medal and given his choice of station. Anywhere he wished to go.

He told the officers he would give them his decision in a month's time. Then he settled into his job in Washington, where he contacted the proper Air Force individuals who would listen to his report of not one, but two encounters with the proper respect. He told them where he needed to go and how it would benefit them. They said they could arrange it.

On the thirtieth and last day of his stay, Ryan told his superiors where he wanted to go. They were surprised, but agreed. He said he wanted to drive there, so they told him to go to the base in New Mexico which was closest to his destination, and they'd give him his clearance and directions out there.

He had spent three weeks driving from Washington to New Mexico. He got onto the remains of Route 66 in St. Louis and followed what was left of the grand old highway out to New Mexico. It had been an enjoyable trip. Ryan hoped this next one would be as good.

The elevator stopped moving with hardly a sound. The trip down had taken at least two minutes. The steel doors opened and Ryan stepped out.

He found himself in a small corridor ending in another set of steel doors. Next to the doors was a guard station. The guard looked at him and came to attention.

Ryan walked over and saluted. "Major Ryan Winters, reporting for duty."

The guard returned the salute and said, "Yes, sir, if I may have your identification, sir."

Ryan surrendered his card. The guard scanned it, then had Ryan look at a corner of the corridor above the guard station. Ryan did so, and saw a small red light, indicating a retina scan was working. A beep came from the guard's console, and the steel doors opened. Ryan took his card back and walked inside.

He found himself in another corridor similar to the first, only this one had large viewing windows set along one wall. Going to them, Ryan looked at the incredible scene below.

The hall he was in was actually an observation platform overlooking a huge room. Even at this time of night, white-jacketed men and women were monitoring computers, aiming video cameras, huddling over reams of notes and printouts, and, in several instances, sleeping at or under their desks. Rows of mainframe computers whirred and clicked endlessly, recording everything these scientists were doing. And what they were doing it to.

The subject of all their experiments and research sat in the center of the room. When Ryan looked at it, all of the various descriptions he had read in the hundreds of eyewitness reports came flooding back to him.

It looked like a giant flying sombrero . . .

. . . like a pancake with a scoop of ice cream on top . . .

. . . like a frisbee with half a tennis ball glued to it . . .

. . . like a flying manhole cover with lights everywhere . . .

It looked like all of those things. And at the same time, like none of them.

It looks like a flying saucer, thought Ryan.

Ryan knew the whole story. He had read it on the Washington computers. He had read even more in the musty archives at Washington. He sniffed the air here. It smelled about the same.

He knew about the recovery of the UFO at Roswell. He knew about the military sightings similar to his Kansas encounter. He knew about the Siberian Explosion, and what the U.S. government thought caused it.

He also knew just about everything there was to know about this project. Operation Greeting, they called it. Only there was one problem. The visitors didn't want to come out and say hello.

The men in this underground cavern had been working on the same problem ever since the 1950s. How to communicate with whoever—whatever—was inside this spacecraft. The alien bodies purported to have been seen at Roswell were just military misdirection, something for the nation to chew on, worry over, and eventually forget about. The real aliens were here. And if they weren't hostile, well, they weren't exactly friendly either.

The scientists, now in their second generation, had tried everything. Peace messages, Morse code, light pulses, microwaves, binary code, hard radiation, lasers, tight-band computer broadcast, tapping on the hull. Every signal known to mankind had been tried, all with the same result. Nothing.

The craft had sat here for almost half a century while the Pentagon's brightest had labored to gain access, to pry off the slightest useful bit of information. Ryan remembered reading something about one group of scientists who had been trying to analyze the spacecraft's composition. They were no farther along now than they had been thirty years ago.

Ryan walked to the door at the far end of the corridor. Unlike the others, this one opened automatically as he approached, revealing a flight of stairs. The rush of noise and activity swept over him, men and women walking here and there, fiddling with whatever experiment they were trying, and everybody involved in hushed conversations, either with themselves or others. Ryan listened for a moment, then realized what it all resembled to him.

If frustration had a sound, this is what it would be. He walked down the stairs, practically unnoticed. Those who did see him barely glanced up from their laptops or sheafs of paper. The craft had been off limits for the first fifteen years, visible only through monitors and leaded glass. As the years and failures mounted, the scientists had gradually taken over the hangar. Their reasoning was, if the aliens had wanted to do anything to them, they would have by now.

The frustration was showing in their reports as well. One of the latest theories was that there was nothing inside the UFO; it was just a decoy to divert attention away from whatever plans the aliens were really implementing. Ryan had thought that was an interesting theory until his trip to Washington, when he had found out the truth.

Ryan set down his bag beside the staircase. Everyone had already gone back to what they were doing. With such a big puzzle to occupy them, mundane things such as one more Air Force officer weren't worth looking at twice.

Slowly walking among the various experiments, Ryan didn't say a word. No one came to greet him. It was expected that you were here for one reason and one reason only. He slowly meandered his way through the maze of computers, monitors, and other electronic equipment, gradually drawing closer to the round ship in the middle of the hall. After a few minutes, he was standing in its shadow. He could see the smooth surface, could catch a brief glimpse of light reflecting off the alien metal or compound, or whatever it was.

Ryan also knew that the Washington brass had pretty much given up hope that the scientists would ever break into the craft without the use of perhaps a nuclear weapon. But the scientists had kept the funding alive until the ideas had started to run out, and a certain president had ensured that funding in perpetuity, or until something happened with the craft, whichever came first. Ryan knew all of this, and a whole lot more.

Basically, I'm giving the United States one hell of a budget cut. He wondered why the aliens didn't just swoop down and rescue their trapped friends. After all, a mile of bedrock shouldn't be too much trouble to a race with interstellar travel. He also wondered why they just didn't make contact, why they limited their interaction to isolated sightings and kidnappings. Whatever their plans were, Ryan didn't understand, nor did he ask to.

But he did understand the desire to be free. And when he had seen them the second time, he understood what he had to do.

There were aliens in this captured craft. Waiting to be released. The ones Ryan had encountered over Vermont were on a rescue mission that had finally arrived after almost twenty years. After much searching, they had discovered where the ship was being held. But they had no way inside that didn't involve attracting a lot of attention. Ryan, however, did.

He had accepted the price he would pay. Once the ship was activated, there would be no going back. Not that he wanted to. After all, it was why he had agreed.

Reaching out, Ryan placed his hand on the smooth skin of the UFO. It felt cool for a moment, then warmed to his touch. The not-quite-black material yielded under his fingertips, as he had been told it would for him alone.

A slight hum started somewhere from inside the spacecraft. The scientists nearest him paused in their calculations, slowly becoming aware that, finally, something had happened. They looked up to see the new Air Force officer with his hand on the saucer. As they watched, the man's hand pushed though the skin of the craft, then his wrist, then his elbow, and his arm to the shoulder.

Ryan was slowly, gently being drawn into the UFO. He looked around at the giant room one last time, seeing the shocked looks on the nearby scientists' faces. He didn't know why he had been chosen, but he knew that what they had asked of him, he couldn't refuse. *Funny,* he thought, *they may not have said much to Jameson, but they sure had a long conversation with me.*

Excerpt from military report PROJBBXCUR892-650385:

CLASSIFIED/EYES ONLY

. . . base was destroyed in an explosion of unknown origin. The craft the scientists had been studying is presumed to be destroyed as well, although no wreckage has been positively identified.

Eyewitness accounts say the explosion began when a power source inside the spacecraft apparently activated and then overloaded. The blast was channeled upward into the ceiling, and extended to the surface. Luckily, the blast occurred several minutes after the craft had achieved active status, so the base personnel were able to reach the bunker quarters in time to prevent serious injury. There were several minor injuries and one missing person reported. An Air Force major, Ryan Winters, had arrived that evening to begin his duty there. As no human remains were found in the explosion aftermath, his current whereabouts are still being investigated.

Base scientists still cannot explain how or why the

craft began functioning. Unverified reports place Major Winters in close proximity to the craft when the accident occurred, but it is unlikely that he had anything to do with the incident. . . .

THE END OF WINTER
by R. Davis

R. Davis currently resides in Green Bay, Wisconsin, with his
very patient wife Monica and his beautiful daughter Morgan
Storm. He holds a B.A. in English from the University of
Wisconsin, and writes both fiction and poetry. His current
projects include a book length manuscript of poems entitled
"In the Absence of Language" and several novel projects
that may never see the light of day.

The snow began during the afternoon of the last Friday of March, and continued into the early darkness.
It came down in blinding white sheets that stuck to everything, though the spring thaw had begun. Danielle
Wheatson sipped coffee and watched the snow through
her back patio window. She was pleased to have already
finished her chores; the horses had been watered and
fed, the dogs coaxed into the kennel. She could sit inside
and enjoy the warmth.

Danielle lived alone, except for her animals. The occasional visit by a neighbor was more in the line of country
friendliness. She was not a social woman, nor was she
attractive. Her limp brown hair fell unevenly over eyes
that could best be described as mud-colored. She didn't
mind the way her life had turned out. Being alone, well,
that was easy—she had gotten used to it. She had
enough money from a modest inheritance to raise her
horses and train her German shepherds. That was
enough. And as for a husband or lover, she knew that
it wasn't really in the cards.

As the last of the gray light disappeared from the sky,
Danielle could hear the dogs barking. "Now what?" she
muttered to herself, a habit garnered from long hours
alone.

She walked over to the window and stared outside. She could see little through the blowing snow, but she could still hear the dogs. She flicked on the light, but as she reached to open the door, someone rang the bell at the front of the house. "Huh, they must have sensed someone coming around, though I can't imagine anyone being out tonight."

Danielle went to the front of the house and turned on the porch light. Then she opened the door, letting the storm in. Standing on the front porch was a man. Or at least she thought so. He was quite tall, and bundled up under a large bulky coat. A scarf of similar material was wrapped around his head. Danielle took an involuntary step backward, even as she noticed that he was soaked. They both just stood there for a moment, regarding each other with the wary eye saved for strangers in the country.

Danielle spoke first. "Can I help you?"

The man slowly unwove the scarf from around his face. "I sure hope so," he said and smiled.

Danielle smiled back, still uncertain what to make of him. The man had dark hair and very large eyes which were almost black. His face was thin to the point of sharpness, and his skin was pale, though it may have been a trick of the light. He was still smiling, and Danielle realized she had been staring. "What can I do for you?" she asked.

"Well, you might start by letting me come in out of the snow. My car broke down about two miles from here, and it's not much of a night to be outdoors." He paused, then offered his hand, minus one hastily removed glove. "The name is James," he said.

She shook his hand out of reflex and noticed its dry warmth and long fingers. "Danielle."

"Mind if I use your phone, Danielle? It's a long walk to town."

"Yes, yes, of course." She remained standing in the doorway.

"Uh, Danielle, I think it's safe to say that the phone is probably inside." He smiled again, and motioned toward the inside of the house.

She jumped a little. "I'm sorry, just a minute, well, I

just don't get many visitors. Please come in." She
stepped into the house. *Good lord,* she thought, *I'm acting like I've never seen a man before.*

James crossed the threshold into the living room.
"Great," he said, "where's the phone?"

Danielle indicated the rotary phone on the table next
to her print sofa. "There. Um . . . do you need a
phone book?"

"No," James replied as he moved to the phone, "It's
broken down enough that I've actually memorized the
number." He looked at the phone. "How quaint," he
remarked as he picked it up to dial.

Danielle watched as James began dialing. She couldn't
help but stare a little. It was true, she rarely had visitors.
But even more, there was something unique about this
man that she could not quite put her finger on. He was
tall, over six feet, and his jacket and scarf were a bright
silvery-white color that she had never seen. *And,* she
admitted silently to herself, *that smile of his makes my
knees weak.* She suddenly realized he was speaking to
her.

"—did you know your phone was out?" he was
asking.

"What?" she said, startled out of her thoughts.

"I said, 'Danielle, did you know your phone was
out?' "

"No, I—what do you mean?"

"I mean it's not working. Come listen." He handed
the receiver to her.

Danielle took it and put it to her ear. She heard nothing, even when she tapped urgently on the operator button and the hang-up switch. "I'll be damned. Must be
the wind. We get that out here from time to time."

Silence descended as the wind slowed outside, and
both of them found they had nothing to say. Even the
dogs had quieted. Then the wind howled again, and
James stood up. "I guess I should go. Thanks anyway."
He started back across the living room.

For a moment Danielle said nothing more, then a
voice that sounded suspiciously like her own when she
was fifteen years younger and not so used to being alone,
shouted inside her head, *Don't let him leave!*

He was almost to the door when she stopped him. "James, no, wait."

He turned toward her. "Yes," he said softly.

"Well, it's awfully nasty out there, and I've got the room. Why don't you just stay, and I'll drive you in the morning." She blushed lightly.

James looked at her, and she thought for certain that he would insist on going. *What am I doing?* Danielle thought, and then answered herself, *Getting away from being lonely.* She was half-holding her breath, waiting for him to answer.

"If you're certain I won't be imposing . . ." The words trailed off.

"No, no, not at all. I could use the company," she said.

"Well, then, I'm sure it would be easier in the morning. I thank you." He smiled again and gave her a strange little bow.

Danielle found herself returning his smile earnestly. "It's no trouble, and you're welcome." She looked at him then and realized he was still dripping onto her carpet. "Why don't you go and get out of your wet clothes? I'll find something for you to wear until they're dry. Then we'll eat." *Great, Danielle,* she thought to herself, *beg him to stay the night, get him out of his clothes, and offer to feed him. Next thing you know, you'll be in bed with him. Which,* she thought with a mental grin, *wouldn't necessarily be a bad thing. Good lord, what must he think?*

"I think," he said, "that getting warm and dry is an excellent idea." He recrossed the living room to hang his coat on the hook by the door.

"By the way," Danielle asked, "where on Earth did you get that coat? I've never seen one quite like it. And the scarf matches exactly."

He chuckled from across the room. "It's unique," he answered. "I had it made for a trip I took last year. Though, apparently, I should have had it waterproofed as well."

Danielle went in search of something for James to wear, while he stood dripping near the door. She found an old but heavy bathrobe and some oversize sweatpants she had stashed in her closet. *Not perfect,* she thought, *certainly not a smoking jacket and silk pajamas, but they'll do.* She brought them back to him. "How about these?" she asked.

He held them up. "Perfect," he said, "Where do I change?"

She directed him to the bathroom. "Why don't you change while I make dinner?"

"All right," James agreed, starting in that direction. Then he stopped and turned around. "Hey, Danielle?" His voice was very soft.

"Yes?" she said.

"Thanks again."

"You're welcome again. Now go get changed." She made a shooing motion with one hand.

James walked to the bathroom, whistling to himself as he went. Danielle did not recognize the song.

Dinner came and went much too quickly for Danielle's liking. James proved to be a charming companion, and she was forcibly reminded of how much she had missed being with someone, had missed just talking with someone. James, she found, was able to talk freely about almost any subject. They talked about her horses, and were just moving on to her dogs when they started barking again. Danielle laughed. "That's them now. My 'shepherds.'"

James also laughed. "Makes perfect sense with you being out here by yourself so much. You probably need them to watch over you."

"Well," she said, "if nothing else, the barking reminds me that I'm still alive."

He looked at her quite seriously, his dark eyes never leaving hers. "Danielle, make no mistake. You're very much alive."

She thought then that he was going to touch her, take her hand, something. But he didn't. She was a little disappointed.

After dinner, they adjourned to the living room for coffee. Sitting on opposite ends of the sofa, Danielle wished that the night would not end, that the storm would keep on blowing.

"Is that what you really wish?" James asked when silence again descended on them.

"Wish what?" Danielle replied.

"That this night, this storm, would last forever?"

"Well, figuratively speaking, I—wait a minute. I never said that! How did you—" Danielle stopped. Her shooing hand raised toward her mouth as though she were warding off the words she had just said.

"I know you didn't say it. But I think it's sweet. And there's more unique to me than my jacket."

"What, what, what do you mean?" Danielle asked.

"This," he said, and leaned across the sofa to kiss her gently on the mouth.

Danielle didn't resist, couldn't resist. She didn't want to. *Anything,* she thought, *to not be alone again.* Her lips parted slightly, and as her breath quickened, she hugged him with a passionate half-sob.

James stopped and looked down at her. "Danielle, is everything all right? he asked.

She looked back at him, her decision already made. "Oh, yes," she replied, "everything's perfect." He kissed her again, stronger this time, and she whispered in his ear, "The bedroom."

He picked her up and carried her.

Danielle awoke when the sunlight from the window reached her eyes. *What about the storm?* she thought, still somewhat dazed and asleep. Then she remembered. She had briefly woken earlier when the wind had finally stopped. The storm was over. She rolled over to wake James, speaking as she did, "Wake up, sleepy."

Danielle realized she was speaking to an empty bed. James was gone. "James—?"

There was no response, and she climbed out of bed. *Surely he wasn't a dream,* she thought. She went out into the living room, noticing en route that his strange coat and scarf were also gone. She knew then that the house was empty. Near the phone she noticed a slip of paper. Wildly, she thought, *A psychic who leaves notes?*

She picked it up and began to read, not even noticing that the script very closely matched her own.

Dearest Danielle,

*As you surmised last night, I am not like other men
you have known, though I suspect that you have known
very few. My kind are few and far between, my home far
from here. I can, however, safely say that a part of me
will always remember this place as home. I was comfortable here.*

*I thank you for the hospitality of last evening. It is
generally not my preference to leave without saying good-
bye, yet I dare not risk too many questions. My superiors
will brook no foolishness. I may have gone too far last
night, and yet I have no regrets. I admit I was drawn to
you from the first moment you opened the door.*

*I came to learn something about human interaction
among strangers. I left not knowing any strangers, and—
I think—having made a friend as well.*

*I have returned home now, and while it is possible I
may return, I do not think it likely. I can say, having
known you but a little, that given the chance I would
never have left. You would do well to remember that only
by giving love can you receive it. You will not be lonely
for long if you do this. Spring is coming to your land,
and with it, comes hope.*

*Yours,
James*

Danielle let the sheet of paper fall slowly through her
hand. "Damn," she muttered, fighting back tears, "he
left me."

A month later the snow had all but finished melting.
The dogs ran joyously through the mud, and the horses,
tired of having spent a winter in the barn, galloped
across the pasture with something akin to glee in their
eyes. Danielle was slowly coming to terms with the night
she had met and spent with James. She thought a great
deal about what he had written in her letter to her, and
concluded that he was right. She had to get out more.
In hindsight, it all seemed like a dream. *Wishful thinking,*
she thought to herself.

Working in the afternoon sun, she didn't hear the old,
beat-up truck pull into her driveway. She turned just as
the man was getting out of the cab. "Howdy," he called.
She still couldn't see his face because of the sun glint-

ing off the door window. "What can I do for you?" Danielle answered back.

"Well," he said, stepping out where she could finally see him. "I think maybe I'm lost, and this old truck here is beginning to overheat. I was hoping I could borrow some water for the radiator, and maybe a glass for myself." He smiled.

Danielle looked at him for a moment, taking in his dark hair and eyes. She smiled back. "Lost, huh?" she said.

"Something like that," he said.

Danielle said nothing, not really trusting herself to say the right words. She walked slowly toward the man, and as she neared him, she held out her hand, "Sure," she said. "Come on into the house."

He took her outstretched hand. "Seems like spring to me," he said. And it was.

HEIRLOOM

by Jim Combs

Jim Combs is an author and critic who lives in Michigan. His fiction can also be found in *Love Kills*.

Jean LaLoise the baker rose slowly and softly out of sleep like a ripening loaf of *pain poilane*. Even before he broke through the crust of his dreams, he was absently scratching his dry, mottled shins, a perpetual affliction produced by the intense heat of the ovens. It was the occupational hazard of bakers, or as Grandmama Marie would insist, "Boulanger, Jean. Baker, non, boulanger, boulanger." It was of no consequence that they were now living in Chicago, where he had been born; it was still "boulanger."

He was in Grandmama's Boulangerie (Bakery) where nearly all his good dreams began and ended. Like all of his good dreams, it was filled with the open door of Grandmama's wrinkled smile and the omnipresent aroma of baking. Baking, always baking, in the boulangerie that was the home of all his memories and the scent of all his dreams.

He grew up there by Grandmama's oven in the fournils. Grandmama would never let him call it a cellar. In this nest of golden warmth, even on the coldest day, he was surrounded by ficelles, palmiers, amandines, the sharp tart odor of the *chaussons au pomme,* the heavenly riots of smells from the fruits and berries in the tartelelles and a finally the baguettes which pointed upward like long, thin fingers of sunlight, glowing with a moist yellow warmth.

Wandering through all his dreams was Gerard, Grandmama's *coutre-maitre,* stripped to his waist and covered completely with a white dusting of flour. He was a ghost with eyes bright from the oven's heat, his movements precise, his gestures part of ancient rituals a thousand years old.

Something was lifting him out of the warmth of the odor of yeast and dough and sweat and into the dark night of his bedroom. Gone were the smells and smiles. Instead, he caught the slightly acid scent of his socks and the musk of his underwear on the floor beside his bed. His nose snorted, and he was awake.

Strange sounds, struggles and grunts came to him. Jean walked nude to the door. The source of the ruckus was Mary, his huge thirty-five-pound Maine Coon cat. She was snarling with frustration, trying to pull some blue-gray mass through the pet door. The cat looked up briefly as Jean approached but returned to the task with a grunt. She braced her front paws and lowered her back haunches. Her long tail stood straight up and fluffed out like a feather duster. With her paws tucked under her black-and-gray, tiger-striped body and the dark round O of her anus under the upright bushy tail, she looked like some bizarre version of an exclamation mark.

Jean nudged Mary out of the way, opened the door, and looked down at what appeared to be an odd mop-shaped object. Then, as his eyes adjusted to the dim light, he could see a slight, slow heaving, as if the object were breathing. He nudged it with his toe and thought he heard a scarcely perceivable puff of air come from somewhere inside . . . whatever it was.

He knelt beside it as Mary squeezed through the door and begin to rub herself against Jean's leg. Jean reached out and nudged what was, or appeared to be, a live thing, albeit like nothing he had ever seen before. Again, he heard a slight puff and again he had no idea from which end of the . . . creature it came. It seemed to be some sort of animal, but there were no legs, tail, head, nothing to give it recognizable form. It seemed to have no fur, hair, or skin, just thick strands of something that could only be called none of the above. It looked like, well, like a dust mop without a handle. Jean gently placed his palm on the creature; he had begun to think of it as a creature. He could feel the faint ebb and flow of breathing. It was slow and ragged as if the creature suffered from congestion. That thought wiped away all hesitation and Jean carefully slid his hands under the creature and lifted it from the floor.

As he moved into the living room, the first appropriate place he saw was Mary's bed, a wicker oval with a plaid pillow which stood by the radiator. The bed was practically new, since Mary had never slept in it, even refused to come near it. He placed the creature in the bed and scanned the area for Mary, whose fluffy tail was disappearing into the bedroom. Jean found a soft towel which he placed over the creature. He tried to tuck the towel around its neck but soon gave up. He found a nearly empty cottage cheese container in the refrigerator, dumped half a cup of curds into a bowl, washed and rinsed the container, filled it with fresh water and turned to take it back to the creature. He halted in mid turn. Mary was sniffing at the creature. Jean didn't dare move or call out lest she should turn predator. The creature made a sharp sound that resembled a sneeze. Mary flinched, flicked that gorgeous tail in the air, and stalked haughtily back into the bedroom.

Jean placed the water next to the creature and lifted the towel. He passed the container over the creature several times and on the fourth pass the creature shifted and a part of the mass under the body moved—oozed would be a better way to put it—toward the water. One mop strand slowly undulated and awkwardly twisted itself around several of its neighbors. The combined strands flattened out at the tips and formed a small snorkel which plunged into the water.

The water disappeared in a wink, just disappeared, without a sound. There was no straw-getting-near-the-bottom sounds. Nothing. Just gone. Jean stared at the creature, astonished at what he seemed to have seen. He quickly returned with more water and the scene was repeated. By the seventh trip Jean was in awe of the creature, but this time nothing happened. It ignored the water. He placed the container beside the creature, and as he sat there on his haunches and watched it, he realized that he was naked.

In the bedroom he noticed that Mary was safely curled up on the bed on Jean's pillow as usual. He dressed in his baker's clothes and checked the time, 1:09 A.M., nearly an hour before work. He wondered how a creature that small could intake a gallon and a half of water without perceptibly altering its appearance.

He was fully dressed when he stepped out into the living room and received a shock that stopped him dead cold. The creature was not in the bed. It lay in a puddle of itself on the end table under the light of a lamp. Jean squinted his eyes and replayed his movements since he had gotten up. He had turned on the light when he got out of the bed and walked into the living room on his way to the front door. But at no time did he turn on another light. He had definitely not turned on the lamp. But there it was. The lamp was on and the creature seemed to be shivering.

Reluctant as he was, Jean could not resist. He gingerly placed his hand on the creature. Its rise and fall of breath, if that was what it was, seemed longer and stronger. The rattle had gone. Then he noticed that one of the strands seemed to be moving. Swelling, plumping—what?

From the kitchen he retrieved a chair, turned its back to the creature, straddled it, and placed his chin on the top rung. He concentrated on the single strand. It was surely growing slightly larger. He racked his brain for a way to categorize the creature; after staring at it and nearly falling asleep several times, he came up with the closest configuration: It was a tribble, from *Star Trek*'s "The Trouble with Tribbles." But this creature was silent, larger, more oval shaped, and had no fur. It also captured only his curiosity, and unless he was dreaming, it was real. He shook his head, looked again, and this time he noticed something. Maybe it was all the water, but for whatever reason, the strands seemed to have lines. He practically ran to the bedroom and snatched the magnifying glass from his desk.

Under the glass it was clear that the strands had a texture. When he moved the glass into focus, he could see the lines. The lines were veins, veins, like a leaf. The obvious conclusion came to him. Light and water: Photosynthesis. The tribble was a vegetable.

It had moved to a light source. How does something

without legs move? How did it turn on the light? Better still: How did it know the lamp was a source of light?

While he was pondering his last question, Mary began to scratch at the bedroom door. He glanced at his watch. Late. He was already late. Quickly he took food, water, and kitty litter into his bedroom, checked the door, took a last look at his tribble, and hurried out the door.

The clack of his shoes on the sidewalk lulled Jean into his usual reverie. He discovered that he was softly whispering a name: Gill-i-an. The three syllables rolled deliciously around his tongue, out, down, then up to the roof of his mouth. Gill-i-an. Gill-i-an. Gillian. And with the sound of her name, like a summons, she came. . . .

It was two months ago, quitting time at the bakery where he had been working since the death of Grand-mama. He was picking up his lunch bag behind the sales-room. As he passed the door, he saw her face framed perfectly in the opening like a painting. It took his breath away. She glanced up, saw him, and smiled. He was filled to bursting with the sight of her, and for the first time since junior high, he knew that his soul was singing that same old, old, song: He was in love.

Later, when he could call her face up in his memory, he could never quite understand what there was about her that had so smitten him. Her green eyes were round, bright, vibrant, maybe a bit too close. Her nose a trifle pinched. Her mouth a tad too large. But then it had to be, didn't it, in order to contain her smile. A smile that gushed out to you, stopped you cold, grabbed you by the shoulders, stared straight in your face, and said, "Hello there." Then there was her hair. Hair that could still the tongue of a poet: a rush of red, red hair that flowed over her forehead, waterfalled over her ears, splashed off her shoulders. It was simply magnificent. . . .

Luck was with him. He arrived at the bakery just ahead of Morand, the owner. Guyot, the other ouvriers, was already there. As usual, he gave Jean his haughty Gallic nod. Jean went to work without a word. He stripped to the waist and was soon a ghostly imitation of Gerard as he moved through the ancient rituals of the fournils. He lost himself to the song of the bread: The whistling voices of the hot gases escaping through the cracks in the crust told him that all was well and it was good, and he forgot about his tribble.

But he did not, could not, forget about Gillian and once again he relived that first day. . . .

He found himself following her, wincing at the thought of what would happen if she turned and discovered him. He continued down the gusty canyons of Chicago by focusing on her baguette, which she swung through the crowded lunch hour streets like a baton. She disappeared into a doorway half a block ahead. He stepped off the curb into a blare of horns and curses. When he had made it across, he turned and shook his fist at the traffic, more out of embarrassment, frustration, and a sense of failure than anything else. He peered down the street at the line formed by the tops of doorways and zeroed in on what he thought was the correct configuration. It was. And more. He could see her inside. He looked up to verify the name: Chanticleer. Jean felt the urge to enter the exclusive store, pretend to be shopping and see if he could ferret out her name. But he knew he would not, could not. He had been born shy and would die shy. For some reason, the only people he could talk to and look in the face were Grandmama and Gerard. No one else, especially not females. He was attracted to them in an intensely significant way, but even glancing at them made him sweat and turned his cheeks the color of apples. In grade school he had been shunned, vilified, teased, and mocked. He was the butt of jokes: They called him Jeannie the weenie. High school was no different, only a bit more sophisticated and immeasurably more cruel. He pretended not to hear their ever-present comments. He pretended not to hear their new nomenclature: Jean LaLoise now became "Lew wah the loser" or worse, "Louise the loser," which, by the time he was a senior, had degenerated to simply "freak" or "fag." He refused to attend commencement, unable any longer to face the open taunts of his peers. He received his diploma six months later, but by then he was already employed by Morand, a distant cousin of Grandmama. That was seven years ago and he still didn't have a friend in the world unless you counted his haughty, and he suspected a bit jealous, fellow ouvriers, Guyot, who occasionally invited him to share a

*bottle of wine at a local café, but who had ceased even
those rare invitations since customers had began to ask
specifically for Jean's bread as "pain LaLoise."*

*Then there was the yearly Christmas party at Morand's
which he attended, but always seemed to wind up lurking
at the wallflower edges of the festivities, where he felt like
a gramophone in a CD world.*

*He would sit and watch the other guests turn to one
another and cover their mouths with a hand. Jean knew
that behind the hands their tongues were wagging, but he
was resigned to a world that would forever deny him his
basic needs: confidence in himself, friendship, companion-
ship, self-esteem and at the far edge of his galaxy, somewhere beyond his richest dreams, his most simple but
most desperate need, that which had unequivocally
flooded and forever flowed from Grandmama—love.
Love unending, love unquestionably given and graciously
received, but forever lost, gone, somewhere beyond the
rest of forever.*

*Jean LaLoise was desperately alone but desperately in
love. Worse, he had discovered that his classmates were,
in fact, essentially correct: He was a pervert.*

*He had followed her when she left Chanticleer with a
coworker. As they talked, the wind gusted off Lake Michigan, lifting pieces of their chatter, pushing their words
down the street like leaves; still, he caught her name: Gillian. Gillian and her colleague parted after a few blocks.
Jean continued until he found her apartment and had
taken to, no, was unable to resist, watching her, nearly
every night, from the fire escape outside her bedroom
window. Although he had the decency to turn away while
she changed into her nightgown, he felt he was degenerate
and grotesque, yet could not help himself. When an occasional male stopped by, it served only to fill him with a
deeper sense of remorse and . . .*

"Are we waiting for the executioner today?" Morand
screamed. In his reverie, Jean had placed a loaf of pain
de seigle upside down. Bread facing hell instead of
heaven had been a bad omen for centuries. No one
would buy it, since the loaf set apart for the public executioner was always placed upside down. Jean hastily

right-sided the loaf, but Morand plucked it from the shelf and threw it in a corner.

"Go home, Jean," Morand said softly but not angrily. "Your mind is not on the loaves. We can finish up here. Go." He reached over, undid Jean's apron, and tied it on himself. "Go," he repeated as he gave Jean's shoulder a gentle push, "It's your weekend, get an early start."

Outside Jean squinted his eyes in the bright sun and was reminded of his tribble. It occurred to him that he should stop thinking of the creature as a tribble and give it a name. His first thought was the invisible pooka in the play, *Harvey.* Pooka seemed appropriate: It couldn't be there, but there it was, a visible Pooka.

Pooka was still there but not under the lamp. It was lying in a puddle of sunlight in the middle of the living room—and it was different. It was green and larger, more vibrant, healthy, alive. Mary, hearing the door open, began to protest with a gargling wail.

Jean started toward Pooka. He was halted by an intense white light which flash-flooded his mind, then was gone, leaving only a feeling. A powerful feeling. A message. The message said, "Stop." It was not articulated. It was not telepathy. It was not a language. It was a feeling. And the feeling was not a command, but the strongest feeling Jean had ever experienced: even stronger than the feeling when Grandmama passed away and left him forever alone, even more overwhelming than the feeling he felt when he first saw Gillian. He was immobilized.

Jean's initial reaction was terror, pure adrenaline-pounding terror; but in the next moment it was replaced by the feeling of gratitude. The feeling grew and filled him and brushed over him like a caress. He was lost in the bliss of gratitude. And when he felt he could scarcely hold more, it washed over him again, and again. He knew he was smiling. He knew he could live in this serenity forever, here in this place, in this incredible moment. Just as he began to feel that it was too much; that he would fill up and burst with affection, it began to ebb, slowly at first, then at a quicker, more liquid pace, as if to carefully extinguish the fires of his desire.

He felt a question: "Why?" Then an answer was forming, slowly, with much effort and difficulty: a stutterer determined to get it right, get it absolutely correct. The next feeling was "Friend." It burst upon Jean like a wave and filled him with an immense sadness and loss of what he had never had. The feeling disappeared and was replaced by "Care" then "Cherish." Which was superseded with "Pet" and haltingly, slowly replaced by "Heirloom."

Then, as if satisfied with the message, the sequence repeated itself, faster and faster, a kaleidoscope of emotions on a carousel spinning out of control.

Jean staggered under what was now a dervish of emotions. Just as he began to lose control and was on the cusp of falling to the floor, the room filled with a flash of white light. It was so intense it stung his eyes. Then he felt "Sorry," and he knew it was an apology for the pain. He sat on the floor until the pain subsided. He cautiously opened one eye. The stab of pain told him it was too soon.

When he could open his eyes he felt "Up." He looked and was astonished: The roof had vanished and in the sky a small white point of light pulsated in the blueness. "Good-bye," he felt, then "Return." Then "Thanks,"

Jean was breathless, drained. He felt withered and desiccated as if he had gone from a juicy plum to a wrinkled prune. He barely made it to the bedroom. He fell asleep nearly instantly, but not before he snatched a quick glimpse of Mary cowering in the corner, every hair on her body stuck straight out. Her back was arched enough to fit over a large pumpkin. Then he was asleep, even before his lids shuttered his eyes.

When he awoke, he wondered why. One moment he was asleep and the next awake. There was none of the slow drowsy passage that normally accompanied the events. Asleep/awake. Like a switch. Off then on.

Mary was beside him like always; it made him realize that he felt good, exceptionally good, better than he had felt since . . . since . . . what? He didn't know, he didn't care. He jumped out bed so fast that it startled a hiss from Mary.

*   *   *

He was so full of energy that he literally skipped into the living room. Pooka was where he had last seen him, he was beginning to think of him as a him, in the middle of the living room in a pool of midmorning sun. His strands were more green and were rising, shimmering, falling, then repeating the pattern—sleep? Jean watched for a moment and then raced into the kitchen.

Over a fresh cup of coffee, Jean remembered that he had ruined a loaf of rye. Morand had sent him home and he had been so tired he took a long nap. He checked his watch: 9:55 A.M., Monday. *Monday.* That meant he had been asleep for, what . . . nearly three days, seventy hours. *Seventy hours.* Impossible.

"Impossible," he was still muttering as he dressed quickly. Impossible, he was still thinking as he stroked the growth of beard on his cheeks. At the door he paused and looked back. Mary was peeking out of the bedroom door. Jean called to her, but she refused to respond.

He shrugged, ran out of the apartment and down the street to the news kiosk. Both newspapers verified his watch. Three days, he had lost three days.

As he slowly climbed the stairs, he tried out some questions: Have I been abducted by an alien? Is Pooka an alien? Immediately he felt a swirl of emotions race through his body. He felt "Error," and the following feeling was so like a blow that it doubled him up on the stairway, not with pain but with the pure pleasure of it: "Heirloom."

He knew that whatever he had been thinking was gone. He tried to remember, but it was no use. But the pleasure remained. It was strong enough to push him up the stairs in a wave of pure joy.

When Jean was finally able to sit at his kitchen table, he could only wonder about what it was that he was wondering about. This made him wonder why he was wondering about . . . Then his mind simply balked. Stopped. Quit. Enough. Like thinking about eternity . . .

Pooka was where he had left him, except for two important differences. One was that Pooka was now in Mary's bed. The other was that Mary herself was snuggled up next to Pooka. He didn't remember moving the bed and he certainly couldn't believe Mary's change of behavior. Mary hated all creatures large and small, even loathed members of her own species. Yet there she was, all toasty and content as she yawned, opened her eyes, stretched out her paws and began to knead Pooka as though he were Jean's pillow.

Air blew softly from somewhere near Pooka. He went in search of Mary's litterbox and found it behind the couch. Mixed in with Mary's sizable chunks were several smaller green cylinder shapes. For a moment Jean considered his discovery, pondered on his ability to accept the incredible, then gave up on it. At least Pooka was housebroken.

Jean got a chair, turned it around, and placed it in front of the creatures. He rested his chin on the back of the chair and mused: Why had Mary changed her tune and how could things move around?

As he sat and watched the pair, he began to realize just how good it felt just to be there. As he relaxed, almost to the point of dreaming, he began to think about Gillian.

She came back the next day and the next . . . always at her lunch hour, Jean's quitting time. He began to watch, to wait for her like the Little Prince waiting for the fox, to anticipate her, and sure enough, it was getting better and better.

Then Gillian asked to meet the baker who made that wonderful bread, pain LaLoise. When they called for him, he came. But slowly, frightened witless that he would surely make a fool of himself.

Then he was in the same room, so close that it was like touching her, so close that he could smell the faint, lush scent of her femininity as it sang in his nose, an aroma far beyond any bakery. He was confused, lost in the intensity.

And when it was over you remember the heat from your face like the hottest of ovens. You remember stumbling when you step up to her. You remember nearly falling into that incredible smile as you mumble, "Thank you. Thank you," an inanity of times. And then there's the swish of her skirt like a wave good-bye as she steps through the sliding glass door and melts into the crowded street, the tip of her baguette bobbing, then slowly subsiding into the tide of the lunch hour crowd. . . .

Hunger drove Jean from his chair. Mary, somehow sensing the approach of food, padded after him. As Jean bit into his Spam-and-ketchup sandwich, Mary crunched noisily at her dry food. He watched a wattle along the bottom of her stomach flap back and forth as she chewed. He made a note to cut her kibbles by a third.

Jean rummaged through the kitchen until he found an extension cord, plugged in the gro-lite he had purchased and placed it over Pooka. He immediately began a series of sharp "sneezes." Jean turned the light off and the "sneezes" were replaced by a soft hiss. He mixed some plant food, according to the instructions on the bag and placed it in a pail beside the creature. The "sneezes" began again. He quickly removed the pail. As he placed the fresh water by the creature, he thought he heard the usual hiss, but he couldn't be sure. He watched as several strands twisted into a snorkel and dipped into the pail. As before, the water disappeared without a trace and without a sound.

Jean returned to his chair, still amazed. He soon found himself lost in memories of Gillian, replaying the memories over and over, like tapes. . . .

In the days that followed that first embarrassing encounter with Gillian, Jean realized that he always found an excuse to be in the shop when Gillian made her daily noon-hour purchase: one pain LaLoise. Each time, Jean was incapacitated by his fear. The inside of his head was a roaring whirlwind. In quick glances he could see her lips move and was aware that she was addressing him, but the internal roar blotted out all sounds. Once, he tried to answer what sounded like "How are you today?" His response came out a pathetic squeak. He was mortified. He fled to the fournils, where he resolved to stay away from the shop and her fire escape. He did manage to stop the excruciating shame of his fire escape visits, but the next day he was back in the shop at the regular time. . . .

As if by some silent alarm, he found himself staring at his watch. It was time to get ready for work.

On his dark walk to the bakery, Jean had the strangest feeling that it was not he but the Pooka who was at the switch replaying his memories. The Gillian tapes, as he had come to think of them, were too vivid to be simply memories. There seemed to be some cutting-edge technology here, some fabulous breakthrough far beyond virtual reality. No, it wasn't Pooka, it came from beyond Pooka. Pooka was the medium and not the source. The feeling pulsed with joy and he entered the fournils with a grin that seemed to swallow his face.

Gillian didn't show that day or the next. Jean paced back and forth as long as he dared in front of Chanticleer. He spent all his spare time in his chair in front of Pooka and Mary. They seemed to always be together these days. Pooka had turned a green that was nearly black. It reminded him of the color called Charleston Green: one part yellow and nine parts black. And then the Gillian tapes began and he was immersed.

That night he had a dream about Pooka. When he woke for work, he ran to the living room. Both Pooka and Mary seemed to be sleeping. Jean smiled. The dream had been a real hoot, but that was all he could remember. He was beginning to accept this selective amnesia of his and thought no more about it; what was the use? He changed the litter, filled the water pail, and left for work.

Gillian came to him on the way, and he concentrated on mentally forcing her to return, to be there. The idea that she might never return chilled him to the quick but was replaced with a bright surge of optimism which carried him through the long, hot night with the ovens.

And return she did. But her smile was only at half mast, her mouth seemed to droop, the fire in her hair had lost its roar and seemed banked like an idle oven. Jean was devastated. So much so that he very nearly summoned up the courage to speak to her. She made her usual purchase, nodded to Jean, and left. He summoned every ounce of energy in his body to follow and comfort her. He failed, fuming at himself.

All the way home he chided himself, cursed his timidity, silently screamed at his shyness. He bloodied himself with insults until he actually stopped at a streetlamp and banged his head against it. He began to muse that it was a sad, sad comment on his miserable life that his sole objective was to sit in front of his only companions in the world: a cranky cat and . . . what, some kind of geranium, or something even more amazing, an intergalactic baby redwood. Whatever.

In his chair as in front of a comforting, crackling fireplace, the tension drained out of him, and as he relaxed, the Gillian tapes switched on. Sometime later, a brilliant white light came and went.

Jean awoke as he had awakened that first night of the Pooka. Asleep/awake. Off then on. And he was happy. No, he was beyond happy. He was pure bliss. And as his mind cast about for the source, it found it. It was something inside him. Something new. Something he had never had before. He felt confident, confident. Confident with a capital C.

And. It. Was. Wonderful. Now he knew what he was missing, knew how people really felt, had felt all their lives and accepted it, taken it for granted. He knew he could look people in the eye, even women. He could tell the whole world to LOOK OUT. Jean LaLoise was up and out and about and ready to grab the world by the tail. Yessir, he was a rip-roaring, ringtailed tornado, and he was on the loose. A *whoopee* formed in his mind, and he very nearly let it out. Then he thought, *Why the hell not. . . .*

As the echo of his incredible whoopee faded, he could hear the frantic flight of Mary's claws tearing the carpet, then the couch and then some other material. He crossed his legs and nearly purred with bliss. He basked in the pure golden glory of confidence. Just as he was approaching smug, all hell broke loose.

Something, somewhere, was screeching, caterwauling in pure angst. Jean leaped from the bed and raced into the living room. There at the top of the drapes hung Mary, who had apparently been terrorized by the deafening whoopee. Her claws were caught in the material, and Jean was greeted by a snarl, fangs, and a jungle quality hiss. It took several minutes of "good kitty, nice kitty" to get her down. As she sat in his lap she seemed a lot heavier. He had remembered to ration her kibbles and was at a loss to account for the weight. He made a mental note to take her to the vet, looked up at the time, and hurried off to work.

As he stirred the ovens, it occurred to him that on the way to work he had looked everyone straight in the eye and greeted them. Not just a measly "hello," but a big, boisterous, cinemascope "Howdy." The memory embarrassed him for a moment but was instantly swallowed up by an uncontrollable insouciance.

His bliss was ablaze throughout the night and morning. By noon he waited anxiously. He was nervous but, hallelujah, not incapacitated. And what a difference a difference made.

She walked in carrying a smile and a sack of groceries. Jean was sliding down the icy slope of panic, barely in front of an avalanche of swirling emotions. But in the emotions was . . . confidence.

Gillian purchased a baguette and then surprisingly turned to Jean and spoke. "I've decided to take the rest of the day off, and treat myself to an expensive pastry. What would you recommend?"

To his vast astonishment, Jean heard himself speak. "The peach tartellelles is a good choice." Gillian nodded.

On her way out she called back to thank Jean. As she turned to face the street, she nearly collided with a passerby and lost her hold on the grocery sack. The purse strap on her shoulder slid down to the elbow. She tugged the strap and gave the bag a lurching snap to get a better purchase. The movement caused the tartellelles to shoot out of her bag. It fell, fruit side down, and was promptly squashed by the passing feet of several pedestrians. Gillian didn't seem to notice.

Jean ripped off his apron, snatched a fresh tartellelles, and joined the crowd. He caught up with her at the first light. He moved beside her at the curb and held out the pastry. "You dropped your other one," he said. He was thinking that it was amazing that something as simple as confidence was surely a gift that most gave little or no thought, yet it made all the difference in the world.

"Oh, my goodness, thank you. Thank you so much." Gillian said as she placed the new pastry in her bag and stepped into the street. The light changed, and her purse strap again dropped to her elbow. A black sedan honked at her as she stood in the street attempting to relocate the strap. Jean reached for her arm and gently nudged her back up on the sidewalk.

"Thank you again. It must be your day to take care of me."

Jean nodded. The light changed, and they stepped off the curb together. Gillian glanced curiously at Jean as they crossed the street together. He had no idea of what to do or what to say; he simply wanted to be near her, and so he said nothing. When they stepped up on the other curb, Gillian stopped and looked at him. A question formed on her face, and Jean struggled for an answer. Together they formed a double impediment to the flow of pedestrians who brushed, bumped, and bounced around them. One man jostled Gillian and knocked the purse strap down again. Jean was quick to pick it up and move it back to her shoulder. It gave him time to think. "I . . . I . . . uhh . . . live in this direction, and I am going home, too. Give me your bag, and you can fix this pesky purse while we walk." Jean had just astonished himself again, he couldn't believe it was happening. Gillian stared at him for a moment, as if trying to decide if she was ready for this or not. She smiled, handed him the bag, and they moved down the street side by side.

"Again, I am in your debt." She laughed. It was the first time Jean had ever heard her laugh and it was even more wonderful than her smile. He laughed at her laugh and it became contagious and they laughed together at their laughter. It provided a thaw and suddenly everything seemed absolutely right.

"How do you fix a purse strap?" Gillian wanted to know.

"I haven't the faintest idea." He was trying very hard not to think. It was better that way. Close your mind down and just enjoy.

"I should hope not," she came back, chuckling at her own joke. "The heck with it," she muttered as she crossed the strap over her head, neatly solving the problem.

The sidewalk traffic had thinned as they came to a stop at the light, Gillian turned to him suddenly and with a mischievous glint in her green, green, impish eyes, blurted out, "What are you going to do when you get home?"

It took him aback and he lied. "Probably read."

"What do you read?"

"Right now, I'm on a nonfiction kick."

"In that case, I know exactly how to repay your kindness . . . I've always relied on the kindness of strangers." Her voice became husky with Spanish moss, sweet with magnolias.

"The Glass Menagerie," he shot back.

"Why, darling, you really do read."

"Yes, Amanda, I do" he replied in his best Southern. Nearly everything he was doing and saying continued to amaze him and he tossed in a quick prayer to all the Gods That Be.

"What's that, sugar bear?"

"Uh, all the time, I read all the time," his accent returned to Midwestern Flat.

Gillian stopped and motioned with her chin.

"I live up there. I'd like to invite you up, but my apartment is such a mess. If you'll wait right here, I'll run up and bring your present. Will that be okay?"

Jean stalled. He wanted to keep the evening going somehow. Then he noticed a small café across the street. "Is it okay if I wait in that café? I could use a coffee, too . . . you're welcome to join me . . . on me, if that's okay, I'm not trying to . . ."

"It's a deal," she said, snatching the groceries from his arm. Then she was up the stairs and through the door.

Jean sat at a booth by the window and finished two cups of Yuppie Arabica, never taking his eyes off the door to her apartment. He was still thirsty, so he drank several glasses of water. Just as he was beginning to wonder if something had happened, he saw her skimming down her steps, her feet in a blur. As she waited at the light, she kept swinging a small paper bag.

"I hope they don't notice I brought my own goodies," she whispered as she sat down. Something seemed to have dampened her spirits. She sipped her coffee. When she saw that Jean was observing her, she perked up.

"What would you be doing if this were the weekend?" She stuck her chin in the air and looked down at him like a naughty, willful child.

"It is my weekend. I'm a baker, remember?" He was trying to look naughty, but he wasn't at all sure it was working.

"That's right, I have my . . . I forgot . . . my tartle, tortle, turtle, what is it?"

"Tartellelles, peach tartellelles."

"And here is my tortele, peach tortele, ta ta," she said with a flourish as she rummaged in her bag and drew it out. It was flat and runny. She dropped it on her saucer where it began to ooze.

"Uh-oh." She pulled a book with an orange smear out of the bag. "This was, is, sorta my present to you." She pulled a slew of napkins from the dispenser and began to blot the book. The napkins stuck, tore, and slid off the book as she blotted. Some stuck to the book, some the table, one latched onto the heel of her hand and another got pasted to her forehead when she attempted to wipe the sweat from her brow.

Jean threw up his hands. She froze at the dramatic gesture. He peeled the napkin from her hand, then the one from her forehead. He folded them and wiped her forehead, then her hand. He wiped the table, then the book. She began to snicker as he worked. She tried to hold it back. The effort made her snort, and with that she began to laugh. He was captured by the laughter and joined in. The people in the next booth began to stare, but it only made matters worse. They laughed until they had to pull more napkins to wipe their tears, then catch their breath and start all over again until the hard work of laughing wore them down.

It set the tone for the rest of the evening. First they examined the book and found it sticky, but readable. It was a history of French bakeries.

The hours slid by, a blur of favorite books, plays, desserts, shops, vacations, museums, movies, TV shows, confections, politics, and finally cafés. And since it was dark and this one was closing, they were ushered out into the chiaroscuro streets.

It sobered them briefly and then they started laughing again. About what, neither knew. It didn't stop until Jean noticed that they were at Gillian's apartment. Neither spoke. Then she thanked him for the wonderful time, and he thanked her for an even more wonderful time.

They each said "Well . . ." several times and "Good night" several more times and Gillian turned and put her hand on the door and Jean turned and took a step down the stairs . . . and Gillian said, "Wait," and came down to the step where Jean's foot waited and sat down beside it. Jean took one more step and sat down beside her.

He took up residence in the lush aroma of her hair. There was a long, lovely silence and then Gillian's troubled voice brought him back to the real world.

"I don't want to be alone. I don't want you to get the wrong idea, either . . . I don't want to, but maybe I should just move."

That got Jean's attention. "Move, you can't move."

"And why not?" she challenged.

"Because I . . . because you . . . because you just said you didn't want to."

"You got a better idea?"

"No."

"Well then . . ."

"Well then, what?"

"Well then, if you don't have a better idea, the least you can do is to kindly shut up about it."

"Shut up about what? I don't even know what this is all about. What is it about?

"It's a secret."

"A secret?"

"It's a secret."

Jean guessed that he could make this a game. He put all the "brat" he could into his tone. "I've got a secret."

"You've got a secret?"

"I've got a secret,"

"Well, your secret is not as good as mine."

"No, it's not as good, it's better."

"Is not."

"Is too."

She didn't respond. Instead, she lay her head on his shoulder and silenced him with her perfume. Then in a voice like a child she said, "I wish I could tell you."

"I'll tell you mine, then you can tell me yours."

"Okay," she said, "tell me."

"It would be much better if I could show you."

"No, just tell me. Tell me your secret and I might tell you mine."

"I could tell you I have a unicorn, but wouldn't it be better if I could show you?"

"Do you have a unicorn?"

"No, but it is as unique as a unicorn."

"Where is this unique thing?"

"In my apartment."

"Aha, right next to your etchings, I bet."

"No, those are in my Yucatán condo, I'll show you them later. Let's go."

Jean stood and held out his hand. "Come on, it's only four or five blocks away."

She hesitated. "Why should I trust you?"

"I'm not asking you to trust me."

"What are you asking, then?"

"I'm asking you for a chance."

"What kind of chance?"

"A chance to trust me."

"Again, why?"

"Because, when was the last time someone washed the peaches from your face and hands, and to whom else have you ever loaned a history of French bakeries, and who else has something to show you that is more fabulous than a unicorn?"

She took his hand, and he pulled her up.

"I thought you said *as* not *more* fabulous than a unicorn?"

"Close enough, who's counting?"

As he led Gillian down the steps, it occurred to him that this night was a fairy tale. If anyone had told him that he would someday be able to say and do the things he had done this night, he . . . Yet, here he was walking down the streets holding the hand of a woman he had fallen in love with at first sight.

She peppered him with pleas the entire journey. At the door to Jean's apartment she stopped. "Is it animal, vegetable, or mineral?"

"All of the above and maybe some more."

He opened the door, made a mock bow, and extended his arm toward the living room. Jean went to the kitchen and returned with a chair which he placed beside his chair and then he extended his arm again. As she sat, he offered her a drink, but she didn't seem to notice the offer. She was staring at Pooka and Mary curled up together when he returned with his glass of water. Gillian turned to Jean and asked if she could pick up the cat. Jean thought it better that he pick her up. Mary didn't resist and even began to purr. Gillian cautiously ran her fingers over Mary's stomach.

"Her name is Mary."

"Let's see, a pregnant cat is *as* or *more* unique, an oxymoron that, than a unicorn . . ."

"What?"

"What . . . What?"

"Did you say Mary was pregnant?"

"No, I said that Mary is pregnant, not was."

"How do you know?"

"My father was a vet, I've seen scads of pregnant cats. I went to vet school for two years. What do you want, an affidavit? A second opinion? What?" Gillian seemed to be getting peevish.

"She can't be pregnant."

"And why not?"

"She's been fixed."

"Fixed?"

"Yea, fixed, altered, neutered. That kind of fixed. Besides, she never met a cat or any other animal . . . that she didn't hate. She can't be pregnant."

"Well then, her name is certainly appropriate."

"How's that?"

"It'll be the first virgin cat birth, if it goes to term."

Jean stood up and let Mary drop from his lap. She returned to the bed and curled up next to Pooka.

"She certainly likes that black dust mop."

"It's not a dust mop. It's the unique thing."

"You gotta be pulling my leg . . . And I'm still a bit suspicious about this change from painfully shy to confident, quite confident indeed. So cut the kidding, kiddo, and take me home. I hope . . . I'm sorry. I don't mean to be cruel about that shy stuff. I've had a wonderful time, Jean, but it's all catching up with me. I'm exhausted. Please . . ."

"Allow me to prove it. Just stay here in this chair and watch. And by the way, there is no earthly reason to apologize. You couldn't possibly be more amazed by my confidence than I am, believe me. It will only take a minute."

Actually it only took an instant. John brought in the pail of water, and Pooka did the water trick. All Gillian could say was, "I saw it, but I don't believe it."

Jean took her hand. "Just sit and think about your secret."

She did. She sat there for hours and never moved, and hardly blinked. Jean sat beside her and watched his latest Gillian tapes.

At a bit past two A.M., Gillian stirred and started to look at her watch. A brilliant white light came and filled the room.

"It's after four, how can that be?" Gillian asked? "It's the most incredible thing. I know but I don't know. I can't . . . can't . . . Jean?"

"Are you trying to say you can't think about what you think you remember?"

"Exactly."

"You'll get used to it. How do you feel?"

"Wonderful, just wonderful, but what is that, that creature? Where did you get it? What is it? My God."

"Mary found him somewhere. He's literally what the cat dragged in. I've named him Pooka. He's an heirloom."

"Whose?"

"Now that is the BIG question. I don't think he's from here."

"Here? What does that mean?"

"Don't ask. I can't think about it either."

"Can't?"

"I can't think about it, so I can't explain it. You sure you feel okay?"

"More than okay. This unbelievable thing is, is, it's all gone away. There is no problem."

"Is the problem your secret? You promised."

Gillian stared at the wall for several moments. "It's all so embarrassing. I'm going to explain it in twenty-five words or less and ask you never to mention it again. Okay?"

Jean nodded.

"In the last two years I've gone through three boy-friends. I blamed myself and decided on the geographic cure. I was giving myself a pity party. I can't believe how dumb I was. It's their loss, not mine. I'm so embarrassed, don't you ever bring it up."

Jean ran a finger and a thumb across his lips like a zipper.

"I also got snappy with you about your confidence. It's a wonderful thing to have, it must have been a misery without it. Again, I'm sorry."

"Forever forgiven."

"Now take me home before you have to carry me. I'm pooped." She turned and took a last look at Pooka. "Good night, Pooka, you wonderful creature. Good night, Mary, you pregnant puss."

On the walk back they held hands and smiled at each other a lot, but no one spoke. Gillian unlocked her door and turned to Jean.

"I've been thinking all the way over here about this. I don't want to say something clichéd like: How can I ever repay you. So, I'll say a wonderful thank you to a wonderful man who came into my life, a shining knight in shining armor bearing a peach torttle. I could fling my arms around you and give you a long, passionate kiss. I could drag you off to bed . . . but I'm old-fashioned and I'm beyond tired, so I'll just give you this . . ."

Gillian left a gentle touch of her lips on Jean's cheek.

". . . And drag myself off to bed." She reached for his hand, held it in hers for a moment, then turned to go. Jean, still stunned by the kiss, had very nearly shut the door when she called out.

"Jean."

"Yes," he answered, his face barely fitting in the crack of the door.

"Thanks for the chance."

"Chance?"

"Yes, for the chance to learn to trust you."

He smiled and closed the door.

"Jean," she called through the door.

He opened it and saw her standing there with a sleepy, dopey smile.

"Can you keep a secret?"

"Yes."

"I didn't just happen to have the book. I bought it especially for you. But I thought I'd had my three strikes and was out of the game."

Jean smiled and crossed his hands palms down, giving her the umpire's signal for safe.

Somewhere on the stairs, he walked into a pinpoint of brilliant white light which spread until it took him into its soft, warm depths. He was a vapor moving through the . . . "Craft" and among some other moving shapes, white on white, more brilliant than light . . . "Benefactors," and as he moved farther, the feelings became more intense. Jean felt a new joy that so surpassed his previous joys he was terrified by the forces that moved through him. It passed, yet remained still within him, and he knew that he was going somewhere, somewhere on a fabulous journey and he opened like a blossom to the sun and let it take him in. And when he had come to the place that he had come to, it was clean and bright and pure. He felt Pooka had been "Taken," but the sharp pang of sadness that came with that knowledge was also taken and he knew that he had come "Back." He looked up through the stairs above him, and as he had before, he could "See" into the predawn sky, where a small white point of light pulsated in the grayness. "Good-bye," came to him and "Good-bye," he felt. He expected sadness; instead, understanding came to him: All of the feelings that had come before, came to him, and then all the other feelings came with them. Faster and faster they came, and he knew what the feelings meant and what an "Heirloom" was. Again he was terrified, and again as that too passed, yet stayed within him, he finally came to understand the miracle of the gift that he had been given.

When he could, he began to walk slowly down the stairs again. He was thirsty and thought he could hear a faint puff of air coming from somewhere, but he couldn't locate the source. He reached within and felt confidence once more and it was good.

As he stepped outside, the dawn broke, the sun washed over Lake Michigan, flooded down the streets and splashed over Jean as he raised his arms and drank in the new day. In the intense sunlight he could see the shadows the hairs on his arms made. And nearly hidden in those shadows, he could see lines. The lines were veins, veins like a leaf.

BUG-EYED METHODISTS

By Bob Morrish

Bob Morrish is one of the preeminent horror critics working today, with reviews in every magazine associated with the genre. He published *The Scream Factory*, a seminal magazine for horror writers and critics in general. He was also involved in operating Deadline Press, a small press that published single-author collections and horror novels.

Saturday, July 27th, 3:14 P.M.

An occasional squawk from the radio was the only interruption to the monotonous crunch of tires over gravel as Frank Wallace navigated the meandering curves of Ross Road with practiced ease and calculated boredom. Off to his right, the Mehatchi River flowed lazily, its currents mirroring the contours of the road.

Frank was in the midst of his latest lament—approximately the 500th such expression since he'd joined the force two-and-a-half years ago—over the lack of job-related excitement to be found as a law enforcement officer in Oak Valley. Outside of the occasional pot-farming bust, the odd drunken and/or domestic dispute, and the by-now routine logging protests, there was precious little to occupy one's attention. It was so dead around here that a few recent livestock mutilations had quickly become the talk of the town. Frank was about to make his customary segue from reality-based regret into fantasy-oriented daydreams, envisioning a move to a big city—maybe Sacramento, maybe all the way to San Francisco—and the Dirty Harry style career that would undoubtedly follow for him, when he was jarred from his reverie by a flash of movement glimpsed from the corner of his eye.

Turning his head and squinting into the midafternoon sun through polished reflector lenses, Frank saw something that made him forget his nothing-ever-happens-around-here complaints.

Frank's jaw dropped in tandem with his foot stomping on the brake pedal, sending dual sprays of gravel from his tires and saliva from his lips. The deputy stared for a few seconds longer, drinking in the sight, and then dropped the gear shift into "park" and opened the door. With one foot on the ground, he hesitated. Procedure. Don't forget procedure.

Reluctant to avert his gaze, Frank fumbled for the radio mike, nearly dropping it before pulling it to his mouth.

"County Base, this is Officer Wallace in car 24. Do you read?"

"Affirmative, 24. We read."

"Base, I'm on Ross Road near Lynch . . . and you're not gonna believe what I'm lookin' at."

Saturday, July 27th, 7:16 P.M.

Neon lights buzzed angrily overhead, but the sound of the electric hive was almost completely drowned out by the general din of the Lassen County Hospital Emergency Room. The shades on the western-facing windows of the ER waiting area were closed, deflecting the bright, seeking rays of a twilight sun that still held an hour's lease on life above the horizon.

Taylor Duncan was long past knowing or caring about the time of day as he weaved his way on autopilot through a shuffling mass of sprained ankles, cut knuckles, bruised faces, and assorted maladies. Duncan's mind was, if not a million miles away, at the very least in the next county. The unceasingly long hours of his psychiatric residency were taking their toll, compounded by last night's frenzied events, a typical occurrence on a Full Moon Friday. In fact, Duncan guessed that fully half of the patients in the waiting room were just now dragging themselves in to have injuries and afflictions from last evening attended to.

Duncan, meanwhile, was troubled not by any Full Moon hangover, but rather by the addled and largely unresponsive young woman whom the police had brought in earlier, after finding her wandering, naked and in an apparent state of shock, in a cornfield. Duncan was initially intrigued by her state, not to mention entranced by her beauty, but . . .

"Taylor! How goes it?"

Looking up from the meditative stance he had just assumed in front of the candy machine, Duncan winced (inwardly, he hoped) upon seeing Harvey Schlichter, a perpetually wired consulting psychiatrist whose mulatto background was strangely reflected in a Don King-style hairdo and mildly Tor Johnson-like features. Duncan had reflected more than once about how disturbing Harvey must be to some of his patients.

"Oh. Hi, Harvey."

"So, I hear you got assigned the naked babe."

"Hmm? Oh, yes. Yes, I did." Duncan felt a vague sense of disappointment that his obviously detached mood was serving as no deterrent to Harvey's curiosity, which was nearly as boundless as his enthusiasm. *Oh, well. I didn't really think he'd take the hint.*

"So. Have you done a prelim on her yet? What's her story?"

Duncan sighed, estimating how long it was going to take to extricate himself from Harvey's enquiring presence.

"Yes, I just finished with her. She seems to be in shock. She's largely uncommunicative and unresponsive, but seems to be okay physically."

"*Largely* uncommunicative? Meaning she has verbalized . . . ?"

"Well, yes. But it's nonsensical. She indicated that she was abducted last evening, apparently by two men, but then . . . she became quite agitated and incoherent."

"Do the police know about the kidnapping angle? And . . . elaborate on incoherence for me."

"Yes, the officer who brought her in was there when I examined her. And . . ."

"Oh, come on, Taylor, out with it! Since when are you so closemouthed about cases?"

Another sigh. Duncan didn't want the attention and teasing this was going to bring.

"All right, all right. It's hard to piece together, but it seems that she thinks she was . . . abducted."

"You already *said* that," responded Harvey, brimming with good-natured impatience.

"No, I mean . . . by aliens."

"By aliens? Hah!" uttered Harvey. "That's the first alien abductee we've had in a while. Did she give a description of the aliens? Did she get a license plate number on the spaceship?"

"You're a riot, Harvey. No, it's not even clear whether she thinks she was taken aboard a ship. I'm extrapolating a little bit. She talked about being abducted by the two men—in a *car,* mind you—and didn't bring up the spacecraft until later. And then she got vague about what she thinks happened. I believe she's simply displacing the trauma she's experienced, and introducing the spaceship to avoid facing what really—"

"Hah! Sounds like you've got a perfect handle on her condition," interrupted Harvey. "We're gonna have to refer all of our abductees your way. Make you our little ET specialist."

"It's not funny, Harvey. That woman was extremely traumatized by her experience. I'd very much like to know what really happened to her. . . ."

Friday, July 26th, 10:34 P.M.
The car took the turn at Lynch Road at a high rate of speed. The '78 Impala wasn't designed to take a sharp corner at 40 mph, and its back end fishtailed across to the very brink of the roadside ditch before the driver was able to correct his skid and resume a relatively straight course.

Jerry Berringer marked his successful display of drunk driving with a celebratory war whoop: "Wooh-hooh!"

The cry was punctuated by an exclamation from his shotgun-riding partner, "Goddammit! You made me spill my fuckin' beer!"

"Aw, so fuckin' what? You always wear more than you drink anyway. And we still got damn near a case in the trunk."

"I'm more interested in what we got in the back seat than what we got in the trunk."

"For once, Ricky-boy, you are making perfect sense."
Jerry glanced at the rearview mirror, eyeing their unconscious passenger. "She is one sweet piece of meat."

Ricky twisted around to get a better vantage point on
the backseat occupant. A low sound issued from his
throat as he reached back and wrapped a length of the
young woman's hair around his fingers. Then the look
of lust slipped from his features, replaced by a furrowed
brow and pursed lips.

"You sure we should be doing this, Jerry? You sure
we ain't gonna get caught?"

"If you ask me that one more fuckin' time, I'm gonna
slap you upside the fuckin' head. For the last goddamned
time, she ain't gonna remember nothin'. I slipped her a
handful of them roofies I got from Tank. We're just
gonna have us a little fun, and then dump her off somewhere. She won't even mind."

"How come you gave her so many of them pills, anyway? Tank said one was all it took."

"I figure if one works good, then a handful'll work
better. What the fuck do you care?"

"I don't. I just don't want her to OD on us."

"You worry too much, Ricardo." Jerry finished his
beer with a guzzle as he braked, slowing to a halt in
front of a ramshackle cabin. He killed the engine and
opened the Impala's bulwarklike door, which yawned
open with a protracted creak. Stepping from the car with
a grunt and a belch, he fired his empty bottle into the
bushes across the road, sending some small creature
scurrying away. Jerry turned back to the car, where
Ricky stood fidgeting, a beacon of nervous anticipation.

"Well, whatchoo waitin' for? Carry her ass inside."

"You're not gonna help me?" Ricky whined, "She's
gonna be heavy . . ."

"Horseshit, Ricky. She probably weighs all of one
hundred ten pounds. And besides, I've done all the work
so far. I scored the roofies, I got her out to the car
before she passed out. What the hell have you done?
Sat there, pulling your pud, that's what. Just shag her
inside and quit bitching."

"You didn't pick up on her, she came right up to you.
And besides . . ." Ricky trailed off, knowing his argu-

ment was futile. He took another pull on his beer and
set it on the roof of the car, then steeled himself—all
five-foot-six and one hundred forty pounds of himself—
for the task at hand. He put the seat forward and
wedged his hands under her arms, pulling her out toward
him. He nearly overbalanced and toppled when her
weight shifted off the seat and into his arms, but he
caught himself at the last instant and staggered on up
the porch steps with his precious cargo.

Beer case in hands, Jerry magnanimously kicked the
front door open for him. "Carrying your woman across
the threshold . . . how fuckin' sweet!

"Set her down on the couch and take her clothes off."

"Okay, Jerry," wheezed Ricky as he dropped the
woman onto a mildewed plaid sofa.

Jerry worked on fitting the beer into the refrigerator
while Ricky stripped off the woman's sweater and jeans.
His low whistle caused Jerry to look up from the
kitchen. Ricky had just removed the woman's bra and
was standing there, staring at her.

"Ain't she somethin'?" said Ricky.

"Yeah, she is. Now finish up, and then we'll chug another beer fore's we get started."

Moments later, Ricky walked over, twirling a pair of
black panties around one finger, and took the proffered
beer from Jerry.

"Like the commercial says, it don't get any better than
this," laughed Jerry, tilting his beer to clink against
Ricky's bottle.

"You got that . . ." Ricky stopped suddenly as a low
rumbling sound filled the air, building quickly to a pulsating roar that began to rattle dishes, doors, and even
the very structure itself.

"What the fuck!" yelled Ricky as he fell against the
counter, the bottle slipping from his hand to crash on
the floor.

"Gotta be an earthquake, a big one," shouted Jerry,
struggling to be heard over the growing clatter.

But an earthquake didn't explain the harsh, unearthly
light that suddenly blazed through every window, every
crack, every chink in the old cabin. An earthquake didn't
began to explain the sudden, drastic change in atmo-

spheric pressure that caused both men to clutch at their
skulls in pain. Exchanging a wordless look of terror, they
broke, stumbling, for the door. . . .

Saturday, July 27th, 8:12 P.M.
The car took the turn at Lynch Road at a high rate
of speed, nearly clipping a panicked squirrel that darted
out of the headlights and to safety in the nick of time.
Frank slowed momentarily until he was back on the
straightaway, and then sped back up. He knew he should
wait for a backup car, but his destination was just ahead,
and he was in no mood to wait. Finally faced with the
opportunity for a little action, Frank was wired and primed.

Based on the brief description garnered from the as-
yet-unidentified woman, and on the area in which he'd
found her wandering naked, Frank felt sure that Jerry
Berringer was one of the assailants. And the smaller one
was likely that little ratfuck Ricky Gomez, who'd been
Jerry's partner in crime lately. In fact, Frank had busted
them both on a D&D charge at One-Eyed Red's not a
month ago.

Frank slowed as he came up on Berringer's cabin,
veering into the rutted parking area in front of the cabin,
which sat swathed in darkness, nearly overwhelmed by
a confusion of oaks, madrones, and towering redwoods.

Clicking on his flashlight, he stepped from his car and
headed up the cracked flagstone path toward the house.
Swinging the flashlight across the front of the house,
Frank saw for the first time that the door was hanging
askew, barely held upright by its upper hinge. He un-
snapped his holster and withdrew his gun, moving up
the steps in a stealthy crouch now.

The silence was so deep it was stifling. There was no
breeze to stir branches, no sounds of animals or insects.
Frank took a deep breath and called out, "Berringer, you
in there? Come out with your hands where I can see 'em."

Silence.

"You hear me? Come on out now."

Still nothing. Frank suspected the house was empty—
there were, after all, no cars in sight, nor any lights on—
but he wasn't exactly experienced at this sort of thing.

Somehow his fantasies of big-city busts had managed to omit a lot of the nitty-gritty details.

Taking another deep breath, Frank stepped through the door in a crouch, gun and flashlight leading the way in hand-over-hand fashion.

It looked as if a small cyclone had passed through the cabin.

Chairs were overturned, lamps toppled, dishes scattered and broken on the floor, pictures liberated from walls, windows cracked.

But nobody home. *And no bodies.*

Frank tried the light switch next to the door. No luck. Moving carefully, he picked his way through the debris and kicked open the bedroom door. More of the same. Things strewn everywhere.

Then into the bathroom. Empty.

Exhaling audibly, Frank reholstered his gun and tried to get a handle on what had happened here. The girl, if she'd been here, might've put up a struggle, but she couldn't have caused all this. *No, something more happened here. But what? Just a drunken rampage by one or both of those tubesteaks?*

It was more than Frank could figure. He was headed for the car to call in a report when he realized he hadn't checked the bedroom closet.

He redrew his weapon and retraced his steps. Paused before the closet door. Fumbled with the knob while trying to maintain his sweaty grip on gun and flashlight. Pulled open the door . . .

. . . And found nothing. Standard-issue closet, albeit one with about half the clothes on the floor.

He nudged the pile to one side with his foot. Something clinked beneath. Curious, he knelt and pushed the clothes aside. Found a canvas knapsack. Flipped it open and looked inside.

"I'll be damned . . ."

Ten minutes later, Frank was finishing his radio report.

". . . and that's when I found the bag. Scalpels, cleavers, tubing, a funnel—the works. If I remember right, Berringer used to work at the meat-packing plant, so he probably knows how to cut.

"Over," added Frank belatedly.

"So I suppose you're thinking what I'm thinking," came the voice from the radio. "Over."

"Exactly. Looks like we found our cattle mutilators."

Saturday, July 27th, 10:51 P.M.

Taylor Duncan turned the corner at a high rate of speed, nearly colliding with a supply cart pushed by a bored-looking orderly.

"Watch it, willya?" Duncan muttered, knowing that the near-miss was his fault.

At the moment, though, he couldn't care less if he pissed off an orderly or twelve. He had bigger fish to fry. An "emergency" page had him double-timing it from the ER, where he'd been doing an eval on a homeless, delusional drunk, back up to the psych ward.

He reached the departmental nursing station and squeaked to a halt on the heavily waxed floor.

"Who paged me? Where's the fire?"

"It's the Jane Doe abductee. She's missing."

"Missing? She could barely sit up, let alone go waltzing off. Have you looked for her?"

"Yes," replied the exasperated nurse, "We didn't page you until we'd conducted a thorough search of the ward and the rest of the floor. She's seriously gone."

By this time, a small group, consisting of two nurses, an intern, and an attending, had gathered around the nursing station. Most of them nodded in unison.

Taylor sighed. *Why me?*

"All right. Let's get word out to the rest of the hospital. And to the police, I suppose. Give as complete a physical description as possible. She was, what, about five-foot-ten, maybe one thirty-five, shoulder-length, curly blonde hair . . ." Taylor stopped when he noticed several faces staring at him, wearing dumbfounded expressions.

"What are you talking about?" said one.

"*Who* are you talking about?" said another.

"It's the *abductee* that's missing," chimed in a third.

"I know that. What's your point?" snapped Taylor, feeling all-too-typical feelings of frustration rising in him once again. *Am I surrounded by imbeciles?*

"Well . . . she wasn't a five-ten blonde, for starters,"

offered a male nurse. "She was a brunette, only about five-four."

"Cut the crap," said the attending. "This is serious business. She was about five-seven with short red hair."

"No, she . . ."

"What are you . . ."

The debate erupted into a cacophony of voices.

* * *

Sunday, July 28th, 12:27 A.M.

With a visibly shaking hand, Jerry Berringer drew his beer to his mouth and took a long swallow.

"Do you really think it's safe to stop here, Jerry?" asked Ricky, gripping his own glass in a white-knuckled fist. His wide-eyed gaze betrayed the levels of adrenaline coursing through him.

"If it ain't safe here, it ain't gonna be safe anywhere. They're either gonna leave us alone, or they're gonna get us whenever they please. But like I said, I think if they was gonna get us, they woulda done it last night. They had us, dead to rights. Why the fuck would they let us drive off if they wanted somethin' with us?"

"Yeah. Yeah, you're right. So you really think they maybe just wanted the girl? Whattya think they wanted her for?"

"How the fuck should I know? Maybe they just wanted to dip their alien schlongs in a little Earth nookie."

The waitress chose that moment to walk up behind Jerry. She gave him a strange look before taking their order for two more beers.

"Hey, Jerry . . . you think we could sell our story to the papers, or TV? I mean, tell them what we saw and . . ."

"You really are a brain-damaged sausage monkey, aren't you? We ain't got no pictures, we ain't got no proof. Who the hell's gonna believe us?"

Ricky stared into his empty bottle, his hyperactivity momentarily derailed.

* * *

Outside the roadhouse, a young woman walking through the parking lot paused momentarily before a beat-up tan Impala, nodded slightly, and then walked on toward the front of the bar.

Across the lot, a middle-aged biker climbing off his Harley stopped to admire the woman. *Don't get many black chicks around here, but that one sure is fine.*

Just then, a happy-hour survivor staggered out the door of the bar. Spying the woman through his alcoholic haze, he propped himself against the fender of the nearest car and stared at her. *Damn, that's just about the hottest blonde I've ever seen.*

SOME BURIAL PLACE, VAST AND DRY

By Peter Crowther

Since the World and British Fantasy Award-nominated *Narrow Houses* (1992), Peter Crowther has edited or coedited eight more anthologies, continued to produce reviews and interviews for a variety of publications on both sides of the Atlantic, sold some fifty of his own short stories, and completed *Escardy Gap,* a collaborative novel with James Lovegrove. A solo novel, a short story collection, two more anthologies, and *Escardy Gap II* are all currently underway.

> What weeping face is that looking from the window?
> Why does it stream those sorrowful tears?
> Is it for some burial place, vast and dry?
> Is it to wet the soil of graves?
> —WALT WHITMAN, from "Debris" (1860)

The first parts of the colossal architectural complex drifted into the town in fragrant traces, myriad vapors floating on the winds of Orgundy like the memory of a cigarette or the promise of a delicate perfume.

The hint of its crenellated towers brought with it all the smells of the past . . . hamburgers and hot dogs, popcorn and lemonade, toffee apples and candy floss, all long-ago faded into a billion sunsets but here again, *now,* wafting across the barren landscape. The scent of its storm-worn, front porches and tall, fluted columns filtered into thousands upon thousands of forgotten wispy rocket exhaust residues and settled like fairy dust onto the softly-sighing stamens of the peach flowers.

The old man looked up from tending his crops beside the glimmering Plexiglas of Dome 12 and stared, responding to the faintest tingling in his bones, a song of sorts which whispered tenderly of youth and mystery, and, most of all, of Earth.

Home.

He stood there, amid a patchwork quilt of rectangular crop partitions, most of which, long untended, had grown over with the ever-present, orange weed of Orgundy, and mouthed the word silently as, above him, the strange yet familiar constructs of the past swooped and glided like summer kites or playful birds.

Home!

It was a mantra of sorts—*aum*—a single word comprising all that was dear and all that was distant. Maybe the two went together, *always* went together.

The grass is always greener . . . he thought, as a thin, gossamer line of picket fencing unraveled like uprooted railroad tracks above the domes and drifted off toward the usual site, breaking apart and then reforming en route. But the grass on Orgundy was not green at all, he suddenly remembered, looking down at the rust-colored sward and the fine, mauve sand he so lovingly—so absently—tilled every day.

He hadn't realized The Day had been so close. The old 2069 calendar thumbtacked on his cot-room wall still showed April . . . a different year, a different month. What year *was* it? he wondered. But that was so unimportant now: The main thing was that today was The Day, come again to entertain him and fill him with wonder and memories.

He laid the crude tilling device on the loamy soil and walked slowly to the dome's hatch, hardly daring to breathe lest his discarded energy should disturb the ghostly constructs that swooped and swirled outside. He keyed in the password, a solemn configuration of uncaring numbers, and stepped back to allow the hatch-guard by his feet to disengage. When it was fully open, he slipped inside and keyed the hatch-door closed again.

The air inside the dome was thin and tainted, redolent with inaction and age. The old man moved through the doorless rooms, suddenly noting the fine covering of years-old dust which lay on the furniture and the piles of books that towered and tottered in every corner and littered every corridor with a literary loam.

He lifted the old Timberline jacket, corduroy and fleecy-lined, from the foot of his cot and shrugged his way into it. It had been a long time since he had worn the jacket. Too long, he realized sadly. The Orgundy climate was constantly early autumn and he needed only his regular workshirt and vest while working in his garden. That was all he did these days, work his garden.

The old man shook his head, scattering the first settlings of self-pity, and then straightened himself up. He savored the stillness and the familiarity of his dome while he tried to gain his bearings . . . not in a geographical sense but a temporal one. How long was it? Fifty years? It must be at least fifty years: The face that stared back from his silver-cracked mirror was now that of a grandfather.

There was a time, once upon a time, when he would walk away from the domes to the distant foothills and visit with everybody. At first, he went with Margaret. But then Margaret left him, too. The old man shook his head again, dislodging the memory and bouncing it around in his mind to stop it from settling and taking root. He zippered up the Timberline and shuffled back into the memory of the coat.

That was the last time he had worn it, he realized. When, on a particularly bad day, when the lonesomeness had tugged at every nerve ending and pounded in his temples like a migraine, he had gone to talk with Margaret. That was the last time he had needed to wear the jacket. That was . . . how long ago was it? *Too* long.

He turned sharply and walked back to the hatch, ignoring the silence and the loneliness that surrounded him.

Back at the hatch, he keyed in the password. Then, as always, he closed his eyes and breathed in deeply.

The smells of Orgundy filled him, sank into his soul through mouth and nose, swirled amidst his creaking ribs before spiraling outward to the very tips of his outstretched arms. Then, pulling the old Timberline collar up to his chin, he opened his eyes and stepped outside.

Like a child's breath across a set of pipes, the Orgundy wind whined and hummed, a calliope melody of false starts and delicate refrains.

He slackened the dirty bandanna around his neck and

pulled it over his mouth, preventing the lavender-hued dust from turning his saliva into purple goo. He raised his left hand to shield his eyes and watched.

Up ahead, near the foothills and the Resting Place, the first parts of the complex were settling, miragelike, a curious but heady amalgam of French chateaux, Italian palazzi and Elizabethan manor houses. He threw his head back and laughed out loud, laughed in spite of himself and his loneliness, laughed both against and with the tears he felt welling deep inside . . . stretching his arms out like a man in a desert feeling the first fulfilling drops of cool rain on his parched body.

"Here it comes," he shouted.

And it did, filling the air with glints and reflections, casting creeping shadows across the mauve sand. . . .

It was the ultimate airborne craft, sky-wide and horizon-deep, a veritable city of lines and curves, the last word in what they used to call unidentified flying objects. But the old man knew every corner and every tile, recognized every piece of stone and every gable-end, every sun-blasted shard of brick and every weatherworn section of polished beech and oak and cedar.

Stuccoed walls, tiled roofs, loggias, open courtyards circled by elegant ironwork; wooden sash windows decorated with thin strips of white marble trim along their sills; dormer windows enriched with crockets and finials . . . square towers, tall chimney stacks, ornately carved balustrades and a million-and-one gargoyles resting, sitting, flying, hiding.

And it didn't stop there.

Gliding above him, shimmering as still it pulled together its composite parts, a colossal potpourri spaceship of construction and style and architectural fashion rode the alien winds . . . fifty—no, one hundred!—times bigger than the tiny, cold and futuristic silver needles that had brought the old man and his wife, Margaret, and all of their friends, here all those many long years ago.

A vaulted banqueting hall pirouetted to his left, its tapestries and enormous hooded stone fireplaces catching the wind and the light while the whole affair steadied itself as it prepared to join the others.

Alongside, like suckling calves, other rooms and

smaller buildings nestled in the shadows of the great hall. Colossal pilasters, arched windows and doors and rusticated bases leveled off amidst a cornucopia of scroll-work, console brackets, fascias, garlands and cartouches as they all approached the foothills up ahead.

The old man spun around, laughing, spittle flecking his lips as he waved to one and all and bade them *Welcome!*

To his right, a shingle-style homestead bumped on the air currents, a single-prop dwelling beside the ostentatiously sleek great-hall airliner. At its back hung a coal chute and from its oak-paneled doorway a flagstone path dangled like an ornate ribbon, trailing the soil as it passed . . . though, miraculously, disturbing not a single spicule of the mauve sand. As he watched, the building leaned to negotiate the wind and its side fell slowly open like a doll's house, exposing bedrooms and servants' quarters, an oak-beamed kitchen area, and a circular wooden staircase whose ornate carvings the old man could make out even from this distance.

Pausing for breath, he steadied himself and watched the latest arrivals settle down into the usual place amidst the gentle rises and slopes of the foothills. He was near enough now that he could make out the weathered markers of his friends and, just for a moment, he felt a wave of sadness wash against his insides. But, like any wave, it passed almost as soon as it had appeared, retreating, perhaps, to consolidate and return, strengthened and more determined.

No matter, he thought. It would not spoil The Day. And just for a second, his mind drifted back to his grandfather telling him about how he would jump up on Fourth of July morning, trampling dogs and siblings underfoot, to race into the Illinois dawn in a frantic effort to be the first kid on the block to let off a firecracker. Orgundy might be a long way from Illinois, Earth, but he reckoned he felt the same way as his grandfather had felt all those years ago. Just the same.

Taking a deep breath, he leaned forward into the thickening breeze and took the first of many steps that would take him Home.

Up ahead, the first parts of the "ship" had landed, its building-sections settling into place, becoming one huge composite of line and curve, stone and wood, plaster and brick.

And now, as ever at the start of The Day, he wondered—marveled—at how this could be. That a planet somehow could transpose memory and feeling, hopes and dreams, wishes and regrets into one mountainous construct of all that once was—and forever would be—Earth.

For this was a strange sentience indeed, a bizarre ability. Perhaps it was even a need. Perhaps the planet sensed his loneliness. Perhaps it sent these corporeal translations of his mind as some kind of reward . . . a payment for attention and affection, for friendship. Whatever.

The Day was his and his alone. It had never come when they were all together, not even when he and Margaret were alone. But then, in the July of—of when? 2068? '67? He couldn't remember. There was so much he couldn't remember, which was, of course, what made The Day so special—the buildings had come. It was the fourth day, the Fourth of July, some year. Independence Day. Which was why he had christened his own personal Eldorado as Independence.

He quickened his step. And as he walked, he thought.

On that first Day, that first and dimly remembered Fourth of July, two thousand and something or other, he had thought the buildings were indeed spacecraft. That they were some huge, intergalactic flotilla, lost in the vastness of space and happening upon his lonely personal world by pure chance.

They had come—as they always had come since that first Day—silently and without warning, darkening the skies above the domes as though a swarm of insects blotted out the light of Orgundy's twin suns. He had rushed outside, responding to the gathering darkness inside the dome, and looked up, covering his eyes. Many of them he had recognized immediately; others he recognized only after time.

And each year, there were more.

He spent the long months between Days structuring his thoughts in the same way that the planet seemed to structure his Independence for him. He fought to remember. And with each memory of buildings and homes, so came memories of the times around them . . .

memories of the people he had been with. But, for a while at least, the planet had seemed only able to replicate inanimate matter.

Then, that, too, had changed.

He shuddered involuntarily. The best was still to come, he thought, and the sudden realization . . . the heart-speeding certainly of what was to follow roiled inside him like a warm storm.

As he neared the foothills, he rested again, turning back the way he had come.

He was already quite high. The domes lay beneath him, scattered on the mauve carpet of Orgundy like droplets of mercury. He looked up into the air, watching the last shacks and bandstands and outhouses shudder across the sky and disappear over his head to take their places behind him. As always, the biggest would come last.

The old man sat down to wait.

The spire showed first, far away, where sky and sand met in a shimmering, fluctuating line, far beyond the broken remains of the smashed rocketships that had brought him and his friends here, sunlight glinting from their still-polished hulls . . . far, far away, framed against the egg-shaped bulk of distant Quextal which lay as though partially submerged in Orgundy's horizon, its twinkling rings sparkling in the encroaching shadow.

Am I the first, old man? said a voice by his side.

The old man turned in the direction of the voice and stared into the eyes of himself—but this was him as he was years ago . . . maybe thirty, forty years ago.

"Yes, you're the first," the old man said with a smile. "I'll call you 'Thirty.' "

The younger man tilted his head to one side as he considered the name, and then he frowned. *But I'm still you,* he said, *Will Gainsborough.*

The Old Man—who was, indeed, William Gainsborough—nodded and turned to face the swelling shape that now seemed to fill the horizon. "Yes, well, it'll make it easier when we're all here," he said. He sensed the other man chew on that and then turn his own head, apparently appeased if not entirely satisfied, and together they watched the end of the first act.

The first half of its 1,454 feet could now be seen: some fifty or more of its 102 stories, one thousand or so of its 1,860 stairs and maybe 200,000 of its reputed 365,000 tons of building materials. It seemed to hover, but the old man knew it was actually moving, drifting silently toward them, filling both the sky and his own mind with all of its majesty.

"You know," the old Will Gainsborough said to his younger self, "she took nineteen months to build and was so strong that, in 1945, a B-52 bomber crashed into the seventy-ninth floor and it didn't even shake her."

Mmmm, said the other Will Gainsborough. *And an elevator operator—her name was Betty Lou Oliver— managed to survive her elevator car plummeting seventy-six floors as a result.*

"You remembered," the old man said.

So did you, came the reply.

"And by the time we left Earth in late '66, thirty-eight people had jumped from her to their deaths," said the elder Gainsborough. "Would have been thirty-nine except that, in 1979, Elvita Adams threw herself from the eighty-sixth floor and a gust of wind blew her back onto a lower ledge."

Thirty-eight, said Thirty thoughtfully. *That's a lot of unhappy people,* he added.

The old man shook his head. "I sure do miss her," he said.

Margaret? Or the Empire State?

"Both. But mainly Margaret. How is she?" As he turned to face Thirty, the shadow of the magnificent Empire State Building fell across them and, for a moment, the air seemed slightly cooler. "How is she right now?"

You remember, Will Gainsborough. She's wonderful and healthy and she fills my every waking and sleeping moment. We've just had our second child—a boy, Timothy.

"Then it's 2064."

Right.

William Gainsborough lifted his head as the end of the building drifted soundlessly above him. "I was twenty-eight," he said.

That mean you're going to change my name?

He laughed. "No, I'll keep calling you Thirty."

How about me? said a younger voice.

The old man lowered his head and smiled at the boy standing before him. The boy had a thick, unruly thatch of brown-blond hair that stood proudly off his head. He wore short pants that stopped inches above scuffed knees, below which two sock tops hovered at different heights on scrawny legs.

"You," he said, "you I'll call Twelve. Is that what you are?"

The boy nodded.

"Good guess," said Will Gainsborough.

You gonna play? Play ball, maybe?

"Maybe, Twelve. Maybe I'll pitch a couple to you later. But first . . . first we have to watch the rest of the show."

The old man got to his feet and turned around in time to see the Empire State Building settle silently into place between an old brownstone that he had lived in when he was a small child and the bandstand that his mother and father used to take him to on a Sunday afternoon, its clap-board sides magically twisting into the exhaust-darkened brickwork of 289 Third Avenue in midtown Manhattan.

It looked just the way it used to look, before his old home became the only brownstone left on the block, cowering in the shadows of the skyscrapers and clashing with, to its left, the blue-glass and stainless-steel of the adjoining French restaurant, with its garish red awning, and, to its right, a concrete block containing a branch of First National.

He remembered its brickwork and its sad window-eyes, each sided by blue, latticework shutters and topped with bracketed moldings, the latter providing the eye-brow curves essential to the Italianate style.

These were the things that had led him to architecture and design all those many years ago. These were his loves—the old buildings, the homesteads, the mansions. They were his children, his friends. Each brick and each board, known to him personally. It was they who had whispered to him, sung to him of their constructive and beautiful magic, first in school, then at college and then at various design agencies until the space program asked him on board to work on the life-support units for the first planned outpost beyond the Milky Way.

He felt a trickle on his cheek and tasted the unmistakable bitterness of salt.

Who's that? Thirty asked, pointing to a figure sitting cross-legged in the sand between them and the collection of buildings, his back to them.

Will Gainsborough squinted his eyes at the figure and immediately recognized the lowered shoulders. "That's Forty-Four," he said, and he started toward the figure, his heart heavy with sadness.

He crouched down by the side of himself so many years younger and felt a strange mixture of emotions. First, he felt jealousy: After all, the person by his side had such fresh memories of the woman he had loved. *Still* loved! But he felt profound sympathy, too, for the younger Will Gainsborough had just lost that woman while he himself had long since come to terms with her absence. For this reason, he felt pleased that those were not his present feelings, not his present suffering. Will Gainsborough Senior (as he liked to think of himself on The Day) remembered those feelings all too well, even though some thirty years or more had passed since he had first experienced them.

"Take it easy," he said. "It gets easier."

Easier? the other said, his words echoing in the old man's ears. *Will it really?*

"Yes. You won't miss her any less, but the pain will become more bearable."

The younger man lowered his head into his hands and sobbed.

William Gainsborough forgot for a moment and tried to place an arm about his younger self's shoulder, suddenly starting as the sleeve of the old Timberline seemed to shudder in mist.

You may not touch us, old man, the figure said into its hands.

He withdrew his arm and clasped his hands tightly. "I forgot," he said.

You must not forget.

"I know."

He got to his feet, rubbing his knees—the first signs

of arthritis, he reckoned—and turned round. There were more of them now, many of their ages making it difficult for him to distinguish one from another. He could only recall the occasions, the landmarks in his life.

There, at the back, running around the dunes amidst the other figures, was Eight, fresh from asking his father one Christmas morning if Santa Claus had really brought the bulging pillowcase of gaudily wrapped presents that stood beside his bed. And there was Eighteen, the round face of adolescence now surrendered to the finer features of approaching adulthood, wearing the stern, proud gaze that came with graduation and the keys to his first automobile.

They were all there: first kisses, winning football games, exam passes, first building design, successful interviews . . . and all the Margaret memories.

They came in a swarm, flooding his mind with pictures of the past. He shook his head, fighting the tears, and turned around, away from them all, to see the finished construction.

It was the greatest building that had ever existed, a castle of such magnitude and invention that it dwarfed all other contenders in both size and concept. Never . . . not in all the years that it had come . . . had it ever reached such magnificent proportions.

Shack stood upon brownstone upon tenement.

There was the Whalers' Church he had marveled at on a long-ago visit to Sag Harbor, butting its Egyptianate boundaries with the stark symmetry of Louis XIV's orangery at Versailles.

There was . . .

There was . . .

Mansard roofs, columns, pediment and entablature, fish-scale shingling, Adamesque fanlights, Italianate porches, Greek transoms, robustly paneled shutters, conically roofed gazebos aside scissors-trusses and pierced-wood paneling, all leading onto old brick sidewalks swept with fine sand and protected by white picket gates which, suspended magically in the air, circumnavigated high stories of the many magnificent and wonderful adjuncts and extensions. Bargeboard frames with elongated quatrefoils, paired dormers opening onto Mosque rooftops which themselves led onto buttressed dormer windows of striking Pre-Raphaelite beauty . . .

William Gainsborough was breathless just looking at it.

It was every building he had ever known, every style he had ever studied and every color he had ever seen.

It was Gormenghast and Tintagel, magnified a thousandfold.

It gleamed and glimmered, catching light and diffusing its rays, sending them spinning and pirouetting across roof and window, gargoyle and gable, dulling brick and shining shingle.

Its highest points scraped the sky, tore its blueness in thin gashes so that its steeples disappeared from view into the strangeness of space. And of all the high points, of all the distant, towering curves and lines of this castle of castles, the Empire State reigned supreme.

It was finished. Now was the time.

Now it would start to shimmer, its bonds and joinings begin to fade, to grow dissolute and drift with the wind. Now it would fall apart, its beams and its masonry stretch and fold in upon itself like smoke dreams cast by the most ancient of tribal pipes.

He waited, watching, staring, drinking in with his eyes and his mind, recharging memory and dreams alike.

But still the Castle Independence remained.

He waited some more.

And still it remained.

William Gainsborough Senior turned around and was startled to see that he stood alone on the sand. He looked again, first one way and then the other, wondering if, perhaps, the many other versions of himself over the years of his life had huddled together to surprise him. But there was nothing, only the distant dome-droplets on the plains below, and the far-off egg of Quextal sitting astride the horizon and, nearby, the marker-clad carpet of the Resting Place. And all about him, the wind sang softly.

Then he heard the rusting grind of metal on metal and the throaty churn of creaking wood.

The old man tensed, hardly daring to turn. There had never been a noise before, never a sound from the col-

lective monolith that visited his space-borne island,
never a whisper from the fluttering drapes or a squeak
from the gently wafting picket gates. The sound continued, growing heavier and deeper, until there came a distant thud and the ground beneath him trembled.

Silence returned.

Twisting himself around, inch by inch, he turned his
head to see what had happened.

The Castle still stood there, its every gable and turret,
its every rooftop and minaret, its every column and
bracket . . . all strikingly complete and sturdy. But, in
the middle of it all, a tiny square on the front of its
seemingly endless facade had opened by virtue of an old
portcullis drawbridge which now rested flat upon the
sand. And, as he looked, the old man could see the
faintest traces of wafting sand released into the air by
the sheer force of the gate, and, within the gaping maw
of the entrance, the vaguest hint of shimmering light,
eating the blackness around it as it grew in intensity.
Something was coming toward him.

Suddenly he felt afraid. The mirage had become real.

Now the castle seemed to take upon itself an altogether more Gothic appearance. Now, it seemed murky
and melodramatic, dreary and dolorous . . . brooding,
lugubrious and woeful.

Now, the building before him seemed a place more in
keeping with surroundings of weeping willows, howling
storms, and subterranean, niter-encrusted crypts . . . a
monolithic maze of secret passages, hidden recesses, and
tattered tapestries.

Now it felt less like the Fourth of July and more like
November, the thirteenth of November, perhaps, with
summer lying long-dead with the bluebonnets in the
fields, and the final stroke of midnight still echoing in
the darkening air.

The old man looked up and saw that it was, indeed,
getting darker. He turned and saw that the twin suns of
Orgundy still seemed to burn as brightly as ever but now
they seemed to burn behind cloth—thick, dark cloth,
that stole clarity and precision.

He turned back and saw that the light now filled the

entrance to Independence. And he saw that, encased in the light, a lone figure stood, motionless. Waiting.

Waiting for *him.*

William Gainsborough Senior took a step back, away from the towers and the wood and the stone. Then, as he was about to take another step, the figure raised an arm and beckoned to him. He stopped and squinted his eyes. There was something familiar about that wave. Something he recognized.

He withdrew that step. And then took one more.

Then another.

His heart pounded and his eyes widened. The figure moved again . . . and he started to run.

Surely it was his imagination. Surely it was a trick . . . a trick of the twin suns, of the desert breeze, a construction of his active mind or a reflection of his inner thoughts or of some distant star whose light had traveled many millions of years to create such an effect purely for him. He felt his teeth jangling together as he ran, his jaw flopping with the effort. And then, suddenly, he had the strength.

It came in a flood into every pore of his body, a rush of energy and determination.

As he ran, the figure stepped back, her arms still outstretched the way she always stretched them to him. And he saw her hair now, blowing around her face and her shoulders.

He ran through the sand, kicking it around his feet in purple gusts until he reached the drawbridge in the shadow of every building he had ever known, all of which now gathered around the skirt-tails of the Empire State Building where, so many years ago, he had first met Margaret.

His feet clattered on the wood and he laughed at the sound they made. He shouted her name, over and over again, and he heard her shout back, his own name spoken again by another voice after all these long years. *Her* voice.

And now he understood this monolithic construct . . . this unidentified flying castle.

He knew that, inside, he would find King Arthur and Gandalf and Steerpike . . . and Herman Melville and

Edgar Allen Poe and Edgar Rice Burroughs. He knew instinctively all of its rooms and its corridors, recognized all of its thick-pile carpets, stone floors, and polished bare-board rafter walkways.

Margaret had stepped back now, well back into the first of those corridors. But now he could see her face and her smile.

And as she bade him welcome, he could hear, above the sound of the drawbridge closing behind him, every single syllable of her words, and every tiny consonant. And each was as important to the message as each slate of Independence's roof and each brick in its sides and each board in its floors was essential to the final construction.

And then he fell once more into her arms, to build again.

Over time, the patchwork quilt of rectangular gardens was covered by the sands though the domes remained, still looking like tiny droplets of mercury on the otherwise arid plains.

Over still more time, the sand covered the distant polished-steel skeletons of the broken rocketships in their silent tombs and, finally, even drifted up to the Resting Place, where the winds had blown down the crude markers whose words had long since faded.

Each year, the airborne domain of memory and hope returned, its ghostly gables drifting again on the strange breezes. And each year, it seemed a little different . . . though there was no one there to appreciate the modifications.

Finally even the faded corduroy of the Timberline jacket had disappeared from sight.

"I raise high the perpendicular hand, I make the signal,
To remain after me in sight forever,
For all the haunts and homes of me."
                    —Walt Whitman, from *Salut Au Monde* (1856)

(For Ray Bradbury)

DADDY DEAREST

By Jack Cady

Born in Ohio in 1932, Jack Cady was educated at the University of Louisville. A former auctioneer, truck driver, lumberjack, English professor, newspaper publisher, and editor, his work has appeared in such magazines as *Yale Review* and *Atlantic Monthly*. His short stories also appear in *Sea-Cursed, Dixie Ghosts,* and *Western Ghosts.*

It began in a tearoom in Seattle, one with rose-colored tablecloths and stained-glass lamps. A tearoom, I ask you. A tearoom with pictures of bunnies and duckies quilted on the napkins, the whole show run by a granny-lady named Mrs. Perkins.

In addition to bunnies, the tearoom sported furniture like riffraff from an antique store, you know the kind: a late Victorian breakfront, nineteenth century reproductions of seventeenth century chairs, and cutesy washboards, trivets, and unwarranted junk from rural America of seventy years past.

Into this tearoom, on one of those rainy Northwest days specifically designed for funerals, slipped two quiet people who murmured to each other while touching hands. One, the man, carried a jar. The man (who looked like someone named Harold but who was actually named Aubrey) seemed nondescript in spite of grooming. His slender frame stood topped by brown hair, and he gazed about with brown eyes, a man eminently suited to brown, a man, one assumed, accustomed to brown thoughts, and he looked as though he'd been thinking them for about thirty years. He dressed not in brown, but in elegant tan cashmere and wool, most expensive.

The woman, smashingly beautiful, tended to the green

of springtime. If the man seemed sad, the woman seemed only mildly serious. A touch of girlishness chased away rain and wind and gloom of streets where cars ran wet and umbrellas turned inside out. Whereas the man looked like a shirt advertisement, albeit a depressed one, the woman looked like an artist, which in fact, was the case. A bit Bohemian, perhaps, but an artist who knew her business. Her piled hair looked Norwegian, her features classic Greek. She stood taller than Aubrey, not so elegantly dressed, but a green wool skirt fell just far enough to display trim ankles, and her green wool jacket snugged tidily around narrow shoulders. Name of Patsy.

The jar was one of those funerary things which hold ashes that crematoriums give the bereaved right after a service. This cream-colored jar carried a gold leaf inscription reading: "Blessed is he who don't dip his finger into this jug-a-trouble 'cause he'll sure-God get it bit."

"I wanted a really nice inscription," the man murmured sadly. "Something from the Bible. But Pop had to be snotty till the end. The whole memorial ceremony was compromised."

"It's been your problem all your life," the jar said. "Making compromises. Cutting deals where you come out on the short end of the stick. I tried to pay attention when you was growin'." The voice spilled from beneath the lid of the jar, no more than a whisper, but steady as wind across Montana. Aubrey looked at the jar, looked mournful, but not a bit surprised. He looked as though he had been expecting something like this all along.

"Being dead doesn't seem to shut him up," Patsy suppressed a giggle.

"I had many a doxie in my day," the jar whispered proudly, "but nobody prettier than you." The jar chuckled, its voice not a little horny.

"I can't say I'm surprised, but I wish I'd known him better," Patsy said. "He's the sort of rascal who seduces entire convents."

"He had that reputation," Aubrey admitted in a brownish voice. He held a chair for Patsy, then seated himself. "This is a nice place," he hissed to the jar. "Just this one time try not to embarrass me."

"I thought the memorial was actually very nice." Patsy looked around the room, at prints of kitties, piggies, and sunny children. She wrinkled her nose.

"My father's friends," said Aubrey, "were various."

"Apple knockers," the jar whispered, "and lonesome cowboys, railroad station agents, bar girls, torch singers, lady truck drivers, plus bozos, battleaxes . . . I'm talking here about ex-wives . . . lumberjacks, used car salesmen. . . ."

"She gets the picture," Aubrey muttered. He also looked around the tearoom, looking at nicely dressed women at lunch. The women chatted about dreams and plans of husbands, sons, grandsons, daughters, nieces, chatted of piano lessons, while making distressed noises about Democrats and orthodontists. A few women cast cautious glances at the jar. They pretended nonchalance. The jar chuckled, the chuckle lascivious.

"I suppose one never gets completely away from his father," Patsy said. "But yours is a special case." She glanced through a menu. Her hair held just a touch of russet. She smiled generously and reached to touch Aubrey's wrist. "I'm not sure why or what you need. . . ."

"For openers," Aubrey said quietly, "what do I do with him? He was a pretty good old dad, but I can't park him on the mantle at home. He'll just hit on the cleaning lady. I can't dump him. He'll turn into dust, and the dust will have a million teeny-weeny little voices. I'll be surrounded."

"We'll think of something," Patsy said, her voice a trifle cool. "You should look at your menu."

"I feel uneasy with decisions unless we've talked." Aubrey blushed while Patsy brightened. He started to speak, then waffled. "There was a time when I dreamed you and I would become much closer."

The jar expressed an alarmed sniff. Patsy smiled. The owner of the tearoom, Mrs. Perkins, arrived to take orders. She hovered above the table like a beneficent deity of doilies, a lacy, gray-haired lady capable of expressing cupcakes with the wave of a hand, capable of cookies.

"Sadie," the jar whispered mournfully in the direction of Mrs. Perkins. "You must have sold the brothel. You and the girls must of retired." The jar sounded appalled.

Then it began to hum, the hum sounding suspiciously like "Long Ago and Far Away."

"Did someone say something?" Mrs. Perkins sounded puzzled. "Is someone humming?" She gave a grandmotherly chirp. "At my age one gets to hearing things."

". . . got a birthmark on her right leg, well above the knee . . . ?"

"Excuse me." Aubrey stood, removed his jacket, and placed it over the jar.

"Cucumber sandwiches, Darjeeling tea, and a pair of your lovely ladyfingers," Patsy told Mrs. Perkins. Patsy smiled happily at the thought of ladyfingers, certainly not at the thought of cucumbers.

"That one's gonna cost." A muffled whisper came from beneath the jacket. "I'll keep you up nights singing, 'cause I ain't sleeping, I'm only dead."

"A period of mourning is appropriate," Aubrey said after Mrs. Perkins left. "I can even get leave from the office. One does not lose a father lightly, even that father." He pointed to the lump beneath the jacket. His eyes shone a little mistily, a man with more to say, a man about to stutter. Then he sat quietly.

"I'm not at all sure you've lost him." Patsy could not suppress a chuckle. "When you stop to think of the power of fathers, and how they live in your life and your dreams, I'm not sure any of them are truly lost." She sat quietly, perhaps remembering her own father, or perhaps wondering when Aubrey would get to the point, if there was a point. "In your case," she said, "I'm sure you've not lost him. Have you wondered why this is happening?"

"Solar flares?" Aubrey asked. "Radiant energy from the center of the Earth? Spaceships? Malicious gods? Time warps, bad luck, karma . . . do you believe in karma?" He reached to touch her hand, his touch tentative. "At first I hoped it was a simple case of madness. Hearing things, you understand? I hoped it was an aberration of grief. But you're hearing him as well."

"And so is Mrs. Perkins." Patsy giggled. "You may be crazy. I may be crazy. But I double-guarantee you that a sweet old bat like Mrs. Perkins is not crazy."

"It's an out-of-body experience. I kid you not." The

jar whispered from beneath the jacket. "Makes a person think."

Tea arrived ahead of the sandwiches. Patsy poured two cups, raised hers in a toast. "To fathers."

"To fathers and to lonely nights," Aubrey replied. Another blush began, although his first blush had not yet finished. "Was there ever a chance for us?" Beyond the windows, in the gray light of autumn, traffic reflected in the polished surface of a store's large front window. Images passed back and forth as people were mirrored in the glass. A teenage boy wearing a red baseball cap strolled past, hands in pockets and with a faraway look. He did not whistle. A policeman waited at a traffic light while three other people jay-walked.

"I love autumn," Patsy told him. "The world is just a little gusty before it goes to sleep for winter." She smiled, but her hand trembled slightly as she rearranged a napkin. "There still *is* a chance for us. Still is, but with alterations."

Aubrey stared brownly into his teacup as if reading leaves or searching for ultimate wisdom. "You're talking about my melancholy."

"You can do better," the jar advised Patsy. "With a bod like yours, a girl could get to Nashville."

Patsy stood, took off her jacket, and piled it on top of Aubrey's jacket. Whispers of indignation barely sounded through the folds of cloth.

And it is true, without the jacket, Patsy displayed a delicate combination of features which would turn the head of any statue, if the statue were male. She touched her shirtfront, realized she drew attention to some assets, hesitated . . . then leaned back in her chair as cucumber sandwiches arrived.

Mrs. Perkins glanced at the pile of jackets as she set plates on the table. "We can't allow pets." Her mouth formed an unhappy line. "You cannot believe the strictness of the health department. If you have a little one there, he'll have to wait outside."

"It's not a pet nor ever was," Patsy assured her. "It's not alive." Patsy looked beyond the window and into the day of rain and wet leaves. She smiled at Mrs. Perkins. "A lovely day."

"I count myself lucky," Mrs. Perkins murmured. "So many friends have gone before me, yet here I am healthy and cozy in my little shoppe." Her voice trembled. "One does miss friends, though. Rather badly, in fact."

Unintelligible whispers rose from beneath the pile of jackets as Mrs. Perkins returned to her kitchen.

"Melancholy," Aubrey said. "It's all around us."

"A brown study," Patsy told him. "That's what old-time poets would have said. You're always in a brown study. Your mind must look like a piece of English tweed." Her voice, though critical, sounded tender. "My dear, dear man, with one life to live, why must you choose only gloom and sorrow?"

Aubrey mutely pointed to the pile of jackets. He seemed near tears. Even his tan cashmere sweater appeared affected.

"Because a girl can't live with gloom," Patsy told him. "At least this girl can't. I'm basically a happy person."

"I think an evil jinn causes this." Aubrey pointed to the pile of jackets. "When I was a child, that . . ." his finger shook as it pointed . . . "that man denied my childhood. He made me clean out a chicken house. Worst day of my life."

"A chicken house?"

"Among other indignities." Aubrey sighed, but did not sound particularly sad.

"I'm looking at you in disbelief," Patsy told him, "because I don't believe a word of this." She stood, carefully removed the jackets from the jar, and hung them over the backs of chairs. To Aubrey she said, "It's the restroom for you, my man. Get in there for at least ten minutes." Her tones were those with which one did not trifle.

Aubrey, bewildered, passed toward the restroom and beyond hearing. Patsy turned to the jar, her voice changing to tones most raspy. "Crap me around one time," she said, "and we head for the ladies' can. A royal flush will be dealt. Only one of us will return."

"Even if you can't do better than Aubrey, you can do different." The jar's whisper sounded impressed.

"I can't do either," she told the jar. "Even if I can, I

don't want to. Artists are surrounded by people with weird egos. You can guess how a quiet and attractive guy . . ." She shrugged. "So, explain love? Go ahead."

"I have the time," the jar whispered sadly, "but you don't. You still have some livin' to do."

"What's this chicken house business?"

"The whole family had chores during a time when we went broke farmin'. He's not feeling sorry for himself, he's protecting his mama's good name. She pretended we weren't broke. Put on a few airs." The jar paused, the pause thoughtful, or almost. "He's his daddy's boy. He's got a sense of humor. He just never learned how to laugh."

"When he returns," Patsy said, her voice grim as graves, "I'll head for the can. You have ten minutes. Teach him to laugh."

"You two kids are gonna get along just fine," the jar murmured. "You are soundin' exactly like his momma."

"Ten minutes. He's on his way back here right now." Patsy grabbed her purse and left.

"One advantage in bein' dead is bein' able to tell the future," the jar whispered to Aubrey, after Aubrey returned looking unsettled, ". . . or rather, futures, because everybody's got a lot of them, depending on their choices."

"Give it a rest, Pop." Aubrey looked like a man who did not know whether to stay or flee. He looked a little lost, and plenty lonesome.

"So I'm gonna tell you about a boy who could be you, a good boy 'til he married the wrong woman. He may hook up with the right one later on, or maybe not."

Aubrey sat, elbows on table, looking into the wet street. He pretended not to listen. He pretended he did not feel befuddled.

"This boy's daddy was a famous buffalo-rider of the old school," the whisper continued. "Won loving cups and stuff. When the buffalo-rider's wife had a little kid, he named the kid Spike; only the wife didn't like it and named him after some artsy-fartsy guy who moped a lot and died young. The kid grew, and wore a lot of brown, and turned into the boy who married the wrong woman."

"Spike?" whispered Aubrey, and he seemed interested. His mouth twitched in a way that said it would be hanged if it was going to smile. "All my life you flipped b.s. Aren't you ever ashamed?"

"Did I ever lie?"

Aubrey considered, looked at wet streets, wet leaves, slicky sidewalks. ". . . told some pretty wild stories."

"Every one true," the jar whispered. "This boy I'm tellin' about married this gal . . . she sold his furniture . . . rearranged his place . . . bought a goldfish named Clarence and a hamster named Rasputin. She donated his suits, all brown and tan, to a home for delinquent Arabs, and she decked him out in stuff that would get him shot in Milwaukee. He had to grow a mustache. The mustache shed down his shirtfront. Hair worked under his belt and tickled his crotch . . . caused a case of the hots . . . he goes home in a hurry . . . she's not home . . . hamster missing . . . goldfish floating belly-up . . . he takes his case of hots to a cowboy bar. Boy gets a snootful, ends up with a bar-girl famous for card tricks, sharpshooting, bareback riding, and occasional hustles . . . they run off . . . live . . . you're chuckling, what'n'the hell's so funny?"

"You're trying to con me out of something. What?" Aubrey tried to make his voice brownish, and only managed something close to dark ivory.

"I got it on the line here, boy. Listen up, 'cause this is what happens if the story gets a different ending.

"Boy still marries the wrong girl. Boy still goes home with the hots. Goldfish intact . . . hamster happy . . . girl is home, copulation certain. Lots of hollering, rolling around, and in nine months out pops a kid. Name of Aloysius. Boy secretly names him Studs. Goddammit boy, there's a third story, quit giggling. . . ."

"Can't help it," Aubrey said. "You're running a con, and I'm seeing through it, and for once your b.s. isn't . . . hush, here comes Mrs. Perkins."

"Is everything all right?" Mrs. Perkins sounded the way a woman might, if a young man sat in her teashop talking to himself.

"Sadie," the jar whispered as loudly as it could. "Long time . . ."

Mrs. Perkins stopped, paused, looked around her tea-room. She checked out tea-drinking ladies, pictures of duckies, doilies, and lace. She quickly took a seat. "One of the boys from better days," she whispered to Aubrey, and looked fondly at the jar. "Give you fifty bucks for him."

"He's my father."

"Forty bucks," Mrs. Perkins said.

"Don't let her shove you around," the jar whispered. "A dozen times I've seen her run that number. You can easy get a hundred."

Aubrey laughed, practically helpless. Patsy, returning from the ladies' restroom, heard the laugh. Aubrey tried not to laugh, made a bad job of it, and laughed some more. Patsy took his arm, smiled happily, murmured something unintelligible, and Aubrey blushed. In the street, watched over by gods and flying saucers, by radiant energy and plain-dumb-luck, rain paused as if pondering a spot of sunshine; a new beginning, a blessed dawn. Then rain seemed to shrug its shoulders, puffed a gust or two, and decided to drizzle.

"I'm staying here with Sadie," the jar said to Aubrey. "You'll know where to find me." To Mrs. Perkins the jar said, "It's you and me, kid. You gonna display me on that sorry breakfront?"

"On my nightstand." Mrs. Perkins whispered so low Aubrey could not hear. Of course, by then, Aubrey had already helped Patsy with her coat and the two were nearly to the doorway, doubtless headed toward intimacy.

"On your nightstand?" the jar whispered, a whisper between awe and mild excitement. "You always was creative."

"We'll figure something out," Mrs. Perkins said, her voice throaty and bright as she watched Aubrey and Patsy step into the wet street. Aubrey raised an umbrella. He looked ready to tsk.

"I expect they'll be all right," Mrs. Perkins said. "But it's just going to be Hail Columbia for the first few years."

"It surely ain't a match made in heaven, plus he had

another option. He could of learned to be a buffalo rider."

"It's a match made in a teashop," Mrs. Perkins said. "You'd be surprised how often it happens these days . . . no, nope, you wouldn't be surprised."

"She's too pushy," the jar whispered, "and he's a natural worrywart. A'course they're both good kids."

"You have to cut them loose sometime," Mrs. Perkins said. "If they've got a lot to learn, it's best to get started."

"I tried to be a good daddy," the jar whispered. "Take it easy, Spike."

And Mrs. Perkins and the jar stood looking into the busy street, a street of sales and traffic where it may be that a beneficent eye hovers godlike in the sky, directing the affairs of men, the affairs of women, and of women and men who have affairs; and then Mrs. Perkins picked up the jar and stashed it beside her umbrella where it would be handy when she closed shop and went home. She heard a slight sound as she turned to attend to customers, but missed seeing the jar nearly tip from the shelf as it gave a small hop and a jiggle, while weeping only a little.

RENEWING THE OPTION

by Elizabeth Engstrom

Elizabeth Engstrom is best known for her dark suspense stories. The late Theodore Sturgeon, one of science fiction's greatest talents, felt that she was one of the best writers of her generation. Other short fiction of hers appears in *Love in Vein, When Darkness Loves Us,* and *In the Fog.*

"I see you as a gambling man," she said with a sly grin. "Are you a gambling man?"

The question caught him a bit off guard, and he didn't know whether to match her directness or back down a little. "Doesn't every man fancy himself a bit of a gambler?"

Her grin faded as she stared straight into his eyes. They were dark blue, navy blue, Stefan noticed, not like any other eyes he'd ever seen. "I'm not talking fancy here," she said, suddenly serious. "I'm talking about high stakes."

He sat back in the seat, wiped his mouth with the cloth napkins, and set it next to his plate. "Stakes?"

"The future," she said with an arch of the eyebrow. "Are you willing to gamble on your future?"

"What do you mean gambling? Don't we do a little bit of that every day? Isn't that what gambling is all about? Isn't that what life is all about?"

"Then you're not afraid?"

"We're all afraid."

"I don't mean 'we all.' I mean you. Are *you* afraid?"

He pushed his plate to the side, eager to be rid of it. "Of course," he finally said. "Terrified. Every day. Aren't you?"

"Not any more," she said as she leaned back and lit a cigarette.

He looked around nervously. "I think there's a special car at the back of the train for smoking."

"I know. I hate going back there. All I need are a couple of good hits, and I can get those before the waiter tells me to put it out." She never took her eyes from his. He was mesmerized by those dark blue shiny eyes.

She took a second pull from the cigarette just as the waiter came hustling down the aisle. Stefan admired the way the conductors, porters, and waiters just took the rocking of the train in stride. They never tripped or fell or stumbled or had to hold on to anything, even with a tray of food in their hands.

"Excuse me, miss," the waiter said, but she was stubbing out the butt even as he approached.

"I'm sorry," she said to him, unlocking her eyes from Stefan's for a moment. "I forgot."

"Thank you for your cooperation," he said, then took their dirty dishes and walked away.

Those blue eyes again. There was a storm behind them.

"Come with me," she said, picked up her purse, put her cigarettes into it, then slid out of the booth. She wore a black sheath dress with black stockings and high heels. She didn't need to hold on to anything either, as she walked down the aisle, through the car couplings, and back to her private room. She walked as if she'd been on the train a while.

Most people wore sweatshirts and jeans on the train nowadays. He felt as though she was from a different era, a time when train travel was civilized instead of cheap, social instead of low-class, a place to meet the crème de la crème instead of those whose fears of flying ruled their traveling lives.

And his linen slacks and silk knit polo were irresistible to her game, whatever it may be.

She had a private compartment, as did he. But whereas his had his business suit hanging in the slim closet, his suitcase in the overhead rack, and his briefcase open on the opposite seat with the latest issue of *Field and Stream* on top, her compartment was highly personalized.

She had framed photos on the windowsill. Silk scarves

wrapped around the lightshades. A calendar with photographs of celestial bodies taken by the Hubble telescope hung on the wall. She had piles of books and magazines. She had dirty dishes, and laundry drying on the doorknobs.

She even had a file folder with mail in it.

"Come in," she said, and cleared off the reclining seat opposite hers. "Sit down."

Stefan looked around in amazement. "How far are you traveling?" he asked.

Those blue eyes again. "All the way."

They sat down opposite each other, the muted reddish-orange light echoing the last blast of sunset out the big window.

"If that window didn't take up the whole wall," he said with a smile, "I'd say you'd wallpaper it and put up curtains."

She didn't find that amusing. Instead, she pulled up the little retractable desktop and pulled a deck of over-sized cards out of a plain cardboard box.

She leaned closer to him. Her eyes were bright with eagerness. "Mix the cards in a clockwise direction," she said.

"Just smoosh them up?"

"Whatever. Take your time."

He was humoring her, but he was beginning to feel a little cautionary, too. This woman could be off balance in some way that could spell trouble. He mixed the cards and indicated the photographs, jiggling on the windowsill. "Your kids?"

"Concentrate on the cards."

He smooshed them, then fiddled them back into a deck.

"Now cut them three times."

He did as he was told and handed them to her. She took them with both hands.

"I'm going to draw one card. Only one. It will be your destiny card."

Stefan smiled at her. Those dark blue eyes had long, black lashes to go with them. And dark eyebrows. And dark hair, and white skin. He wished she weren't quite so intense.

"Okay," he said.

She looked up at him, her eyes locked onto his, and she flipped a card over and laid it face up on the table. Neither one of them looked at it; they were looking into each other's eyes. Finally, Stefan looked down.

Death.

He smiled up at her. She was still looking at him. She picked up the card and put it back into the pack. "It was the death card," he said.

"I know," she said, but she hadn't looked at it. "It always is."

"Let me see," Stefan said, and took the cards from her. He'd seen tarot decks before, but didn't know much about them. He quickly shuffled through. They were beautiful, with intricate artwork and many strange symbols, but there was only one death card, and it was not to be mistaken. The hooded reaper with his scythe.

He put the deck back onto the table and smooshed them around again. This time he concentrated. He did it very well, mixing them up, mixing, mixing, mixing. Then he assembled it back into a deck, cut it three times, and handed the deck back to her.

She flipped over a card and didn't even look at it.

Death.

Stefan sat back as she calmly put the card back into the deck.

"What do you mean, it always is?"

"I mean we're going to die on this train."

He stared at her. She looked calmly back at him, the intensity in her eyes replaced by a resigned, peaceful acceptance. "One more time," he said, and took the cards from her.

Death.

He took the death card, ripped in it half, and threw it on the floor. He reshuffled the cards, cut them, handed them to her, and she turned one over.

Death.

He slumped. "How can that be?"

"The cards are bigger than that," she said, indicating the torn card on the floor. "You can't expect a puny act like that to change destiny."

Stefan thought for a moment. "Everybody on this train?"

She shrugged. "You and me. That's all I know so far."

He took the Death card and stood it up on the windowsill, next to a picture of two teenagers. Then he reshuffled the deck and turned over a card.

Death.

With calm, deep blue eyes, she lit a cigarette.

"This isn't funny," he said.

"You're right."

"It's a good trick. But I don't like it." He stood up, and she stubbed out the cigarette. He looked at her, but he had nothing to say. She frightened him, and he didn't know what to do about that. He had no experience with women like her.

He left, and tried to walk down the hall without holding on to anything. He stumbled when the train lurched, and slammed his shoulder into the wall.

Inside his own compartment, the porter had made up the bed, so there was no real place to sit. He undressed, turned on the reading light, got into bed, and picked up his magazine. But he was in no mood to read about fly-fishing.

He clicked off his light and watched the lights pass by the big dark window. He thought of Jane, his wife, a talented violinist, and Stefanie, his daughter, just starting out as a freshman at Juilliard, herself a gifted musician. He thought about his parents, and his job, and his friends.

How would it happen, this death? Train wreck, certainly. If it was to kill them both, then it would surely be a wreck. Would he wake up to the jolt, hear the scream of wrenching metal before it wrapped around his body and ripped it in half?

Or was a bomber aboard? Would a firebomb vaporize him so swiftly that he would not even have time to awaken?

Or would a crazed gunman open fire in the dining car at breakfast, spraying his brains all over the people sitting across from him?

Would his last thought be of his wife, his daughter?

He looked wistfully at the window ledge and wished he had their pictures in a little frame.

Or would his last thought be of that woman, that other woman, that scary woman, and her death's head tarot card?

Stefan got out of bed, pulling on a pair of jeans and a sweatshirt and walked, barefoot, back through the car to her compartment door. He turned the knob and pushed the door open.

She sat, just as he left her, in the chair with the tarot deck on the table in from of her.

"How?" he asked.

She shrugged.

"I'm getting off at the next stop. Get off with me. We'll rent a car or something."

A slow pitying smile tweaked up the corner of her mouth. "This train doesn't stop for us anymore," she said.

And with a shudder, he tried to remember the last time the train had stopped, and he couldn't. He sat down in the chair opposite her. "Where did you get on?"

She shrugged again, and he couldn't remember the name of the city he lived in. Absurd. It was on the top of his tongue. His address was . . . was . . . His wife's name . . . His daughter's . . .

He closed his eyes and felt perspiration bulge out of his pores. He took a deep breath, then indicated the photographs in the frames on her windowsill. "Your family? Your children? What are their names?"

She looked passively at the photographs, then looked back at him, slowly shook her head and shrugged.

Stefan jumped up, his nerves on fire. "I was fine until I ran into you," he said. "Everything was going along just fine until you and your . . ." he pointed at the tarot deck. He looked at her for a moment in frustration, then spun around and left the compartment.

In the hallway, he took a deep breath of train-recirculated air and tried to think, but there was some sort of a Saran wrap feeling about his brain. He leaned his head against the wall and felt the rhythmic motion of the wheels on the rails. He loved that rhythm. He loved riding trains. He'd always loved it.

If he couldn't die in the arms of his wife, he guessed he'd just as soon die on a train.

He looked back at the woman's compartment door. He could probably die in her arms, if he wanted to.

And he wanted to. Never had he met a woman more baffling or more appealing.

He went back to her compartment, opened the door, stepped in, and took her hand. Wordlessly, and with complete understanding, she stood and let him lead her down the aisle to his compartment, where the bed was made and waiting.

In the terrifying urgency with which a dying animal breeds, they clasped lips, tore clothes and merged before falling onto the moving bed. And there, in a wrestling match more aggressive than loving, fighting the movement of the train rather than letting it soothe them, they kicked away restrictive clothing, then clawed and screamed their way to violent orgasms.

She sat up afterward, huddled naked in the corner, one bare shoulder against the cold glass. Stefan lay on his back and looked at her, watched her watch the passing scenery. Now the movement of the train lulled him. The fear and fury of his impotence in the train situation had spurted out along with his bodily fluids, and he felt relaxed and able to deal with whatever was coming. For the moment at least.

She looked at him just before his eyes closed. Those navy blue eyes of hers, against that milk-white skin. How long had she been on the train, he wondered. How long? He'd have to remember to ask. . . .

Stefan startled awake.

She was still sitting at the end of the bed, so he couldn't have been sleeping for long.

"Did you feel it?" he asked. "The train. It stopped."

She looked at him with sadness. "Maybe it did. There's a thing that the train does, perhaps it's just exactly that. Stopping. But I only catch it . . . like out of the corner of my eye." She smiled. "The corner of my id."

She touched his foot. "But the train doesn't stop for us."

"This is fucked," Stefan said, and got up. He pulled

on his jeans and a T-shirt, opened the door, and stepped out into the hallway.

He walked through car after car, seeing no one, finally arriving in the dining car. People were having breakfast. He stopped a waiter. "Excuse me?"

"Sir?" The waiter looked at Stefan's bare feet and frowned.

"What is the next stop?"

The waiter consulted his watch. Then he spoke, and it seemed to Stefan that he spoke in a foreign language. "Pardon?"

The waiter repeated himself, but Stefan still didn't understand. His fear was turning into anger, and its potency had increased.

Stefan stepped closer to the waiter. "I still didn't understand you. Please speak slowly and distinctly."

The waiter spoke again, slowly and distinctly as asked, but it was a word and then a phrase that made no sense to Stefan at all. He looked around, at the woman and her two children sitting at the table next to where he stood.

She spoke, reaffirming what the waiter had said. Then the children said it, as if he was stupid or something, but it was no stop that he had ever heard of before, and chances were, he'd never know it when they did stop.

"Where are you getting off?" he asked the lady.

"There," she said, "at the next stop."

"And what is that?" he asked patiently.

"We just told you," she said, and turned to her menu, frowning at the children to do the same.

But the young girl, she looked up at him with a question mark in her eyes, and he knew that she didn't understand either.

He crouched down and looked at her at eye level. She was about twelve, and had beautiful blonde hair, light blue eyes, and pink pouty lips. "Do you know the name of the next stop?" he asked her gently.

Wide-eyed, she shook her head no.

"I just told you," her mother said.

"Dummy," her brother said.

"Tell me again," she said, and the mother and the brother and the waiter all said it, but it sounded like noise from the throats of otherworldly beings. It sounded like a recording that had been electronically elongated. The girl looked up at Stefan with what appeared to be growing terror. Stefan knew the feeling.

"You're one of us," he said.

The girl clutched her brother's arm.

"Car forty-eight, compartment C."

"Call a cop," the mother said to the waiter.

Stefan stood up with weak knees and reassured her. "That won't be necessary. I mean no harm." He looked again at the girl. "Car forty-eight, compartment C."

The girl nodded, and without a backward glance, he walked away from them, boldly returning the stares of the other diners.

The navy-blue-eyed woman had dressed, and the porter had made up the bed.

"I don't know your name," Stefan said.

"The driver's license in my purse says my name is Mary, but I call myself the Mother of Wands."

Stefan had no response for that remark. Finally, he said, "You don't look like a Mary."

She shrugged, a gesture which was becoming an irritating part of her whole demeanor. Stefan sat down opposite her. "There's another," he said.

"Well," she said. "The event must be getting close. For a long time there was only me. Then you, the Father of Cups, and now, so soon, another."

"How long? How long was there only you? How long have you been on this train?" But he couldn't look at her answer, at the shrug. "It's a little girl."

And with that, a timid knock on the door.

Stefan opened it and she stood there, her hands clasped nervously in front of her. "I'm afraid," she began, "I'm afraid . . . I think they got off the train without me," she said, then began to cry. "I can't find them anywhere." He put his arms around her, then brought her in, and set her in his seat.

"The Daughter of Stones," Mary said. She pulled out her tarot deck, pulled up the little table, and coached the girl on how to shuffle the deck.

Mary flipped over the card, and Stefan didn't even

have to look at it. The sharp intake of breath from the girl told him everything.

Death.

He rang for the porter, who brought a ginger ale for the girl and a bottle of brandy and a bucket of ice for the adults.

"Okay," Stefan said as he poured two stiff brandies, then gulped half of his, "enlighten me."

Mary shuffled through the deck of cards and handed one to him. It was long and smooth, heavy and felt authoritative. On the back was a painting—why hadn't he noticed it before?—of a train. A train at night, the track weaving through a skyscape of stars.

He turned the card over and there was the Father of Cups. It looked like him.

"Let me see the others," he said.

She handed him the Mother of Wands and the Daughter of Stones. There was no doubt. Pictures of Mary and the little girl.

"How many cards in the deck?" he asked.

"Seventy-eight."

He sat down on the arm of the girl's chair. Do you think this train is collecting an entire deck?"

She shrugged.

"Do you think we'll die when the deck is assembled, or do you think we'll be set free?"

"Some group karma to be settled, I imagine," she said.

"Why me? Why you? Why *us*?" Stefan asked. "Is there something else we have in common?"

"I saw a flying saucer once," the girl said, and Stefan remembered a dream he had a long time ago, a dream that terrified him with its implication of the magnitude of his responsibility in the greater scheme of things. The dream made so much sense he sat straight up in bed, saying, "Of course!" and then, with consciousness, the dream vaporized. He couldn't even remember the gist of it. But it was a dream the likes of which he'd never had before or since. It was an extraordinary experience, the residue of which still dusted his psyche.

When the girl said, in her twelve-year-old way, "I saw a flying saucer once," Stefan knew exactly what she meant. She could have said, "We all like the train." Or, "We all have blue eyes." Or, "We're all Americans." Instead, she said instinctively, "I saw a flying saucer once." So had he, after a fashion.

He looked at Mary. She looked back at him, her expression no longer blank and vague. No telling what Mary had experienced, but she resonated with the girl's statement just as he did. Another weirdness to add to the pot.

He finished his brandy and poured himself another, then picked up the cards, turning them over and over in his hands. They felt like a living thing, squirming, almost, in his grip. "Where'd you get these?"

Mary shrugged.

"Don't do that any more," he said. "Don't just shrug. Help me out here. I think there's a way out of this predicament, but we have to work together like a team, like a . . . like a deck, and shrugging doesn't get it."

"I can't remember," she said. "I think they were in my room when I got on the train."

Stefan lay the Daughter of Stones card on the table.

The girl regarded the card with what seemed like adult composure, then turned her pretty eyes up to his. "Looks like me."

"It *is* you," he said.

Stefan turned the cards up one at a time on the table. Some of the faces were familiar. One man he'd seen in the dining car, another was the porter.

"It's happening," Mary said. "Finally."

"Do we go along with it?" Stefan asked.

She shrugged, and caught herself, mid-shrug. She smiled up at him. "What else?"

"Change things."

"One of us could leave," the girl said. "Jump off the train. Then there'd never be a full deck."

"Then the rest of us might just travel on this train for eternity," Mary said, "never fulfilling our destiny."

"But the cards are here for a purpose. To tell us. To alert us. Group karma, you say? Don't you think that happens all the time? People who go to war in the same unit, people who work in the same office, people in the same families. But what about us? We've been gathered."

Another knock on the door. Stefan opened it to find a young woman holding an ice bucket. "Hi, excuse me, but the porter said you had ice," she giggled.

"Seven of Swords," Mary said.

Stefan looked at her. She held up the card, and the woman came in, took it, and looked at it wonderingly. "All four families are represented," Mary said. "Cups, Swords, Wands, and Stones."

"Maybe we should have a meeting," he said.

"I have a feeling we don't have time," Mary said. "As soon as the deck is assembled . . ."

"What's going on in here?" the woman with the ice bucket asked.

Stefan looked at her, smiled, and shrugged the way Mary did, then emptied half the ice bucket into hers. "Party it up," he said, then turned to the little girl. "I want you to take these cards, and match them up with the people on the train. I want to know how close we are to completing the deck."

She nodded, took the tarot deck, and solemnly left, instinctively knowing the gravity of the mission.

"And then what?" Mary asked.

Stefan shrugged. They smiled at each other. "Something to do while we wait," he said. "Although . . . Come on." He grabbed her hand, pulled her up and out the door.

They went down the stairs to the loading platform. The sense of the train's speed was more evident, louder, scarier.

Outside the window, the wide open countryside passed. If he jumped here, assuming he didn't break something in the process, he'd have a long walk to civilization.

Stefan looked for a conductor, but seeing none, he opened the heavy door and pulled it aside.

What passed outside the door was like nothing he had seen before. It certainly wasn't the outdoors scene that showed outside the windows.

The windows looked out on countryside, with trees

and fields, fences, livestock, blue sky, clouds, country roads.

Outside the open door was what appeared to be a continuous sheet of brown paper. Cardboard. There was no horizon, there was nothing beyond the tracks. Stefan thought if he had a long stick or something, he could reach out and touch the paper, perhaps he could tear it and see what lay beyond.

He stuck his head out and looked up. Seamless, dark blue ceiling. The train seemed to be going through a tunnel of cardboard that melded into a dark blue at the top. Stars? Were there stars up there? The train was going too fast to tell. It made his stomach queasy.

He turned and looked out the window in the door on the opposite site. They were passing a pond. Brown ducks floated lazily and white, long-legged birds fished in the shallows. In the distance, dust trailed a tractor.

Stefan looked at Mary, who looked at the floor. Wordlessly, she turned and walked back up the stairs.

Stefan closed the door. Out the window, he saw the outskirts of a small town with a big balloon flying over something—a new shopping mall probably. Never had he felt so hopelessly out of control.

He followed Mary back up to his room, where the little girl waited breathlessly. "They're all here," she said, "except for these ones."

"Major arcane cards," Mary said. "Sun, Moon, Wheel of Fortune, Fool, Hanged Man . . . These don't have people on them. This is it, then. We're all assembled."

Stefan's mouth dried and he sat down in the chair, pulling Mary into his lap. She struggled for a moment. It was such an odd thing for him to do, and yet it also felt like the perfect thing to do.

He flashed for a moment on seeing a tarot layout. Two cards were crossed. He and Mary were crossed.

The compartment door opened. The girl with the ice bucket came in again, and with her came another boy.

"Two of Swords," Mary whispered. "I think we've been shuffled, laid out, and now we're being read."

The idea could not have been more absurd or more appropriate. Everyone stayed still, almost holding their breath. Stefan had an eerie, goosebump feeling that he was being examined, that the lid on his life—whatever it contained—was being pried open and the contents poked around in and stirred up.

Eventually the feeling passed, but then he felt Mary stiffen in his arms, and he knew the same examination was passing through her.

And the train zoomed past towns and cities, through stockyards and switching stations, and on toward twilight.

Several times during the long, strange night, people changed places. Stefan found himself walking through the corridor, passing people whose faces were blank, only to sit, compulsively, next to someone he had never met. They would sit side by side, or facing each other for the duration of that horribly intimate examination, then he would stand again, and walk through the train, zombielike, until the next chair in the next car beckoned irresistibly, and he sat.

While he waited, he looked around and saw a perfect cross-section of humanity. A beautiful teenage girl; a retarded little boy. An old man with years of wisdom on his face, an old woman ravaged by disease and reeking of alcohol. Stefan couldn't remember the details of his life before boarding the train, but he had a feeling about it, kind of a spirit shadow image that felt okay, but not great. A fair amount of satisfaction resided in his habits, but there was a time, he could tell, where he didn't live up to anywhere near his potential, and spent time embarrassing himself and those who loved him.

He wondered if those who were reading his life saw all of that. Was it true that they read his intentions and not necessarily the results of his actions? Or were the results all that mattered?

The train lurched, and everyone in the club car looked around at each other. The train slowed, the wheels grinding, and a new landscape began to show itself out the windows.

Dachau, and the ovens are smoking.

Dresden, and people on fire run screaming through the ruins.

My Lai, and machine guns cut a row of people in half before they fall into the ditch.

Iraq, and burned corpses sit at the wheels of a hundred miles of military jeeps.

Turkey, and bloated, gassed peasants feed flies in the sun.

Los Angeles, and a man is dragged from his truck to be beaten almost to death.

New York, and a jogger is gang-raped, beaten, and left to die.

Cincinnati, and a woman slaps her child and calls him stupid.

Are we the temperature of society, Stefan wondered. *Are we the periodic cross-section that is examined to see whether or not there is hope, whether or not this experiment called "humanity" should continue?*

Whose experiment are we, anyway?

He looked around at his training companions and knew that though his past may have been murky, for the most part, as an adult, he felt he had done the best he could with what he had to work with at the time. At least he hoped he had. He searched his soul and found it wanting, but not by much. He hoped to God that the others found peace in their souls, too.

The grip on him eased as the view out the window returned to normal. It appeared as though they were entering a large metropolitan area. People outside waved to the train as they had always done, all across America.

Stefan felt almost normal. He looked around and saw the others stretching and standing, as if awakening.

We've passed, he thought. *We must be making progress.*

Mary.

He rushed back to her compartment, and she was there, sitting in the seat, her bags packed, the tarot deck on the table before her.

"It's over," he said. "We didn't die."

"Shuffle the cards," she said, her gaze as steady and as intense as ever.

He sat down opposite her and did as he was told. She took the deck from him with both hands. "I'm going to draw one card. Only one." He nodded. She turned up the card.

Judgment.

His eyes locked onto her infinitely deep navy blue eyes.

Heavy footsteps came down the corridor. "St. Louis," the conductor said. "Next stop, St. Louis."

"That's my stop," she said, grabbed her bags, and stood up.

"Will I see you again?" he asked, and even as he did, he knew the answer.

She shrugged.

He helped her with her luggage, and stood on the platform as she disembarked, but aside from a vaguely comfortable, uncertain smile, and a cursory wave, he was pretty sure that she didn't remember him.

But it didn't matter, because he'd be home in the arms of his lovely wife in—he tapped his watch—less than an hour, if the train was on time.

THE ONE THAT GOT AWAY

by Kristine Kathryn Rusch

Kristine Kathryn Rusch has worked as an editor at such places at Pulphouse publishing and most recently *The Magazine of Fantasy & Science Fiction,* though she is currently a full-time writer once more. Forthcoming novels include *Hitler's Angel* and *The Fey: Resistance.* Her short fiction appears in *Mystery Fairy Tales* and *Wizard Fantastic.* A winner of the World Fantasy Award, she lives in Oregon with her husband, author and editor Dean Wesley Smith.

It happened at the Thursday night blackjack tournament, and we were miffed. Not because it happened, but because of *when* it happened. And to get to that will take a bit of explaining, both about the tournament and about us.

There are about ten of us, and we call ourselves the Tuesday/Thursday regulars because we never miss a tournament. The local Native American casino—the Spirit Winds—held an open tournament every Tuesday and Thursday. Anyone could play if he put up twenty bucks, and if he won, he got a share of the pot. The pot consisted of the buy-in fees, and the buy-back fees plus another hundred added by the casino. The casino made no money on the tournament. The game was a freebie designed to get people into the place—and it got me there twice a week.

Me, and nine others. There were more regulars than us, of course, but we were the ones who never skipped a week. I was a pretty good player—I'd made a living counting cards in the mid-seventies—and I'd swear that Tigo Jones had professional card-playing experience as well. Five more of the regulars played basic strategy, and the rest, well, they relied upon luck or God or their moods to supply their strategy. It worked for them every once in a while.

In blackjack, you learn to honor luck.

The good players just try to minimize it. They try to rely on skill. But luck can win out, in the end, if you're not careful.

On most nights, pot's only worth about two hundred to the winner, a hundred to second place, and fifty to third, with four dinner comps to sop the folks who made it to the final round. What that means is that there's good money in this for me and Tigo because we place every four tournaments we play. A few regulars are losing money each time they play, and about five—those basic strategy guys—are giving their gambling fund an occasional shot in the arm.

It's all in good fun, and we've become a family of sorts—the kind of family that barflies make or old ladies make when they work on church social after church social. We look after each other, and we gossip about each other, and we tolerate each other, whether we like each other or not.

We also know who's crazy and who isn't, and, except for Joey, the kid who is pissing his inheritance away twenty dollars at a time, no one who shows up for the blackjack tournaments at Spirit Winds is crazy.

Or, at least, that's what we hope.

That night, I noticed a few strange things before I even made it to Spirit Winds. For one thing, the ocean was so black it was impossible to see. Now, the ocean is never black. It reflects light—and even if the sky is completely dark, the ocean isn't because it's reflecting the light of nearby homes. In fact, I like the ocean on cloudy nights because it has a luminescence all its own, a glow that makes it look alive from within.

The second strange thing was that there was no wind. None. Zero, zip, zilch. We usually have a breeze in Seavy Village and often have more than that. The ocean again. It is a major part of our lives.

And the final strange thing was the power outage that swept through the neighborhoods like anxious fingers pinching out candles. I didn't know about that until later—the casino has backup generators—and if I had known, well, it would have made no difference.

I would have been at the tournament anyway.

I have nothing better to do.

You see, I call myself retired, but really what I am is hiding out. I'm good enough to play in big tournaments, but when Spirit Winds holds its semiannual $10,000 tournament, I'm conveniently out of town. That way, I don't have to fill out a 1099, and I don't have to show three pieces of ID, and all the correct tax information. Because I don't have three valid pieces of ID, and I haven't filed taxes since 1978, the year I fled Nevada with the wrong kind of folks at my heels. I moved too fast to get any fake ID, and so I lived off cash for far too long. By the time I had settled down, I didn't know anybody in that business anymore. The government had closed the loopholes making fake IDs simple for anyone with half a brain, and I really didn't want to put fingers out to the criminal element, since it was the criminal element I'd been running from.

I confessed to a local banker with hippie sympathies, let him think I had been underground since my college activist days, and had him set me up a checking account. It's amazing what a man can do with a checking account—the lies he can tell to get him a real life in a small town.

But it couldn't get me a driver's license, nor could it get me a credit card. I still use cash much of the time, and a lot of that cash comes from my safety deposit box in the aforementioned bank. The gambling at the small casino is just incidental. I figure I'm old enough now that no one would recognize me and my problem is so out of date that the folks who were looking for me are either dead or in prison. But I have learned to be cautious by nature. I don't rub anyone the wrong way.

And I never, ever call attention to myself.

The tournament was big that night, bigger than it had ever been. Later I learned the reason: the power outage. The casino was packed on a Thursday because much of Seavy Village had lost their lights, their heat, and their cable. I had been in the casino since midafternoon. I'd

been on a roll at one of the regular tables, parlaying my
lucky hundred dollar chip into six thousand. Normally
that puts you in tax declaration territory, but I would
get five hundred on one table, then pocket it, and move
to the next. I was hot that afternoon, and it felt good.

Lucky streaks are important. Knowing how to max-
imize them is even more important, and that's what I
was doing. Perfecting the old skills.

When I reached six grand, my brain shut off, and I
decided to replenish it with food. I had a solitary dinner
at the buffet, and then wandered to the tournament
tables.

There were a lot of unfamiliar faces around the table,
and I was burdened with a small fortune in chips, stuck
in my pockets and my fanny pack. I couldn't take anything to the car because I didn't have one, and I also
didn't have time to walk home. I'd been in that situation
before, and I'd learned not to be too friendly. The last
time I'd told one of the regulars about my run and a pit
boss overheard, I had to spend a good fifteen minutes
making a show of losing the money at various tables.

Normally the pit bosses don't tell on me. They tolerate
me and Tigo and the other local professionals. It's the
out-of-towners they kick out of the casino. Oregonians
and their dislike of "foreigners." Gotta love 'em.

That night, though, I wasn't taking any chances. I
leaned against one of the slot machines and smoked a
cigarette, adding to the thick, slightly bluish air already
growing around the tables. The casino is new and modern—no tokens for slots, only cash and cards—high ceil-
ings, good traffic flow. The place feels more like a spa
than a casino, especially the casinos of my heyday. I still
miss the chink-chink of tokens as they clink out of the
machines. I'm not sure I'll ever get used to those electronic beeps. But not even the modern recycling system
was taking care of the cigarette smoke. In a blue-collar
town like Seavy Village, card players get nervous when
more than $50 is on the line.

That night, forty players had signed up for the tournament, and the pot tipped a grand for the first time since
the casino opened.

*   *   *

I'll leave out the detailed descriptions of the rounds, although I can recite all of it, every card, every bet, from the first round, the semifinal round, and the buy-back round. I know by what percentage Tigo beat the odds when he doubled down on eighteen and got a three. I know the exact moment luck abandoned Cherise and it wasn't when she drew a twenty to the dealer's twenty-one. I even know that I made a small mistake on the twenty-ninth hand, and if the cards hadn't gone my way, I would have been out—deservedly so—and it would have peeved me to no end.

I rarely make mistakes.

I can't afford it.

No. I won't say much about the game except that tempers flared early, even among the regulars, because of the amount of money on the table. And people left angry when they were eliminated because everyone could taste his share of the pot.

When it came to the final hand, only the players and the regulars were left.

Tigo and I were on the table, of course, along with the idiot Joey, whose luck was running better than usual, and Smoky Butler, who was a dealer at another casino on the other side of the coast range. The rest of the players weren't regular. Two were bad bettors and even worse strategists who managed to get the right cards at the right time, and the other one was a black-haired woman who'd caught all of our attention.

She looked like she should all be in Monte Carlo, not Seavy Village, Oregon. She wore a black cocktail dress cut in a modified V that revealed more cleavage than I had seen in years. Her hair was pulled into a chignon and over it she wore a cloche hat complete with small veil. Her lips were dark red, and she smoked a cigarette through a cigarette holder.

And she wasn't lucky.

She was good.

Almost as good as me.

The cards were running hot and cold that night, and our pal Joey's luck ran out first. He was off the table in five hands. Then we lost the first of the two bad bettors.

The second was holding in, but not worth our time. He was out by the eleventh hand.

The rest of us, though. The rest of us had a game.

For our buy-in, the casino gives us $500 in tournament chips (which you can't carry to the real tables) per game. The winner, of course, is the person with the most chips after fifteen hands.

By end of the eleventh hand, I had fifteen hundred eighty-five dollars in phony chips.

Tigo had fifteen hundred seventy-five.

Smoky Butler had fifteen hundred and fifty.

And the woman, well, she had two thousand even.

For the first time since I'd left Nevada, I was in a blackjack game where everyone knew how to play. That meant they knew how to draw cards, they knew how to bet, and they knew strategy.

I damned near licked my lips and rubbed my hands together in glee. Instead, I crouched over my chips as if I were protecting them from prying eyes.

We all put out our bets.

The lady put out a hundred.

Smoky put out a hundred and fifty.

Tigo a hundred and twenty-five.

And me, a hundred and fifteen.

Then Rosco, the dealer, began the hand. I was first base (a revolving position), and he gave me an ace of clubs.

Followed by an ace of diamonds for Tigo, an ace of spades for Smoky, and an ace of hearts for the lady.

"They should be playing poker," someone said from behind me.

Rosco gave himself a three of hearts. Then he reached toward the shue for my next card.

At that moment, the lights went out. The place was pitch-black except for several small red dots made by the tips of a hundred cigarettes. I fell across my cards and chips, and Rosco yelled, "Freeze!" to the tournament players. The pit bosses were yelling and the dealers were shouting orders, and some old lady near the slots was wailing at the top of her lungs.

All the time, I kept thinking that this shouldn't be happening. It couldn't be happening. The casino had generators. They should have kicked in. (At the time, I didn't know they'd already kicked in, which meant that they shouldn't have gone off—at least, not all at once.)

Then the lights came back up, or I thought they did, until I realized that the overhead lights in the casino were white, not green. Everyone looked as if they were peering at each other through a fish tank. Even the mystery lady looked green. She was holding her cigarette holder over her chips, and glaring at us all angrily, as if we had caused the problem.

The pit bosses were looking mighty scared. I don't know how much money they had to protect, in chips mostly because the cash disappeared into slots beneath the tables, but I knew it was a lot. And there were more civilians in the casino than pit bosses. Security guards had stationed themselves near the casino banks, and other employees had fanned themselves around the room.

I had never seen anything like it, but it made sense. The casino had to have a drill policy for all types of emergencies.

The place was hot and smoky and everything was green. I kept my hands over my chips and scanned for the source of the light.

As I did, a wind came up. First it licked my hair—or what's left of it—and then it cleared the smoke. At first, I thought the air recycling system had turned back on. Then I realized something greater was happening here.

The source of the green lights were small dervishes the size of my coffee saucers at home. They looked like the alien spaceship out of *ET,* only shrunk down into toy specials for MacDonalds' Happy Meals. Except they worked. Their top was a dark cone, and their base was a rotating series of lights, all various shades of green.

And there must have been thousands of them in that small space. Maybe even millions of them.

They hovered over various tables, avoided the slot machines, and disappeared into the back. The poker room was filled with them. I could see them from my vantage point, lined up like tiny aircraft carriers facing a city, the poker players backing against the wall, hands up.

Five crafts found their places over our table, and a sixth placed itself above the dealer. The woman pulled a small pistol from her handbag, and a pit boss immediately grabbed it from her—firearms are illegal on Indian land. He pointed it, wobbling for a moment, at one of the little crafts, then Rosco said, "If you shoot one and it explodes and we get that green goo all over us and we die, you're going to regret that."

"He'll regret it more if the bullet hits one of us," Smoky said.

"It could ricochet," Tigo added.

The pit boss let the weapon fall to his side. The woman glared at him.

"I wouldn't have missed," she said, as if she blamed him for taking away her opportunity.

The little crafts were above us, whirling and creating the breeze. Rosco had his hand on the money slot. So, it seemed, did every other dealer in the place. We all stared at the things.

"What are they?" Tigo whispered.

I took the question as rhetorical, and apparently so did everyone else because no one answered him.

One of the pit bosses was on the phone, talking with the 911 dispatch. He was whispering loudly, so loudly he may as well have been shouting: "No, really, I'm not kidding. Please . . ."

Aside from the whirs, the soft mumbles of scared patrons, and the wailing woman, the casino was eerily quiet. No electronic beeps and buzzes, no blaring music, no tinkling chords of winning slots. The silence unnerved me more than anything.

"What do they want?" Tigo whispered.

"Ask them," Smoky snapped.

"I feel like I'm in a James Bond movie," the woman said, and that started a ripple of panic through the pit bosses. They apparently hadn't thought of the things as high tech theft devices.

"If you were in a James Bond movie, my dear," I said, "you'd have better lighting." No one looked good in that ugly green. Not even the most beautiful woman in the place.

Then, as if on cue, green lights flared out of the bottom of the tiny crafts. I backed away from the table, chips forgotten. So did everyone else. Rosco let go of his hold on the money slot, and one of the pit bosses screamed at him but—I noted—did not make a move toward the money, the table, or any of the lights.

The lights hit the table and I expected to see big burning holes appear. I was ready to run for cover—all of this going through my mind in the half second it took, mind you—when I realized what was going on.

The cards rose off the surface, whirling and twirling as if they were in a tornado. For a moment, the entire casino was filled with swirling cards. It looked like an elaborate fan dance, or as if green seagulls were swarming the beach, or like an electronic kaleidoscope performance designed especially for us.

Then one by one the cards slid into the crafts through a slot in the sides. They made a slight ca-thunk! as they entered. Then the green tractor lights—what else could they be called?—went out, and the little green ships whirled away.

The doormen and the folks in the parking lot at the time all say the little ships sped out the doors and into a larger ship that had been hovering over the ocean. A number of green slots opened on it, letting the little ships through, and then they disappeared into the night.

The ocean, which had been dark, regained its luminescence, and slowly the lights flickered on all over town.

At least, that's what the outdoor folks said.

Inside, it was chaos. People started shouting and screaming, and that wailing woman continued. A few people stampeded toward the door, and one relatively fit young man got trampled just enough to later attempt a suit against the casino.

Then the lights came back on. The slot machines groaned as they started up, then beeped through their start-up protocol. The slot players, the video poker players, and the keno players all continued with their games except for a few sensible folks who decided to call it a night and left.

I have no idea what happened inside the poker room, but at the tournament table, we counted our chips. The pit bosses put the game on hold as they made sure the money was fine.

It soon became clear the only thing missing from the casino were the cards.

All of them.

Including the decks stored in the back rooms, and the discards waiting to be trucked off the place, and even the little souvenir cards in the gift shop.

Gone.

All gone.

The pit boss who had called 911 was off the phone, saying the police were going to arrive soon, but I suspected it would take them some time. If, as people were saying, things were a mess all over town, it would take the police a while to get anywhere.

"We still have money on the table," Smoky said.

"And a game to finish," Tigo said.

"How do you propose we do that with no cards?" Rosco asked.

"We know what was dealt," the woman said.

"But we don't know the order in the rest of the shue," I said.

"We're going to shuffle a new shue and start over," Rosco said, "just as soon as we get cards."

"We need the other three players," Tigo said. I glanced around me. Joe was standing behind me as he usually did after he got knocked out of a tournament, but the others were nowhere to be seen.

"We're going to have to put this game on hold until the cops arrive anyway," the pit boss said.

"Until we get cards," Rosco added.

"Besides, everyone'll have to report what they saw," Smoky said.

At that point, the woman and I both stood up. "I think my luck has just run out," the woman said.

"Mine, too," I said.

We left the table and headed toward the door.

"Hey!" Tigo said behind us. "We can't replay the game without you guys!"

"I think the game is forfeit," the woman said.

"Yeah, have the casino put the pot in for next week," I said, knowing they never would.

Then she and I walked through the casino, side by side. The conversations were strangely muted, only a few people discussing what they saw. As we stepped outside, we ran into chaos, cars cramming the parking lot, attendants staring at the sky, a warm bath of light all over the town.

A familiar bath of light.

I had missed it more than I realized.

I turned to her. "There's a nice coffee place about a block from here. Care for a walk?"

"I'd love it," she said.

And we had a nice cup of coffee, and a nice evening, and a nice night, and an even better morning. I never learned her name and she never learned mine, but we both knew that we had left the casino for the exact same reason.

We didn't need to see the police.

Or the media.

Or anyone else, for that matter.

"What do you think they wanted with the cards?" she asked long around midnight.

"I don't know," I said. "Maybe they use bigger shues than we do."

And a little later, I said, "That, by far, has to be the strangest thing I ever saw in a casino."

"Really?" she responded. "I've seen stranger."

But she never elaborated and I didn't ask her to.

Some stories are better kept close to the vest.

You see, that isn't the strangest thing I'd ever seen in a casino either.

But it's the only one I'll admit to.

And I only do that because I'm a regular and it's a shared group experience. A bit of local legend—the one game that never finished, the pot that got away.

Well away. The casino had to shut down both the poker and blackjack tables for two days while it ordered cards from all over the country. During the time, regulars gave interviews on every show from *CNN* to *Hard Copy*. Except for me.

I laid low for a while even after my lady left. Laid low and watched the skies.

And wondered—

What would have happened on the thirteenth hand if we had all blackjacked on the twelfth?

What would have happened then?

THE MAN WITH X-RAY EYES

by Richard T. Chizmar

Richard T. Chizmar is the author of over forty published short stories, and the World Fantasy Award-winning editor of *Cemetery Dance* magazine and numerous anthologies, including *Cold Blood, Thrillers, The Earth Strikes Back,* and *Screamplays.* His first short story collection, *Midnight Promises,* was published in hardcover earlier this year.

My father died when I was just a boy.

There was an accident at the mill where he worked. One man lost a leg. Another lost the vision in his right eye and most of his scalp. My father got the worst of it, though—he was crushed to death.

We buried him two days later on a sunny June morning. After the service, most of our friends and relatives came back to the house. A somber parade. They stood in the kitchen and sat around the living room and the den, whispering, crying, nibbling on little sandwiches, and drinking from paper cups.

I stayed outside mostly, sitting in the shade of the front porch.

Most folks didn't know what to say to an eleven-year-old who had just lost his father, so they pretty much left me alone.

After a time, my grandfather came out and sat down next to me on the step. He put his arm around me and we sat there in silence, listening to the grass grow and the birds sing. After a while, I asked him if he felt like crying. He slowly nodded his head and told me what it felt like to bury his only son; how his heart ached with sorrow and swelled with pride all at the same time. He told me that my father dying the way he did was a cruel reminder that life has a way of playing tricks on all of us, that sometimes things aren't the way they seem. And then he told me how much he loved me, how proud he was of me, how much I reminded him of my father.

That was just like Grandpa. He always knew the right thing to say, the right thing to do.

And he was right—life does have a way of playing tricks on all of us.

That was a long time ago; seems like forever. I'm much older now, just turned forty-two last month. My grandfather is gone, of course, and so is my mother. I stayed with her in the old house until she passed away from ovarian cancer in the autumn of '76, and then I sold out to a young couple from somewhere east of Boston. I left town at the age of twenty-one and spent the next five years at the university.

After graduation, I moved back to Coldwater. Just across town, on the other side of the tracks, right next to where the old Lexington Bed and Breakfast used to be. A nice little house with a decent yard and a white painted fence.

I've been there ever since.

I don't date very often. There's just not many opportunities in a small town like Coldwater. At least not for a guy like me. Last time I had a date—six months ago, at least—was with a woman I met at the library one evening. Anne something-or-other. A tall redhead from over in Windhurst. We went to a movie and then out for pizza. She spent most of the night staring at her wristwatch and playing with her hair. We never had a second date.

I'm not lonely, though. I guess I've gotten used to this kind of life. Besides, I always have my kids. I see them at school five days a week and around town most every day. They call my name and wave and sometimes stop to talk. So, it's a rare day that I feel alone or without company.

I teach history over at Coldwater High School. Six classes a day, three with the seniors and three with the sophomores. Been there almost fifteen years now.

My teaching philosophy is simple: work hard and have fun. I try to make all my classes interesting for the kids, plenty of films and graphics and student participation. I think they learn more that way—and that's what's important.

Every year the kids tell me I'm one of their favorites. And every year it means the world to me.

My coworkers don't talk to me much, but that's okay. Sometimes I think they're jealous.

I've never seen a UFO.

I've met a few people who claim they have.

Roy Weideman, a gym teacher from the high school, swears he saw one fly directly overhead one night when he was crappie fishing out on the lake. He told me (and this is a direct quote): "Hell, I almost shit my pants right there in the boat. That's how scared I was."

A lady down the street from where I live—an old friend of my mother—told me she was actually abducted by a UFO when she was a teenager. Said it flew down and landed in the field behind her house early one morning and when she walked out there to investigate, she was zapped unconscious and abducted. Said she woke up in bed, naked, all covered in grass and dirt, her feet cut and bleeding. When she checked the alarm clock on her nightstand, four-and-a-half hours had passed.

Weird stuff, huh?

Sure, like most folks, I've seen them on television and in pictures, but I've never seen a UFO up close and personal.

I wish I would.

I'm not sure how the aliens got here, or when they first arrived.

I saw my first alien the summer I turned sixteen.

Her name was Jenny Glover, and she was new in Coldwater. The weekend after the Fourth of July, her family moved right across the street, into the old Sumner place. She was fifteen, and just like me, an only child.

God, she was beautiful. Long, shiny hair the color of summer wheat. Eyes like an angel. And she liked me.

She actually liked me. She always used to say that I made her laugh.

Those first couple of weeks, we spent all our free time together. Showing her around town. Going to the movies. Playing card games in my basement. I can still remember how my heart felt every time she came close to me or brushed against my skin: like it was going to jump right out of my chest. Jesus, she drove me crazy.

But then, one day, everything changed . . .

We were walking on the dirt path that runs alongside Hanson Creek, taking a shortcut back from the grocery store. About halfway home, we took a break and sat down on an old, fallen log. For a long time, we just sat there, shuffling our feet in the dirt, not looking at each other, talking about nothing. Then she took my hand in her hand, and I knew we were going to kiss. If I didn't faint first.

I looked up into those ice blue eyes, *really* looked for the first time . . .

. . . and I saw something that wasn't human.

Somehow I *saw.*

And then in a flash of sudden understanding a flash of absolute *knowing,* I *knew* what she was, what she intended to do.

And I knew right then and there that I had no other choice.

So I killed her.

The second one was many years later.

I was in college at the time. It was summer break, and I was at Fenway Park, watching the Red Sox and the Mariners. An extra inning game in the middle of a gorgeous August afternoon.

Between the tenth and eleventh innings, I moved down a few dozen rows to a better seat along the third base line. I excused myself and sat down next to a plump, bald man with a smear of mustard on his chin. The man looked up and smiled at me.

I nodded, but didn't return the smile.

He was one of them.

After the game, I followed him home to the suburbs and killed him in his garage.

I've only been wrong once.

And once is enough, believe me.

Happened about a year ago. I was vacationing by myself in Florida. I'd never been to Disney and had always wanted to go.

There was a little girl at the park with her family. Cute as a button, and about that small. Maybe six or seven. She was waiting in line ahead of me with her older sister and brother. She kept looking at me and smiling . . . looking right into my eyes.

And I knew.

Later on, back at the cabin, I discovered my mistake. And it almost killed me. Honestly it did. I couldn't believe it.

Somehow, I had been wrong.

She wasn't one of them after all.

I had killed a human being.

The doctors and the detectives like me. Despite what they suspect, despite where they fear all this is leading, they can't help it. I can tell . . . I can see it in their eyes.

They asked me to write down everything in my own words.

They recorded all of our conversations, but they want something down on paper. Something official, I guess.

First, they want a little history about myself. About my life—past, present, future. That's easy enough.

And, then, about the aliens. They want to know every last detail—starting with the first one I killed out by Hanson Creek when I was sixteen years old and ending with the old lady from just last week.

They want to know how many others I've been able to find over the years. Where? When? How?

They want to know where I've traveled to during my summers off from teaching. Visits with relatives? Vacations? They want to know all of it.

And they want to know about the eyes. The eyes are

very important, they tell me. How do I know the things I know? How do I see the things I see?

They're all very nice to deal with. Very pleasant. And they're patient, too; they never rush me with anything.

Of course, I'll give them all the answers they need. They're on my side now. Or at least, they will be very soon.

Earlier this morning, when I finished telling my story, I gave them directions to my grandfather's cabin in the woods. They left a few hours ago by helicopter, so they should be there by now.

Any time now, I expect a phone to ring somewhere down the hall. Then they'll come for me again. With more questions, I'm sure.

After that, I expect a lot of phones will be ringing. All over the country, probably.

Or maybe not . . . some things are better kept secret.

I took precautions, of course.

Aliens walking our streets is not a very believable story—*Jesus, don't you think I know that?*—so I took some safety measures, just in case.

I cut off their heads.

Each and every one of them. Cut off their heads and saved them. Took them up to my grandfather's cabin. Took Polaroids. Then stripped the flesh with chemicals. Then took more photos. Carefully labeled each one of them—date of death, gender, age, and identity (whenever possible).

Inside my grandfather's cabin, I have all the proof anyone will ever need . . .

Skulls. Hideous looking things.

Skulls of various shapes and sizes—none remotely human, none constructed of anything resembling human bone.

Skulls that will forever change our history.

Over forty of them in all.

They're back from the cabin.

About twenty minutes ago.

They haven't been in to speak with me yet, but I can

see them talking outside in the hallway. The two detectives and the doctor with the long hair.

They're scared. Real scared.

I can see it in their eyes.

CLOSED: DUE TO CURIOSITY

by Robert J. Randisi and Marthayn Pelegrimas

Robert Randisi and Marthayn Pelegrimas live and write in St. Louis, Missouri. Her short fiction has appeared in *American Pulp, Cat Crimes Goes on Holiday,* and *Love Kills.* He is the author of the popular Joe Keough Mystery series, and has short fiction appearing in *The Fatal Frontier, Careless Whispers,* and *Murder Most Irish.*

The first sign appeared a year ago. Someone had used a Magic Marker to hastily write the words: CLOSED DUE TO CURIOSITY. Soon the others were duplicating the sentiment, because there was no better way to say it.

The once gleaming surface of the ship had dulled during the course of the year. The weather, the pigeons, the kids, the tourists, they had all contributed to the demise of the ship's appearance.

The first day it landed—the first day anyone noticed it—it had reflected the sun, intensifying the heat and the glare of the already blinding summer rays. Now it was summer again, and the rays—though still blinding—received no assistance from the metal surface.

At least, everyone had assumed the surface was metal. Once the military appeared and their experts took a look, they decided that if it was metal, it was a type they had never encountered before. Their x-rays couldn't see through it, or scrape it, or mark it in any way.

Stanley, Nebraska, claimed a population of five hundred. An even number, but not the eight hundred and forty it had boasted back in the seventies. Times had gotten hard, and farmers were forced to move up to the big city. When times got better, there seemed no reason to move back to the dinky place. Omaha could offer so much more entertainment, more stimulation.

"I think the first one was Bill Lawrey." Roy sat on a splintered bench with his feet propped up on the UFO.

"Then he told his wife," Kevin said.

"God, they certainly were an ugly couple."

Kevin tossed the silver wrapper from his candy bar into the wind. "My dad says it isn't nice to talk about people that way."

"Just bein' honest. You're gonna have to learn to take life a little easier, boy." Roy patted Kevin on the shoulder.

"I know. So after Mrs. Lawrey came Mrs. Freeman."

"Nora the Mouth. But that was a good thing, her bein' such a gossip, considerin' she owned and operated the *Stanley Sentinel.* People came to her with every bit of news—good and bad."

Kevin kicked at the ship with the toe of his sneaker. "My mom was her friend and didn't even know nothin' until she read about it in the paper. Same as everyone else."

"If your family lived in town, there wouldn't have been any need to read about it. There was so much commotion when the sun came up the next day. A UFO! What a shocker!"

"It looks like it belongs in some alien movie." Kevin kicked harder at the thing he hated.

"That's what everyone said at first. We all thought Nora was out of her mind for callin' the government people like that. What she wouldn't do to get a story. She was somethin'."

"I was standing right there with my dad when the tanks came."

Roy looked past the ship as he remembered. "I've lived in this burg my whole life. Seventy-one years and never seen anythin' like that. It was terrifyin'. We thought we were done for. All those other times—Germany, Korea, Viet Nam—they were all out there, somewhere." He waved his hand like he was swatting away insects. "But this thing," he studied the UFO for a moment, "it was here. In our faces . . . in our park."

"I wish it would get the hell outta here," Kevin complained.

Roy could feel for the boy. His parents had been killed in one of the many riots this thing had started when it first landed. After the shock wore off, end-of-the-world scenarios began and then came the panic. The fear had been so intense it bound logic like a straitjacket.

Roy had felt it, too. Cold, deep in his soul. But it wasn't the same brand of fear the kid or even his folks had felt. That unthinking, blind hysterical fear that told you to run. Run for your life! Run far away before the pod people get you. No, Roy Kenwood had outlived his entire family—even Roy Junior. He wasn't afraid of getting sucked into the ship, being taken away by hideous monsters who would do experiments on his withered body. He was afraid of the nothingness. No excitement for anything. He'd seen a thousand Christmas trees, blown out too many damn candles, and there wasn't any new gadget or gizmo that could make his life enjoyable. But the UFO, now that gave him hope, a reason to get up every morning, eat his breakfast, dress, and wait to be a part of something really important.

"Maybe today it'll open up and someone—or something—will walk out, pretty as you please."

"I'd run home and get my shotgun! Kill 'em all! I'd make 'em pay for the trouble they caused." Kevin stood up and spit. His hatred landed right between the neon pink peace symbol, spray painted by Herbie-the-hippie and a dried pile of pigeon poop.

"If it's hate that keeps you alive right now, more power to you." Roy tried to extend a comforting arm but the fifteen-year-old moved away from the old man's reach.

"Want something to drink? It's only eleven and already too hot." Kevin stood with his hands buried deep in his worn jeans pockets.

Roy shaded his eyes with his right hand and grinned. "Sure. I always liked those flavored teas. Pick me up one at the Convenience. Peach. And don't forget to say 'hey,' to Brenda for me."

They both laughed.

The young farm boy played along. "I think I'll even

tell her you're wondering if you could have a date with her."

"You do that." Roy added another joke. "Do you need some money?"

Kevin turned and shouted over his shoulder, "I'm in a dangerous mood today, Roy. I think I'll just walk in there and take what I want."

Along with the military had come the warnings. Yellow tape was draped around the spacesphip, and citizens were warned that an epidemic could erupt. That was the first wave of panic to hit the small town established in 1830.

But when the local cats and dogs and birds all thrived, in fact seemed to enjoy stretching out on top of the ship to have a nap, things got relaxed.

The guards were allowed to remove their decontamination suits when the temperatures climbed to an unseasonable ninety-eight, sometime around the middle of October. That's when the press moved in for a closer look. *Newsweek* was the first to do a cover story, at least one that was credible enough to entice the tourists. And for a while, it seemed as though the UFO was the best thing to happen to Stanley, Nebraska.

Neglected Victorian homes were suddenly transformed into quaint Bed and Breakfasts. The Holiday Inn on the outskirts of town was booked solid, weeks in advance. Disposable cameras and film sold for three times their normal price. Every citizen became either tour guide or innkeeper.

Dorothy Appleman, who ran the Craft Boutique, a small storefront filled with quilts and handmade dolls, realizing her place suddenly could boast the best view of the UFO, bought four white wrought-iron tables with matching chairs. Her sidewalk cafe had a galactic menu specializing in Neptune cakes and lunar lemonade. Profits were so large she could finally afford that fancy sign. But instead of ordering it with the old name, her shop was resurrected as The Boutique Zone.

The grocery stores all had to hire on extra help. Campers claimed every vacant lot and unpaved space in and outside of town. Supplies were needed—lots of them.

A local artist set up his easel by the fountain and for ten dollars a person with fifteen extra minutes to kill could have his or her portrait sketched with a real life UFO in the background. There were UFO buttons, T-shirts, songs, and even a documentary shot on location starring that guy from the *X-Files*.

Then Joey Dexter spoiled everything by telling his sister he saw something moving around inside the flying saucer. He claimed to have stayed beneath the spacecraft all night, positioning himself so he could watch through a small vent. Joey's sister told their father, and the next day they were packing, warning neighbors that something terrible was soon to happen. It didn't help any that Joey's father was the Lutheran minister, one of the most respected men in Stanley. If such a steadfast, honest man, a person directly connected to God knew it was time to leave town, the rest should follow his lead. It was in that second flood of panic, when cars packed with hysterical drivers and passengers rode the streets and sidewalks to escape alien annihilation, that Kevin's father had been killed.

The owner of the shiny black pickup had gotten impatient waiting in the line of desperate deserters. He had swerved, cutting through the parking lot of the grain store, and pinned the farmer loading his overpriced feed against his old Camaro. Seeing her husband struck down, his wife ran to help. A minivan, following the pickup along the new escape route, ran the screaming woman over in the Co-op's parking lot.

"I still can't get used to just takin' stuff. I keep thinking I'm gonna get arrested." Kevin handed the cold drink to Roy and then plopped down beside him on the bench.

"Nobody to arrest you; nobody to take your money. Enjoy it while you can, boy." Roy took a gulp of the peach tea. "You're never gonna have an opportunity like this again."

"How long do all the people have to be gone before

they think of a place as bein' a ghost town?" Kevin asked, uneasily.

Roy thought a moment. "Longer than a month. And that's all it's been since the last of 'em left. But there's still the two of us, and I figure as long as we're here . . ."

"Yesterday you said just a few more days."

"What's your hurry? We have all this space and quiet, not to mention the food." Roy could never understand youngsters. But Kevin MacDonald wasn't your typical teenager, that was for sure. All the things he had seen, so early on in his life, surely had to have left more fears than a regular person could dream up in a lifetime.

What had been left of Stanley's citizenry, after the Dexter exodus, gathered around the UFO for days . . . waiting. The mayor organized a twenty-four-hour watch plan and all men eighteen years and older were assigned four-hour shifts. And they waited, around the clock . . . for movement from inside, a beep, a glow . . . anything.

That lasted for about three weeks. And then a renewed nonchalance settled in. The holiday season was celebrated as usual. Pumpkins were carved, thanks were given that the little town had survived, unharmed, and Christmas presents were brought. The UFO was even strung with red-and-green twinkling lights, a plastic wreath was stuck to the side, right above the door, or hatch—whatever it was.

Jacob Morgan was out one day, walking his cornfield after a heavy snowstorm. The toes on his left foot had gotten frostbitten the year before so he turned for home because he was starting to feel a burning. At first he thought some kids had come in with snowmobiles, but then he recognized the burned markings as one of those crop circles he'd seen on TV.

Nora the Mouth called a famous researcher in England to report the phenomenon. He told her it was a sign and to expect other spaceships to land in Stanley, Nebraska, very soon. He was positive that the spot had been chosen for an invasion site.

Some people believed it, but most ignored the report. They were so past the point of being scared, they even laughed. Besides, the youngest Morgan boy had been in and out of trouble for years, probably staged the whole thing just to get himself noticed.

No new crop circles were ever reported. Winter brought on comfortable boredom. The UFO became just another tourist attraction. Until three cows were found slaughtered at Ed Wolf's place.

The absence of blood around or inside any of the animals could only mean that alien experiments were being conducted in the night. Autopsies were performed by experts flown in on private jets. They were interviewed by television, radio, newspapers, and magazines. Their inability to explain what was happening unleashed the final and most severe wave of hysteria on the town of Stanley.

Neighbor accused neighbor. Fear gripped reason and logic. Friendships dissolved in the matter of a moment over a single accusation. Threats came to the *Stanley Sentinel* by way of letters, faxes, and scribbled notes tied to rocks that were heaved through the front window.

Money. It came down to money as it always did. Farmers so sure the government was staging the threat to clear the land for their own use. Grocers lost their money and blamed everyone: distributors, afraid to deliver to the doomed town, consumers, afraid to eat anything grown in local soil, even the box boys and cashiers. While tempers raged and threats grew louder, violence moved right in and made itself at home.

Furniture and television sets, smashed or still in their packing crates, lay on sidewalks where the looters had dropped them. It wasn't the property itself but the act of stealing taking it away from some no good, rotten, corporation that was slowly plotting the destruction of the town, the people, the family unit as we know it today. Truth and the American way had to be respected. Hadn't their forefathers rioted in the name of peace, too?

Kevin climbed the ancient oak that had been rooted in the center of Evergreen Park centuries before he had been born. His father used to lift him up on the lowest branch and tell him how he used to climb the very same tree when he was a kid.

"The food can't last forever. And the last delivery to the Hy-Vee only came because of a mistake."

"Praise the Lord for good old-fashioned computer errors," Roy said.

"Aren't you lonely?" Kevin asked.

"Nah. But I do suppose I would be if I were your age. I still don't see why you don't move into town. You could stay at the Stanley Inn, in the Presidential Suite. Could drive out to your place and fetch some things in their Lincoln. I saw it parked in the back yesterday when I was nosing around."

"The tractor's fine. Besides, I'm not old enough to drive a real car yet."

Roy had to laugh at the boy, even at the expense of hurting his feelings. "Kevin, Kevin, Kevin, my boy. Rules and laws, they don't matter here. You're in a special place. Drive a car, for Pete's sake! Eat caviar, get a bottle of the fanciest champagne over at the Liquor Barn. Do whatever you want to do. Have some fun!"

"Ya know what I want to do? What I really, really want to do?" the boy shouted. "I just want to go back to my old school. I guess that ain't gonna happen. I want my mother alive and wakin' me up in the morning. I want to play 'Mortal Kombat' at the arcade with my buddies, and I don't want to be here no more. This place isn't home, it's creepy." He dropped back to the worn-out grass. "I hate it here!"

"What about relatives?" Roy had never wanted to bring up the subject of Kevin's parents for fear of reminding the youngster. But he did think it strange the boy would drive back to that old farm every night and stay all by himself. "There must be someone to come get you."

"My grandpa died last year; that was the last of the old people. My mother's sister lives in New York. They never got on that well and last we heard, she was afraid to come out here. I wouldn't fit in there anyway. I was thinkin' maybe people from some government place would take me to live with a family. I see that on the news all the time."

Roy stood up to stretch his bad leg. "Tell ya what, you come with me. We'll take that old tractor of yours out onto Highway 29 and see what's happening up in Euclid City."

"Now you're talkin'," Kevin ran excitedly around Roy.

"But not today." Roy stretched his back out.

Kevin stopped in front of the old man. "Why not today? Euclid's only thirty miles from here."

"We have to prepare. I need to get my things together—so do you."

"Okay, tomorrow. Positively, absolutely tomorrow, right?"

"If it cools down some." Roy clamped his hands down on the boy's shoulders. Kevin was tall for his age, but Roy still had to look down at least six inches to make eye contact. "Now, listen to me a minute. My eyes can't see good enough to allow me to drive, and you insist on takin' that antique machine of yours. I watch you roll into town every morning. The thing looks like it can't go no faster than ten miles per."

"It can do twenty-five," Kevin corrected.

"Excuse me. But it'll still take us more than an hour to get to Euclid."

"No big deal."

"Not for someone your age. But look at me, son." Roy backed away so Kevin could take him in. "I'm old. I can't take sittin' up there without anything to keep me cool . . ."

"You could wear a hat . . ."

"And the heat?"

"We'll go after sunset."

"Okay. I'll wear a hat, we'll leave when it's cooler. How do you think my back will take more than an hour's worth of all that jigglin' around?"

"I'll fix pillows for you, Roy." Clutching the old man's arm, Kevin pleaded. "I'm afraid to go without you. Please. I'll drive the Lincoln—anything—just don't make me go alone."

Roy embraced the boy. "We're in this thing together, doesn't matter if we're in town or on the highway, we'll stay together."

"Thank you," Kevin said into Roy's warm, damp shirt. "Thanks, Roy."

Nora the Mouth had driven the last car out of Stanley, Nebraska. She didn't have much left worth packing. The rioters had stolen her computers, and supplies and furniture had been destroyed as she watched in terror from the sidewalk. She tried convincing Roy Kenwood to leave with her; she'd known the strong-willed man since he'd married her cousin Wilma, more than forty years ago. She wasn't surprised at all when he declined her invitation.

Roy had lived in the small apartment above the *Sentinel* office since his wife's passing. His tiny room had gone unnoticed when the violence came. But then he didn't have much of anything worth taking.

As he sat in the air-conditioning, rocking, he wondered how long he could tolerate life in the big city of Euclid and why on earth he would want to leave the paradise that his home town had now become. Only one reason he could think of—Kevin. He'd promised the boy and Roy was a man of honor. No matter how comfortable or happy he was with all the quiet and food he could ever want, that frightened look embedded in the poor kid's face haunted him.

But once the boy was settled . . . hell, there was no reason Roy couldn't return to Stanley. The thought cheered him. If he gathered all the canned goods, and his health held out, he could make it.

And then the power went off. The radio fell silent. Roy sat, waiting for things to get back to normal. He could feel the heat seeping through the window, up through the floor. His chair creaked as he slowly moved back and forth. As if signaled by the outage, his thirst became overwhelming but he remembered his wife always cautioning him not to open the refrigerator whenever the electricity went out.

Twenty minutes passed slowly; the thermometer nailed to the wall, registered an increase of ten degrees. Opening the window, Roy searched for the boy. "Kevin? Are ya there?" he shouted toward the park.

"I'm here, Roy."

"We can leave early tomorrow morning. Go home and get ready now. Meet me here around seven."

Kevin walked into town with the blue gym bag slung over his shoulder, convincing himself that a Lincoln Town Car was just lower to the ground and had more metal stuck out in front. He could manage the vehicle . . . no problem.

There it sat, dusty, the front fender missing and all its windows smashed out. The temperature was already in the eighties, but Kevin figured the air-conditioning in the vehicle probably still worked. That should make Roy more agreeable.

Slinging the bag into the back seat, Kevin brushed broken glass onto the driveway. Positioning himself behind the steering wheel, he reached down before realizing there were no keys.

Having seen Kevin turn the corner, Roy came looking for the boy.

"No keys!" Kevin shouted.

"Did you think there'd be a set just waitin' for ya?" Roy sat his Samsonite down on the gravel. "Let an old pro show you how it's done." Lifting the hood up, the old man was stunned to see a greasy cavity where the engine should have been.

Kevin got out of the car and was standing at Roy's side. "Geez. Guess that's why this was the only car left behind, huh?"

Roy let the hood fall loudly back into place. "Guess so."

"I told you I should have driven the tractor."

"I know."

Afraid Roy's resolve would lose them another day or even more, Kevin spoke quickly before his friend could change his mind. "I know! You stay here, sit in the shade, and I'll run home and come back for you. You won't even have to bother yourself, Roy. I'll bring the pillows and one of my dad's old hats. I'll bring us some Cokes too, they should still be cold, even though the fridge stopped working. Guess the electric company figured why bother with a ghost town, huh?" Kevin paused, waiting for Roy to laugh at his joke.

"Calm down. It's okay." Roy knew what the boy was doing and had to smile at the kid's effort. "I promised you we'd leave town together."

"I know, but that was when we thought the car worked."

"No matter. We'll go to your place together. Now pick up your bag."

Kevin reached passed the jagged glass and retrieved his things through the rear window.

Roy picked up his suitcase. "We'll stop by the drug store, they had a big freezer in the back, packed with ice. We'll pick up something for the walk."

"Great thinkin', Roy. Here, let me carry that for you . . ."

Roy started to protest.

". . . just until I get tired and then you can have 'em both."

"Okay, thanks."

It took them ten minutes to find a six-pack of cold drinks, beneath the melting ice. Kevin stuffed the remaining four into his bag, and the two last survivors of Stanley, Nebraska, walked slowly out of town.

The hatch of the UFO creaked as it opened.

No one was there to notice.

"Hello?" A low voice, sounding as though it were amplified over a microphone thick with static, asked, "Is there anyone there?"

HERE'S LOOKING AT UFO, KID

by Lawrence Schimel
& Mark A. Garland

Lawrence Schimel is a coeditor of *Tarot Fantastic* and *Fortune Teller,* among other projects. His stories appear in *Dragon Fantastic, Catfantastic III, Weird Tales from Shakespeare, Phantoms of the Night, Return to Avalon,* the *Sword and Sorceress* series, and many other anthologies. Twenty-four years old, he lives in New York City, where he writes and edits full-time.

Mark A. Garland is the author of several novels, including *Dorella, Demon Blade,* and *The Sword of the Prophets.* His short fiction has appeared in *Xanadu III, Monster Brigade 3000,* and various other publications

Of all the gin joints in all the towns in the world, she walks into mine!

Well, that's not really true. It isn't strictly a gin joint. And it isn't mine. It belongs to my father. And for that matter, she wasn't really a "she."

Yeah, I know that last bit sounds odd, but it's true. She wasn't human.

I'm not sure I wanted to mention that so soon in this account. Some of what I'm going to say gets a bit wild. That's why I wanted a grand opening sentence like the one I used. Something with an air of mystery and intrigue to it.

Besides, it's a line from *Casablanca.* Around here, everything has something to do with *Casablanca.* My dad and I run a restaurant called Rick's Café Americain. It's from *Casablanca,* too. My grandfather built it right after Dad came back from college. He worked in Hollywood as a set designer before he retired to Chicago and opened the restaurant. He built the sets for *Casablanca;*

naturally, the restaurant looks exactly like the one in the movie.

Dad's name is Rick, too, just like in the movie. So's mine. He hasn't come right out and said so, but when Dad retires, I hope to take over for him. I think it's inevitable. I never knew the alien's real name. I called her Ilsa Lund. It just seemed right. Like how everyone calls our piano player Sam, even though his real name is William.

Of course, when she first walked in, I had no idea what to call her. Or what to do. All I knew was, of all the gin joints in all the towns in the world, an alien had walked into ours, and she was wounded.

It was obvious from the start she was an alien, but nobody knew whether to believe she was real or not. That's one of the problems of living on a movie set. Everyone thought it was a joke, an actor wearing an alien mask, hired to play *Casablanca* meets *War of the Worlds*. I did, too, at first. Then I saw the mask hanging out of her hip pocket.

Most of the aliens look just like you and me. They're built like us, pretty much, and they wear faces, human faces, in order to "blend" in. That's what was odd about our alien visitor, she looked . . . *alien.*

Everyone watched her when she came in, but no one moved to help her.

I was certain she was real. Maybe it was the high-pitched, muffled cry as she crossed the room and slumped onto the bar, or the pulsing way her purple skin glowed. Whatever it was, I knew this was more than just a joke.

Dad normally handled anything out of the ordinary like this, which was fine with me. Dad's always cool-headed, always in control, just like Grandad. It's something I've never been able to master. But Dad was on the road trying to find cheaper wholesalers to buy from.

So I handled it. Someone had to do something. She looked like she would die otherwise.

"Sam, help me carry her upstairs."

He got up from the piano and turned on the CD player. We brought her up to the apartment above the café. She was bleeding—thick yellow blood—and for a moment I wasn't sure where to put her. Then I realized it was more important that we save her than the furniture, and put her on the couch.

She held a small, stubby blue cylinder in one hand, which I thought might be a weapon. I took it from her. The finish was dull, and nothing moved anywhere on its surface. I put it down on the coffee table.

"See if you can stop the bleeding," I told Sam. "I'll be back in a moment."

I went downstairs into the café. Everyone was watching me, curious, wondering what was supposed to happen next. I wondered myself.

When in doubt around here, you can always turn to *Casablanca* for a line. I took a Humphrey Bogart stance, faced the customers, and said, "I'm sorry there was a disturbance, folks, but it's all over now. Everything's all right. Just sit down and have a good time. Enjoy yourselves."

But was everything really all right? I wondered, as I went into the kitchen to get a clean tablecloth to tear up for bandages. It was easy enough to repeat a line from a movie. But the alien looked like she'd been badly wounded. I didn't even know how to help a human who'd been shot, let alone a creature from another planet.

I thought it was best not to move her, so I brought a blanket from my bed and tucked her in on the couch. She was asleep now, breathing softly, and the pulsing of her skin seemed more normal. She looked frail and vulnerable lying there, like Mom had been while she was in the hospital, right before she died. I hoped Ilsa wouldn't die as well. I was a bit surprised at the strength of this desire, and the more I thought about it, the more I began to worry. For no sensible reason at all, the longer I sat with her and watched over her, watched her gentle breathing, her purple skin pulsing softly as her chest rose and fell, the more attracted to her I became. It was a feeling I'd never had before; impossible though it was, I seemed to be falling in love.

I wondered if she would like me, if she would want

to speak to me at all? I wondered if she would mind that I had seen her naked; Sam and I had cut her suit from her to bandage her up properly.

It was foolish, I knew, to fall in love with an alien. But I've always been something of a fool for sentimental stuff. If I weren't, I'd probably have been more surprised that aliens even existed. And I probably wouldn't be contemplating spending my life in a café from a movie.

I let her sleep, and fell asleep myself, sitting there at her side.

The next day Ilsa looked better somehow, the color of her skin, smoother breathing. I sat with her most of the day, imagining what it would be like to talk to her, to touch her, to have her touch me back. But she only lay there, recovering. I sat watching her until early evening, when there was an explosion outside. It was too loud to be a car backfiring, I was sure. I went to the window and saw a long furniture delivery truck burning nearer the street corner, just up from the café. When I turned around I saw that the sound had awakened Ilsa. As I stared into her eyes, I expected her to say Ilsa's line, "Was that cannon fire? Or was it my heart pounding?"

What she said was, "They're still chasing me."

I felt very foolish. I hadn't even thought to wonder if whoever had wounded her was still on her trail. It could be dangerous harboring an alien fugitive. *I guess we've become accustomed to danger,* I thought. At least, that's what I wanted to think. What Dad and Grandad would have thought. It just seemed so much easier for them.

I heard a sudden commotion downstairs. Dad wouldn't be back from his trip to the distributors for several weeks, so it was up to me to handle everything. He kept a small revolver in his desk drawer. I had no idea how to use it—I'd never fired or even held a real gun—but just the same I went to the desk and took the weapon out, checking if it was loaded. It was. I stood there a moment, thinking of what I would do with the gun, thinking about what might happen. There was just no way. My Dad reminds me of Rick Blaine, but I couldn't fool myself into thinking I did. I suddenly wished he would get home early.

I put the revolver back and closed the drawer, then

took a deep breath to steady myself. "I'll be downstairs for a while," I told Ilsa. "Try and get some rest. Is there anything you need?"

She smiled at me, a faint smile, but it made me feel weak as a baby. Then she closed her eyes, so I went downstairs to see what the problem was.

The café was silent. Four more aliens had come in, no masks, not even street clothes. They each wore what looked vaguely like tunics and slacks, but were less familiar. They were searching the place: looking under tables, banging through the doors to the kitchen, and generally ruffling the customers. All of them held stubby, blue cylinders like the one Ilsa had, but theirs glowed, brightly toward one end, dim at the other. I wondered if they'd used them to shoot the truck outside?

They had just decided to try the stairs as I came down them. I stood at the base of the stairwell, blocking their way. Desperately, I tried to think of what Bogart would say in this situation. I wished I were Bogart, or Dad.

"I'm sorry, sirs, this is a private residence. Your cash is good at the bar."

"What?" The aliens looked at each other, puzzling over the line. It was only half Bogart's, the other half a line Abdul the bouncer says. But it seemed to work fine in stopping them. Then the leader advanced toward me once more, waving the arm with the weapon, and said, "Do you know who we are?"

"I do," I replied. "You're lucky the bar is open to you." I motioned to Sam, and he started playing.

The leader glared at me, his purple skin pulsing rapidly with anger. I stood my ground, running through all of Rick's lines in *Casablanca*. I knew that if I thought of anything else, I'd realize how much danger I was in and break. I couldn't let Ilsa down. *Here's looking at you, kid,* I thought.

The leader turned and carefully looked around, eyeing every corner of the café. Finally he nodded and stormed out, the others trailing after him. For a few minutes after they had disappeared I stood on the stairs. My legs had forgotten how to move. They felt weak with relief that I was still alive, and I was afraid that the moment I moved them I would tumble down the steps.

Sam left the piano. He came up to me and asked, "Is everything all right?"

"Yeah," I answered. "I'll be upstairs. Let me know if they come back." Somehow, I managed to keep that Humphrey Bogart cool until I was upstairs and out of sight. Then I collapsed.

"Who are you?" I asked her in the morning, when she was again awake.

She opened her mouth to answer, but seemed unable to. "It doesn't translate," she said at last. Her face began to pulsate slowly. I wasn't sure what that meant.

"If it's okay," I said, "we'll call you Ilsa."

She just nodded.

"I'll have Sam bring you up something to eat." I stood up to go downstairs again. "You want anything in particular?"

"It is all the same. We do not taste."

"No taste, huh? Maybe I'll hire you as the cook."

She seemed to grasp the humor. The glow beneath her skin began to ripple. I wanted to tell her she looked beautiful when she laughed. I kept quiet and forced myself to leave her.

There were loud noises outside again. They weren't explosions, but construction sounds: hammering, diesel machines running, men yelling to one another. I had a feeling the aliens were responsible.

"What's going on?" I asked Sam when I got downstairs.

"Those four who were in here yesterday, nosing about, bought the place across the street."

"Thanks, Sam."

I got Ilsa some breakfast, then went back upstairs and looked out the window. Ilsa came and looked over my shoulder. "Do you have any idea what they're up to?" I asked. A crew of construction workers was refacing what used to be a hardware store. A long furniture truck like the one I'd seen burning was parked in front of the dry·cleaners next door.

"None."

We watched in silence. The construction was proceeding amazingly quickly. I said, "They sure work fast, these friends of yours."

I sat with her on the couch and watched her eat. No taste, I wondered briefly. Mostly I just watched her. When I looked across the street again, I saw a crane hoisting something up . . . a sign. When it was in place the crane rolled away. The sign read: *The Blue Parrot.*

I guess I must've had a pained expression, since Ilsa asked, "What's the matter?"

"This doesn't look good," I answered. "Someone's been doing their homework."

"Something's not right," I said. Ilsa and I were down in the café, standing in the front window, watching the aliens across the street. They had disguised themselves now, so they looked human. All four of them were wearing identical masks—of Ferrari. Ilsa wasn't wearing her mask. I'd asked her not to. They smiled and waved at us when they noticed us watching them.

I guess I must've had that pained expression again, as I tried to figure out why all of them were Ferrari.

"It's that movie again, isn't it?" Ilsa asked. "Can so much revolve around one movie?"

"Yes."

She regarded me quietly, as if waiting for me to continue.

"Come on," I said, turning toward the stairs. "It's about time you saw it for yourself. Maybe it'll help us figure out what they're up to. After all, they obviously went and saw it after coming in here. Aside from the fact that the Blue Parrot is the rival of Rick's Café Americain, I can't guess what it is yet."

I had Sam get one of our copies and bring it upstairs. We sat on the couch where she had recovered from being wounded. She had a natural talent for healing, it seemed, since the wound had completely closed up without a trace. One of the benefits of her alien metabolism. I popped the tape in the VCR and we began to watch *Casablanca.*

It wasn't long before Ferrari showed up on screen. I found myself leaning forward slightly, I was paying such close attention.

Ferrari: Hello, Rick.

Rick: Hello, Ferrari. How's business at the Blue Parrot?

Ferrari: Fine, but I would like to buy your café.

Rick: It's not for sale.

Ferrari: You haven't heard my offer.

Rick: It's not for sale at any price.

Ferrari: What do you want for Sam?

Rick: I don't buy or sell human beings.

Ferrari: That's too bad. That's Casablanca's leading commodity. In refugees alone, we—

I hit pause on the VCR, then began to rewind. My stomach felt like it was turning inside out as I thought of the four Ferraris across the street. "I think we just found what they're up to," I said, as I replayed the scene. "Play it again, Sam."

We watched the rest of the movie. Partly, because it was something she just had to see, but also in case it held any more clues.

When Ingrid Bergman showed up on screen, Ilsa turned to me and asked, "This is the Ilsa I am named for?"

"Yeah. Do you mind?"

"No."

She turned back to the movie. I watched her for a little while, then I picked up the dull blue cylinder on the coffee table. "Is this a weapon of some kind?"

"It is a multipurpose tool, used to operate many devices, including my ship. It can also be used as a weapon, yes, but that one is useless. Its energy is gone."

I thought for a while. "Could you make more of those masks, like they did? Any kind of face?"

Ilsa kept watching the movie as she answered me. "Not another one. I can vary the one I have, but that's all. If I had my ship, I could make them easily. But they destroyed it."

"That's what the explosion was?" I asked. "That burning truck was your ship?" She nodded.

"They look uncomfortable," I said, holding up her mask of a woman's face.

"They are."

I turned back to watching the movie as well. "That's okay. I like you fine the way you are."

When the movie ended, I decided it was time for some serious questions and answers. Ilsa and I were still sitting together on the couch. "I know so very little about you," I said.

"Isn't that my line? In the movie, at least."

I smiled. She had paid close attention, then. From now on she'd understand when I quoted things. Soon, I figured, she'd be quoting the movie at me.

"Who are you really?" I asked her, Humphrey Bogart to Ingrid Bergman. "And what were you before? What did you do and what did you think?"

"We said 'no questions.' "

"Here's looking at you, kid."

Her skin rippled deep purple with gentle laughter. She was enjoying our game of quoting from the movie. I was warm inside, and felt that my skin was rippling purple as well. Perhaps it was just the reflection of the glow from her skin on mine.

"Be serious," I said, sinking back into the couch as I stared at her. "Who are you really?"

Ilsa thought for a long moment before answering. "It is fitting that I wound up here. I am indeed very much like the characters in this movie, around which so much seems to revolve. I am like someone fleeing from the Germans. From the Nazis?" She looked at me for confirmation, and I remembered suddenly that English was a foreign language to her, despite how fluently she spoke it. I nodded that she had used the correct word, and she continued.

"But I think perhaps you should have named me Lazlo instead. Like him, I am a leader of the revolution. Some of us do not approve of the things the . . . ah, high command does, the way they exploit or destroy every civilization they discover. The four who are chasing me are like Major Strasser, or worse. They are busy with their new enterprise now, I think, but eventually they will get back to me. They have no intentions to bring me away with them or to keep me here, though.

I will simply be gotten rid of, once they're finished with me."

The warm feeling inside had disappeared, replaced by an unnatural chill. "Finished?"

"They want me to tell them the names of other members and leaders of the revolution. I will not."

My head was swimming with questions to ask her. But some were more important than others. "Do you think I'm right about what they're doing, then, across the street in the Blue Parrot? Smuggling people on a black market, like in the movie?"

Ilsa sighed, which made the pulsing of her skin slow. "It is likely. They will start with the street people, those no one will miss. They take a few humans here, a few there, but in time they will take more. They have subjugated many different worlds. It is hard for the resistance to keep up these days. Here, they have found another mission. And there is nothing anyone can do. They destroyed my ship. I have nothing to fight with, and no way to contact the resistance."

"Your friends could help?"

She nodded. "But there is no hope of that now."

"Don't talk like that," I said, shaking her gently. "There has to be a way to fight them still. We've got to! Everyone's got to. We can't let them kidnap people. What will they do with them?"

"First they take specimens to study and observe, so they know how best to conquer and exploit this world. Then they take some for amusement, the newest toy, the new pet. The rest will likely be taken for slave labor."

I tried desperately to think of a plan. Maybe I couldn't get her off the planet, but if I had enough money I could get her, and myself, out of Chicago. We could disappear until . . . Until when?

I got up and went to the window again. The construction crews had gone home for the day, leaving only the neon BLUE PARROT sign out front, and a furniture truck next door.

"I'd call the police," I said, "but we don't have any proof, and it all sounds so implausible. Aliens invading the Earth. They'd lock me up."

My mind was racing as I tried to think of a solution.

"What we need," I said, "is your letter of transit. After all, you're Ilsa Lund. No matter what, we'll get you away."

"Sam, I need a favor from you. Go to the Blue Parrot and tell them I'm not happy here. Ask them if they'll do better for me over there. Tell them I can't handle things here, that I just want out, and I'd probably sell the place for the right offer."

"We should wait for your father," Sam said, eyeing me with obvious distress. I was straining his loyalties.

"We can't. We have to act now. Will you do that for me, Sam? It's terribly important. Not just for Ilsa. For the entire world."

Sam glared at me, then looked over my shoulder, at Ilsa. Her skin glowed imploringly as she begged him, "Please." I could tell he was thinking about my last line, "For the entire world," that it was running through his head over and over again and he was realizing that these were really aliens we were dealing with.

"All right, all right," Sam said. "I can't believe I'm going to do this. When I get back, I'll need a drink." Sam turned and started toward the door.

I smiled at Ilsa. The plan was underway. But I think she realized it was a weak smile. Inside, my stomach felt like an octopus doing gymnastics.

We waited for Sam to come back. I began to sing "As Time Goes By," softly, almost under my breath. It seemed fitting. It's the song Sam plays in the movie. I hoped it would bring him luck.

Ilsa turned to me from the window and asked, "What is a kiss like?"

I moved closer to her, and held her in my arms. Leaning forward, I kissed her. I could feel the warm glow of her skin on my lips as our breath mingled.

"Don't men and women do that on your planet?"

"On my planet there are no men and women. We have three genders. Kiss me again."

Three genders? I knew I was a fool to fall for an alien. I leaned forward and kissed her again.

*   *   *

"They want to talk to you," Sam said when he came back.

I felt my shirt growing wet under my arms. "Thanks."

"Tell me," Sam begged, "that you really know what you're doing."

I looked him square in the eye, but only said, "I hope so."

"You shouldn't even be interested in politics," he went on. "The problems of the world—or the whole universe—aren't your department. You're a saloon keeper." He glanced at Ilsa, then quickly looked away.

I knew he was nervous and afraid. He was quoting Rick's lines from *Casablanca,* just like I did when I was scared.

"I stick my neck out for nobody?" I replied, Bogart's line.

"Yeah," Sam answered.

"But Rick did, and I think my dad would, too."

Sam's expression changed, a slight grin. "Yeah, maybe. But you're not your father."

He was just saying it, just pointing out the fact. But it hurt.

"I guess it's time to go," I said.

Sam considered me a moment longer, then nodded. "What's the plan?"

"We close the café, then you and I go over there."

Sam looked concerned, that same look I imagined I wore a lot lately. "If Ilsa is left here alone, they might come search the place for her."

"Yes," I said. "I know."

We decided on a direct approach. We took our time crossing the street, then we walked in through the front door of the Blue Parrot. Two of the four Ferraris were at the bar. The other two were waiting at a table near the door. As soon as we got past them they both got up and left, headed, I was sure, for the other side of the street. The two remaining Ferraris moved toward a table in the corner where we joined them.

Ferraris: Hello, Rick.

Rick: Hello, Ferraris. How's business at the Blue Parrot?

Ferrari: Fine, but we would like to buy your café.
Rick: It may be for sale.

One of the aliens invited me to sit down. We stood.
"We're leaving, Ilsa and I. We need the money."
"Why would we let you do that?" the Ferraris asked.
"Because you don't need her around, and my way,
she won't be. It's as simply as that. Everybody gets what
they want."
Both Ferraris smiled. "Very well," one of them said.
"We've taken the liberty of drawing up some papers for
you to sign."
One Ferrari handed the papers to the other, and they
spread them on the table. Sam stayed where he was as
I went around the table. When I stood between them, I
looked up at Sam, and nodded. He pulled the revolver
out from under his jacket and pointed it at the aliens.
They looked at him, then reached into their ample pants
pockets, but I put one hand on each of them and said,
"I wouldn't get careless, if I were you. Take those out
slowly, and give them to me."
The little blue cylinders glowed brightly as I handled
them. I backed away from the aliens, then traded with
Sam, the two cylinders for the pistol.
"You'll never get away with it," one Ferrari told us.
"With what?" I asked.
"With whatever you're trying to do," the other Ferrari
said. "We will have her, and you."
"I think you'd better watch the movie again," I said.
We directed them to a storage room, then locked them
inside, and hurried out. We ran down the street to the
furniture truck. With one of the fully charged cylinders
it took only a moment to get the hidden panel in the side
to open up. I helped pull the Sam mask off Ilsa's face.
"I must get back to the revolution," she said. "They
need me. But I will return someday. Plans must be made
to protect your planet from subjugation. And the revolution will need you, Rick."
"We might stay closed until my father gets back, let
things cool down a little. With you gone, they'll leave
me alone, for the time being. I figure I can stay closed

about three weeks, and still keep everyone on salary. But I'll be around."

She turned toward the door of the ship, then back to me again. "Not just the revolution, Rick. I will need you, too. Kiss me once more."

I stepped forward, and we embraced. I will always remember the feel of her skin as it pulsed softly beneath my fingers, the soft purple glow.

When we pulled away from each other, she turned and entered the ship. I stepped back and watched as it silently rolled a few doors down the street, then took off. I thought of her last words, and compared them to Ilsa's line before she abandons Rick, "Kiss me. Kiss me as if it were the last time." She hadn't said that.

I think this is the beginning of a beautiful friendship.

LOVE LIES BLEEDIN'
by Billie Sue Mosiman

Billie Sue Mosiman is the author of the Edgar-nominated novel *Night Cruise*. She has published more than ninety short stories in various magazines, including *Realms of Fantasy* and in various anthologies such as *Tales from the Great Turtle* and *Tapestries: Magic the Gathering*. Her latest novel is *Stiletto*.

Jo Bettle stooped in the flower bed beneath the dappled shade of a weathered homemade trellis pergola, her glasses slipping down the bridge of her nose on the fine film of sweat that coated her face. She pushed the glasses up again with her middle finger and let out an exasperated sigh. Without glasses, the world was a place of aquarium green swimming with motes of gold from the sun. She couldn't see a thing clearly.

Al sat in the wicker rocker on the narrow cement porch that ran the length of the ranch house. She could feel his gaze through the muslin material of her shirt and gloried in that quiet, unobtrusive attention. Though married thirty years, she adored her husband with something bordering on worship. When he watched her as she worked the gardens, she glowed with an aura of happiness.

Jo pulled out a few more weeds that were trying to strangle the heavenly blue morning glory vines. When finally she looked over at Al, he was smiling. A rare occurrence these days.

She returned a tentative smile and said, "What were you thinking?"

"How nothing can stop you from working in the flowers. Not heat, not rain, not the Delerias . . ."

She made a face before she could stop herself. Then

she looked behind her and up above, at the sky, afraid there might be a Watcher near to hear him. They weren't supposed to discuss the Delerias. You could be imprisoned in one of the national compounds for many years if they thought you were speaking ill of them.

"Oh, you're so afraid all the time," Al said, looking away from her to watch a lemon yellow butterfly dance over the scarlet heads of the lobelia, the cardinal flower.

"Please . . ." She unfolded from her crouched position near the ground and stood to massage the small of her back. She wasn't as young as she wished she were, but except for a few minor aches and pains, she could still work hard in her gardens without too much complaint. Flowers were her passion and, except for Al, her reason to exist. All other activity and entertainment had been stripped from them with the coming of the Delerias. They were encouraged to garden, especially herbs and vegetables, in order to help feed themselves.

She remembered the proclamation, a bit of stilted rhetoric that was flashed over the globe: "Henceforth Man shall plant seed and grow as much of his own food as possible. Population growth is out of bounds. Over-production of children will force you into starvation unless you follow our directives. Even small urban plots of Earth shall be made productive. This is the law."

Jo had already been growing food for years, so she did not feel as deprived as most other people who depended on grocery stores to feed them and the television and computer networks for their fun. She had to admit she rather missed movies after Hollywood had been dismantled and made into a distribution center. But then they all missed a lot of what they'd taken for granted before.

Al stared at her again, this time without smiling. "Why are you so afraid?"

"Why do you persist in bringing this up? You know it's dangerous."

He took the beer from the small table to his left into his fist, the dark bottle dotted with droplets of moisture. He gripped it a moment then shook it in front of him, slopping some of the beer onto his knees. He hadn't shaken it at her. She knew he shook it in outrage at how the world was managed, how truly dangerous it was to be an individual with independent thoughts.

·"I can't *not* speak of it. Your timidity gets on my nerves, Jo. You used to have some . . . fire . . . about you. Remember when we marched with Martin Luther King? Remember protesting Vietnam?" The pain in his voice lessened until it was no more than deep sadness. He said, "I remember. I remember the way you were. They can't take that from me."

Jo wiped down the knees of her jeans to loosen the soil from where she'd kneeled. She didn't want him to see her face. She nursed her own sadness at the losses they'd endured. It was true she used to be a fighter. Al laughingly called her "The Protest Kid" when she was young, when she was riled and determined to engage the devil of inequality or the demon of poverty. Nothing, it seemed, could stop her. She joined organizations, sent out flyers, wrote pamphlets, participated in sit-ins and protests and marches. She gave speeches, gathered supporters, wrote letters to Congress and the president.

She had been a firebrand in her day. For all the good it did her. How were they to know it was not mankind who would bring about total change, but invaders from the heavens?

But no more was she a fighter, it was true; Al was right to mourn for her. Since the invasion, since the day the sky filled with dull metallic saucers bringing down a dominating force and one world order, she had become more and more silent, less and less involved, until now, in her fifty-sixth year on Earth, she was but one more crippled, frightened citizen dominated by the terror of reprisal.

"I'm sorry, Jo." He stood up from the rocker and met her as she walked slowly down the brick path to the porch. He took her into the circle of his arms and brushed his lips across her cheek, burying his face in her hair. "Jo, Jo, I'm sorry."

"Come inside where it's cool," she said, stepping away from his embrace. "I'll make sandwiches for lunch."

The big problem was how much time they had on their hands. Al had been an engineer for the army, but now the military was disbanded and every job Al could do had been taken over by robots, sending Al into early retirement. He was not a man who could sit around the house all day with nothing to do. It made him brood.

She had no idea that it also allowed him the time and gave him the incentive to plot.

In the Reign of the Dark Mind, brought on by the Delerias, Jo and Al Bettle were named outcasts early on. For one thing, by the new decree that favored youthful entrepreneurs, they were too old and mired in the past to be useful. For another, they hadn't any skills deemed strictly necessary to the betterment of the new age and the civilization the aliens meant to erect.

When Al was forced into retirement, he was first taken to a reeducation camp and thoroughly questioned, probed, and drilled in what he could and could not do in his new life of leisure. He had never forgiven the invaders for that. It was enough that they had come down by the millions and taken over Al's mother planet, enough that they had dismantled the United States government (and all other governments) to install their own brand of governing, enough that they caused fear and panic to spread so deeply that too many Americans died in revolution and battle. But that they would take him from his work and then tell him he was not to congregate with other men, he was to remain at home away from society, and he would, by damn, *like it*—that was too much.

Jo tried in the first year to involve him in gardening with her, but although he would do the heavy tilling and weeding when required, he had no interest in growing things. She tried, also, to talk him into writing about his early life when he was a drafted foot soldier in Nam and had saved his platoon from disaster one muggy hot night in the jungles. At least that would have kept him interested and engaged.

Al resisted any effort to get him onto another track. Nothing, he told Jo, would alleviate the boredom, the strain and stress of oppression they were under, the failure of the dominating species to mark out dependable paths for the disenfranchised such as he.

Jo took the change better than most. She had stopped

working as a mystery novelist the year before—just gave it up as a bad job and inconsequential—and had devoted herself to home and land. Their two acres on the outskirts of a sleepy Southern town were all that mattered to her. Her aim was to turn it into a paradise unparalleled this side of Eden. Gardening was more than providing food for the table. It was an addiction that led her into the land of no-mind, the source of bliss other people often searched for relentlessly using the aid of chemicals.

If she and Al were to be outcasts and ignored, it was all the same to her. She had never had many friends, not dear ones, and most of her family had moved to the East Coast to take jobs with the new order.

If only Al would settle down, she thought she could be content despite how all the world and her life had changed.

She hadn't the hint of an idea what might be the trouble the day two members of the Scream Team came to their house and asked politely to see her husband.

It was early, the sun just rising, dew still on the roses she could see beyond her windows. Al was in the shower. Jo hurried to the back of the house to the bath off their bedroom and shut herself inside. She reached through the shower curtain and turned off the water.

Al said, "Hey! I'm not through yet. Jo? What the hell?"

Jo faced her husband, her stunned gaze and trembling telling him all he needed to know.

"They're here," he said.

"Yes. They want to speak with you. Al, what have you done?"

No one was visited by the Scream Team unless he had broken some rule. The title of this squad of goons was a misnomer. They did not scream. In fact, they hardly raised their voices above whispers from the attached boxes on their chests that translated their words into English. What they did to deserve their title was to make whoever they visited scream with despair. They were always bearers of bad news.

And now they were here for her husband.

"Tell me, hurry, they're waiting. What have you done? Why are they here? Is it a mistake?"

Al stepped from the shower and toweled himself dry. She couldn't stop looking at the rounded cheeks of his buttocks and the hard muscles in his back. He was still in excellent shape for a man nearly sixty years old. Just the sight of his naked flesh infused her with torrid longings to lie in his arms, to feel him inside her.

He turned, the towel drooping in his hands. "I formed a coalition. Those days I go shopping for you in town? You complain how long it takes me? I brought together some . . . like-minded individuals. I guess the Delerias found out despite our best efforts at subterfuge."

"You what?"

"I can't live this way, Jo. You must have known I couldn't."

She wanted to burst out crying. She wanted to tell him that it was true, he couldn't live this way, not if he went against the order laid down by their invaders. He would be separated from her, perhaps forever. She wanted to smack his face, hard, for deceiving her, for doing something so insane, so *useless*. She wanted to grab him into her arms and protect him, never let him go. Oh, God. Oh, God, no.

The Scream Team stood exactly where they had been when Jo left them to collect her husband. Al walked in front of her, pushing her behind him. He went up to the Team and said, "I am Al Bettle. What can I do for you, gentlemen?" He made it sound as sarcastic as he could, though it was all lost on the alien minds behind the immobile humanlike masks they wore.

"You are accused and convicted of bringing together an alliance against us. We cannot have an uprising. Your sentence will be carried out at oh-six-hundred tomorrow morning. You have one twenty-four-hour period to say good-bye to your mate." With this, the one speaking made a military turn and his companion, a small silent observer, followed him out the door.

Jo stood at the window, the curtain in her hand, watching them leave in one of their flying machines that defied gravity and logic. It was a small cigar-shaped ship that zoomed its passengers straight up into the clouds in

so few seconds it was as if it disappeared rather than
ascended. She had never understood the logistics of
faster-than-light travel that had brought them here in
the first place, much less how their Skimmers and Fleet-
men worked.

When they were out of sight, Jo slumped. Al came
up behind her and put his arms around her waist. He
whispered, "I couldn't help it. You know that, don't
you? It was out of my control."

"Oh, Al, what's going to happen now?"

"I don't know."

"Will they do something to your mind? Or will they
just kill you?"

"I honestly don't know."

"Either way, I've lost you. Al, I can't live without . . ."

He turned her around and hushed her next words by
kissing her hard on the lips. When he pulled back, he
looked down into her brown eyes watering with tears.
He removed her glasses and smoothed away the damp-
ness on her cheeks. He said, "You have your flowers.
You can go on without me."

She laughed harshly, drew away, and sat down at the
dining table. She had her flowers, her gardens. She had
her silences and her solitude and the passion born of
making things live and prosper in the soil. But none of
it was worthwhile if she didn't have Al. She might as
well be dead and she knew he knew that.

They did not murder Al Bettle, but should have.

Jo stood over him in the wicker rocker, grieving. They
had come a week ago, at six o'clock, just as they said
they would, to mete out punishment. They had restrained her and made her listen while her husband
screamed in agony. She buried her face in her hands,
refusing to watch the destruction of the man she loved.

When they were done, they dropped her to the floor
from the force field that had her bound, as if in an iron
collar, from waist to ankles. They left the house, stiff
manlike creatures, heartless, cruel, and extremely effi-
cient in their methods to still dissenters like Al.

Jo ran to him, dropping to her knees, taking his limp
body onto her lap, crooning into his face, dripping new

tears over his closed eyes. "Oh, Al, please talk to me, can you talk to me?"

When he came to, he did not recognize her, nor where he was or who he might be. He could hardly speak, his words blinkered by memory loss. He was no longer Al, not the Al Jo had known all these years. He was mindless as a dried sponge lying dead along a seashore. He needed help walking. He had to be spoon-fed. He could not go to the bathroom alone or be left in a room without watching over him for he panicked, forgetting where he was and why.

He was definitely no more threat to the Delerias.

Now Jo stood over him and could hardly withhold her fury. She felt the fire she used to have return, kindling the coal-black depths of her soul to flame.

"They won't get away with this," she told the top of her husband's nodding head. "They'll pay for this if it kills me."

She didn't even bother to check her surroundings for a Watcher. She was beyond caring if they heard her or suspected her of subversion. Let them pounce on her from the wood's edge or abruptly descend out of the sky, lighting above her green lawn like a hovering giant horsefly. She was no longer afraid of what might happen to her now that they'd taken Al away. Frontal engagement would suit her fine. She would claw away their masks and embed her nails in their bulbous eyes if they came for her. She would do what damage she could and damn the consequences.

Now that they'd taken Al away.

Jo lay on her back in bed next to Al, feeling his body warmth beneath the sheet. On the ceiling above her head twinkled a fluorescent star galaxy she and Al had put up in a moment of childish fancy. They had found them at the discount store and stood on the bed's mattress giggling, naked as jays, while sticking the little stars in place. When the overhead light was turned off, the room took on a phosphorescence that glittered like new worlds circling lazily overhead. They had fallen together onto the bed, admiring their handiwork, their hands exploring one another, stimulating the lust they shared.

Who could have imagined that the real sky was seeded with life? Hungry, alien, ambitious life?

Now Al cared no more for the ceiling stars than he did for her thrumming body. He could not make love to her, had no urge for sex, was impotent as well as mindless. She thought she missed the intimacy of sex more than their quiet talks together. When they'd made love, she was lost to the original world and entered one of euphoria. Unlike many long-married couples, she and Al led an active, steamy sex life. Until now.

Now Jo was relegated to lying on her back in the dark, staring into the starred distance on her ceiling, imagining the light-years the Delerias had traveled to come here, trying to still her rapid heart.

She still talked to Al, though less than before. She felt herself slipping into muteness since she already lived with a ghost, who if he did mutter something, made absolutely no sense.

She blinked her eyes, holding them closed for long periods, then opening her lids wide to see the stars overhead swirl as if set off into great looping movements by the hand of God. She said in a soft voice to the sleeping Al, "Maybe if we'd had children, I could have found solace in a family."

She bit down on her tongue. "I don't mean to sound regretful. It wasn't your fault. We both agreed, we made our decision. But this . . . this Death in Life, I'm afraid that's all your fault. You admitted it the day you came from the shower and knew they were here. It was the most selfish thing you ever did, Al, starting that group to conspire against the aliens. And look what good it did. Your coconspirators are all dead like you, and nothing has changed.

"Didn't you know you couldn't win?"

It had always been self-evident to her. If the military could not contain the Delerias, who could? Why begin a cabal that is doomed from the start? It was the ultimate in foolhardiness. Hadn't she warned him against following his rebellious nature?

She turned onto her side to cradle one of his heavy arms against her breasts. She slipped his limp hand down between her drawn-up thighs and shut her eyes to dream.

Delerias roamed every city and hamlet, keeping the peace, ordering around humans, watching for insubordination. The only place they were not in evidence was in the homes. That is where Jo knew she must start her mutiny. Even though she knew she would not have much better luck than her husband, she had to try. If someone had taken away her land, her home, her flowers, she could forgive him. But there was no forgiveness for taking away her husband.

There had been such paranoia in the beginning of the invasion that many people believed the aliens had in some manner bugged their homes and grounds. This was widely thought possible until they understood it was an unnecessary precaution. The aliens had the Watchers. Small, sky-blue, automated flying eyes that were shaped like boxes with hairlike antenna. It was understood the Watchers taped and recorded any unusual movements or gatherings around home sites. If there were more than two humans at a time entering a home, a report was sent back to headquarters.

As Jo worked in the front garden bed, setting out divisions of daylilies, she thought about the problem of the Watchers and how to circumvent them.

What if people came to her one at a time, over a period of several hours? Would the little sky-spies notice and make a report? Or better yet, what if she went to her neighbors to plead for their help?

This afternoon she would go to people who lived in her rural neighborhood and try to start trouble. Trouble was to be her middle name. Trouble was to be her way of life.

She tamped down the earth over the transplants, watered them thoroughly from the watering can, and sat back on her heels. She said to Al, sitting in his place on the porch, "I should have known it would end this way."

Spittle ran down his chin as his head drooped forward onto his chest like the heavy bud of a rose. His fingers danced on the arms of the rocker, tapping out the minutes of his life.

She thought once again that soon she would have to put him to sleep. He was no longer her Al. She couldn't stand watching his deterioration much longer.

Appropriately, Jo took small bouquets of Love Lies Bleedin' with her on each neighborly visit. The small pendulous red flowers became her statement and her plea. The neighbors grew vegetables, not flowers, so they did not know the name of the flower she brought to them, or its significance, but that wasn't the point. Jo had no need to make her symbolism understood, only her true aim.

Flagg Johnson lived alone at the end of the road. He was the sixth neighbor she visited, trailing her sorrow like a widow's veil. She knocked on his door and when he opened it, thrust forward the bunch of pendant flowers. He looked surprised to see her, perhaps to see anyone at all at his door, for it was well-known on the street that he was a hermit and didn't care for the intrusion of company.

His expression adjusted from surprise to mourning when he took the flowers from her hand. "What is this? Has someone died?"

It was Jo's turn to show surprise. "You know this flower?"

"Love Lies Bleedin'. Difficult to grow in our hot humid summer. If you've grown it successfully and you've picked it to bring to me, it must mean something special. Will you come inside out of the sun?"

He held open the screen door and allowed her entrance. He gestured toward an informal setting of chairs around a big square oak coffee table littered and piled with books. She watched him at the sink, filling a vase with water. The house smelled fresh, like watercress found at a stream's edge. The windows stood open and a breeze circulated with the help of ceiling fans.

"It's my husband," she said.

"Al? How is Al these days?"

She had forgotten they had once gone hunting together in the woods surrounding the neighborhood. Though not bosom buddies, they had been slight friends.

"I guess you haven't heard. The Scream Team came for him and . . . and they . . . destroyed his mind."

Johnson stopped arranging the flower stems in the vase, frozen for moments, his gaze downcast. Finally he brought the vase from the adjoining kitchen and set it in the front window. He turned to where she sat in one of the old comfortable chairs and said, "He tried to undermine them?"

She nodded and looked away form him to keep from puddling up. Her visits had been difficult when she spoke of Al. This was no less so.

"Your love lies bleeding," he said softly. He crossed the room, sat in a chair near her, and took her hands into his own. "How can I help you, Jo?"

"Do you think there is any way to hurt them back? Am I crazy for even thinking there might be?"

He let go of her hands and sat back deep into the chair. He let his gaze wander over the books on the coffee table as he contemplated an answer to her questions. She realized how old he was, nearly eighty, his white hair scraggly and thin. How was this old man to help her?

He finally leaned forward and took up what looked like a plant textbook, opening it to the contents page.

"Do you believe in magic?" he asked.

Magic! She never would have thought him, a former military man like her husband, into the black arts. "I'm not sure magic can help me," she said carefully, not wishing to mock him. "Can it?"

He smiled at her. "Well, I don't believe in magic either. But I've found something close enough to it." He still studied the book, running a gnarled finger down the listing on the page of the contents. "Here it is." He turned the book around on his lap and showed where he pointed. "I wish Al had come to me before getting involved in whatever plans he had cooking. But now the evil is done, this could be what you're looking for."

She took the book from him and read the entry. "Poison sumac. A swamp shrub (Rhus vernix) of the southeast United States, having compound leaves and greenish-white berries and causing an itching rash on contact with the skin. Also called poison elder."

She glanced at him. "Oh, I know sumac. How is this . . . like magic?"

"I worked for military intelligence up until five years ago—when the invasion occurred. I suggested the aliens couldn't possibly be stopped with force. There were too many. But they couldn't be much like us. Physiologically. Surely some of our earthly poisons could affect them. You know that they eat their own foods that they grow for themselves. Strange things, grown from seeds we can't even imagine. But they do drink H_2O. Just like we do."

"And did the military try to give them sumac?"

He shook his head. "I hadn't come to the sumac yet. During the time we had, once they landed, we did try a few things. Hemlock, DDT, poison gas, paraquat, cyanide, ratsbane, dioxin, strychnine, Agent Orange, prussic acid, teratogens . . ."

"God."

"They were immune. Crazy. Any of those things would take us to the grave within hours. It seemed not to bother them even a little. That's when the plan was given up and, besides, we hadn't any time left for fighting back."

"So you've tried things on your own?" she asked.

He closed the book and leaned back, closed his eyes. She thought he might not answer, but soon he began to talk softly.

"They came for my son. That was before I moved here, so you never knew of him. He was a bright, articulate boy who couldn't abide these impossible days. No matter how I tried talking sense to him, he went his own way." Despair and loss transfigured Flagg Johnson's face into that of a gargoyle, sharp and contemplative. "I hadn't found the right poison yet. He had no chance at all against them."

"I had thought of bringing together people to join the Underground," she said. "I never thought of doing it all myself, of trying to fight them alone." She didn't want him to talk about his son. She didn't want to think about Al or any of the millions who had been lost. Grief, hers or another's, paralyzed her.

He opened his eyes and looked at her from beneath

shaggy gray brows, and his expression softened. "There is no such thing."

"There's no Underground? But we've heard of it for years now. Barbara Allen said it was there. Surely . . . ?"

He shook his head. "No, it's a myth. Barbara is misinformed. We were a weak-kneed, subjugated people before the aliens arrived. We were ripe for the plucking. We bought into the idea that any higher intelligence must be humanitarian. There haven't been many like your husband and my son who had the will to fight back. They are rarer than you think. There's never been enough like them to form or support an Underground."

Jo flipped through the book to the page on poison sumac and began to read where the plant grew best, what soil it needed, how much sun and moisture. She slowly folded closed the covers and let the volume rest on her knees. "So after losing your son, you discovered this . . ." She tapped the book. ". . . would kill them?"

"Absolutely. The berries distilled into a syrup—or just powdered—and added to their water is a most potent pesticide."

"But they're still here. They're everywhere!" She hadn't meant to rebuke him, but she had been hoping for more than a poison. It unsettled her, too, that there was no Underground. It was nothing but fanciful illusion. They were truly and well doomed.

"Do you expect," he said, "that I could kill all of them myself. Alone? I am not powerful enough to rid the world of every single invader, Jo. I haven't found anything that can do that. But it's enough to target a few at a time. I've been using it for five years now and, even though they won't let the news leak out, I'm convinced more and more of the enemy has fallen. For instance, we are having this open conversation now, one punishable by death, but do you see a Watcher anywhere to report it?"

Jo hunched her shoulders, fear crawling up the back of her neck. She glanced toward the open windows and shivered.

"Don't worry. They're not out there. When was the last time you saw one?"

She tried to recall. It had been more than a year! "A long time," she said.

"Did you never stop to wonder why?"

She shrugged. "No, I guess I didn't. But then Al and I didn't have these sorts of discussions. He went into town and started gathering people for some kind of an assault on the local headquarters. He kept it a secret from me. To protect me."

"Well, let me tell you something. The Watchers aren't omnipresent the way they once were because there are fewer of the invaders to send them out and to monitor their feedback. I have hopes the whole governing body will collapse eventually. If enough of us take the battle to them and we are stealthy . . ." He rapped on the book in her hands. ". . . perhaps they will be brought low. I've even sent the news of the sumac to interested parties in England, Iran, Japan, and Argentina. It's being slipped into the aliens' water supply worldwide—at least the ones they don't share with humans." He stood, nervously rubbing his hands together. "I don't expect I will live to see the eradication of this new species, it won't occur in my lifetime. But you're twenty years younger. You can carry on and find others who will help."

"You really know it works, then?"

"All I can tell you is to try it yourself. It's the only weapon we have. I assure you it does work."

He took the book from her hands and gestured for her to rise and follow him. "I've had to special order some of the plants, the same as you will have to do. I couldn't find any growing naturally around here. I use every berry my bushes make. My supply is dwindling, or I'd share it."

Jo stood and followed him, watching from the sideline, intrigued with the old man and his apparent sincerity. He really believed what he was telling her.

She watched him grind something dry and gray in a stone pestle. She watched him sift this powder into a small envelope and hand it to her. "Take this. Try it on one of them yourself. You don't have to believe an old man."

She took the packet and thanked him. He told her, as

she left the house, "Be careful, Jo. There is no forgiveness for what you are about to do."

"I know," she said. "And I wish for none."

She stepped through the screen door into sunlight. She
had come bearing a bouquet of flowers and was leaving
with a small square manila envelope of ground sumac
seed. If it worked, it was more than an even exchange.
She would bless Flagg's name if what he told her was
the truth. He might even be the savior of the entire
human race. One day. She must find out quickly if it
worked. She must not be caught. She must kill them. All
of them. Or at least, dear God, as many as she could. . . .

She had sneaked onto the alien base at night and
poured the little bitter powder into a soldier alien's bot-
tled drink. He had set it down on a concrete wall, his
back to it, and she reached up and grabbed it quickly,
spilled the powder inside, shook it gently, and replaced
the bottle. She sat in hiding behind the wall, holding her
breath, trembling with anxiety, listening. They spoke in
their strange language—well, strange to her despite how
some humans had learned to communicate in it. She
heard another alien approach the soldier and stand with
him talking a bit. Then she heard the scrape of the bottle
as it was taken from the concrete wall top. She put her
hands over her mouth and breathed shallowly.

Suddenly she heard a high wail, like that from some
sea creature, a dolphin, perhaps. She heard the soldier
fall to the ground and heard him writhing and wailing
in that awful high-pitched voice. Footsteps came running
over as she crawled away from the area and made her
way from the camp.

They did not catch her until she was on her tenth
mission to the alien compound to taint their water with
the sumac. It was six months after her talk with Flagg
Johnson. She had ordered sumac plants and put them in
her garden. She gave them the best possible care, babied
them more than any plant in her garden, and they
thrived.

On the day she was caught, she was dressed as a cleaning woman, blending in with other menial workers employed as slave labor. She had Al with her, waiting in

the car, his right wrist tied to the armrest so he would not wander away. When she returned to him, her heart racing as it always did when she was on a sortie that could turn disastrous, they were waiting for her.

The tinny electronic translation of the alien's voice caught her unaware just as she was opening the driver's door. She twirled on the command, "Turn around, Jo Bettle."

"Yes?" she said, trying to look into the eye slits of the mask the beast wore to camouflage his real face.

"You are unauthorized for this compound. This is an offensive action. Please accompany me to the office."

"But my husband . . ."

"He will be brought along later. Come with me *now*."

Her heart sank. She had no way to dispose of the incriminating little plastic baggies secreted into her clothing, all of them gray with the residue of poison. At least she had already cleared a fourth or more of the number of aliens who lived on the boundaries of her area. It was a good thing she had already explained everything to Barbara Allen who already was working at another compound, spreading the poison. Barbara had promised to also pass on the knowledge to someone else. In her own small way, Jo had started the rebellion her husband had tried to instigate. Or rather, Johnson had started it for her. No matter what happened now, the dying out of the alien race would never end until they were all decimated. From one person to the next the news would wander and spread and bring forth death to the invaders.

In a cold featureless room, Jo was searched and the plastic baggies found. "What is this used for?" she was asked. She refused to answer. She was left alone and then another of the invaders entered. He braced her with different questions and she suspected he was an officer in charge. You could never tell who held rank over another for they all wore the same mask, the same clothes, but Jo knew they had brought in someone serious.

"I have gone over the little plastic containers and do not know what you might have been carrying in it. Does it have something to do with the plague that has afflicted us recently?"

Jo stood rigid and silent. She bit into her lower lip, anticipating torture. What worried her most is that they would realize the powder came from the sumac. But could they really eradicate the plant from off the face of the Earth? Before it was used against them? She did not think so.

Oddly, she found herself thinking of her gardens, how they would be in full late summer bloom soon, the regalia of nature transporting her small home place into a veritable wonderland of color and scent. Only this morning she had noticed the first blooms on the veronica, the blue blossoms softening the gay multicolored daylilies behind. Without her to water and prune, to plant and divide, to fertilize and love, the gardens would go to seed and fall to ruin. Even the poison sumac. Just like the world had done, over and over again, since the beginning of time. But it always rebounded, didn't it? Always came back stronger than before. Seed flew on the wind, was carried by bird and animal, and it took up residence in unlikely ground.

"Jo Bettle, you are instructed to answer my questions."

She heard the officer as though from far away. She was cocooned in her own thoughts, thinking now of Al and how she had loved him so. His broad hands soothed her flesh, his kisses were balm, his love finer than the tendrils of a fern, deeper than the roots of the peony.

She interrupted the officer's stream of questions abruptly, "Have you ever heard of the plant, Liveforever?"

"We are not familiar with that Earth flora."

"I am a gardener. I love flowers. Do you understand gardening just for the love of beauty? Have you heard of soapwort, creeping thyme, lavender, lobelia, sweetpea, baby's breath, nandina, phlox, chrysanthemum, iris, coreopsis, calendula . . . ?" She went on and on, naming every flower and plant that came to mind—*except* the sumac—knowing that by doing so she was annoying the alien. If she continued, she would force him to put her to sleep to shut her up.

So she continued, bravely, smiling as she spoke, content to die now since there was no reason to live and she had done her best already to take revenge for her husband. Besides, she was too alone, too lost without Al. Only providing death for her enemies had kept her alive this long.

"What about yarrow, red hot poker, parrot's feather, bird of paradise, oxeye, goldenrod, foxglove, chamomile, campion, daisy, gentian, Jacob's ladder, passion flower, and Soloman's seal?"

The officer touched the door behind him and another of his kind entered carrying the appliance that injected lethal volts into the necks of dissenters. He might even be the same one who had taken her Al from her, thought Jo, smiling at him, stepping forward so that he could reach her easily.

All the while she named her beloved flowers to force them to quiet her. She would fall by the wayside like a seed from the clawed foot of an eagle, be swept away, she knew that, and Al with her now that he had no one to care for him, but hope springs eternal in the smallest bud, in the tiniest seedling sprouting from harshest ground, and so would the poison sumac be handed on, one remedy against the onslaught of night consuming the human race. They would never stop them, never.

Her last whispered words were, "Don't forget . . . you must never forget the fragile Love Lies Bleeding . . . Love Lies . . . Love . . ."

SCIENTIFIC ROMANCE
by Kevin J. Anderson

Kevin J. Anderson has written excellent fiction in a number of genres, from novels set in one of the most famous universes ever created, that of *Star Wars* (*Jedi Search, Dark Apprentice, Champions of the Force*) to near-future techno-thrillers with Doug Beason (*Ill Wind, Ignition*). He has also worked on comics with Dark Horse, and written several stand-alone novels. He lives in California.

Late after dark on a chill November night, young Wells followed T.H. Huxley up to the labyrinthine rooftop. The air felt damp, tinged with a clammy mist, yet the sky overhead was dark and clear and sparkling with stars.

The meteors would begin falling soon.

The minarets and gables of London's Normal School of Science provided nooks, crannies, gutters, and eaves where students could hold secret meetings, perhaps rendezvous with young girls from the poorer sections of South Kensington. Wells doubted, though, that any of his classmates would climb to the sprawling rooftop for the same purpose as his teacher and mentor led him now.

Huxley's creaking bones and aching limbs forced the old man to move slowly along the precarious shingles. Wells knew better than to offer the professor any assistance. Huxley finally found a spot against a gable and eased himself down. Leaning backward, he propped his head up and stared into the depths of the universe.

"Is this your first meteor shower, Herbert?" Huxley asked. "The Leonids are a good place to start. We should see about twenty per hour."

Wells, at only eighteen and much more limber, struggled to find his own comfortable observation place. "I've seen shooting stars before, sir," he said, "but I've never actually . . . studied them."

Huxley gave a wheezing laugh. His voice sounded strange to Wells, a private conversational tone instead of the forceful oratory for which he had become famous across England. "From what I can see, young man, you study every facet of life with those quick and darting eyes of yours."

Wells blushed, then ran a hand across his face to hide his embarrassment. His unkempt dark hair fell over his forehead, and his mustache showed gaps where the whiskers hadn't yet filled in enough.

He fidgeted, working himself into an awkward squat, holding onto a gutter for balance. Huxley intended to stay out here for hours, but the conversation interested Wells more than his personal comfort. Ideas made mankind superior to other creatures . . . and superior men had superior ideas.

The flash in his peripheral vision took him completely by surprise. "There!" he shouted, gesturing so rapidly that he nearly lost his precarious balance on the angled roof. A streak of brilliant white light shot overhead, then evaporated, so transient it seemed barely an afterimage on his eyes.

"The first meteor of the night," Huxley said with a smile, "and you spotted it, Wells. I'm proud of you. But, of course, your eyesight is much better than mine."

"But your eyes have seen more things, sir," Wells said, then hated the reverential tone he had let slip.

"Don't flatter me," Huxley warned. The old man's wit and intellect were as bright as the sun, but his personality remained acerbic and abrasive. Wells would tolerate any number of rebukes, though, for the insights the professor had given him during his biology lectures.

Even now, Huxley fell comfortably into the role of teacher. "Make note of the meteors we see this evening, and you will be able to envision their radiant point in the constellation Leo."

Wells settled back to continue watching. Bright in the western ecliptic, the ruddy point of Mars hung like a baleful eye, not twinkling, though the other stars around it glittered and flickered.

He shivered from the chill in the air, then tapped his foot, always moving, trying to get warm. Due to his severe financial situation, Wells was underweight and scrawny . . . even cadaverous, if one were to believe his roommate and friend, A.V. Jennings. On Tuesdays, the day before weekly pay for the scholars, Wells occasionally could not afford lunch, and Jennings would take him out to fill up on beefsteak and beer so that they could return replenished to the workbench in Huxley's laboratory.

Wells' wardrobe was meager, consisting of grubby dark suits and worn celluloid shirt collars. His thin jacket was insufficient against the chill of the November evening, but he had no desire to go back inside the school building.

A second meteor appeared overhead like a line drawn with a pen of fire, eerie in its total silence. "Another!"

Around them the city of London made its own nighttime noises. Horsecarts and black cabs clopped quietly by, while prostitutes flounced into dim alleys or waited under the gas streetlamps. Across the park, in the boarding house at Westbourne Grove where he and Jennings shared a room, Wells knew the other residents would be engaged in their nightly carousing, brawling, singing, and drinking. Here, high above it all, though, he enjoyed the peace.

Within moments a third meteor passed overhead, far from the trivial human concerns around him. This shooting star was larger and louder than the others, sputtering. Mentally tracing the fiery line back to its origin, Wells saw that the meteor radiated from a point in the sky not far from Mars itself, almost as if the red planet were launching them like sparks from a grinding wheel.

"Do you ever imagine, Professor Huxley, sir," he said as an intriguing idea formed in his mind, "that perhaps these flaming meteors are signals of a kind, even ships that have crossed the gulf of space?" Wells had had many outrageous ideas since the age of seven, and he often spoke his speculations aloud, sometimes to the entertainment of others, sometimes to their annoyance.

Huxley shifted position, looking over at his student with keen interest. "Ships?" His eyes held a bold challenge, as did his tone. "And from whence would they come, Wells?"

Wells rose to the occasion. "Why not . . . Mars, for instance?" He indicated the orange-red pinpoint of the planet. "According to theory, as the solar system cooled, each planet became hospitable to life in relation to its distance from the Sun. On Mars, therefore, intelligent life could have begun to evolve long before any such spark occurred on Earth."

At the mention of evolution, Huxley perked up—just as Wells had known he would. The professor had spent his life as a proponent of Darwinism, had debated buffoons and ill-educated orators in so many forums that Huxley became infamous as "Darwin's Bulldog."

Another shooting star passed overhead, as if to emphasize Wells' point.

"Martians," Huxley said with a wry smile. "Interesting. And what do you suppose a Martian would look like?"

Wells folded one leg over the other, in spite of his precarious rooftop position, and restrained himself from answering instantly. Huxley did not suffer foolish or glib answers. "I would suppose that since the Martians are a much more ancient race, they would have minds immeasurably superior to our own. Their bodies would be composed almost entirely of brain."

Two more faint Leonid meteors danced overhead unnoticed. Wells uncrossed and recrossed his legs.

"And what would such beings look like?"

Wells frowned, letting his thoughts flow. "Natural selection would ultimately shape a superior being into a creature with a huge head and eyes. He would have delicate hands, tentacles perhaps, for manipulating tools—but his mentality would be his greatest tool."

"An interesting exercise, Wells. You have quite an imagination." Huxley leaned from his cramped position against the gable, scooting across the roof tiles so that he could speak in a low, hoarse voice to his protégé. "But why would Martians want to come to our green Earth? What is their motive?"

Wells was ready for that one. "Mars is a dry planet, cold and drained of resources. Our world is younger, fresher, more vibrant—filled with all the things they have lost over the course of their evolution. Perhaps even now the Martians are regarding this Earth with envious eyes. They might even be drawing up plans for invasion."

As a boy, Wells had studied military history, staging mock battles in the park and observing the movements of one historical army against another. But an interplanetary war was beyond his comprehension.

"A war of the worlds?" Huxley actually chuckled at this. "And you believe that such superior minds as you propose would engage in an exercise as trivial as military conquest? You must not consider them so evolved after all."

Wells kept his thoughts to himself, for he had suddenly realized that perhaps Thomas H. Huxley was a bit naive himself.

In his life, Wells had seen the gross divisions of the upper and lower classes and how each fought amongst the others for dominance. His hard-working, sweet mother had sent him off to be apprenticed to a draper, where he had labored as a virtual slave. After escaping that fate through his own calculated incompetence, Wells had lived with his mother where she was the head domestic servant in a large manor, and she had commanded the workers beneath her. His angry father had once been a gardener, but for years had found no better employment than occasional cricket playing. . . .

The hierarchy remained, no matter what their social standing, powerful and powerless. It proved to Wells' satisfaction the Darwinian basis that all humans had been predators at some time in the past.

Wells answered his professor carefully. "If the Martians are a dying race," he said, "it would be survival of the fittest. The Martians would see Earth ripe for conquest, humans as inferior cattle."

"Survival of the fittest—I'll concede that point, Wells," Huxley said. "We must hope the Martians do not invade." He shifted back to his former position, where he watched for further Leonids.

The two sat in silence, looking into the clear sky.

Wells shivered, partially from the cold, partially from his own thoughts.

They watched the stars fall as the red eye of Mars blinked balefully at them.

The following day in the bustling laboratory section of Huxley's biology course, Wells felt feverish. He wondered if he had caught a chill from the previous night's vigil.

Nevertheless, the sounds of clacking beakers, the smell of old chemical experiments, and the chatter of students engaged his mind. He soon became totally absorbed in the setting up of microscopes and experimental apparatus for the morning's exercise.

One of Huxley's assistants—a demonstrator who delivered occasional lectures when Huxley himself was too ill to speak—prepared the laboratory activity. As if he were a prize French chef, he presented a pot in which he had prepared an infusion of local weeds and pond water. The resulting murky concoction was infested with numerous fascinating microbes.

Wells' workbench partner, A.V. Jennings, was the son of a doctor. He received a small stipend, which allowed him much greater security than Wells, though they both lived in an unpleasant boarding house an intellectual world away from the high atmosphere of Huxley's lecture hall.

Now, while Jennings set up their shared microscope on a narrow table against the windows, Wells went forward with his microscope slide to receive a drop of the precious infusion, as if it were some scientific communion. He carefully slid a cover slip over the beer-colored droplet and returned to where his partner had finished preparing the apparatus.

Under watery light shining through a veil of gray clouds, Wells focused and refocused the microscope. Jennings had a sketchpad, as did Wells, to record their observations. Wells feverishly sketched the alien-looking creatures he observed: protozoans of all types, alien shapes with whipping flagella, hairlike cilia vibrating in a blur . . . blobby amoebas, various strains of algae.

As Wells scrutinized the exotic creatures swarming

and multiplying in the tiny universe of a drop of water, he felt like a titan. His looming presence stared through an eyepiece to observe the tiny struggles of pond microorganisms. . . .

Wells realized that the other students had stopped their conversations and stood at attention, as if a royal presence had entered the room. Professor T.H. Huxley had deigned to visit his laboratory this morning.

The intimidating, acerbic old man strode around the various workbenches where his students diligently studied the infinitesimal animals they found on their microscope slides. Huxley nodded approvingly, made quiet sounds but little conversation, and moved from station to station.

When the great man came to where Wells stood proudly beside his microscope, Huxley said in a gruff voice, "Morning, Wells." The professor bent over to study their slide, adjusted the focus ever so slightly as if it were his due. "Lovely euglena you have under the light." He made another noncommittal sound, then moved on to the other students.

Wells stood looking after his mentor, disappointed. Huxley had made no mention of their shared experience with the meteor shower, their imaginative conversation. He had come here for no purpose other than to scrutinize his insignificant students . . . in the same way that Wells and Jennings had been studying the microbes.

His cheeks flushed, and the cool feverish sweat swept over him. He extended his imagination farther, wondering if other powerful beings might even now be scrutinizing *Earth* in the same manner, curious about the buzzing and swarming city of London.

The hair on the back of his neck prickled, as if he could sense the probing eyes watching him from afar.

He was startled to find Jennings regarding him oddly. "You don't look at all well, Herbert," he said. Jennings reached over with practiced ease and touched Wells' forehead. "In fact, you're burning up." He frowned. "I think you should go home and rest before this grows more serious."

*　　*　　*

The fever caught hold with nightmarish strength, and Wells fell into a labyrinth of delirium fostered by the powerful resources of his own imagination.

He saw meteors falling and falling, huge cylinders accompanied by green fire that blazed across the sky. The interplanetary ships crashed to Earth, pummeling England like quail shot.

In the great impact craters where they settled and cooled, the cylinders opened up to reveal that they were warships from the red planet, carrying hordes of invading Martians—hugely developed brains with tentacled limbs evolved under a lower gravity.

Their vast mentalities had turned toward the conquest of Earth. The most insignificant of these extraordinarily developed creatures had a military intellect far superior to the combined genius of Napoleon and Alexander the Great.

Using their whiplike appendages, the Martians built war machines, clanking metal things on tall stiltlike legs that surpassed even the imagination of Leonardo da Vinci.

The clanking machines strode about the English landscape like industrial contraptions he had seen among the dark factories of the dirty towns where he had worked as a draper's apprentice. But these machines were equipped with weapons, powerful heat rays that burned everything in sight.

Hot like Wells' fever.

And overhead the meteors continued falling, falling. . . .

When the fever finally broke, Wells awoke in his narrow, lumpy bed to find Jennings tending him, laying a cool rag over his forehead. A patch of bright, hot sunlight spilled through the window, warming his skin.

Wells croaked, his voice uncooperative, but he spoke quickly, not wanting his roommate to get the best of him with a first witticism. "What now, Jennings?" he said. "Are you practicing to become a doctor like your father?"

Jennings smiled. His eyes were red-rimmed, as if he hadn't gotten much sleep. "You've had quite a time of it, Herbert. Been sick for days, feverish, haven't eaten a thing but a bit of broth I managed to acquire for you.

"Worst of all, you've missed three of my lectures," said another voice.

Weakly, Wells managed to prop himself up enough to see another man standing in the small, stuffy room. T.H. Huxley himself.

"Since you are one of only three students who has so far proved worthy of a first-class passing grade," the old professor said, "I wanted to see why you were so rude as to forsake my class." Huxley's voice was stern but subdued, as if he were restraining his normal booming tone only with great difficulty.

"Not to worry, sir," Wells said. "I'm sure Jennings took good notes."

It embarrassed him that Huxley had to see how poorly his student lived. The room in South Kensington had a crowded, squalid appearance, with too many brutish noises that carried through the walls as other boarders came in drunk at all hours. The air was cold—no one had brought up coal for some time—and smelled rank from unemptied chamberpots sitting out in the hall.

The professor maintained a mock stern expression. "I should have been quite disappointed had you died, Wells. Though you are only eighteen, I see great potential in you."

Huxley paced the room as if searching for something significant to say. Wells waited for him. "Quite humbling, isn't it?" the professor finally said. "A superior creature such as yourself, highly evolved and possessed of a grand intellect—laid low by something as crude and insignificant as an Earthly germ."

Wells gave a wan smile in response. "I'm sorry, sir. I shall try to prove my evolutionary superiority henceforth."

Huxley sighed reticently and paused at the door, ready to leave. "You may wish to know, Wells, that I have decided this will be my last semester teaching. I've spent far too many years trying to show everyone the obvious truth, and I shall give it up and retire out of sheer exhaustion."

Distraught, Wells cried, "But, sir, there's so much more we can learn from you!"

"I have wasted far too much time and energy in debates with fools over the correctness of Darwinism. I've earned myself a rest. But I will need someone to carry on, eventually."

Huxley opened the door, adjusted his hat, and frowned back at his sick student. "With your imagination, I think you can make something of yourself, Wells," he said. "Don't disappoint me."

Then Huxley left, heading out to far more pleasant surroundings on the other side of the park.

Wells leaned back into his bed while Jennings stared at him in awe. "That was quite a benediction, Herbert."

Wells lay back and closed his eyes, dizzy with residual weakness from the fever. But his mind was already whirling and spinning, filled with a thousand thoughts.

"I think I'll rest for a bit, Jennings," he said.

After all, he had to restore his health before he could begin his life's work.

THE S-FILES

by David Bischoff

David Bischoff is active in many areas of the science fiction field, whether it be writing his own novels such as *The UFO Conspiracy* trilogy, collaborations with authors such as Harry Harrison, writing three *Bill the Galactic Hero* novels, or writing excellent media tie-in novelizations, such as *Aliens and Star Trek* novels. He has previously worked as an associate editor of *Amazing* magazine and as a staff member of NBC. He lives in Eugene, Oregon.

TRANSMISSION 41222.X—GALAXY WEB

Your Neuronal Extresence Ichor,
   In routine analysis sweep, this exploratory mind-knot has located again the atmospheric phenomenon mentioned in previous annual clickings of this solar orb life-composite.
   It is a glackoid being, of corpulent dimensions, riding in a null-grav vehicle, fronted by null-grav quadrupeds with bony head crests. In this vehicle's rear reside numerous boxes of different dimensions, containing artifact-effluvia of the various civilizations currently under scrutiny. Previous records merely visual, plus this audial snippet: "Ho ho ho!"
   Unlike previous sightings, subject did not escape tractor beams. Subject has been procured and is presently awaiting testing in Egg Lab of the Deci-craft.

TRANSMISSION: 41223.X—GALAXY WEB
Your Sinoid Gangloid-Drip Lappings,
   Glackoid subject detained and analyzed.
   Physical parameters unrevealing.

Anal probe inclusive. Tagging effected. Brain-scan negative. DNA alteration begun.

Cell structure indicative of abnormal glackoid age. Dream-screen mappings reveal much crystalline frozen water, tiny glackoids in unusual suits, an old female glackoid preparing confections in food-preparation unit, and the polishing of shiny black boots for subject's unusual glackoid costume.

Unlike previous subjects, however, old red-clothed glackoid not responding to fear-injections. Paranoia transducers, indeed, overloaded and short-circuited. Replacements behind effected.

TRANSMISSION 41224.X—GALAXY WEB
Your Holy Sphincter Product,

The Cause seems ineffective on present bearded glackoid. DNA shifting inconclusive. Species preparation for mind-meld worship of the Great MudDroolGod ineffective. Instrumentation failures frustrating.

Termination procedure commencing, with usual biological immolation. Sterilization of probe-chamber immediately following.

Bone-crested quadrupeds shed glackoid offerings more in spirit of Universal Terror/Harmony, creating delicious bacterial aroma in Cell 10. These beings will be spared and studied to determine gravity-control faculties.

TRANSMISSION 41225.X—GALAXY WEB
Your Urinal Endorphin Gulpings,

During mid-Evacuation Vespers, red-clothed glackoid subject has somehow escaped! Quadrupeds have been released through hatch and have attained sufficient distance to negate possibility of pursuit.

Immediate ped survey reveals no sign of white-bearded glackoid upon any deck, yet sodar readings indicate he did not accompany quadrupeds in atmospheric evacuation.

We can only assume that this large specimen of glackoid is hiding in the extensive ductwork of Primary Vessel.

This astonishing ability has not been exhibited in any

other abducted glackoid specimen, due to rigid skeletal structure in each.

Conclusion: Subject's ability similar to Homeworld CloudElf's ability to squeeze through Elimination Chimneys to snap with claws at unwary ventral buttocks of defecating pupas.

TRANSMISSION 41226.X—GALAXY WEB

Your Enzymatic Digestive Eructions,

Great Alarm on Primary Vessel!

White-bearded glackoid chimney squeezer has struck several times, absorbing Primary Vessel's Intelligence Units in a large frontal sac similar to container of jelly. Sensors indicate expanding genetic structure.

Sudden vegetative matter has made its appearance on deck, containing red berries and green prickly leaves. Unsettling frequency variation emanations containing glackoid verse communication radiates through hallways.

Result amongst your Loyal Droppings:

Fear and Constipation.

Please advise.

TRANSMISSION 41227.X—GALAXY WEB

Your Divine Original MuckWorks!

White-bearded glackoid has absorbed all members of crew, save for myself. Now he thunders through the hallways, bellowing for "Milk and cookies!"

As no advice has been received, for safety of Mind-Net, I am forced to enact automatic destruct sequence and thus—

Ahh! The glackoid has squeezed out of ductwork.

He speaks of "naughty boys" and "lumps of coal." He is indeed a fearsome, hypnotic creature and though my hand is stayed upon Automatic Destruct Sequence, my constipation has been dramatically cured.

He nears—

Ahhhhhhhhhhhhh!

TRANSMISSION 21448.X—GALAXY WEB

YOUR SUPERNAL BIRTH CANAL DRAINAGES,
Ignore previous message.

All Intelligence Units have been returned and re-formed, in high state of serotonin flow.

White-bearded glackoid cheerfully smoking pipe containing aromatic vegetative matter by a fire of wooden lab materials in "hearth".

All assembled partaking of exotic gourmet offerings "milk and cookies." Newly bipolarized sexes gather under "mistletoe." Groups in pleasantly warm clothing gathering in snow patches, bearing candles and singing "hymns."

Reflection: Perhaps our mission was wrong-buttocked. Forced abduction seems now repulsive.

New spectrums of meaning shuffle through the collective Net-Mind here.

We have altered course and are returning home, to bear good tidings.

Good will to Consciousness, and Peace in the Galaxy.

Message from white-bearded glackoid:

"Ho ho ho! Merry Christmas . . .

. . . and a happy new DNA!"

THE KINDNESS OF STRANGERS

by Alan Dean Foster

Alan Dean Foster was born in New York City and raised in Los Angeles. He has a bachelor's degree in Political Science and a Master of Fine Arts in Cinema from UCLA. He has traveled extensively around the world, from Australia to Papua, New Guinea. He has also written fiction in just about every genre, and is known for his excellent movie novelizations. Currently, he lives in Prescott, Arizona, with his wife, assorted dogs, cats, fish, javelina, and other animals, where he is working on several new novels and media projects. His latest book is the next in the Pip & Flinx series.

Harry Landusky wheeled himself out the door of the sun-baked trailer ("mobile home" was far too grand a designation for the place) and down the metal ramp that pointed toward the abandoned gas station. Inside the trailer, the alarm had gone off, signifying the arrival of that rare and precious commodity, a customer. Despite the minimal charge of one dollar per person, not many travelers stopped at the old station on State Route 163 to view Harry's mini-museum of pickled rattlers, scavenged hubcaps, rusting license plates, paperweight tarantulas, lovingly tended succulents, and other engaging detritus of the desert. But enough did to supplement his Social Security and SSI without drawing the notice of the IRS or any other avaricious government acronyms.

The visitor was tall, in his early thirties, and well-dressed. Overdressed for the high Nevada desert, but not for Reno or Carson City, both of which lay a modest distance yet worlds away to the west. Gamblers sometimes came Harry's way, slumming just long enough to remind themselves how badly they missed room service and air-conditioning. They always had the dollar price of admission. Those that did not, didn't come this way.

The man smiled tolerantly as the bearded occupant of the wheelchair rolled up. "Morning. I was just passing through."

"What else would anyone be doing out here?" Harry cackled. "You're welcome to have a look around. Admission's one dollar." He squinted up at the supercilious visitor. "Guided tour's another dollar."

"Name's Rick Boyes." Already bored, the visitor shrugged indifferently. "Guess I'll spring for the guided tour. I'm trying to kill a morning."

"Gonna make me an accessory to murder, eh?" Tilting back slightly, Harry spun the wheelchair on its axis. "Follow me. But not too close. I brake for critters."

Looking suddenly uncomfortable, the visitor glanced down at his feet, not neglecting to peer behind him. "Your sign didn't say anything about live exhibits."

"Not exhibits." Harry grinned. "Neighbors. There's not much living around here that can't get over, under, or through a chicken-wire fence."

Boyes looked on politely as Harry proceeded to enumerate the details and delights of his modest collection. "That snake in that big jar over there, that's the biggest rattler I've ever had on the property," he would declaim. "And that's a coyote skull. I'd like to have a whole skeleton, and God knows, there's plenty around, but coyotes don't like to kick off in accessible places, and until they build one of these grocery carts with tracks instead of wheels, I'm kind of limited in my roaming."

The visitor nodded somberly, eyeing the chair. "Nam?"

Harry shook his head. "Bosnia. Land mine. Christ, how I hated those little suckers. Didn't care who they killed or maimed. Our side, their side, little kids, some sorry-ass sheep. Step on the wrong spot and your ass goes ka-boom. Only in my case, it was only from the ass down."

"I'm sorry," the visitor offered quietly.

"Sorry, shit." Harry spun the chair and pushed off in the direction of the old garage that he had renovated to hold his indoor exhibits.

They were coming up on his favorite part. The part that invariably startled and amazed his visitors. While some were gratified by the sight, and some were indifferent to it, and not a few were openly sarcastic about the limited appeal of his museum, there was nary a one who failed to be impressed by the gadget in the box. He called it a gadget because he had to call it something and he had no idea what it was. But then, neither did anyone else.

"You strike me as a smart guy," he told Boyes as the visitor trailed along behind him. "Let's see if you can tell me what this is." So saying, he parted the wooden doors to the homemade display cabinet. Revealed on its improvised stone pedestal within was the gadget.

The foot-high, silvery cone had an integral curl at the top, like a just-dispensed soft ice cream cone. Through this curl and around the cone's grainy, patterned surface darted a thumb-sized cylinder of light. Bright yellow, two inches long, it was not constrained by glass or any other visible mechanism. Its cone-orbiting path appeared random, sometimes circling the base, sometimes the crest, occasionally passing through the loop of the small curl at the top. The mechanism was absolutely silent, emitting not a whir, not a hum, not an isolated electronic buzz.

Appropriately intrigued, Boyes leaned close and stared at the simple, orbiting light. "You're right. This is very interesting. No, extremely interesting."

Harry tried not to grin. It was a reaction he'd witnessed many times before. "Worth a buck?"

Ignoring Harry's request for a fiduciary evaluation of the object, his visitor inquired sharply, "What is it?"

"Beats the hell out of me. I call it the gadget, because that's what it looks like." He wheeled himself forward. "Watch this."

Extending his right arm, he timed his reach so that his fingers would make contact with the swirling light as it swung around the base of the cone. Upon contact, a second cylinder of orbiting light appeared, bright red this time. Repeating the gesture produced a third orbiter, this one lime-green. The lights not only circled the cone, they passed through one another, changing colors whenever they briefly merged. Soon Harry had half a dozen lights darting like overgrown fireflies around the cone and through each other. They gave off no heat and no sound. When Harry made a show of blocking their passage with his hand, they went over or around his outthrust fingers, seemingly of their own volition.

After a while, the newly conjured lights winked away one by one, leaving only the original orbiting yellow cylinder.

Standing next to the wheelchair, Boyes was staring, his eyes just a little wider than normal. "What powers it?"

Harry shrugged. "Batteries, I guess. Though I'm damned if I can figure out where they go in. I haven't been able to find the compartment lid. Maybe you need a special key to get inside it."

"How long has it been running like this?"

"Every since I found it. 'Round the clock, twenty-four hours a day." He grunted softly. "Damn good batteries."

"You found this?" With undisguised reluctance, Boyes tore his gaze away from the cone. "Where?"

This was the best part, Harry knew. His favorite part. He spoke slowly, savoring every word. "It fell out of a flying saucer." He pointed eastward, toward the Saltlick Mountains. "I was camping, out looking for turquoise and jasper, and this big metal disk about the size of a Lear jet popped right out of an arroyo not a hundred yards from where I was parked. Wobbled a little, like a fawn taking its first steps, and then pow-bam-good-bye-ma'am it went straight up out of sight. But while it was hanging there, doing that little wobble, the gadget fell out."

He waited, anticipating the usual hoots of derision, the sarcastic comments, the smarmy sideways glances. But Boyes surprised him. The visitor's voice remained calm, his attitude respectful.

"I don't know how it's generating those lights, and I've never seen metal like that. If it is metal. And you say it's been running ever since you found it."

Harry nodded. "That's right. Nonstop. Like I said; good batteries."

"Or something. That trick you did with your hand.

Do the lights always appear in the same order, or can you bring up different colors at different times?"

"Sure can." Harry proceeded to demonstrate. "See? It's all in where you put your fingers."

After the second light display had gone the way of the first, Boyes turned to the man in the chair and announced calmly, "I'd like to purchase the gadget from you."

Harry smiled knowingly. It wasn't the first time someone had tried to buy the gadget from him. "Sorry. It's not for sale. It's the one real out-of-the-ordinary in my collection. If I sold it, I really wouldn't have anything special to show people. I'd lose my big draw."

"Yeah, I can see how many customers it draws. But I don't want you to think I don't understand," Boyes told him. "I will sign a proper notarized bill of sale and give you five thousand dollars on deposit. I'd like to have some tests run on the gadget. If they come out the way I'm hoping they will, I will then pay you a balance due of one hundred thousand dollars."

Well, Harry mused, this was a first time. "I'll be damned. You believe my story, don't you? You're the first one."

"I don't believe your story. Not yet. That's why I want to have tests run." Boyes nodded in the direction of the gadget. "But I believe in what I can see with my own eyes strongly enough to make the offer, and give you the deposit."

"A check, I suppose." Harry found himself stalling for him. His visitor's offer, coupled with his apparent earnestness, had thrown him off-stride.

Boyes nodded toward his car. "I had a good week in Reno. I have twenty-two thousand four hundred dollars and change in a money bag in a hidden compartment in the trunk of my Cadillac. Five down, one hundred thousand on successful completion of tests. I can provide you with telephone numbers, credit card numbers, dozens of personal references. I'm a pretty successful guy, and I can deliver on what I promise." He leaned forward solicitously. "What do you say?"

"If you think the gadget is worth a hundred grand,

that says to me maybe it's worth more." Harry grinned up at his visitor, showing missing teeth.

Boyes' return smile was forced. "Like someone's going to come along tomorrow and offer you more."

"Might," Harry declared. "Or maybe I'll get a hold of a professor or two at the college and have them run a few tests for me."

"That's hardly fair. I'm the one who suggested that course of action."

"Fuck 'fair.' " Harry took a swipe at the place where his legs should have been. "Don't talk to me about 'fair.' "

"All right." His visitor took a deep breath. "Ten thousand now, two hundred thousand if the tests prove out."

This time Harry had to think a little longer, and his reply came harder. "Man, the more you look at it like the way you're looking, the more I think maybe I'd better have this checked out on my own."

"They'll take it away from you," Boyes warned him. "You're a nobody, you have no clout, and if you let others get a hand on it, they'll steal it right out from under you. The government, some big corporation. They'll screw you out of your rights of ownership, and nobody will give a damn."

"Let 'em try. I'll take the story to the media."

Boyes chuckled, and the sarcasm that heretofore had been absent from his voice materialized in his laugh. "And they'll all believe you, right? Even if you can get some tabloid to print your story, and find a lawyer to take your case on contingency, whoever rips you off will tie your claim up in court until you're dead or don't care anymore. Why not accept my honest, straight-up offer now? Two hundred grand would buy you a lot of creature comforts. New handicapped-equipped van, all kinds of amenities for that dump you're living in, trips, live-in help if you wanted it—what do you say?"

"If it's worth ten grand to you on the spot and two hundred thousand later, it might be worth my while to try and find another legitimate buyer. If I could get it auctioned, nobody could steal my claim to ownership."

His visitor stepped back. "You think too much. That's how people lose in the casinos. Doesn't matter whether its craps, or baccarat, or keno. They all start thinking too much. You have to be quick enough to react instinctively." Turning, he started for the door. "Think about my offer, Harry. But don't think about it too much. I'm going to give you some time to think, and then I'll be back."

As soon as he heard the Caddy fire up and spit gravel, Harry wheeled himself out onto the porch of the old gas station. His visitor had left in a hurry, accelerating far faster than was necessary in the direction of the Sierras and the civilization they concealed.

Who could he call on for help? The nearest sheriff's deputy was based in Palo Verde, thirty-five miles to the south, and the chances of getting him to come out to the place on a supposition and a suspicion were about as good as Harry holding the winning ticket in the next lotto. A natural loner in a lone place, there wasn't really anyone he could call to come keep him company while he waited to see if his visitor made good on his promise to return.

He worried about it, because he hadn't liked the look in Boyes' eyes when he'd departed, hadn't liked the cant of his jaw or the hostility implicit in his posture. None of it boded well. Harry had a couple of guns, but he didn't fool himself about any imagined ability to repel boarders.

He could take the gadget, climb in the old station wagon, and drive into town—and do what? Sit in his car until something happened? Until Boyes found him? He had no doubt that anyone who could make a legitimate offer of two hundred thousand dollars for the gadget could find him. He had no money to run with, and even if he did, where would he run? Metaphorically, of course, he thought bitterly.

Maybe the smart thing to do was make the best of it. Until his visitor returned, he could at least do what Boyes had suggested. He could think about it.

The glow was very subtle. It would have awakened a dog immediately. Ex-soldiers required only a little more exposure before their field-sensitized senses kicked in and responded. Despite the passage of years, Harry had not lost that.

So it was that he found himself carefully picking up the shotgun from its resting place next to the bed, hauling himself into the wheelchair, and heading cautiously outside the trailer. If the sight of his shaggy, unkempt self clad only in slippers, underwear, and oil-stained sweatshirt wasn't enough to scare off any intruders, maybe the shotgun would suffice.

As he neared the crumbling stuccoed back of the old garage, wheeling his way silently between lovingly tended cacti and poorly labeled rusty mining implements, he saw that there were actually three lights. By far the brightest issued from the dry riverbed that wormed its way through rock and dry soil half a mile north of the station.

The others were nearer, and flickered within the garage. That was where he kept those few items of his collection that could be considered valuable. That was where he kept the gadget.

Whoever was inside had not only broken the lock but also disarmed his admittedly simplistic alarm system. His lips tightened. If that slick son-of-a-bitch Boyes had come back early and with help, they weren't going to leave without participating in a twelve-gauge discussion of the merits of breaking and entering.

But there was no car, unless its headlamps were the source of the light illuminating the edges of the distant wash. Why park way out there? he wondered. Even if they had a four-wheel, it seemed unnecessary.

Slowly he made his way around to the rear of the station and worked his way up the ramp that led to the back door. It, at least, was still closed. Good time to have a power chair, he told himself. Another luxury he couldn't afford. He couldn't have cared less, except that in order to get his chair up the ramp to where he could open the door he had to use both hands, which meant putting the shotgun down on his lap however momentarily.

The door opened silently: not surprising, since the alarm system had been disarmed. Easing himself inside, he closed the door behind him. No doubt Boyes wasn't expecting trouble from a reclusive double amputee. He was in for a serious surprise. You didn't have to pull triggers with your toes.

On silent rubber rims he rolled into the museum and headed for the nearest light switch. He never reached it. Mentally prepared for falling fists or clutching hands, he did not anticipate being halted by a glow—but that was exactly what happened.

There were two of them. The largest stood nearly seven feet high, tall enough to have to maneuver between old hanging lamps and a rotting crystal chandelier. Its companion was considerably smaller, topping out at maybe four feet. Lean and lanky, clad in what looked like fleecy gold, they revealed pale white skin that would not have lasted five minutes in the northern Nevada sun without burning.

Skinny, they were, with long thin legs and arms that terminated in two sucker-tipped fingers apiece. Their faces were comparably elongated, with loose flaps of brownish skin on either side that could as easily have been gills as ears. Jet-black hair trailed from midway down the back of the neck and was gathered together in an incongruous ponytail by more of the woven gold material. Their eyes were vertically oval, black, and fitted with slightly concave dark blue pupils. The mouths were small, round, lipless, and toothless. The distinctive glow they were emitting came not from them but their attire.

They might be advanced, but they were not omnipotent. They had not detected his entrance, and were clearly surprised when he rolled into view. At least, he chose to interpret their slight retreat as surprise. Captivated by their alienness, he gingerly laid the shotgun down on the floor and rolled slowly toward them.

"Hello." He raised one hand, palm upward, because that seemed to be as proper a thing to do as anything else.

In response, the smaller one looked up at the larger and mouthed something that sounded like wind whispering through holes in rock. The larger replied, and then both turned to gaze at him. Emboldened, he resumed his advance.

"You two look like you could use a good feed. But I have the feeling this isn't a social call. Let me guess: You're here for the gadget."

There was no reply. They simply stared, following him with their unnaturally prominent pupils as he wheeled himself over to the display case. Parting the doors, he lovingly removed the gadget from its pedestal. As always, the intensely bright yellow cylinder continued to circle its silvery cone. He spun the chair.

"Guy who came by today wanted to buy this. Two hundred thousand he offered me. I have a feeling I can't do anything to stop you if you insist on taking it back, but I just want you to know that I could sure use that two hundred thousand. Like I told him, if I shopped it around, I could probably get more. Especially now that I know it's, well, genuine."

Again the shorter visitant looked up at the taller and spoke. Receiving a reply, it stepped forward. Harry held his ground, a simpler decision to make in the face of conflict when you don't happen to have any legs. But he had the feeling he would have held it anyway.

Two long arms extended in his direction, the sucker-tipped fingers outstretched toward him. The meaning of the gesture was plain enough. So was Harry's response. Tense but with little to lose, he held onto the gadget, and waited, and watched.

After a minute or so, the more diminutive of the two aliens stepped back. It had not tried to take the gadget, had made no threatening gestures. What it did next surprised Harry almost as much as its initial appearance. It also explained some things.

The smaller alien put one two-fingered sucker-tipped hand on the larger one's arm and turned its head away from Harry. It did this by rotating its skull almost a full hundred and eighty-degrees on its neck. The larger creature wind-whispered something to the seated human, then started to turn. It struck Harry then that they did not intend to take the gadget from him by force. Maybe an interstellar version of the old finders-keepers law applied here. Or maybe there was something going on that he did not understand.

Either way, he thought he had it figured out. Their

shape might be alien, and their posture, but the relationship between them could only be interpreted in one way. At least, given his limited store of knowledge and imagination, he could only interpret it in one way. For all he knew he could be completely wrong, galactically off-base. But what the hell. . . .

"Hey, wait a minute! If it's that important to you . . .

They turned back at the sound of his voice, not because they understood the words. Smiling even as he wondered how it would be interpreted, Harry held out the gadget. He was going to miss it; miss the looks on the faces of the astonished who visited his museum, miss playing with the bright little lights, miss the extra dollars it brought him in tips—but what the hell. . . .

"Here you go, kid. I lost a toy or two when I was your age, too. Or your size, anyway. Next time, don't be letting it hang out the window when you take off. Or wherever it was hanging when you forgot about it."

As the smaller alien accepted the gadget, one of its fingers made contact with Harry's. It was amazingly cool to the touch, like tinfoil that had spent an hour sleeping in the refrigerator. Then the hands withdrew, clutching the gadget.

The two aliens never changed expression. They might be incapable of doing so, he realized. But neither did they leave. Instead, both approached and began to examine him more closely, running those strangely flexible fingers over his face, his body, the chair. Up close, he found that their golden suits generated not only soft light but soft heat. Sitting in the chair in his underwear, he could sympathize. The high desert got plenty cold at night.

A sucker-pad touched him in a sensitive place and he laughed, causing both his gentle examiners to draw back sharply. "Hey, watch it! That tickles."

When he reached out to touch the smaller alien, he was infinitely delighted to see that it did not pull away from him.

"What do you mean, it's gone?"

Boyes hovered menacingly over the man in the wheelchair. The two unimaginative types flanking him scowled

down. They were hot and tired. It was evening, the sun
was down, and already they were regretting having left
their regular gigs in Reno to haul all the way out here
to the middle of nowhere. But the guy who had hired
them had promised that there would be little or no trouble, and thus far he had certainly delivered on that. As
much as anything, they had been brought along to intimidate. It annoyed them that they did not appear to be
having the desired effect on the clown in the chair.

Harry spread his hands. "I told you, I gave it away.
Back to the original owners. They showed up last night,
and I gave it back to them."

"I can't believe this," Boyes muttered. Ever since he
had arrived to find the gadget gone, he had been muttering it a lot. "Wait a minute. You just gave it back?"

"That's right. I gave them back the gadget, and before
they left they gave me an old bike. Looks like a classic,
but I thought the idea was pretty funny. Giving me a
bike, I mean."

"Watch him." Fury bubbling from his eyes, Boyes
strode off toward the sad-looking garage-museum, leaving Harry waiting under the baleful gaze of the two
hirelings.

"You guys get out this way much?" he inquired
conversationally.

"Shut up, jack," the nearest meat ordered him.
"We're not liking this any better than you." He wiped
at his forehead. "Christ, it's hot out here! How do you
stand it?"

"I've been in hotter places. Arabia. Bosnia."

The other dog showed a flicker of interest. "You were
in Bosnia? That how *it* happened?"

Harry snorted. "Didn't happen crossing Silver Creek
Road in Tahoe."

His transitory nemesis nodded. "My dad was in Bosnia. Worthless bastard, except for that. They say he did
good there."

"Sorry."

"Hey, don't you be sorry for us. You'd better hope
that . . ."

"He's telling the truth." They all turned in the direction of the gas station as Boyes came stomping out. "It's

not there." Approaching the chair, he leaned over its occupant and glowered.

"You don't think I believe a word of this, do you?"

Harry shrugged. "What are you gonna do? Tear the place apart? If I did still have it and wanted to hide it from you, you know you'd never find it. I know this country, and you can't dig it all up." His eyes rose to meet those of his visitor. They did not swerve or fall.

"As for beating it out of me, I've taken worse than anything your hired donkeys can hand out."

"You think so?" Unexpectedly finding himself pinned by that unwavering stare, Boyes suddenly blinked and straightened. "One thing at a time, I suppose." He eyed his companions. "Search the trailer first. Then we'll start in on the museum and the rest of this junk out here. And if we don't find it pretty quick," he paused meaningfully, "maybe we'll find out whether you're as tough as you think."

They did not bother to keep an eye on him. After all, it wasn't as if he was going anywhere. As for the possibility that he might have a gun stashed somewhere, Boyes secretly hoped that he did. It would give them an excuse to shoot him, useful in the event the law became involved. Not kill him, of course. Just shoot him. In that event, it would be a simple matter of their trading a call for medical assistance for the gadget. He was not concerned about Harry's possible prowess as a sharpshooter. The two men he had brought with him were professionals, and he had been assured they were competent.

They were working their way through the tired, slovenly bedroom, ripping out drawers and tearing apart storage boxes, when they heard the boom and the subsequent ascending whine. Rushing out back, they saw the small silvery disk rising into the remnant blue of late evening. It trailed a pale pink streak and a somehow triumphant howl behind it. Very quickly, it was gone.

Gone where, Boyes could not imagine. But he would have given a great deal to know.

"What the hell . . . ?" one of the hired pair mumbled. His partner swallowed hard, his gaze focused on that impossible patch of prevaricating sky.

Boyes found himself nodding knowingly. "He said they gave him an old bike. I should have paid more attention to what he was saying. No—I should have *thought* more about what he was saying. He called the generator a gadget I wonder what it was he called an 'old bike'?"

Next to him, the meat whose father had been in Bosnia shrugged. "You got me. But whatever it was, it seems to work fine without pedals."

ALSO AVAILABLE

MERLIN

Martin H. Greenberg, Editor

ISBN: 0-7434-8728-1

SPELLBINDING TALES ABOUT THE WORLD'S MOST RENOWNED MASTER OF WIZARDRY

Merlin is one of the most popular figures in the literature of fantasy, the quintessential wizard, and, aside from Arthur himself, probably the most important figure in Arthurian legend.

Such modern-day bards as Diana L. Paxson, Charles de Lint, Jane Yolen, Andre Norton, Lisanne Norman, Jean Rabe, and Michelle West spin their tales for you in this enchanting collection, where you'll find: the truth behind the fall of Camelot and Merlin's disappearance; a wizardly confrontation with a foe defended by a power Merlin had never faced before; and a new look at the moment of destiny that could put Arthur on the throne.

MY FAVORITE FANTASY STORY

Martin H. Greenberg, Editor

ISBN: 0-7434-8744-3

WHAT DO TODAY'S TOP FANTASY WRITERS READ—AND WHY?

This was the question posed to some of the most influential authors in the field today. This book is their answer. Here are seventeen of the most memorable stories in the genre, each one personally selected by a well-known writer, and each prefaced by that writer's explanation of his or her choice. Includes such tales as:

"Ghosts of Wind and Shadow"
by Charles de Lint
chosen by Tanya Huff

"Troll Bridge" by Terry Pratchett
chosen by Michelle West

"Shadowlands" by Elisabeth Waters
chosen by Marion Zimmer Bradley

"Homeland" by Barbara Kingsolver
chosen by Charles de Lint